'Ann Devine is one of our most endearing literary figures'
Irish Independent

'Warm, funny and charming'
Business Post

'[O'Regan] again proves himself one of the foremost
chroniclers of rural Ireland'
Hot Press

'Ann is an honest and endearing creation . . . She embodies
the spirit of uplift with a refreshing Irish pragmatism'
Sunday Times

'Very funny indeed and actually very heart-warming . . .
A great read'
Brendan O'Connor, RTÉ Radio 1

'Prepare to laugh and grimace at the antics of the Irish
Mammy'
Irish Times

'Hilarious and heart-warming'
Irish Examiner

D1103193

www.penguin.co.uk
www.transworldireland.ie

TRANSWORLD IRELAND PUBLISHERS
Penguin Random House Ireland, Morrison Chambers,
32 Nassau Street, Dublin 2, Ireland
www.transworldireland.ie

Transworld is part of the Penguin Random House group of companies
whose addresses can be found at global.penguinrandomhouse.com

Penguin
Random House
UK

First published in the UK and Ireland in 2020 by Transworld Ireland
an imprint of Transworld Publishers
Transworld Ireland paperback edition published 2021

Copyright © Colm O'Regan 2020

Colm O'Regan has asserted his right under the Copyright,
Designs and Patents Act 1988 to be identified as the author of this work.

A CIP catalogue record for this book
is available from the British Library.

ISBN
9781848272491

Typeset in Palatino by Integra Software Services Pvt. Ltd, Pondicherry.
Printed and bound in Great Britain by Clays Ltd, Elcograf S.p.A.

The authorized representative in the EEA is Penguin Random House
Ireland, Morrison Chambers, 32 Nassau Street, Dublin D02 YH68.

Penguin Random House is committed to a sustainable
future for our business, our readers and our planet. This book is made
from Forest Stewardship Council® certified paper.

MIX
Paper from
responsible sources
FSC® C018179

Ann Devine

Handle with Care

COLM O'REGAN

TRANSWORLD IRELAND

For Marie, Ruby and Lily

CONTENTS

1.

THE FIRST MAN FOR THE HOIST

Gone. Not even the crusts are left. There was plenty last time I checked. But now not a crumb. And one prime suspect sprawled across the couch, texting away to beat the band.

'What happened the Keytone, Rory? Aren't they supposed to be fierce against bread?'

'It's keto, Mam. I've knocked it on the head. I was starving.'

'Are you on some other diet now?'

I'm thinking of my fridge and what concoctions might be in it over the next few weeks. The house was full of whey at Christmas. It was like a creamery.

Rory stretches out and makes a yawny roar. 'No more diets, Mam. If there's one thing being on the non-stop sesh on the beach taught me, it's to learn to love your body. All of it.'

He pats a belly that isn't there. Oh, don't worry, my lad, that will come, if any of the genes from my side have made it through the mix. The exposed bit of belly reveals another bit of writing. I leave that tattoo for another battle. I want him to go out to the shop and get bread first.

'I don't think there's any fear of you not loving yourself, Rory. You're *in* love with yourself.'

'Harsh, Mam. Words like that can damage me and make me distrustful of affection. You need to update your parenting skills. You're creating an atmosphere of trauma.'

'I'll create more trauma now in a second if you don't get your feet off the couch. There was a whole sliced pan there.'

'That lack of empathy is dangerous, Mam. I need to be able to grow in a loving environment.'

'I'll give you empathy. What are you going on about anyway with your empathy?'

'When I was in the library studying, there was this girl near me who kept leaving all these books behind about attachment parenting, and basically I read them to avoid studying and now I can't stop thinking about how you neglected me as a child. I could sue you.'

I throw a wet tea-towel at him, which catches him nicely on the head. He howls with pretend pain. I'm acting annoyed, but it's great to have the smart-arse in the house again. Even the things I was glad to have gone. The smell from runners, the clattering on the stairs, all the times I know he wants to record me on his phone, doing something that's 'classic Mam'. Rory is after coming back from a week away with the college lads. They were in one of those resorts that mammies lose sleep over. I was worried sick while he was there. I was even praying. Well, I got Mam to do the praying. She has a good success rate. I didn't tell her the specifics of what I wanted – that Rory wouldn't end up on *Banged Up Abroad* being deported because he didn't know *that*, or some other quare-hawkery, was illegal. I just told her to pray he'd get back safe.

Thanks be to God and my blessed mother, he arrived back in one piece with only one more piercing, which he swears he doesn't remember getting. And a tan, a hangover and no money. Denis's side can take a tan, so at least I don't have to worry yet anyway about the Malignant Melanoma. Speaking of which, I'm hoping he won't be working with Patsy Duggan, our local TD, this summer.

'Have you heard from The Professor yet?'

He grunts what I think is a no.

'He'd want to be getting his skates on, wouldn't he, Rory? So we can organize things? Do you think he'll need you below in Cork or can you do teleworking?'

'Teleworking, Mam, teleworking, yes.' He repeats the word with an annoying smile, like it's so old. Like I've suggested he use a butter churn.

'Or whatever *you* call it, if you're so up to date. You know what I mean – working from home.'

Tracy, my boss, has started teleworking. It's a small blessing because I see a bit less of her. She is on me like a stain these days.

'I dunno, Mam,' he says cautiously.

The Professor is a Professor Mulqueen below in Cork who thinks Rory is the bee's knees and has a big future ahead of him. He's not the first to think this. The whole reason Rory is down there at all is that Patsy Duggan sent him down by pulling a stroke. He got Rory classified as a special disadvantage case so he could transfer from The Tech halfway through a year and now he's getting four years of college without spending a bob. Even his digs is thrown in. All because Patsy Duggan thinks my boy is an electoral genius. Rory has been working for Patsy for years. He's done everything. Put up posters, carting the elderly to the polling station, wrote an election song called 'The Dugganaut', canvassed up mountain lanes, told farmers that Patsy would defend them from the Greens, told the Greens that Patsy would cover the place in pollinators. Patsy sent him down

3

to do Politics and Auctioneering and learn the ropes of being a TD. But while he was there, even though he made shite of his exams, The Professor gave him a job working for him researching his book, and by all accounts, mainly Rory's, he wrote half of it.

'Any word from Patsy in the last while?'

Another grunt from Rory. There's a bit of trouble in paradise between Patsy and Rory over what happened last month.

'I mean, if you could get another stint with The Professor, what was he saying, you'd be a shoo-in for one of those doctorates?'

'That's not how it works, Mam. You still have to do the degree and a Master's, and I'm not sure I'm that pushed.'

'Didn't he still say you could get one? Imagine you, Rory, one of these election experts on the telly with all the bigwigs. Telling the country about voter turnout and swings. Not a bad line of work. You wouldn't have to be up poles taking down other people's posters and plastering Patsy's mug up instead.'

'I never took down anyone's poster.'

'You took down everyone's poster. And I had to hear about it on the radio. If I guessed who it was, you may be sure others did too. A dirty tricks campaign, they called it.'

'Pffk,' is all he says.

'Rory, someone rang in to *Jake Shakes the Nation* on the local station and told Jake 'Shakes' Shakey they saw a young lad up a pole taking down posters.'

'That could have been anyone, Mam.'

'The fella ringing in said that when he challenged the young lad on the ladder, he was pure brazen and told him to *Chill the beans, Grandad*. Now who else could that be, Rory?'

'Water under the bridge, Mam,' he says.

4

'And you threw them into the river as well. There's me out every week with the Tidy Towns group and my son is throwing posters in the river and we're hauling them out and I'm tut-tutting in front of them about the state of the country. Covering for my own son.'

'Thanks for having my back, Mam.'

'And as far as I'm concerned, I'm much happier with you being under the wing of this fella than Patsy. You don't see The Professor up to dirty tricks campaigns. He's way more respectable.'

'All of them are up to it, Mam. It's just done on the QT. Everyone thinks academics are just going around in their tweed jackets with a pile of books and don't know what's going on. But they're all on the take. Didn't you see the fella who spent thirty kay on a desk?'

'It would still be *way* more respectable. I might be able to finally start telling my brothers in England how you're actually getting on.'

A clattering of keys at the front door interrupts his reply and my niece Freya whooshes in the door, plants a kiss on top of my head, pucks Rory in the shoulder.

'Greetings, normies!'

She's coming in for her lunch.

'Is Auntie Ger gone off to Yogatown yet, Waldo?'

Rory calls Freya Waldo after a fella in *Game of Thrones* called Walder Frey who has a load of wives. He knows she hates it.

'Not yet, Incel.'

Rory takes a deep breath, as if he's been wounded. 'Ooff. Another assault on me by women and the media won't report it. Anyway, it's not involuntary, Freya. Just waiting for the right girl. And actually, there's nothing celibate about me. Let's just say the holidays were absolute carnage in that area.'

5

'Yuck. And also you're totally lying. You're just trying to be like the college jocks, but you're failing miserably. Which is good.'

'F.R.O., Waldo.'

You'd think they were annoyed with each other, but this is what they're always like since they were small.

Freya will soon be staying here for a few weeks. Her mother, Geraldine, is going to become a yoga teacher. The hotel is gone very quiet and her hours were cut back and Dinny wanted her to do cleaning instead of the front desk, so she's *taking the plunge, not the plunger, and trying a new direction.* Geraldine is rarely without a plunge. She was doing reiki last year, but no one wanted it around here because the mindfulness has taken off in a big way and it's cheaper because you can do it on your phone. Before that she was into therapeutic stones. They're still everywhere around her house. Stones with things painted on them to rebalance you. Mam nearly lost her balance tripping on them once. Before the stones were the angels. You could go around for a consultation about what angel was looking after you. Freya said you'd want to see the state of the people who showed up. 'Which angel will get me the ride?' she overheard one of them say. But all of those were just *essential parts of the steps towards my self-actualization, Ann.*

And now she's putting a big chunk of her money into becoming a yoga teacher. But not down the road. In India. *You have to go to the source, Ann*, she says. *Goa, Ann. I need you with me on this journey*, she says. *Can you mind Freya?* So what she meant was that she needed me not to go on any journey. *And you love looking after Freya, Ann*, she says. I do. But I didn't tell Geraldine that out loud. I wanted to make her understand she was still asking for a favour. Which was pointless. Geraldine doesn't 'do guilt'. *Those who make fire need fuel, Ann.* Well, this bag of sticks will get tired one day. But not yet.

Freya bounces back into the room, checks the kettle for weight and clicks the button. She searches the bread bin, frowns and glares at Rory.

'Did you disappear all the bread again?'

'Yup.'

'There's soup in the fridge, pet. Heat that up before you get cranky.'

She strokes her phone and makes a big exaggerated smirk. 'Patsy's video is doing serious numbers. Does he blame you?'

Rory shrugs.

'I swear, Rory, if you were involved in that I would *end* you.'

'I told you before, I had nothing to do with it. On Mam's life.'

'Rory! Don't be bringing me into your swears.'

It's Patsy's referendum result video. Patsy was evasive about which side he was on all the way through the campaign. There wasn't a peep out of him. Or no obvious peep. You'd hear so-and-so say that Patsy was saying it should be a Yes and then he told someone else apparently outside Mass that he was No all the way. Speaking out of every side of his mouth. After the referendum he had a video up saying, *Ireland has changed and we must embrace the change and I will work with the government to heal division*. But then a few weeks ago Patsy put up another video, saying that we *should all move on now and accept the result and heal the divisions thrown up during the campaign* and that he would personally help to *bridge the divide* and all the things he was going to do, and that was fine and grand, only the further you got into the video, you realized something was up. He kept saying, *The Yes side have to accept the result, no matter how tight it was*. And by the end, it was plain as day. He'd made two videos and put them both up.

7

'I still don't understand why he didn't take it down straight away, Rory.'

'He got so many notifications the battery got used up on his phone and he couldn't take it down. He tried to ring me on a landline, but I was at Skitchy's twenty-first, balubas. Gee-eyed. Then he rang The Leech, but that fella wouldn't know what deleting was. Patsy was calling out passwords to him and The Leech was writing them down on a docket. Lads, it was farcical. The Leech is old-school.'

Larry Leach is Patsy's handler. The first man for the hoist at election time. He probably held the ladder when Rory was pulling down posters. Whenever there's a crowd, you'll see Larry easing himself in between Patsy and any potential awkward customers and getting right up close with them so they move away. No one likes eye contact around here. They call it the Leach Treatment.

'And when Larry did log in, he didn't have his glasses with him and he just wrote "delete" underneath it. He's not made for these times. By the time I had it taken down, the thing was copied all over the shop.'

It certainly was. People kept posting it on our Tidy Towns page and I had to pretend to be saying that the page was just for Tidy Towns business, but I didn't delete them either. I was having too much of a laugh.

'And actually, Waldo, he *doesn't* blame me. He just said it would have been better if I'd been on the ground a bit more. That's fair enough.'

'Sounds like blaming to me,' says Freya, stirring the pot. 'So anyway, Patsy's a meme now.'

She comes around to me to show me pictures on her phone. Rory sighs. He must have seen them already.

'It's a hashtag, Auntie Ann. #CageyPatsyDuggan.'

Someone has put Patsy in a load of photos from the past. Patsy in 1922 standing next to a British soldier and written underneath it is: *I hope now we can move on in peace and harmony within the Empire.* Patsy in 1945: *It was a good fight and the Nazis won. Fair play to them. Now we need to move on.* Patsy's face on a fella from *The Simpsons: I, for one, welcome our new insect overlords.*

Rory seems philosophical. 'Could have been worse, Mam. He made four others for different results. There was one he made for a landslide No decision that said he thanked God Ireland was still a Catholic country.'

'Why did he make them so early?' I ask him.

'He was going to be on holidays when the thing came out. And he didn't want to look like he had a tan. And where he was on the safari, he knew it wouldn't look like Kilsudgeon. He can't be all like a statesman with a load of palm trees and, like, a million crickets riding away out in the forest.'

'And you work for this dude, cuz. This is your boss.'

'He's a practical man, Freya. This is a complicated world. You'll learn that some day, when you have friends.'

Freya lands a thump on his shoulder.

'Mam, see this? This is the new generation we're raising here. What hope have we for the future? And this is not about videos, this is about jobs and . . .' Rory goes into a long impression of Patsy's 'I am of Kilsudgeon and Kilsudgeon is made of me' speech, which he made before there was any such thing as memes. You can only get it on tape now . . . 'And I say this as a proud Kilsudgeon man,' he finishes. Word perfect.

'You're turning into him, Rory,' says Freya, even as she smiles.

He leans back and stretches. 'There could be worse things. Anyway, I had nothing to do with any referendum video. I've been telling him he needs more chill. Now, Freya, how about making your favourite cousin tea? Since you're going to be living here, you'll need to pay your dues.'

Freya makes another swing at him.

'Now, now, I don't want ye fighting like cats and dogs while yere all under the same roof.'

'Don't worry, Mam, I won't even be in the country.'

'What do you mean?'

'I'll be away for the rest of the summer.'

'What? Where? Oh, are you going to Cork after?'

'Mam . . .'

'You fecker, you had me going there for a second. So you will go working for The Professor? Now, promise me you'll take it handy on the drink when you're there. You need a break after the holiday.'

'Mam . . .'

'You'll be set up for life if you play your cards right.'

'No, Mam, even better, I am going to the real seat of power. Where all the decisions are made that affect you, the little people.'

'Drumfeakle?'

'Drummfffe . . . No, Mam. Brussels!'

Somewhere in the house my phone starts ringing.

'Brussels?'

'More sliced pan for me so,' says Freya.

'Brussels!'

'That's it, Mam. The capital of Belgium.'

'BRUSSELS!'

'Also the seat of the European parliament,' chips in Freya.

'Did you know about this, Freya?'

'No, Auntie Ann. I just enjoy drama when it's not about me.'

Somewhere in the house my phone is still ringing. It sounds like alarm bells.

2.

A REAL DICK MOVE

I don't agree with corporal punishment, but there are times when you'd like to hit your child a good clatter with something stronger than a tea-towel. This is one of those times.

'What are you doing in Brussels, is it too much trouble to ask, and when were you planning on telling me?'

RING RING! The ringing phone is giving me hives, but I won't be interrupted on this.

'The second time you've done this, Rory, just made big plans without telling me a single thing. It's always the same. I'm the last eejit to know.'

'I was going to tell you before, Mam, but things kept coming up.'

'COMING UP. All you had to do was open your gob and tell me. And what are you going to be doing in Brussels?'

'Auntie Ann, you should answer your phone. No one rings you twice. It might be a death.'

Freya knows exactly where my buttons are.

11

'I will answer it now in a minute. Tell me, Rory, what are you going to be doing in Brussels? What's there except for a load of MEPs having an easy life and . . .'

The penny drops . . . Patsy.

RING RING!

'Someone could be collapsed on a bathroom floor, Auntie Ann. You have to answer it.'

When I find the phone, hopping about beside the kettle, it's Deirdre's photo that pops up on the screen. I'm about to put it away and then I remember why. Oh, SUGAR!

'Deirdre, I'm sorry, I forgot all about it,' I say as soon as I answer.

'Where are you, Mam? Ailbhe keeps looking out for Nana Devine. Her other nana is here ages. You're letting the side down.'

I dash around the house shouting about car keys. Freya follows me, nibbling an apple. Being unhelpful.

'I can't believe Deirdre is taking part in all of this,' she says. 'It's a charade. She voted Yes and now she's basically sending her children as offerings to the head of a criminal organization.'

'Just look for the keys, Freya, will you? Can you manage the soup yourself?'

'You'd better go quick, Auntie Ann. Ailbhe and Adam will start thinking they've only one granny.'

'Thanks for your help, Freya. Now will you go looking for the car keys?'

She finds them on the windowsill and announces that she wants to go as well. She wants to *see what a cult looks like.*

'Don't be doing any campaigning at this now, Freya, and take off that jumper, will you? You'll only provoke them.'

'Appeasement,' she mutters, but takes off The Jumper, which says *Repeal* on it.

I'm all in a knot on the drive over. I haven't minded Deirdre's two that much over the years. I was gazumped by the other side of the family. When I first met Hughie's mother, Nora, I thought she was a very laid-back character, that she and the husband, Johnny Pat, were of the old stock. They wouldn't be into all this socializing for the sake of it. They're the kind of people who'd prefer to meet you at a do rather than organize a do to meet you at.

They weren't even that keen to meet us before the wedding. *Shur we'll see ye in the church*, says Nora. *We know ye anyway*. But Deirdre insisted on an occasion. It was a Sunday in June, and that's in the middle of The Silage. There we were above in the golf club and Nora arrived alone in the Vectra. *Johnny'll be on in a while*, she says, and sure enough Johnny arrived in the Massey, towing a silage trailer, and took up the Captain's, Lady Captain's and the committee's parking spaces. He brought half of his field in on the tyres. But the golf club was quiet that time. The receivers had it then, so you could have driven a tank in and they would have said nothing. Johnny Pat gobbled down the beef and spuds, didn't touch the asparagus, took a bun away in his pocket for dessert and went off to finish a field 'before a shower that was threatening'. At least Denis and him had a great chat about drive-shafts and axles.

I thought we had bonded at the wedding. Johnny Pat made ribbons of my toes doing the parents' dance, but me and Nora were sitting beside each other all night, talking away like mad. She was confiding in me. Telling me she was delighted with us. That she was afraid *Hughie'd turn out gay* or, worse, marry some high-maintenance flighty one. Deirdre would do grand. Deirdre was solid. I remember agreeing very strongly with everything she was saying. The way you could only agree with someone at a wedding. It's like a one-night stand for agreement.

They were waiting hard for a grandchild. It was going to be the first grandchild for both sets of grandparents, but it was business for Johnny Pat and Nora. It was all about the farm. Nora had spoiled her own boys when they were small. They wouldn't go out helping on the farm. Hughie hated farming, the middle fella is a gambler and they won't let him near anything in case he puts the tractor up on *Buy and Sell*. The youngest lad is 'concentrating on his football' and is always in the gym eating that powder. Big muscles on him, but he can't hold down a calf for dosing.

There was a small war over Adam not being called after his grandfather. *Adam is not a farmer's name*, Nora kept saying, even though, as Mam said, it was the first farmer's name, but Deirdre refused point-blank to name any child Johnny.

She won that battle, but she lost the war. Johnny Pat has Adam out farming with every spare minute he gets him. I wouldn't be surprised if he's already driven a tractor. His bedroom is covered in posters of them. He's been at the Ploughing Championship every year of his life. He had a toy with him the last time he was over. I had to ask him what it was.

'A ROTAVATOR, Nana,' he says, as if it was the most obvious thing in the world.

We get to the school. The small car park is full and I have to park along the road outside. I'm sweating, but after all Deirdre's guilting the thing hasn't even started and most of the crowd are outside, talking about the warm weather.

TALENTS ARE GOD'S GIFT says the big banner across the wall in front. KILSUDGEON WELCOMES POPE FRANCIS. The Pope isn't coming to Kilsudgeon, but Kilsudgeon is going to the Pope and one child will get to meet him in person. But just to be on the safe side they're having a talent competition so that the child that's picked

14

doesn't make a show of us. The story Deirdre told me was that one of these lay organizations is picking children all over the country from specially selected parishes and they picked on Kilsudgeon because it voted slightly Yes in the referendum, even after voting against Divorce twice. The bishop himself is coming to make sure we don't accidentally pick an atheist. The word is that the hierarchy blame Father Donnegan. They think he's too wishy-washy. He didn't want to have the magazine *It's Faith!* at the back of the church. He only relented because he says there's a 'young mullah down from Maynooth' eyeing up his spot. 'The only one in his class and he's savage for the doctrine.' I don't know who buys it or where the money goes. They had a 'Pray for Gays Month' in one edition last year.

Deirdre looks a bit cross. Ailbhe is over with her full-time granny. She's looks like she's practising lines from a poem.

'Honestly, Mam, I'm there trying to convince them that the children have two grannies and then you don't turn up to Ailbhe's big day.'

'Auntie Ann was standing up against hypocrisy, Deirdre.'

'I was not standing up against hypocrisy, Freya. I've no problem with hyp—I mean, I was dealing with another . . . I'm sorry, pet.'

Mam shuffles over. Who brought her? Then I see Bim Geraghty trailing a few yards after her. The chauffeur, no less.

She gives Freya a warm hug. 'YOU TOOK OFF THE JUMPER EVENTUALLY, FREYA. YOU'D HAVE BEEN ROASTED. I THINK IT'S TOO WARM MYSELF. I DON'T MIND THE HEAT BUT IT'S GONE HUMID NOW AND I CAN'T STAND THE HUMIDITY.'

'Mam, can you put on the hearing aid?'

'HAH?'

'MAM, YOUR ELD-EARS. PUT THEM IN.'

'I DON'T LIKE THEM. I DON'T TRUST THE FELLA THAT'S HAWKING THEM ON THE TELLY. HIS EARS ARE A DIFFERENT HEIGHT TO EACH OTHER. HE'S BAW-WAYS.'

'Please, Mam.'

'YOU'RE HERE ANYWAY AT LEAST. THAT'S GOOD. THE OTHER WAN IS TAKING ALL THE GLORY.' And she looks over at Nora. I hope she hasn't heard.

I whisper right into her ear, 'Mam, the bishop will hear you.'

'I DON'T CARE WHAT HE HEARS.'

'But you don't want him knowing your business, do you?'

Mam will do whatever it takes to protect her business. Especially from a bishop. Mam likes sound nuns and priests and popes but has little time for any middle men in between. She fidgets in her bag and presses the small remote for the Eld-ears.

'I can hear everyone gossiping now,' she says, and is pleased with that.

Nora comes over with her (and my) granddaughter Ailbhe.

'She's a great girl altogether for the recitation, Ann. A great memory, godblessher. Her grandad can still remember the price of every calf he ever bought. That's where she must have got it from.'

'We had a good memory too on our side,' I say, though I can't remember any examples as specific as calf-prices.

'I'm sure you did. Tis a sin to be inside though, isn't it, Ann? Little Adam is off with his grandad for the silage. Isn't it gas how he took to the farming?'

Deirdre throws me a look.

We go into the school hall. It is boiling hot in there. It has that smell of warm crayon, of a school that hasn't been opened for a while. The back of me is already drenched from

16

the car journey and we're all fanning ourselves with the leaflets.

'I'm melting, Freya.'

'It's climate change, Auntie Ann. Or God punishing Kilsudgeon.'

'You brought it on us with all the campaigning.'

'I fought to create the space for you, Auntie Ann. You'll thank me.' She looks around. 'I still can't *believe* they're doing a talent show to see the Pope. I am so *over* this village.'

There is a murmur from the back of the room that could only come from a bigwig making an entrance. Sure enough, it's Bishop Scotius Murphy, of the diocese of Fleek and Rathoon. He tells us it's an honour for Kilsudgeon to be chosen, a chance to show what Kilsudgeon is all about.

'I swear he's looking at me,' Freya whispers. 'He knows. I should have worn my jumper. That'd show him.'

After the bishop, Ms Foley is up explaining what's going to happen. The children are in the front couple of rows, fidgeting and swinging legs and whispering. Their 'handlers' are sitting behind them. Nora is there for Ailbhe. Deirdre leans into me and points out a girl with twin ponytails.

'That's the one to watch, Mam. Iseult Deasy's sister. Amelia. She goes to Speech and Drama. She's always trying to be on the *Toy Show* but keeps getting nowhere. Iseult claims it's a Dublin fix.'

Iseult walks up the side of the hall to check on Amelia. She seems to be giving her a pep talk. Iseult was the local girl who got a part as a bit of a hoor in *The Celts – Hound of Destiny* when it was being filmed in Kilsudgeon. She was *raging* it was cancelled. She thought she was going to be the next Saoirse Ronan. She put coloured contacts in to get the green eyes and everything. I wonder did she ever find out that it was partly my fault that filmset went belly-up?

17

The first girl gets up and sings 'Here I Am, Lord'. The poor thing hasn't a note, but the Lord will find her anyway. He'll hear her a mile off.

A small lad is up now, dancing. His mother seems to be in charge of the music. I haven't seen any of the dances before. Or heard the music. *Watch me whip, watch me nae nae*, says the music.

'It's a *Fortnite* medley,' Freya explains. 'I wonder will he do the . . . Oh, he is . . .'

The young lad seems to be doing something to the ground.

'That's The Hump,' Freya whispers.

The boy's mam goes up to get him off the ground. 'I never saw him do the full thing,' she says to Ms Foley. Mortified.

Ailbhe is up next. She's doing a poem she wrote called 'Holy God'.

> I love Holy God with all my heart,
> He is there when in games I take part.
> He helps me be good and true,
> And Jesus and the Holy Spirit too.
> And every night before I go to bed
> I pray before I rest my head.
> That God will keep my families safe,
> They will still be there when I awake,
> Especially my Granny Nora who gives me cake.

That cuts deep. But Mam looks very proud. She leans across to Deirdre. 'She got some bit of religion anyway, Deirdre.'

I can tell from the back of Nora's head that she's pleased as Punch. Deirdre looks at me as if to say, *That's what happens, Mam.*

The children continue to do their pieces. There are Irish dancers, of course. Then small twins, one dressed as the Pope and one dressed as an ould lad, who do a skit about the Pope lost in his little Pope car, looking for directions off a fella on the side of the road. 'How much would she do to the gallon?' asks one of the twins. 'It's electric,' says the other one. We're laughing, but the bishop isn't smiling, so they won't get through anyway. In fact, I would say Ailbhe is in the lead with 'Holy God'.

Even Freya says to me, 'We have this one in the bag.'

'I thought you said it was hypocrisy?'

'Family is everything, Auntie Ann.'

And then young Amelia Deasy pops up. It must have been organized for her to go last. The father probably leaned on the teacher. He runs the NCT centre and he's been known to fail cars if he didn't like the owner.

Amelia comes across the stage. Iseult is up conducting her. She's carrying a little box. Nothing happens for a few seconds.

'Hang on, I'm just pairing it,' she tells everyone. Not a bit embarrassed. And we all have to wait for 'it' to be paired. *Pairing*, says the speaker. *Paired*, it says.

Music comes out of the small box. Old church music. It takes me a while to recognize it.

'*Salve, Regina . . .*'

She isn't.

'*. . . mater misericordiae . . .*'

'What's she saying? Is it Italian?' asks Freya.

'*. . . vita, dulcedo et spes nostra, salve. Ad te clamamus, exsules filii Hevae.*'

I can see Mam mouthing it. It's coming back to me as well. I last heard it at a funeral.

The bishop looks transported away. There's going to be only one winner.

Mrs Foley and the bishop confer for a few minutes, then the bishop steps forward.

'Thanks to all the boys and girls for a very special afternoon here. We were blown away by the standard,' he says.

Bishops are allowed a few lies, it seems. 'But one act,' he says, 'stood out. Amelia DEASY.'

Of course.

'Singing in Latin is a real dick move,' whispers Freya.

'They're all Opus Dei too,' Deirdre mutters to me. 'They were in a photo in *It's Faith!* last year.'

The bishop continues. 'Now little Amelia will represent Kilsudgeon in a special children's ceremony during the papal Mass in the Phoenix Park on 26 August. The theme will be Local Pride. She will take all the prayers and intentions of the parish to Pope Francis and he will say a special prayer for us. And we need it now more than ever.'

That's the end of that. We gather around the teary Ailbhe as the show breaks up.

'You were totally robbed, cousin-once-removed,' says Freya, and she hugs Ailbhe's head into her side. Ailbhe snuffles there for a while.

'You were looking forward to Dublin, weren't you, bub?' says Deirdre, in full Mammy voice. 'We'll go and we'll have a day out that day, won't we?'

We're not all upset. Nora is still smiling after her mention in the poem.

Iseult comes over.

'Ah, Ailbhe, the poor pet. *Such* a high standard of competition. I mean, obviously, it wasn't a competition. What a great showcase. Ailbhe, you're such a wordsmith. Maybe you'll write a part for me one day. Deirdre, isn't it? I think you trained me at under-fourteens.'

Ailbhe sniffs. Deirdre encourages her through gritted teeth. 'What do you say, Ailbhe?'

'Thank you.'

We all stand around, trying to think of something to say. We're not good losers, it turns out.

'Are you busy with the acting, Iseult?' I don't know why I asked her that, seeing as how it was me put the kibosh on her last outing.

'I'm actually focussing on other things right now, Ann,' she says. 'I'm concentrating more on being active locally. Like yourself. Don't get me wrong, *The Celts* was amazing for me personally. But when they pulled out it just opened my eyes. No one is going to look after us. We have to fight for ourselves. I'd be interested in having a chat some time. Have a look at my Facebook, Ann.'

She's staring at me. She knows. She definitely knows.

I start babbling. 'How's the NCT, are you down there much? We have the car due in there in a while. You'll go easy on us, won't you? You won't even need to check the emissions or the windows . . . haha.'

Why did I say windows? You'd never spot the window shaking if you weren't looking for it. *Shut up, Ann.* She doesn't seem to notice.

'Just helping Dad out. But I'm working on a pretty exciting project. I can't say too much yet, but let's connect on Facebook. Maybe our paths will cross on the litter trail, haha.' And she touches my arm. She goes over to Amelia, takes out her car keys and blips a swanky Kia nearby. We watch her leave.

Deirdre bustles Ailbhe into her car. Mam is standing next to me when Bim scuttles up. He's a smallish, slight man. He always wears overalls and a flat cap and for some reason a pencil over his ear, which he doesn't use. I have my suspicions of Bim. I think he's after the house. I've seen it happen before. Someone helps out and then they become indispensable and the son or daughter might take their eye off the ball and, before they know it, they're hearing the name called out at the will. I wouldn't put it past him. But Mam can't see that. She says he's just a handyman who does a few jobs for her because she has no sons to do them. But I think he's overstepping the mark. He gave her a phone. I had got her a phone, but she said it was too fiddly and Bim's one was a Doro with the big buttons. *It belonged to his own mother and she swore by it, Ann.* Even now when you leave a voicemail – which she doesn't check anyway – you have to leave it with Bim's dead mother.

'I'll bring you home, Mam.'

'Bim will bring me. I have a few jobs for him to do and I want to pay him too. Now, listen to me, Ann. Make. Sure. You. Get. Me. Tickets. For the Pope, do you hear me now? I don't want to miss it. Promise me now, won't you? Bim?'

She calls Bim over like *Driving Miss Daisy*. He gives me a look as if to say, *I'll take it from here.* And off they go.

'Well, none of that was weird at all,' says Freya. 'Maybe I'll see what Iseult's up to for my local round-up on the podcast. There is literally nothing to round up in every episode.'

Freya has a podcast. Everyone has a podcast now, by the looks of it. I should get one. I don't know what I'd say, though. Give out about my family. Sure, there'd be no one listening. Freya's is called 'The Culchie Feminist', and I'm ashamed to say I haven't listened to a full one yet.

We go back to the car. It gives a funny whine when I'm reversing.

'Go easy on her in the podcast, Freya. Until after the NCT anyway.'

3.

A PURE CHURCHILL

'The door was open, Ann,' says Patsy Duggan as I walk into the kitchen. He is sitting at the table. The cheek of some people.

'I'd rather they broke in than broke the door, Patsy. Freya, will you make tea?'

'Will you have tea *and* coffee, Patsy, just to keep your options open?' she asks, pure innocent.

He doesn't notice and just says, 'Tea will be grand.' He shifts from his left arse to his right arse. 'I thought I might have a word with Rory, Ann, before he goes away on his adventure. Thursday wasn't long creeping up on us.'

'N— next Thursday? Next Thursday, yes, of course, next Thursday. That's right, yes. True for you, Patsy, it *has* snuck up on us. We'd better get him packed up.'

'Is he about?'

'Ah . . .' And I see him coming around the kitchen side on his bicycle. He has a sliced pan. A bit of a peace offering, maybe. 'There he is now.'

I go out to intercept him at the back door.

'Thursday, Rory?' I roar-whisper at him. 'THURSDAY! Were you going to tell me at all?'

'Mam, chill. Do you need to take your HRT?'

'Get in there and say hello to your feckin' STEPfather.'

I let him in a few seconds ahead of me while I compose myself.

They are talking when I go in.

'You'll have a biscuit, Patsy,' I say with angry politeness.

'I found a few anyway, Ann. They'll do me.' And sure enough, he has a couple of Rich Tea in his paw. He's even opened a new packet.

Rory has taken off his hi-vis and I see he is wearing a T-shirt that says 'If you can't love yourself, how the hell you gonna love somebody else?' I can't but smile at him, despite wanting to kick his arse. Biology has us completely handicapped when it comes to our children.

Freya comes back in from the sitting room and pounces on the sliced pan.

I hear the growl of a lorry outside and soon after I hear Denis at the door, brushing dust off his trousers, clearing his throat with a big CHOOOOARGH. Denis doesn't stand on ceremony when he's in lorry mode, but I wish he'd take note of a visitor's car in the yard. I can hear him spit out across the yard. Maybe he recognized the car after all. He comes in full of talk.

'Jaysis, lads, such *dust*. I never saw the bate of it. Patsy, how are you? Are you canvassing or what?'

'Denis, good man. Where are you these days? Still above in the quarry? Plenty of work there, good man.'

'That's right. They're putting in a flyover for the Huawei factory. Some operation up there. They've a hole dug, I swear will they ever fill it? The Chinese must be up to something

24

big there. First the Saudis, then the Chinese, hah, Patsy? I suppose you're involved?'

Patsy's face doesn't change. He's oblivious, or brass-necked, or both.

'No better man to be drawing the cement to that. Good man. Good man. No better man.'

'Kilt I am, Patsy. This'll be my last boom, I'd say. I'm going to retire and become a consultant or one of these influencers.'

'Freelance like meself, Denis.'

'I'm nearly free at the moment with the price of the diesel and the insurance, but anyway, that's a story for another day.'

'I've a letter written to the minister about the diesel and another one about the insurance costs.'

'You were always good for writing letters, Patsy. A pure Churchill.'

It's relaxed between them. Denis mustn't know about Brussels.

'I was just over talking to Rory about Brussels, Denis.'

'Brussels? What are they after doing now? Banning lorries, is it?'

'Haha, no Denis, Rory's trip to Brussels.'

Sometimes Denis acts as if he's slow on the uptake, but it's all for show. You should see him when he's caught on the hop. He wasn't going to let Patsy know he knew nothing about Brussels. He says, 'Oh, right,' and asks is the tea new and pours it and sits down. All the time processing the news. Unflappable.

'What's the latest arrangement now?' he says. 'About Brussels, Patsy?'

'Well, as you know, Rory is going out as an intern for Mick the Lamp . . .'

'Who?' Freya laughs.

'He's our MEP, Freya.'

25

'I never even heard of this dude, Auntie Ann. Was there an election?'

'In 2014.'

'I have litch never heard of him. Why is he called The Lamp?'

'Mick the Lamp Cadogan. He's The Lamp because when he first got elected he said he would be a beacon to the Irish out in Brussels.'

'The light went out fairly lively,' says Denis. 'You only see Mick the Lamp now when he's trying to get credit for something. Isn't that right, Patsy?'

'My lips are sealed,' he says, but Patsy always has a bee in his bonnet about credit. 'Anyway, this lad will be learning the ropes of the European Parliament. With the Brits acting the maggot we'll need more and more of a presence out there. Someone a bit more useful than Mick the Lamp.'

'Someone like you, Patsy,' says Denis.

Patsy smiles and draws his finger across his lips.

'Remind me again how long he's going out there,' says Denis. 'Ann told me, but I've it forgotten.'

'Just the two months.'

'TWO M—' I can't contain myself. 'For FECK's sake, Rory! You are going away for two months and you didn't even . . .'

I get up from the chair and go over to ferociously boil the kettle. I swore I wouldn't let Patsy be meddling in our family again, and it's happening.

'Well, I . . . I suppose I'll leave ye to it,' says Patsy.

'I'll walk you out there, Patsy,' says Rory.

They are there muttering on the doorstep for a while. The only sentence I get is Rory saying, *You know what she's like.*

I'm in such a mood that Freya has to boil the spuds for the dinner. Denis handles it the way he always handles things – by worrying about parking and traffic at the airport.

I see a text from Tracy, my boss in Mellamocare, on my phone. *Hey hun x ok if you could upload the events report, know I pain tx byeee x*

Normally, I hate the paperwork I have to do for the people I mind in my job, but it's nearly a relief to do it this evening. Just to take my mind off things. That feeling doesn't last long.

Mellamocare are the 'elder-care provider' I work for and every single thing has to be documented in The System. What's more, they're after bringing in a new system, and it's as shite as the old system but in a different colour. And they're going to change the name to Soothocare. We got an email about it: *We are reflecting the changing dynamic business environment as we move to NextGen™ elder care.* Which is much better than saying: *The Saudis who own us got into a bribery scandal last year.*

This is all miles up above me in the 'corporate ladder'. All that matters to me is that when I want to Add Update, I still get a message saying, *Contact an Administrator.* I wish I could contact an administrator when it comes to my own children. Who's my ombudsman when my son neglects to tell me he's leaving the country in a few days' time? Ah, I suppose he's finding his path in life. And it's *some* life-path, I can tell you. Patsy had been our TD for years and there was talk he was gone a bit stale. That he'd lost his fight. Rory was only fifteen and on Transition Year work experience when he first went into his constituency office. By seventeen he was coming up with Patsy's election slogans.

RURAL CRIME: DUGGAN PROTECTS HIS PEOPLE.

FOR BETTER BROADBAND, DOWNLOAD DUGGAN.

DUGGAN TAKES YOUR POINTS AND GETS THE GOALS and a picture of Patsy playing football from his younger days.

DUGGAN: ONE LEG BUT TWO FEET ON THE GROUND.
Patsy has only one leg after an accident in London.

Patsy said it was *revolutionary*. And it was, compared to what he used to send out. A cousin of his did his slogans before Rory and the slogans were as dry as bran. We would get leaflets in the door saying: WHAT THE SUCKLER HERD DIRECTIVE MEANS FOR YOU AND YOUR HERD. Rory told him his election literature was 'tragic' and set him up on Facebook and Instagram and the whole shebang. Patsy was entranced.

'He has gumption, Ann,' says Patsy to me time and time again. 'You have all these young lads waiting around for something to happen now. Millennials, they call them. *Oh, I'm so offended at this, that and the other thing.* Rory is a pure throwback. If he was around a hundred years ago, he'd have run away to the Merchant Navy or been building railways out in Africa. When you get to my age in this business, you just know who has it.'

Even Mam thought he'd have made a great priest. 'He'd have ended up a celebrity and all, Ann. With the hair. If he could sing, he'd be a millionaire priest. But no one wants to be a priest now.'

I manage to finally get InfoMinder to believe me about how many adult nappies I've used this week and I press Submit on the four Sanitary Events. Rory knocks on the door. He's caught me at a better time. He sits down next to me.

'You're on The System.'

'I am.'

'Sanitary Events – four. Is that a good week?'

'Rory, you are terrible at making conversation.'

'I know you're upset, Mam, and I was putting off telling you. But I was going to be going away anyway. What did you think I was going to do this summer? Go out with Denis in the truck?'

28

There was no fear of that anyway. Denis and Rory are not a pair I would imagine delivering cement to a farmer building a new piggery.

'I just thought you'd go working for The Professor.'

'I did too, Mam, but Patsy says this is a great opportunity. He wants me to learn everything, Mam. Patsy might try for the European Parliament in a few years, when he gets sick of it here. It's a nice place to retire to. And when he retires, who do you think will take over? Who could be the next kingmaker from Kilsudgeon?' He points his thumbs at himself and says, 'THIS GUY, Mam.'

'Oh, Rory.'

'What's the *Oh, Rory*, Mam?'

'I don't know about being a TD for a career. They do terrible hours. It's not good for a family. I mean, if you had a young family.'

'Mam, do you see any small family around me right now?'

'No, but . . .'

'Mam, the money's good. You can make real change. Think about it. Your son the local TD.'

'I see. I'll think about it.'

He kisses the top of my head and switches on the football. I plug in earphones so I can finish off The System.

What I don't tell Rory is this. I see too much of my father in him. The charmer, the fella who thought things could be done quickly and easily. Who had schemes and plans and who could walk into rooms and have everyone eating out of his hand. And like Rory, he thought he had it all sussed out. He knew it all. But my father was easily led. And he got led into trouble. By fellas who were a bit better at deluding than him.

I didn't grow up on a farm, but for a few months, donkeys years ago, my father owned more cattle than nearly everyone around us in Clonscribben. When Ireland joined up to the EEC, the Europeans started giving money to farmers. Magic money. Spare money from leathery old Germans who didn't know what to spend it on. Headage payments for the cattle and the sheep. And sure enough, when a scheme like that started up in a country like Ireland, where everyone was on their uppers, it wasn't long before people were on the take. It wasn't Daddy's idea. Big Eddie Duggan – another relative of Patsy's uncle, who was a councillor at the time – and some latchiko up in The Department – who we never knew the name of – figured out a way to get money for nothing. Eddie was in school with Daddy and they always *thought they were miles too clever for normal work*, to hear my mother tell it. And she told it a good bit years ago when she'd be giving out to my father for leaving the buttery knife in the marmalade or some other small thing. Because this was brought up against Daddy for the rest of his life.

So the scheme was that Daddy was to pretend to be a farmer. Nine farmers, as it turned out. The man in The Department got them forms with stamps on them, Eddie the Pump would bring them around and he and my father would fill them out and apply for payments for cattle that didn't exist. A Guard would stamp it. If you look hard enough, you'll always find a Guard involved in these kinds of schemes.

I remember Daddy at the kitchen table with a pile of forms and he trying to think of names. When he'd think of a name, he'd look it up in the phone book to make sure it wasn't anyone too real or too close. He'd practise the signatures and Eddie would get his Guard to countersign it and then go off to the post office with letters addressed to the 'Department of Agriculture', only not our own post office, in case the postmistress would get suspicious. I was in my teens then and Ger was ten or so, and we were thinking this was great gas and wasn't it nice to be playing a game with Daddy. *How about Algernon Thompson, Daddy?* and Daddy would say, *No, that's too Protestant.*

At the height of it, he had a hundred cows. We joked the house was four farms and every bit of it was a field. If you were putting stuff up in the attic, you were bringing the cows to the Top Field. Under the stairs was The Byre. The hedge outside was known as the Long Acre.

Mam wasn't One. Bit. Happy. She had her lips pursed over it for the whole few months it was going on. I think by this stage the charmer she had fallen for was starting to tire her out. *He just wouldn't do things the way he was supposed to, Ann, ever! He'd take the longest way round to find a shortcut.* But me and Ger were pure giddy over it. We were the only ones left in the house at that stage. The brothers were gone to England, so there were no grown-ups to tell my father to cop on to himself. Ones that he would listen to anyway. It was easier to get away with that kind of thing then. You could even make up townlands and get away with it. Now everything is watched with satellites.

The thing about it was that he made shag-all money out of it. The money was always *on the way*. Once it had been 'processed' by Eddie the Pump. But that didn't stop Daddy spending like it was a sure thing. I remember he came home one day with a crate of bottles of lemonade.

The guard who stamped the forms was caught for telling the IRA about arms seizures up in a bog in the mountains in Lismeekan, and when they moved him they found the blank forms in his cubby. That led them to Eddie, and Eddie wriggled out of it, and dumped half the shite on Daddy. It would have gone very public, only that it would bring Eddie down and Eddie's cousin was a TD whose vote was needed to keep a coalition afloat. But it was public enough for us at the time. Charlie Hoare caught on the take. Mam was floored for a long time. She wouldn't come out of the house only to go to Mass. Even then she went to another Mass, which indirectly brought us to Kilsudgeon, because it was at that other Mass I got friendly with a few people and one of them was a friend of Denis's sister. So it was good for me but not for Daddy. When his scheme didn't work he got depressed and withdrew into himself. He was never the same man afterwards. And that's what I worry about when I see Rory now. Is some of it in my genes, seeing as how I've turned a blind eye to what Rory and Patsy are up to?

But if Rory gets stuck in any more Patsy Duggan stuff, he'll be the one to get caught. I'm sure of it. The likes of Patsy get away with it. If I can direct Rory away from the world of Patsy and all that shenanigans at all, I will.

4.

SOUNDS YANK

It's another beautiful hot summer's morning but, as I expected, Gordon and myself are the only two in the church car park. And the big Tidy Towns clean-up has a fierce look of 'no one else coming' about it.

Bing! *Hey guys, Can't make it on holidays this week* ☺ *Keep up the good work.*

If you're not going to turn up, don't be sending me WhatsApps with smiley faces, Bernie.

A car pulls in. A 181. Another volunteer? No, it's Andy Walsh, and he isn't going to be helping us. He goes around to the other side and gently edges his mother-in-law, Bessie Doran, out of the car. Bessie is bent half in two and half blind, but she points the walker in the direction of the church like she's laser-guided.

'Small turnout, is it, lads?' Andy says as he's passing us. Me and Gordon are standing there with so many pickers it looks like they were seized in a raid. And no one to use them.

'Grand day for it anyway.' He folds his arms and sits on the car bonnet.

'She's gone away on you, Andy.' I point at Bessie, who has continued on in unaided towards the church. Her face is set for some hard praying and she doesn't even look around.

'Oh, Janey, she is. There's no stopping her when she's heading for Exposition.' He scuttles after her.

Gordon leans back against the car-park wall. 'An intimate gathering, Ann,' he says.

Bing! *Me neither. Clodagh has training.*

We blink into the sun, watching the road, listening out for cars slowing down. But they only do so to gawp.

'Will we leave it, Gordon?'

'We cancelled the last one too, Ann. It sends out the wrong message.'

'There's no message going out at the moment, Gordon. Only ones coming in.'

Bing! *Oh sorry, was that today. Clean forgot, sorry.*

Three cars pull in over the next few minutes. Everyone gives us a salute and goes in to watch the Blessed Sacrament. They say the Church is in trouble, but there's a bit of life in it yet, by the looks of things. It's mainly women the same age as me and older. But we're keeping going much longer now. With all the scanning. When it works. And they do mindfulness there on a Thursday. 'As long as no one tells the bishop,' says Father Donnegan.

Bing! *Can you get milk gerry and not the low fat*

Bing! *And get yourself a couple of cans x*

A big night ahead for Gerry and Lorna.

This message has been deleted.

Sorry lol

'We'll do our bit anyway, Ann,' says Gordon, taking a picker.

We walk up the village and stop and stare. Four bags dumped over the wall at the house where Tadhg the Bear used to live. He's long gone now. A tank of a man. The house has an old planning notice on it announcing someone's intention to build retail and residential units. Nothing came of it. An old planning notice is practically an instruction to Throw Your Shite Here.

After all the fuss and publicity we got last year, the Tidy Towns has fallen away. 'A lack of strength in depth', Gordon calls it. That's Kilsudgeon all over. We're always one thing going wrong away from despair. It's the same with the footballers. They went on a run two years ago in the championship. They absolutely leathered Drumfeakle. We had a fifteen-year-old playing like a Brazilian. Then, against Clonscribben, the fifteen-year-old was being wound up by an ould lad on the sideline, calling him gay because he had a nice haircut, and the young lad ran to the sideline and milled into him and got sent off. The team had been leading, but didn't score again for the rest of the match. And they didn't win a match again for a year.

'What are we doing, Gordon? This is gone to the dogs. I can't even take a photo of us for Facebook.'

We carry on in silence, apart from giving out about the state of the place and a few more Bings! from the WhatsApp.

'Will we knock it on the head for the rest of the summer, Gordon? Start over in September?'

'Maybe, Ann. I'm not around much this summer. Flora has booked us on to a wine-tasting tour, followed by a holiday villa. It's our anniversary gift to ourselves.'

'That'll be lovely, Gordon.'

'We've no one else to spend our money on. Flora's always saying we need to enjoy ourselves. When we got over not having children, we said, we're a family too, aren't we?'

'A fine family, Gordon.'

I see a slight little bit of a pain in his eyes, but it's gone again. He claps his hands together.

'I'll get the jeep and we'll pick this up. We might as well be depressed on a clean street. We need more impetus to get more people involved,' he says.

'Well, if you're heading off, I can't do it on my own.'

He nods. 'I know, Ann. You're right. We shall dissolve for now and regroup in September.'

'That's fine by me, Gordon.'

We go to our cars.

Bing!

Who has cancelled now, I wonder, after it's all over? But it's a text from Jennifer and three missed calls.

Mam call me? Declan's gone weird.

I wave Gordon off and then lean against my car and call my other daughter, Jennifer. Her boyfriend, Declan, was always a bit odd, as far as I'm concerned, so I'm wondering did she just spot it or is he just gone odder.

'He's planning my birthday, Mam,' says Jennifer as soon as she answers. 'He says he wants to take charge of it, that I'm too busy to celebrate myself. He's making it a family thing, he says.'

'No, that's true. It's not like him at all.' It would be a normal thing for anyone else to do, but it's not Declan's scene.

'He's booked Slaughterhouse & Winch, Mam. He says, *Only the best for my girlfriend.* He said he's sending out invites to you and all the sibs and God knows who else.'

'Declan? Sending out invites? Is he well?'

'Stop, Mam. It's very weird. I blame that therapist. I mean, he's not even a therapist. He's just this celeb life coach that shy lads love. Lance Paxman. Declan went to a few of his talks and watched him on YouTube, and he's not the same since.'

'Lance Paxman. I haven't heard of him. That's not local. Sounds Yank.'

'More local than you'd think. Longford. Lance Paxman's not even his real name. He's Liam Padden. He says he changed it because of the country-music singer from up that way, but you just know the young lads in their Jack & Jones will fall for it. He's just a Dealz Jordan Peterson, if you ask me.'

'Would you believe I was in Dealz for the first time in my life there the other week, Jennifer? The *stuff* you'd get in there for half nothing. Denis even got a coin-collecting book and he was *delighted* with himself. One euro fifty! Where do they get it from? Is it the back of a lorry or what?'

I hear a sigh on the other end of the line. I get back to the subject.

'So anyway, you don't like the cut of this Lance Paxman?'

'He's a fucking chancer, Mam, sorry for cursing. I blame myself, actually. We had a bit of a row. Or, more accurately, I got annoyed with Declan. He doesn't argue, or rather he didn't used to.'

'What were ye arguing about?' I'm not hugely interested. I'm just hoping they'll break up and she'll tell me when it's done. My children always overestimate how interested I am in all the details of their love lives.

'What happened was, Mam, Declan doesn't like going out. He's not bothered seeing anyone except for me. He never had many friends and, you know, at the start that suited me just fine. I was sick of going out with lads in London I thought were nice and then you'd meet their friends and they were just gobshites. So I liked just having Declan to myself. And I wasn't living with him then, so I could suit myself. But when I moved in with him I felt like we should do the same things in the evenings together, so I tried to bring him out with my friends. It was actually funny. Because

37

he's blunt and it gets uncomfortable and, you know me, Mam, I like uncomfortable. Like one time, some of my old London workmates were over for this conference about maximizing returns in Dublin, which is basically squeeze more out of renters, and I had dinner with them. It was only because it was suggested in the place I work now that I needed to "sweat my network". Fuck sake, Mam. Like, I never really liked them. And they're three lads with a bit of a rep, so I brought Declan along. And they were being *verrry* Londony. Being all, like, *So JenJen, are you gonna bring us to a titty bar?* and *Decs, mate! What's your deal? How do you put up with this mad bint?* and all that, and Declan was like, *She's not mad, you shouldn't talk about her like that,* and they were all, *It's OK, mate, only a bit of banter,* and Declan says, *What do you mean, banter?* And it was, oh my God, Mam, *incredibly* awkward, but I was all like, SWOON, my man's standing up for me.

'But then, as I've been in Dublin a while and trying to reconnect with friends I actually like, so I bring Declan out a few times and he Doesn't. Say. A. Word. All. Night. Long. He just sits there. And that's *not* my kind of awkward. So I said to him, *Declan, you can't just sit there. You have to work on this.* And he says nothing to me, and I'm going, *SAY SOMETHING!* Then one day he announces he's going to see Lance Paxman . . .'

'Remind me who he is again.'

More sighing.

'Lance Paxman is telling lads there's a war coming and all the men are too pussy-whipped.'

'Pussy-whipped? Is that what I think it is or . . .'

Jennifer carries on. 'He's just exploiting fellas like Declan.'

'Like Declan?'

'You know, Mam, a bit different. Socially awkward. Odd. I know that's what you call him when he's not around.'

I'm silent for a second. Choosing my words carefully.

'Well, maybe it might do Declan some good, you know, to be more of a man about things.'

'What does that mean, Mam?'

'Like, weren't you saying he's kind of helpless a lot of the time? Didn't he get his mother to change light bulbs for him?'

'I suppooose. But he just needs a bit of confidence. And I thought *I* was the one giving him confidence. Paxman says all this stuff about men are really slugs and that only a few can get down the path in the rain without getting squashed and you don't see a slug stopping to worry about whether he's offending anyone. *Be one of the slugs that gets through*, he says.'

'And the dry weather as well. That's bad for slugs.'

'What? OK, whatever, Mam. This isn't really about slugs. Anyway, Declan goes to this Paxman show – *Ladz for Life* or something. He goes on his own. Comes home. Buzzing. Talking about all the lads he met. Talks more about other people in half an hour than in months before. *Gaz is a good laugh, Odran is big into gaming*, all of this. I think this must be good. We can build on this, you know. And then Lee Anne calls me. Lee Anne of Lee Anne and Barry. Lee Anne is lovely, but she's a pain in the hole at the same time, you know the way?' I definitely don't know the way, but I don't think it matters so I don't interrupt.

'Lee Anne was in college with me and we've had this like . . . competitive thing going on and I hadn't seen her in ages. I hadn't seen them in ages, and they've so much going on since. They've children and I'd been avoiding them until I had a fairly long-term fella. And I thought, cool, Declan's a bit looser. Now would be a good time to go, and he's like . . . you know, presentable. And I'm such a shit for thinking that way, you know? But it *is* important after a while, you know? When you're happy they're ready for their debut.'

I know what she means. Denis wasn't presentable. He left an oil mark on a wall from his trousers the first time he met Mam. And I was trying to hide it, but he says to Mam, *Is that tap leaking?* And the tap was leaking for *years*. And he went out and got wrenches and fixed it. Mam says, *A man of action, Ann. Keep him. We'll clean the oil stains after.*

'So, me and Declan go over, and they've put the children to bed and a lot of the talk is about children and Lee Anne is Instagramming throughout the dinner and she's hashtagging the shite out of Barry. Saying how blessed she is that Barry is really good at understanding the burden of emotional labour and that that's really gratifying and, to be honest, I'm bored out of my tits, but I want to rebuild my social life in Ireland since coming back and . . .'

'What is emotional labour? Is that worrying and fussing?'

'And then Declan says it, Mam.'

'What does he say?'

'He turns around to Lee Anne and says that Lance Paxman says that emotional labour is a fraud perpetuated against men already struggling under the weight of *actual* labour by feminists who have no sense of historical context.'

'Is that bad?'

'It's very bad, Mammy, if you're Lee Ann. She even goes on Instagram afterwards with a photo of a heart with thorns around it and how she was at dinner with *someone who I consider a friend* and suggesting I'm a prisoner trapped by a toxic man. Hashtag Run Melania Run. And I don't think I can really talk to her again.'

'Janey.'

'Janey is right, Mam.'

'What do Des and Phil make of the new Declan?'

'Des loves me anyway and she's just happy Declan is happy. Phil doesn't say much about anything.'

'So you're not splitting up with him any time soon?' I ask, trying not to sound hopeful.

'No, Mam, I'm going to stick it out. I love him, and he's kind and, of course, still hot.'

'That's always important. And how's life with the parents?'

'It's very cushy, Mam. The place they call a granny flat is like a house on its own. I'm going to hang in there with the new Declan for a while. Des was so happy I moved into it. She says I made it smell nicer.'

Des – short for Desdemona – and Phil are Declan's parents. Jennifer moved in with them when she moved back from London. Not straight away. She tried renting for a while and discovered she hated living with strangers. *That would be like, I don't know, Mammy. I can't be living with some Forever 21-wearing Script fan who's bringing lads back from Coppers and talking non-stop about banter. I didn't move back from London to go back ten years in time.*

My second daughter has had an interesting few years. She was in London making big money in financial something or other and then got an attack of conscience and came back here to recentre herself. She recentred herself right on to Declan, who was our lodger while he was being an extra during the filming of *The Celts*. They were the most unlikely couple at the time and, to be honest, I still don't see the attraction. I mean, I suppose you could say he is good-looking. *Well fit*, says Jennifer. Anyway, for all her talk of recentring, Jennifer gets a hankering for money again and next of all I hear she's working for CapitaVistaprise. And guess who owns them? Some other big Saudi oil company. Jennifer was never a martyr to her principles, even as a child. *No way* was she going to make her Confirmation, and then she heard you got money for it and she made some deal with the Holy Spirit and everyone was happy. Except the bishop, I suppose.

'So when's this birthday do happening?'

'Two weeks, Mam. Oh, I'm dreading it. It's hard enough thinking about turning thirty without my boyfriend going through the Change.'

'Hard turning thirty? There was no talk of thirty when I was thirty. I barely noticed it. We didn't bother with roundy numbers. Forty, now, that'll soften your cough. What did we do for my fortieth?'

'We went to the chipper, Mam. I wouldn't be using you as an example of celebrating birthdays. And it was different for your generation. You had it all sewn up at that stage. You had your children and your house, but what do I have? That's why the new Declan is giving me the heebie-jeebies. I don't want to start all the dating shit again.'

'Haven't you a great career?'

'No, Mammy, I have a high-pressured job.'

'And savings.'

'Not that much, Mam. I spent most of it on rent.'

'It can't have all gone on rent.'

'London and Dublin, Mam. Rent has been crazy expensive. And I might have sort of spent it as well.'

'Jennifer, you were always so savvy about money.'

'And I might have lost it.'

'How did you lose it?'

'I might also have bought a few shares.'

'But I thought shares were handy enough at the moment.'

'Well, Warren Buffet, not all shares all the time. Sometimes things go tits up. Anyway, look, it's fine. Declan is fine. It's all fine. He's still kind and sweet and fit, and I'm grand, Mammy, it's fine. Forget it.'

This is Jennifer all over. Brings a load of worries home to me like a bag of washing and then tells me not to worry, that it's grand. I should forget it. But I can't forget it now. That's why I was always a mother who didn't ask too many

42

questions when they went on a night out. I couldn't take the knowing. I was always better off in ignorance. And as far as I was concerned, I was finished rearing Jennifer until she had children. *And* I thought she had a few bob and might throw some of it our way when we wanted to put our feet up. If I'd known the generation that followed us were going to have no money, I'd have had more fun along the way.

'Hang in there, Jennifer.'

'I will, Mam.'

For both our sakes.

'Will you be staying here for long?'

'It'll be at least a couple of nights because the day before my birthday dinner I'm going to the wedding with Stephanie, so I'll stay the night with her.'

'Wedding? Stephanie?'

'Yes, Mam, Stephanie. Your daughter-in-law Stephanie? The wife of your eldest son? I told you I was going with her to Vivian Towey's wedding – you know, the horsey one. I sort of know her.'

'You told me about a wedding, but when you said Stephanie, I didn't think it was Stephanie *Rourke*? And . . . are Kevin and the family coming?

'No, just Stephanie. Kevin didn't tell you?'

'Kevin doesn't text much, Jennifer.'

'Yeah, your first-born son, not letting you know his wife was coming home. That's not strange at all, Mam. Anyway Stephanie is bringing me along as the plus one. Stephanie wants some girl-pal time, as she calls it. She wants to catch up with you too, so buckle up, Mam!'

And she says goodbye and hangs up.

It never rains but it shites down. Buckle up? I'll need a new buckle. Stephanie is married to my eldest boy, Kevin, and they live out in Dubai. The Rourkes have money. Or look like it anyway. We're matt, they're hard gloss, says

Denis. Her father is Derek Rourke, the auctioneer and a few other things besides. They look down their noses at us and don't even hide it. The mother is a piece of work. Fidelma. *I'm glad Stephanie found someone, Ann, and while Kevin wouldn't be our first choice, he seems to be a good man*. She told me this at the wedding! Poor Denis took out more money to buy drinks at the wedding than he did for the deposit on the only new car we ever got.

Kevin and Stephanie have two children and I barely know them. When I hear Stephanie is visiting I get an ulcer with the worry. The house gets a deep clean. I don't know why the Rourkes get to me so much. It was just that it was my first family wedding and we felt so *small* at it. I can't be sure, but I swear there were digs in the speeches. *We're delighted to welcome Kevin into the family. He will be well looked after. You won't have to bring him out on the trucks anyway, Denis*, says Derek. The only time I ever saw Denis angry. He stopped buying anyone a drink after that.

Fuckem, he says. *They can buy their own. It's all mixers with them anyway*.

Denis doesn't mix well with mixers.

I'll have to break it to him gently that Stephanie Rourke is on the way.

5.

SOME TYPE OF AN IRAQI

Cutting an old man's hair is not part of the official work of a carer, but I've become more unofficial this past while. According to The System, I'm responsible for three old people. I'm not allowed to mind more because I'm on probation. But then I have a few unofficial clients as well. I don't tell Tracy about them because I'd be contravening such-and-such a policy within the whatchamacallit protocol. It wouldn't be best care practice, but going around and cutting a bit of hair, keeping people company and getting a shnakey few bob in cash isn't the worst way to work either. Rory tells me I'm a hypocrite to give out about Patsy when I'm unofficial myself, but that's different. I think.

Johnny Lordan is a sweet old fella who I used to mind 'officially' when he hurt his leg. He's so grateful to get company. His wife was a bit of a tramp and ran off with a burglar-alarm man. Then she turned the daughter against Johnny. But just as Johnny's leg healed up, he and the daughter had a reconciliation. She has a habit of looking for money off her father when she's a bit skint after partying because she's her mother's daughter, but Johnny turns a blind eye. When I go in, he gives me tea with old milk and a biscuit that's as soft as a bun, but my constitution is well used to ould lad's food. I don't really know anything about cutting hair except not to leave him bald and not draw blood. I ask him how the daughter is and he knows from my voice that I'm really asking if she's been around looking for money again.

'Ann, don't be worrying about me. I'd rather feel like an eejit. It's better than feeling nothing.'

He gives me twenty euro, which is far more than he'd pay for a better job anywhere else. I feel guilty about it. I tell him he should try the Turkish lad in Drumfeakle.

'Ah I don't want men to be fiddling with my head. And those fellas aren't even Turks, I heard someone saying. He's some type of an Iraqi.'

'Shur it doesn't matter where he's from, Johnny. Hair is hair. Denis loves going up there.'

'I don't like people looking at me when I'm leaning back in a chair. People would be laughing at me.'

'No one would be laughing at you, Johnny. Denis gets his ears done there. And that's a big job, I can tell you. The fella burns it off like he was killing weeds. It's some operation, Johnny. Pamper yourself. You said yourself you wanted to feel something.'

But I don't think he'll go up unless I drive him. Which I might do someday. Since he's unofficial, I could bring him anywhere he wanted to go.

My next visit is for Neans Dolan, who is officially rostered to me. A mighty little woman who keeps me filled in on all the gossip. Poor Neans has it hard at the moment. She got shingles, of all things. The curse of the old. When I get there and let myself in, I can tell the mood of the house is down.

There's no radio or telly on and she's sitting there looking glum. I have lotions and potions to give her.

'I was going well, Ann,' she says as I put the compress on her side. 'I was thinking of getting out of the wheelchair. I went back playing cards. That was the mistake I made. Thinking I was on the mend. Got too full of myself. That's the punishment when you get old, Ann. You get a good box in the mouth for trying to go against nature and enjoy yourself. I said the same to the priest, Ann. Not Father Donnegan. The spare one. He said, *We must offer it up, Neans.* I said I would in my fuck offer it up, Ann. That shook him. You should have seen the look on his face, Ann.'

I've never heard Neans curse before, but shingles is a pure curse.

'I should never have gone to that christening, but Orla wanted me to be there and I'm nearly sure there was a spotty child at it. And you know, they'll have the christening, but no notion of taking the child to Mass. And I'm the one who gets punished then.'

I didn't tell Neans at the time that you can't get shingles from someone with chickenpox. She had her theory and it was giving her a bit of comfort to blame the daughter so I let her sound off. It's certainly a bad dose she got. All around her side. She is tormented with itching. As I'm washing her feet I see her rosary beads broken into bits on the floor at the skirting board. It looks like it was thrown against the wall.

'Blast them all, Ann – Him, the Son and the Holy Ghost. Doing nothing there, only laughing at me from their holy pictures.'

After Neans, I have to pop up to Babs Cronin. She is Gary Cushin's aunt. Cushin was Kilsudgeon's only Communist, but then he got married and she's not as into it as he is. So he resigned from himself. Cushin the Russian they still call him, though. Because you can't resign from a nickname.

Gary is there when I call in. Dropping off a big box of books.

'Are you moving in, Gary?' I say, half joking.

'Aisling wants some of these out of the house,' he says sharply.

We are there in the sitting room while I am taking Babs through her physio after her turn.

'Now once more with the other leg, my darling. That's it now. Good woman.'

'Tis warm, Ann.'

'Tis, Babs.'

'I don't mind the heat, but I hope it don't get close. I don't like it when it's close.'

I tell her that my mother was, in fact, only the other day going on about the humidity. She is happy that she's not the only one.

Gary is sitting over at the table, somehow not being enthralled with this. He's reading *The Anti-Fascist Handbook*. Every so often he takes notes. He catches me looking at him and sniffs. He's out with me because he knows I think he took plants from my boats last year. I had no way of proving it. I just know that suddenly his mother's place looked like Homes of the Year and she knew nothing about it. I said nothing for a while, but then I told Denis and Denis said it to the Twins and the Twins offered it out to the parish as fact.

'You're kept busy with the anti-fascism, Gary.' That's the best I can do for a conversation starter. 'Freya is on about it too, on her podcast, Gary.'

'Your niece is one of the few around here who is awake, Ann. We are sleepwalking towards disaster.' He puts down his book and looks right at me.

'And no sign of Davey with you these days.'

Gary looks hurt. Davey Finnerty used to be Kilsudgeon's other Communist but he and Gary fell out a while back.

'Davey has joined the dark side, Ann. It is very sad. We soldiered together to show the people around here that the real enemy is the cosy cartel of late-stage capitalism and the apathy of the masses. But they were too busy going to Mass. Davey still thinks we need a revolution, but I fear he's gone in another direction.'

'Has he left?'

'Ideologically, Ann. I called to him one day. I didn't even go in. He's on YouTube non-stop now. I could see it through the window. His mam and dad have to watch their telly in their room. He has it taken over. There's something gone wrong there, Ann. Dark forces that are a bigger threat than the military-industrial complex.'

'Your aunt is keeping well all the same, though. She'll be up and about in no time.'

'She is, Ann. We will need everyone for the battles ahead.'

'Grand so, Babs. I'll leave you so. You've a busy few months ahead of you with the war.'

'My nephew is very good to me, Ann.'

In fairness, he is. Although I suspect he likes having some-where to go and read his books in peace. There's a small baby below in the house with Aisling. Gary had a family late in life and I think he's still in shock.

I finish up with Babs, and I'm about to go up to Nonie when Tracy texts me.

Hey Annie D! Just checking you are ok with the roster change for this week. Nonie moved to tomorrow. Tx T x!

The first Tx is Thanks and the second T x is T for Tracy and a kiss. The x's annoy me. There's nothing wrong with kisses, but Tracy is not on the kissing list. There wouldn't be many who are, because I'm just not that kissy in writing. I don't even x Mam. She isn't kissy in real life either. I'd do a kiss down on top of her old small head when I'm saying goodbye, and I can feel her tense up. She'll hold my hand,

49

so I think it's just she has a sensitive scalp. Rory is fierce for the kisses, but he always was an expressive boy. The first text he ever sent to me was *TANKS 4 FONE U LEDGE MAMMY XXXX.* Tracy has been putting them in for a good while. With the phones these days you can see a whole year's conversation in the texts. So I see all Tracey's x's and nothing from me. It makes me look awful cold. Mind you, if I go back far enough in the texts there are no kisses. Just Tracy being cross. *Not Acceptable Ann* and *I'm struggling to understand Ann* and a few *???*s.

That was when I got into trouble and was nearly sacked. They tried to make out I was interfering in a will, but I wasn't. When I came back from suspension I was put on a thing called Continuous Presence Probation Programme, which means that Tracy had to come out with me to all my visits. It was a trial for both of us. As soon as I completed any task, she would take me into another room and log it into The System on her tablety thing. She had to log every single thing I did into The System.

Please outline the task you've just completed, Ann, she would say.

The task I just completed was the wiping of the patient's arse, Tracy.

I can't put in wiping the patient's arse, *Ann. This is being recorded to protect you as well, you know.*

How about I was cleaning the patient's bits, *Tracy, will that do?*

Tracy would sigh and write *performing hygiene assessment and remedial action.* After a few weeks of this she changed me to Low Intensity Intervention and Autonomy Enablement Probation, which meant Tracy only had to turn up the odd time. Then she went on a course about Conflict Resolution in the Caring Industry and that's when the x's started in the texts. The WeCareALot Caring Industry Awards were coming up, and she wanted one, badly. She was always obsessed with awards. She even had a debating award from school on a shelf in her office. *St Siofra's 5th Year Christmas Debate runner-up*. And *The Pioneer and Total Abstinence Society Starving Poor Debates 1988 Highly Commended*. I'm nearly certain you only get certs for Highly Commended. Maybe her father got one made. The wife died young and she was an only child, so he doted on her, or so they say. The only other one was the *Mellamo EMEA Employee Engagement Journey Best Promotion of Inclusion and Diversity 2015 award goes to the Ireland Rural Sector H team*. There was no sign of Tracy's name on the trophy, but she seemed to have claimed it for herself and made a small name plate from cardboard that she put in. And even that got taken away after I got into trouble, after the Tidy Towns and the Saudis. She was heard bitching about me that it was my doing and she would get it back if it was the last thing she did.

I only know this because her secretary took a shine to me. I got into the habit of bringing in a few Double Deckers for her if I was passing. She was always on a diet and couldn't buy the chocolate for herself, but if *someone* happened to leave it there . . . I wasn't fishing for information at all, but she took me into her confidence. Mellamocare seemingly brought in new Engagement Targets. And if an Area Sectoral Leader like Tracy didn't hit them, she was for the high jump.

Engagement is the new word for 'happy', or 'no complaints, grand, thanks'. They make us fill out pages and pages on The System about how engaged we are. I don't like it. It's one of those questionnaires where you think they're trying to trick you. Like, if you answered (a) to the first one and (d) to the fortieth one, they'll call the police because only serial killers have that pattern.

Tell Tracy you want help filling it out, says the secretary. *You're her project. The prodigal daughter. If you return, she'll get her award back.*

51

I text Tracy now to say *thanks* and I force myself to throw in an *x*. The phone beeps immediately with her thanking me with two x's. She's upped the stakes. If this carries on, we'll be x-rated.

Then she rings me. 'I've just thought of something, Ann.'

I know well she's spent the whole day thinking of the something.

'So, Ann, it's been a great few months, I guess, realigning with you again, and I think you're ready for the next step. I think we can help you take on more challenging work packages. It's a vote of confidence from the organization. I'd like you to take on Sylvester, Ann.'

'Ah . . . I . . .'

'Ann, before you reply, I know he has a reputation. I know some of the younger staff are unwilling to engage with him. But all the safeguards would be there, and I think a lot of it has just been misunderstandings. The younger generation are not used to his ways, but someone older would be able to handle him. Also, you might be safer because you . . .'

'Because I'm an ould wan and he wouldn't touch me, is it, Tracy?'

Tracy clears her throat. She senses my Engagement scores dropping.

'Oh no, Ann, of course not, I didn't mean anything of the sort. I mean, with your experience you are better at reading the signs. Our other experienced carers are very stretched at the moment, so that's why I'm asking you. I mean, I can't force you, but it is something that would put a positive light on your record with us. Sylvester is someone in basic good health, but he's also in good financial health and we would love to be able to give him some real value-added care.'

'I'll think about it, Tracy.'

'Thanks, Ann.'

I think about it, and in the time it takes me to hang up I know the answer is no.

It's not that I couldn't take on Sylvester. I've tamed randy old men worse than him. I just couldn't be bothered taking on a load of grief just so someone else can win an award. Not that I wouldn't be a bit nosey about getting a peek inside his place. Sylvester has a story. He's one of the last few characters left. They say he was a merchant seaman. They say, years ago, he married some type of an aristocrat abroad and that they parted on good terms and she left him a pile of money sitting in Switzerland. They say a lot of things about him, but no one knows for sure. He used to come home once every few years. There was a time when Sylvester Barrett's return would send a ripple down the town. He always seemed to have money and he stationed himself in the pub for weeks at time, holding court.

I heard about Sylvester's sessions from Tommy Mullins. When Tommy was alive, himself and the nephew, Noel, had no one to make dinner for them so they used to go up to the pub every day for their lunch. And for a few weeks every few years they watched the Sylvester show. *Shortland Street* was turned down in the background, three or four men were gathered closer around Sylvester, and a few more looked at him over the top of their pints, pretending not to listen.

Occasionally a silageman would come in, get half the story and be asking questions and be waved away because they were interrupting the flow. The flow of Sylvester Barrett telling the mountainy men about the wonders of the world.

My dear men . . .

Sylvester Barrett has a way of talking that would make you believe it's normally congressmen he's dealing with and you would do well to listen because you might learn something.

Cape Town, men. That's where it's at . . .

And by *it*, Sylvester was meaning the kind of action they had never got before and never would in the future. The kind of activity that would have them needing the Stroke Warning Signs Chart. Face Changing, Arm Weariness, Speech Gone Quare, Time to Call.

Go to Cape Town. The women there are from another world . . .

And mountainy men like Petey Welch in for a sandwich would nod and say, *Oh, Cape Town, that's right*, and mull over the situations they might find themselves in.

The women, gentlemen, all different races and colours. You'd see them every colour under the sun. A history of pain and human cruelty has created the most beautiful women in the world. Tommy quoted him word for word. He remembered it because he was nearly ready to head out there himself. He remembered it word for word because he was nearly ready to head out there himself. *Only who'd look after my nephew, Ann?* He wasn't going to bring Noel with him, you'll notice. Sylvester had them all convinced that they only had to open their mouths out there and it would be women from heaven. *They love the mellifluous tones of the Irish accent out there. I had them in the palm of my hand, my dear men. As soon as I told them my name and where I was from.*

And to hear Tommy tell it, the lads were lost in thought, thinking about the coffee-coloured women that were only too delighted to talk about how it wasn't a summer for hay at all. And then, when the conversation dried up, what the coffee-coloured women wouldn't *do* to them in some back-street away from the main tourist areas.

When Sylvester came back he used to stay with Nonie's people – he's a distant cousin of Nonie's, and they had a small mobile home out the front and that's where he slept. But that's not where he is now. He lives in Wilderbook House. The old home of Lady May. They say she is some sort of royalty going way back, a cousin of Lord Something of

Somewhereshire in England who had a spare house in Ireland. Her father used to throw parties for all the children around here every Christmas, but then the hunger strikes happened and the mood changed. Even around here. Some old IRA lads *made it known* that people weren't to be kowtowing to the Brits, even though she and her father were Catholic. She never went to Mass in Kilsudgeon. I remember for years on a Sunday a taxi picked her up and brought her to Town to go to the cathedral. She only wanted to deal direct with the bishop. Then that bishop was mentioned in a report about abuse because he did nothing to stop it and he was shunted off to Rome to do whatever shady bishops do when they're retired.

Lady May never got another taxi to Mass again. She went against the Church completely then. One day, her taxi man got a call from her saying, *Bring me to the pub*. She tottered into Johnny's, opened her purse, put a twenty-pound note on the counter and said, *Throw me out a rum there like a good man, I've an awful thirst on me*, as if she had just finished bringing in the hay. And she drank the first drink in her life that wasn't Communion wine.

That's where she met Sylvester. I don't know the exact ins and outs, but they got talking and they got drinking and the little mobile home was pulled down the road to go outside Wilderbrook House, and after a while it was towed away again, to the scrapyard. They lived together for three years before she got cancer and died.

But still no, I'm not keen on taking him on. The other women say the house is in an awful state. And that he keeps going on about his *native carvings*. One woman found a load of jars of pee in there. No, I've enough to be doing and I want to spend whatever spare time I have left before Thursday with my young boy.

6.

THAT'S A NASTY GATEPOST

One of the things I have to be doing is, the following morning, calling to Nonie. May God forgive me but she's an ould witch. She's given me nothing but unpleasantness, for all the time I've looked after her. When I arrive into her place, I know I've made a mistake. I am wearing a new chain around my neck. It's not even that swanky. It has a little bee on it. It's cute, like. I got it with the Carer's discount. But Nonie sees it and latches on to it straight away.

'YOU'RE FOOLING NO ONE WITH THAT CHAIN. IS SHE, BRIAN? IT'S NOT GOING TO MAKE HER LOOK YOUNG, IS IT?'

And her long-suffering husband Brian says, 'Ah no, Nonie, there's no need for that,' but he doesn't go much further in defending me. Which I understand. I wouldn't be arguing with her over another woman's chain.

Nonie has hated me since I first stepped in the door. And I can never figure out why. She is married to a saint of a man who swears to me she's much mellower when I'm not there.

And indeed, Freya came in with me one time and Nonie was all smiles for her, while glaring at me over her shoulder. She gets a couple of hours a week to give the husband a break, and no one else wants to look after her because she's so unpleasant. Denis keeps asking me why I do it. Maybe it's for Brian. She's in a chair for fifteen years. He loves her to bits, but she's had rows with nearly everyone she knows and he doesn't get a rest. When I go up, he just goes and sits in the other room with his eyes closed. I can't leave him.

She still lets me come over, though. She won't hear of it if I ask does she want me to get a replacement. She knows she could complain about me, but she still tolerates me changing a dressing on her back or bringing the prescription, or all the other little jobs that I do. It's like she wants me close enough so she can reach me with her words. They get the care-hours for nothing off the Health Board, even though I'm told there's money from a dead aunt's house keeping them ticking over. People don't appreciate what they get for free at all.

When I'm finished, Brian walks me to the door and thanks me, and I nearly run to the Škoda, so happy to be done for another visit.

I get back to the house and, for the second time that week, Patsy is waiting for me. Leaning against the car, sunning himself like a cat. He's bristling with enthusiasm, rubbing his hands together.

'Well, Ann,' he says by way of greeting.

'Twice in one week, Patsy. If I'd known, we'd have got a list of potholes we'd like you to fix.'

'How was the rounds, Ann? Good, good, good.'

He doesn't wait for me to reply.

'Trojan work you do, and the Tidy Towns as well, mighty stuff altogether. A credit to the community, yes, yes, have ye a clean-up coming up?'

'We had one this week, Patsy.'

'Ah, that's good. Heroes in the hi-vis, isn't that what the *Sentinel* called ye?'

He follows me in towards the house. Praising me all the way. He hangs back a little, or he'd have his chin on my shoulder as I open the door. I usher him in and go through the house looking for Rory, and I find him out the back, eating a Magnum with earphones in.

'Rory! *House of Cards* is looking for you.' I don't care if Patsy can hear me or not.

'Not an appropriate joke any more, Mam, since Spacey got cancelled,' Rory replies.

'Actually, Ann, it's you I've come to see. I forgot to mention it the other day. A very special thank-you for giving Rory your blessing for Brussels.' He pulls an envelope out of an inside pocket. 'Rory had said to me last week that he'd love to have a bit of time to catch up with his mother, so we were thinking maybe you'd go out with him for the first couple of days to help him settle in.' And he hands me over the envelope and there's a printout of a ticket inside. Flexiconomy class Ann Devine DUB-BRU.

It was funny how neither of them mentioned that the other day. I see the email with the booking was sent *after* the time he called around.

'Well, Ann, now what do you make of that, off to Brussels?'

'Ah, it's . . . I suppose . . . yes, of course, that'll be grand . . .'

How do you react to Brussels? I don't know is it a place would many get a surprise trip to.

Rory appears at the door. 'So you've heard, Mam. Brussels! Happy Mother's Day.'

'Easter was very late this year.'

'That's one for the bucket list now, Mammy.'

'Brussels, yes, it is, yes.'

'And you'll be staying in a very exclusive apartment on the Rue d'Idalie, right near the European Parliament, Ann.'

'An all-expenses-paid trip, Patsy?'

He looks uneasy. 'Well, I suppose not all expenses, but you'll have a great time, won't you? You will, good woman yourself. It's a very cosmopolitan city, Ann. The Paris of Belgium. The shopping is great there, all sorts of boutiques, and the perfumeries. Women go mad for that.'

He's taking the wrong angle with me there anyway. I have about as much interest in shopping in Brussels as I do in clothes shopping in Kilsudgeon.

'Oh, I don't know, Patsy. I wouldn't like to risk buying anything out there. What if a zip gave in or it was the wrong colour and you wanted to send it back? Geraldine is having awful trouble getting her money back for a top. *Send the barcode*, they said, *send this, send that*. And when you ring there's no one there. Only you get on to someone in Bombay.'

Rory makes an impatient noise.

'Mam, I think you're focussing on the wrong thing here. I'm going to be at the heart of power. I'll be laying the groundwork for the Brexit negotiations. And I'll start by telling the Brits to shove it up their holes. But in a diplomatic way.'

'That's the boy,' says Patsy, almost proudly. He nearly ruffles his hair. It's a bit late for him now, I suppose, but I wonder, if Patsy had a son of his own, would he be so obsessed with turning my son into his heir?

Denis comes out of the toilet. If he's surprised to see Patsy again, he doesn't show it.

'I was just presenting your good lady wife with her tickets to Brussels.'

'Are we going to Brussels?' says Denis.

'Unfortunately, my good man, I could only get the one flight. But there'll be plenty of chance with Rory out there.'

59

I can see the little shadow of disappointment go across Denis's face, but he deals with it straight away.

'Ah, it's just as well. I wouldn't be able for travelling in this heat now. Those planes get stuffy.'

Says the man who spends twelve hours a day in the cab of a lorry.

There is no further chat and we all spend a couple of seconds looking at nothing in particular and then Patsy rubs his hands to break the spell and announces he has to head away, and that there is, it turns out, no rest for the wicked.

I go out with him on to the road to his car. I suppose it's only fair, since the man is giving me a holiday. As we get near the car, I notice there's a big scratch all along the length of it. I don't comment on it as I've had a few scrapes in my day. But Patsy sees me looking at it and he runs a finger along it casually.

'Just a scrape, Ann. Matt Moran's pillar. I was in there about getting the young lad bumped up the waiting list for his operation. That's another scandal now, how a young lad can't see a doctor on time and, before you know it, he'll be crippled. CRIPPLED. Anyway, when I was coming out the door, didn't I scrape the car on a gub of an old gate hook. It could have been a lot worse, couldn't it? We're all healthy, isn't that the main thing? Unlike poor young Jesse Moran.'

It isn't like Patsy. He doesn't give an explanation unless he's asked for it. That's how he keeps going in politics, while the younger crowd around him talk too much and say something stupid. He gets into the car with a final *Grand so, g'luck*, and drives off. And as the car drives away I see that the scratch goes all the way around. That's a nasty gatepost.

Rory appears at my side and I mean to ask him does he know what all of this is about, but he's straight away in with more sweet talk.

'We'll have some craic, Mam. The two of us. The two messers on the tear again.'

He catches me right in the gut with that one. Rory was born a few years after the other three and we got to be fierce pals, especially in the first few years. The pair of us had all sorts of outings. I'd pick him up after school and we'd go to Drumfeakle to the library, or even the odd time over to Town, where they had a playground. If Denis was in before us, he'd say, *Where are the two messers off to today?* and we'd look at each other and laugh. That's hard to shake off, no matter what they do.

We go back inside.

'You can plámás me, Rory, but I'm still not happy about all of this. You'll get into trouble. The likes of us are always the ones caught by the guards. We're not able for the spotlight.'

'What guards, Mam? Seriously. What are you talking about?'

I'm not going to tell him about Daddy now, so I peter out. Rory takes over.

'Mam, you keep talking about *the likes of us* as if we're, like, I dunno, the peasants. I'm the likes of me. I'm different. I'm a disrupter. Pushing boundaries to get through to people. The world is changing, Mam. It's connected. No one is pure any more.'

'What do you mean, pure?'

'Well, look at you making profits for a company owned by the Saudis. The Saudis, Mam. You might as well be working for Roose Bolton.'

'Who?'

'*Game of Thrones*, Mam. The fella that killed his ould lad and threw his stepmother to the dogs. Anyway, Mam, no one is squeaky clean, so it's about getting the knowledge.

61

Me going to Europe. It's my apprenticeship, Mam. It's like I'm going off to be fostered. Like Fionn and the Fianna.'

'Don't mention the Fianna to me, Rory. It gives me the shivers after last year.'

'And The Lamp is like the old guy with the Salmon of Knowledge. I'm just going to get the knowledge. I'm all about the knowledge. Here's how it is, Mam, OK? I've seen the state of them in the college societies, those young Fine Gael and Fianna Fáil types. Chinos with Ben Sherman shirts tucked in. And then the lefties are just forty-year-old lads in bandanas repeating English for, like, the fucking thirtieth time. Patsy wants a third way. A more practical one. I'm part of a movement, Mam. The new Independents. Patsy is letting me play in Cork and now in Brussels. Mam, there's lots you don't know about me. I know where I'm going with my life.'

He's right, I don't know enough about him. And if I'm ever to get him away from Patsy's clutches, I should at least find out.

Denis waves two cans at me. We go outside to our two chairs. Looking at the sunset with our cold cans. Saying nothing for a while.

'The first summer we get a heatwave and you get sent out abroad. Doesn't that bate all?'

I don't reply, and he asks me what's wrong.

'Am I a good mother, Denis?'

'It's a bit late to be asking now, isn't it?'

'Kevin didn't even tell me Stephanie was coming over. Are we that distant? Deirdre thinks I've abandoned her to the farmers. Jennifer is staying with her fella because she's in love with *his* mother, and now Rory, off again. It just feels like I've lost control. Did I do something wrong?'

'The way I see it, Ann, our job is to get them to eighteen alive and they can do whatever they want afterwards as long as they don't get a drugs debt that we have to pay off.'

'What drugs debt?'

'You see it on the news. The gangs would be around kicking in the door, taking the telly over a debt one of your children owed them.'

'I'd like to think we'd be expecting a bit more than that, Denis.'

'The break will do you good, Annie,' he says. 'You deserve a bit of a holiday.'

'My break. *Shite!*'

'What, Annie?'

'I have to ask Tracy for the time off.'

7.

THEY'RE TALKING ABOUT VAJAZZLING

'No, Ann.'

This is what Tracy says when I ring her the following morning. It's the plainest she's spoken to me in months.

'I can't give you the time off. Not at this notice. I know it's an important time for you personally, but I just can't organize a roster change at this stage.'

'But . . .'

'Yeah, it's just that, well, with your recent record, I guess it's all about having, um, credit in the bank, as it were. So unless . . . let me see now. I'll just pull up the global roster.'

I can hear tapping on the computer and murmuring on the other end of the phone. *Click*, the sound of a pen. *Tut tut. Hmmm.*

'Yeah, there is one opening. Sylvester.'

'Sylvester?'

'Ann, if you can sign him up this afternoon, maybe I can sort something out.'

'I'll do it.'

Wilderbrook House is up a lane off the main road from Kilsudgeon to Drumfeakle. How many times have I passed the entrance over the years and never had reason to go in? It had old-style iron gates once upon a time, and as I come in the avenue I can see them discarded. Lady May had a man in to maintain the place, but since she died it's been neglected. The fields on either side of the lane are covered in ragwort. There is grass down the middle. Big trees line the avenue. There are a couple of half-finished walls in some of the gaps in the ditches and I can see in others where rubbish has been dumped.

As I round the last bend before the house there is a large monkey-puzzle tree on the lawn in front of the house. That's how you know you're dealing with Quality. You don't see a monkey-puzzle tree in front of a scrapyard. But as I get closer I see that the rest of the front of the house is a scrapyard. There are bits of Puntos and a couple of HiAces, an old sprayer, a battered red tractor with no wheels. He must be renting it out. He hasn't driven in years . . .

Sylvester is standing at the front door. A big head of white hair and a moustache and a beard. He is wearing a suit and looks quite smart from a distance. He has a pipe in his mouth and stares at me as I get out of the car and get my bag from the back. I walk up to him. I don't know whether he's a hand-shaker or not. Solitary old men around here don't normally be handshakers unless they're after doing a deal. They wouldn't be used to the contact. But you wouldn't know with a sailor.

'Vajazzling, Ann,' he says as I stop in front of him.

'Sylvester?'

I can hear the theme tune to *Loose Women* up loud inside the house.

'Come in, come in, they're just talking about it.'

I step over a couple of cats that are in the hall. They don't seem worried. The hall is long and the floor has newspaper with yellowish stains. The paper is from a couple of years ago. The smell of cat pee is old and new.

'Move yourself now, Lady. Look lively, May!'

The cats move the bare minimum.

'They only move for the gentleman who reads the ESB meter, Ann. Now look!'

He brings me into the room that was the living room and is now the everything-room, as far as I can see. There's a small telly on a big antique sideboard, and it goes across the room to the plug through an assortment of extension leads. He has a microwave and a fridge and three couches and four armchairs and dressers and a large, dark brown table covered in envelopes. He finds two chairs by sweeping more papers off them and waves me to sit on one of them. Everything else is cat-litter trays, magazines – from what I can see, an awful lot of *Cosmopolitan* – and then the walls are lined with bookshelves. I see the carvings now that the other carers were on about. A whole shelf of figures. Big boobs and backsides and bits out front. Fertility symbols, no doubt, from all over. Geraldine has ones like them in her little cottage, only they're Celticky. *Celebrating the glory of the female body in a world that shames us for having curves*, according to her. He watches me looking at his women. I can see him half smiling.

'Now, Ann, here she is on again now. They're talking about vajazzling. This woman is in *Emmerdale*, you probably know her. She plays Tiffany Brown, the one who turned up after the second plane crash and said she was Henry Wilks' granddaughter. It was in all the papers. Listen to her now.'

'*Well, personally, Bianca, it's not for me, I wouldn't gerrit done but . . . yeknow, each to their own that's wor I always say.*'

'Each to their own, Ann. That's my motto. The good woman has hit the nail on the head. But I'm intrigued, Ann, about vajazzling. You're familiar with it, are you?'

I nod that I am. Luckily for me, I'd found out what it was myself only about a week before, otherwise I might have had to endure him explaining it to me.

'I know among certain indigenous people there is adornment of these regions, but it's often permanent. It's quite curious. Have you ever vajazzled, Ann?'

'They never have it in my colour, Sylvester. Now if you ask me any more questions like that, I'll do permanent adornments on you, do you hear me? Behave yourself.'

He slaps his thigh and laughs a big, dirty, sailor laugh. 'You're the woman for me, Ann. I knew you were anyway after I saw you in the newspaper that time. With the Tidy Towns. Now, what is it you want with me?'

'I thought it was you wanted us.'

'Your boss, Tracy, the queen of prolix and bollix, has been in touch with me numerous times on the telephone. She doesn't say it in so many words, but she would very much like to get her hands, via direct debit, on Lady May's filthy lucre, such as it is. I hardly know where half of it is myself. These are interesting times, my dear Ann. The middle-aged are competing for the custom of the aged. I am in good health, but your lady boss sees a lot of potential in me – potential for decline. So she is trying to capture me for her Saudi masters. I have dealt with the Saudis before, Ann, mainly in unscrupulous deals in the Levant. Your face suggests that you are aware of at least some of this. That you are here to sell it to me.'

'I look after people, Sylvester. I'm not a saleswoman. Tracy said you were interested in the . . . what was it? . . . the Low Dependency Preventative Care package.'

'What would that be in plain terms, Ann?'

I take a chance on speaking a bit of sailor to him.

'Clean the shite out of here so that you don't get E. coli and die and end up getting eaten by your cats.'

He is silent for a while. I'm afraid I've overstepped the mark.

'You're no shill for Madame Tracy, so. Or if you are, you're a very good one. But I have been thinking about how I am to pass my days. I am just about sane enough to know that I might go mad soon. I am in good health, but I am lonely, Ann, and that'll kill me faster. So what would you do? Would you call in when I needed and leave me alone when I needed? Would you help me go through personal effects and keep your mouth shut about what you saw? Would you only rearrange and tidy what I let you do?'

'I'd do one version of our time for Tracy and the rest would be between you and me.'

'A platonic affair so.'

'Any kind of tonic you want, Sylvester.'

I've warmed to the old man. But I'm dreading what I'll find upstairs. He seems to read my mind.

'It's not as bad as it looks, Ann. Most of it is locked up. I find it hard to go into those rooms since Lady May died.'

'I'd call into you as much as I could. If you told me to go away, I'd go away. I'd help you tidy up this place enough so that you wouldn't trip over something, but we'd go slowly. If you're not dead of the place by now, you won't die any time soon. I'll organize our cleaning unit to come in first, for the worst of it. But I'll tell them to only do what you let them.'

'I appreciate your candour, Ann. A sailor always thinks about when and where he will die, and I don't get that feeling yet anyway. Right, off you go so. They'll be talking about labia piercings next and I don't want to miss that. By the way, Ann, did you ever yourself . . .'

'G'way outta that, you dirty fecker.'

'That's the spirit, Ann, hahahah . . .'

I leave his house laughing and come away from there livened up by how I clinched the deal just by being myself. As I'm getting out of the car at home, feeling all proud of myself, I get a text.

ANN WILL YOU BRING ME TO DEVOTIONS TOMORROW?

Ah, Mam. Now, since I'm feeling all assertive and salesy, I write back, *Geraldine will take you, Mam*. Then I ring Geraldine.

'No, Ann, I can't. You know me now and churches. I'll burst into flames in there.'

'Ger, I'm looking after your child while you'll be on the tear in Goa.'

'But I might be working and, anyway, why can't you do it?'

I tell her about Brussels, leaving out some concerns about Rory. I can't be giving her ammunition.

'Oh, so you're gallivanting, are you?'

'Ger, the one time I go anywhere . . . now, are you working or not?'

'I might be.'

'You're not, I can tell. Just do it, Ger, will you? You don't even have to go all the way into the church. Just go a bit of the way, and if you feel like bursting into flames the holy water will put you out.'

'OK, but I'll need you to look after Freya tomorrow.'

'Deal. She can come to the airport for the spin. She'll keep Denis awake on the drive home.'

Denis is inclined to nod off, but there is no way he'll get a chance with Freya giving all his opinions the once-over. I text Tracy that Sylvester is signed up.

Rory is packing for tomorrow's trip when I get back, so I get to see the full glory of his wardrobe for the first time. I sit on his bed and watch, jaw wide open.

'Where are your long socks, Rory?'

'Mam, Mam. Ann, can I call you Ann?' He puts his arm around me. 'The world is changing, Ann. And socks are not the hill we need to die on. I have a number of looks. In this bag are boring clothes I'll wear when talking to the kind of politicians you and Daddy vote for. But I need to reach out to the alternative politicians too. The ones elected by people who put down Full Time at Mad Bastard for 'Job' on their Facebook. The lads elected over turf-cutting or whaling. That's where the real power is.'

'The jeans, though, Rory. Are your legs even that thin? How did we rear you with such thin legs? Your father has massive calves.'

Then, in the middle of all this, Rory holds up a T-shirt where the holes for the sleeves are nearly down to his waist and it says *Manslut* on the back.

'Who are you going to schmooze in this get-up, Rory, the Lagarde woman from the IMF?'

'No, Mam, but I like the way you're thinking.'

As he packs, there are messages from Deirdre and Jennifer in the family WhatsApp group, wishing him well on his trip. There are a few family WhatsApp groups: Family, Extended and Don't Tell Mammy. I found out about the last one accidentally when Deirdre sent a message to Family saying, *She'll go ape if she hears that*, and it was deleted. Then Jennifer added me to it as a kind of a joke, so there's probably a Really Don't Tell Mammy group there now.

You've to be fierce careful in Extended because that has all the in-laws in it. Only very safe stuff goes in there, like when Stephanie puts up a photo of Dubai swankiness. I've never put anything in it because I feel like her mother, Fidelma Rourke, would be judging me. But Declan doesn't seem to know the rules of Extended. His goodbye greeting to Rory looks very odd just after a photo of Stephanie drinking champagne at sunset.

Hi Rory, Declan (Jennifer) here. Good luck in Brussels. Don't be afraid to speak truth to power and the global elites.

Fidelma replies with a thumbs-up. She must think it's a compliment.

8.

RIDDEN SIDEWAYS WITH THE PRICE

Denis is full of beans the following morning as we pack up the car.

'We don't do this enough,' he says. 'Going off in the car on a summer's morning. What do you think, Freya?'

Freya yawns and shivers and rolls her eyes at his enthusiasm. 'Doesn't matter what I think, Uncle Denis. I'm just a pawn between Mam and Auntie Ann. It's always the children who suffer.'

Denis isn't put off. He's just happy to be on the road but not in the lorry. He gets excited about setting off early in the morning in a cool car on a hot day. It brings back memories of going to the seaside when the family was small. He's made a flask and sandwiches.

I'm driving because Denis told me once he had a 'micro-sleep' on a motorway and now I can't relax sitting next to him. If I know he's on a long trip in the lorry, I keep ringing him, which he says is more dangerous. As we pull out of the house, Denis is prodding at my phone stuck up in its holder near the radio.

'Put Brussels into the satnav there for the laugh. How do I tell Shirley we want to go to Brussels?'

'She's Siri,' Rory mutters sleepily from the back seat.

'Shirley would be a better name. Why did they call it Siri anyway?'

None of us knows. Freya takes out her phone, unable to not know.

'Says here it's from the Norse, meaning beautiful woman who leads you to victory.'

'Beautiful woman who leads you to victory. That could be you, Ann.'

'Denis is such a charmer, Mammy. Pure player. You'd want to watch him now, delivering cement to all the ould wans. He'll be all, *Do you want to see where the cement comes out of the truck?*, and then all housewives will be over to look at his pour.'

'Housewives. Nice,' says Freya.

'Can you put the airport into the map, Rory, please, like a good lad?'

'We're miles away yet, Mam. Anyway, you can get Siri to find the airport with your voice if you want. Say, "Hey Siri, Map, Dublin Airport."'

'Map, Dublin Airport,' I say.

'I'm sorry, I didn't quite get that,' says Siri.

'AIRPORT.'

'It doesn't understand your provincial accent, Mam. It's only been trained on a range of normal voices.'

'There's nothing wrong with my voice, Rory. At least I have the same accent coming home in the evening as I had going out the door in the morning. I wasn't the one who went to Cork and came back with a Dublin Telly accent.'

'Burn,' says Freya.

'*Burn: a burn is a type of injury to skin or other tissues . . .*'

'Shut up, Siri.'

There is silence for a while.

'You don't be delivering cement to housewives, do you, Denis?'

'Housewives don't order cement, Ann.'

We're quiet enough for a while after we get on to the motorway. Denis wants to put on Country Classics FM.

'It's all songs about women leaving their man, Ann,' he says.

'Fleeing toxic relationships, more like it,' Freya says. She takes out her little recorder yoke. 'I'm just doing a bit of real-life stuff for the podcast. Auntie Ann, how do you feel about your son helping keep the corrupt in power?'

'I'm driving, Freya.'

'Rory, what are your thoughts?'

Rory pretends to be Patsy and tells Freya he understands her concern but that he has secured funding for a brand-new signpost for Kilsudgeon, and the two of them are joking away goodo in the back.

'That's off the record, Freya, OK?' he says, after telling Freya he'll get her planning permission for her podcast studio.

Ryan Montana comes on then – the big country star that you can't avoid. We shout at Denis to turn him off before he can launch into 'All She Left Me Was a Text'. He switches the station and it's the news.

'It's always good to find out what bad news you'll be missing,' he says.

'. . . the branches have not yet been named but it is believed that this round of post office closures will be the most extensive yet . . .'

'I hope they leave us alone now. It's the only thing we've left to close,' says Denis.

'In three kilometres, take the left two lanes for M50,' says Siri.

'Good girl yourself, Shirley,' says Denis.

*

74

We're sweating as we take our seats on the plane. Rory and me were both trying to shove his carry-on bag into the locker and the air hostess was right behind us saying we would need to clear the aisle. Everyone was looking at us, and my chest came out in blotches, which is a special performance I save for the worst possible time. Rory has to bring his bag of shoes – just shoes! – down the back of the plane.

'EFF EMM ELL,' he says, 'I've to wait for all these plebs to leave first before I can get my bags.'

'Aren't we plebs too, Rory?'

'Remember our chat, Mam. We are no longer the likes of us. We are leaders. Repeat after me, "We are leaders."'

I don't repeat it.

He sighs and checks his phone and whistles.

'Feck, there was another incident with Patsy. Graffiti on his wall. After they did the car. They wrote Soros on it.'

'Who's Soros?'

'George Soros. They're saying Patsy is in league with the Jews who want to take over Ireland. And that he's part of the globalist conspiracy to replace the Irish with Muslims.'

'Jews and Muslims? He's busy, isn't he?'

'Listen, Mam, you're dealing with the thickest mentallers out there. You should see them on Facebook. I go on some-times under another name to see what they're saying. They're saying he's corrupt.'

'But he is, though, Rory.'

'No more than anyone else.'

'Way more than anyone else, Rory. He took money for planning permission.'

'Alleged, Mammy. Patsy aided the application. It's a hand-ling fee.'

'But wasn't he looking for money from that . . .' I stop myself. I don't think Rory knows about Patsy getting caught in the sting last year. The one I helped set up. When I *think* of the caper I got up to by accident. I'm telling you, I'm keeping my nose clean this summer.

'They're saying Patsy took a load of money off some Saudi developer as a bribe as well.'

'Who's they?'

'Clean-up Ireland. It's just this group of absolute spacers going around the place in hi-vis . . . threatening Patsy. They're messing with the wrong man, though. He has a few bad-asses in his corner too.'

'Is that you?'

'No. I'm a strategist. I don't get involved in this.'

'Except when you were taking down posters.'

'That was just work experience, Mammy.'

I change the subject. 'Do you want a sandwich?'

I haul a lump of tinfoil-wrapped sandwiches out of my pocket.

'How did you get that on board, Mammy?' he asks. 'That's metal.'

'I don't know, it didn't set off the machine. They still nabbed me with the shampoo, so I don't know what that achieves. It's only tinfoil. Am I going to bring the plane down with baking or what?'

The sound of the unwrapping attracts a few looks. Mad jealous they are. They'll be ridden sideways with the price of the mangiest sandwich. Rory takes half my sandwiches. We splash out on the can and the wine too, though. We're on holidays.

After an hour the pilot comes on and tells us we've begun our descent. My ears are gone doollaly. 'Welcome to Brussels,' they say in a few languages. The Dutch version sounds like they are fairly laid back while the French girl sounds more expensive.

'C'mon so, Mam. Brussels won't know what hit it.'

9.

THE BOXERS ARE FAIRLY SNUG

There's a fierce tall black fella waiting for us in the terminal with Dǫǫ#Gʜʏɪǫʜ#) #Uʀᴜ|#Gʜʏɪǫʜ written on an iPad. He says his name is Celestine.

'Mr Devine,' he says to Rory. 'Madame Ann,' he says to me. Madame, no less. 'Did you have good flight? From where you coming?'

'Ireland.'

'What region of Ireland you live?'

'Kilsudgeon,' I say, straight out. Normally I'd give the names of fifteen other places people might have heard of by way of locating Kilsudgeon.

'Aha, I hear of this city. Patsy Duggan a great man, hehehe. He is your leader. A strong man. He tells me, "Celestine, I am the beating heart of Kilsajion and Kilsajion is the beating heart of Ireland."'

Rory grins at me. 'See, Mam? Patsy's representing us on the world stage.'

'H-how did you hear about Patsy?'

77

'I drive car for Mr Cadogan and Mr Duggan he comes often to Brussels. We talk many times about Jesus. He is a man of God.'

Rory and me look at each other. We can agree on this much anyway. Whatever Patsy is a man of, it is not God. I know he's been to Lourdes, but mainly to 'tie down the votes of that demographic', Rory says. Because 'they're a captive constituency' when they're stuck on the tour with him.

The car pulls up outside a big tall building of apartments. We say goodbye to Celestine. He tells us that we should have much good fortune because we are friends with Patsy Duggan and he hopes to visit Kilsajion one day. I wonder does he expect us to have statues to Patsy Duggan there. One thing's for certain, if Celestine comes to Ireland, I can guarantee Patsy will have his vote as soon as the man gets a PPS number.

'He must be the fella Patsy was telling me about, Mammy. He met him the first time they came over. Celestine has a wooden leg, too, from the Congo.'

'He travelled a fair bit to buy that.'

'Patsy was telling me Celestine practically dragged himself here twenty years ago. *That's ambition, Rory*, he says to me. *This is what's wrong with the Irish. You have to put yourself outside the comfort zone.*'

'I did that last year, remember, and I nearly ended up being ran out of the village and going viral.'

'And how did it make you feel, Mam? It took years off you.'

'It did, Rory, but not in the way you think.'

We're standing outside the door now.

'Is this the place, Rory?'

The bags are piled around us. Celestine has gone, with a fiver I insisted on putting in his hand.

Rory reads out the address from his phone. 'Residence Uriel, Rue d'Idalie.' The door of the lobby is open and we walk across a tiled floor covered in mosaics. There's no lift. We take hold of the bags and start trudging up. Rory sprints ahead of me with most of his bags, and I'm grunting away up these concrete steps, grumbling about carrying my son's shoes. A young couple pass us on the landing and give me a good stare. No one offers to help. That's the continentals for you. Minding their own business. I could do with them being a bit nosier now.

We're at the top and Rory knocks on number 7. There is no sound from inside. He finds a doorbell and rings that. Again, not a peep from behind the door. He rings the doorbell again and gives the door another thump. Eventually there's a sort of a shout. We hear scuffy steps approaching and the door opens.

This tall fella opens the door in his boxers. He has a tattoo of a dragon all across his chest. And the boxers are fairly snug too. It would be hard to stop looking down. The room is full of smoke and it's not a Carroll's 5 he's after lighting up either. I'm hoping Rory will do the talking, but Rory is sort of transfixed.

'Hallo? Ja,' the man says.

Rory stutters a bit. 'Hey man, we're supposed to be staying here. I'm Rory. I'm doing interning? For The Lamp.'

'Delamp? Who is the Delamp?'

'No, he's in the Parliament. Michael. He owns the house. Patsy Duggan? Said I could stay here. From Ireland.'

'Arra for fuck sake, come in, boyeen! No one calls him The Lamp out here. That's why I was confused. And I'm stoned out of my fuckin' bin.'

'And this is my mam, Ann.'

He sees me and straightens up a bit.

'Oh shite, is this your mam? Come on into our humble abode. I'm JP. Oh Jeszhus, look at the shate of me. I hope you're not shtuffy, Ma'am. The place is in a fuckin' hape around us. We had a heavy night.' He waves around the room, showing us the heap it's in. 'Hold on a second now till I warn herself. Arra shite, we're too late. Watch this lad now having his conniption.'

A fella comes out of what I take to be the shower without a *stitch* and gives a little yelp and says something in a foreign language. He runs off down the corridor to a room.

Our friend goes off after him. He seems to have locked himself in the toilet. JP is knocking on the door, trying to reason with him. He seems to have taken on a different accent.

'Fabueno, man, you gotta chill, bro. For real, bro, check yourself.'

'I thought it was a house to yourself, Rory,' I whisper to him.

'Me too,' he whispers.

'I don't think this set-up is . . . ideal, is it, Rory?'

'You're not homophobic, are you, Mammy?' he whispers back as we listen to the voices coming from the room.

'No,' I whisper, 'I don't mind what anyone does, but it's just that it's very dramatic here.'

'Do you think I'll catch the gay off them, Mammy?'

'*Of course* I'm not thinking that. Will you stop that talk? I was just . . .'

JP comes back down the corridor, followed by his friend, who now has a towel around his waist.

'THE FUCK, JP?'

'Arra Fabby, now c'mere to . . .'

'ENGLISH, JP!'

'Fabueno, please calm down, OK? Everything's going to be fine.' The man in the towel walks off. It turns out the towel is barely a J-cloth so we can see he has a tattoo of a lion and a unicorn on his left arse.

'He's some operator, isn't he, Ann?'

His accent is back to home. I must be gawping at him because he smiles and says I look confused.

'Fabueno can't understand an iota of what I am saying when I use my Kerry voice. The English language wouldn't always be great by him, and when he doesn't understand he gets frustrated and then I get it in the neck. He jusht had a little bit of a bad trip last night, and the boy is not right at all.'

'A bad trip? Oh, was his flight delayed or something?'

'No, Mammy . . .'

And then I cop on to it. 'Oh, I see. Right. Does he need a doctor?'

'No, Ann, just a bit of the oul TLC. Anyway, ye musht be parched. I can't give ye tea just yet. There's a café there down the street and I'll be down to ye when I get Neymar here out of his sulk.'

We ask to leave our bags there. Not before I take any bit of good make-up and perfume out. You wouldn't know what the boyfriend might do with it if he's *in a K-hole*, whatever that is. JP gives us his number in case we go astray and we go down the stairs again. When we get outside, Rory looks up and down the street, trying to get his bearings. His face is doubtful. For a second, he seems almost like the gorgeous little lad who used to be fierce anxious when he was small. He'd give us this look when he was worried about something and he was such a dote I could nearly have eaten him. Don't you know the way you'd be with small lads? You'd want to inhale them. But they get too big to cuddle. I go for the next best thing. Drink.

'Tea my foot, Rory. Bring your mother to the pub. Isn't this what they're famous for?'

Rory gives me a big smile. 'We're in cahoots now, the two messers.'

After a bit of tapping and swiping, Rory announces he's found a place. After five minutes' walk we arrive outside a pub called Lambic of God. Lambic is a type of beer, Rory tells me.

It's dark inside and still early in the day so we have a corner to ourselves. I flop down into the chair. The early start is hitting me now. The menu is like a phone book and along the counter there's a big row of taps of every kind of beer. I've heard of none of them.

'Don't even think about wine now, Mam,' warns Rory. 'This is the home of beer.'

He picks something for both of us and arrives back from the counter with two brown bottles. He hands me one and I take a sip.

'It tastes like oranges or something, Rory. Or there's another taste in there too. Phoof! It's strong.'

'Bernardus Wit, Mammy.'

'I'd want my wits about me with this, Rory, hah?'

'I'll just keep setting them up and you just keep knocking them out of the park, Mammy.'

Too tasty, it is. He pours the rest of it into a little stubby glass and before long the little stubby glass is drained. They have an individual glass for each beer and they're all shapes, which must make it an ordeal to load the dishwasher here.

The woman comes over and asks do we want more. Rory reads from the menu to her. I have given over responsibility to him. After a while the woman brings over chips that turn out to be manky. I thought this place was supposed to be known for chips. *Famed for its frites*, said the airplane magazine, but you wouldn't get these from a van at a horse fair. Greasy, rubbery things.

We drink the next order at a fair clip as well. The drink has gone down lovely and I'm well on. The next drink comes in a contraption like what you'd see in a laboratory. I figure now is the time to ask Rory what's been nagging me.

'Rory, tell me something.'

'What, Mammy?'

'What's the story, Rory?'

'You're on the sesh, Mammy. That's most of the story. And you're buckled.'

'No, but, like . . .'

I'm struggling to get a handle on things here with the weight of this Belgian beer. Rory reads the label on the bottle.

'Absolute scenes, Mammy. This stuff is 10 per cent. You'll have to be hospitalized.'

'I will not. Stop trying to confuse me. I want to ask you something.'

I am silent then for a while, trying to figure out what the something was.

'Will I get another round in, Mammy, while you're coming up with the words? Have you the money there?'

I hand him across a fifty without so much as a murmur out of me, like Denis at the Rourke wedding. I must be in some state all right.

'Habila,' I say to him as he leaves.

He comes back from the bar having had what seems to be a bit of a giggle with the woman behind it, no doubt at my expense, but it doesn't seem to bother me. I am on a different level to them and they don't understand what I understand. Or at least I think that's what I'm thinking.

'You were saying, Mammy?' He comes back all smiles, waiting for me to say the next stupid thing.

'Habila.'

'That's what I thought you said. Here, Mammy, go on WhatsApp with me there. I want to let the Don't Tell Mammy group know you've lost the plot.'

'Fugarra.'

He sits in next to me, puts the arm around me, holds the phone out.

'Halloooo,' I say. The feeling of being on camera tidies up my brain a small bit.

'Hello, go on, say something there, Mammy.'

'This is me . . . Ann. Over here in Belgian with Rory, helping start his internment.'

'Brussels,' says Rory. 'Me and the Mam are getting scuttered.'

He presses Stop on the recording and starts to tap away.

'Where is that going? Now doan send that to the fffamly, Rory, pliz.'

'I won't, Mammy. This is just going to a private WhatsApp group me and a few others have where we post stuff that our parents do when they're lamped.'

I can see the name of the group. It looks like MAMS GO WILD.

'No, Rory, stttoppit.' He stops.

We sit saying nothing for a while. Rory texts JP to let him know where we are. I think I might be sobering up a little. I don't touch the Hofsturgleburger or whatever it is that he has bought me. It's gone flat and I'm even less inclined to have a cut off it. I wave over the wan and ask her for water. I try to talk to Rory again.

'Are you seriously thinking of being a politician, Rory?'

'I just want to serve, Mammy.'

'But Patsy just serves himself.'

'Look, Mammy, no one is whiter than white. We're all part of something.'

'What do you mean?'

'I told you already – you, Jennifer, Kevin. Everyone's working for oil money. Kevin is building headquarters for a company that makes bombs for Yemen, Mammy. And you're worried about me working for a fella that all he's doing is taking a few bob off developers?'

My brain is tired. If none of us are doing the right thing, how can we tell anyone else? How good do you have to be to give advice? It doesn't look like anything I say is going to convince him. I just don't want Rory starting off like this. God only knows what he'll be like by the end. Putin or someone.

'Being pure is hard, isn't it, Mam?'

The barmaid comes over and leans over us, asking are we OK for a drink. I can nearly see her breakfast. She's quite fronty. Rory notices, too, and he's smiling away at her.

'Anyway, forget Saudis, I fffeel like . . .'

'What, Mammy?'

'I never have a chance to talk to you these days. You hardly came home from college during the year.'

'This is the time for living, Mammy. I was busy making my name.'

'And is there any girl on the horizon with you these days? You tell me nothing.'

'Do you want to know everything?'

'No, but even enough to tell someone who'd ask me in the shop. Catherine Allen was asking me the other day how you were getting on and were you doing a line with anyone.'

'Doing a line? As in cocaine?'

'Cocaine?! Do I need to start worrying about that as well? Doing a line, you know, going out with. Seeing. Meeting. What do you call it now?'

'I dunno, Mammy. Friends with benefits. Shifting. Seeing. Tapping. No, I'm not doing any kind of lines.'

He sits back with his hands behind his head and gives me a big grin. His chipped tooth from the time he fell off his bike is still there.

'What about Sarah Whassername, the girl you brought to the debs? She's a grand girl altogether. And I think she went off doing Business, didn't she?'

'I'll bet she's doing business, Mammy. And she brought me. I mean, like, we had a shift at the debs, but she was way more into me. I didn't want to embarrass her so I went along with it.'

'But Rory, when Catherine asked me, I felt . . .'

I'm trying to remember how I felt. The drink is fighting me again now.

'I felt . . . Rory, like I didn't know enough about you and that I was a bad mother. Catherine was looking at me that way, I could tell.'

'Yeah, but Catherine, like, is still practically breastfeeding Clodagh and Conor. Sorry, Mammy, but they're saps. They're older than me and they can't wipe their hole. We're all out the door doing our own thing.'

'Your father said that too.'

'Listen to Denis, Mam – he is wise.'

'But I worry, Rory, you know? Like, you might think you know it all but there's young wans out there. And they'd be looking to trap the likes of you, and before you know it you're accused of something.'

'Accused of what, Mammy?'

'I don't know, something. You hear about these accusations and I'd be afraid someone in your position . . .'

'What do you mean, *trap me*, Mammy?'

'You don't know young wans, Rory. They have their ways.'

'Is that how you got Daddy? Actually, how did you get him? How did you seduce the lorry man?'

It's no question for a son to ask his mother. I should give him short shrift, but the beer is telling me, *G'wan Ann, there are no secrets any more.*

'Seduce. Oh, I wouldn't put it like that now. He was actually doing all the . . . AH, RORY!'

I look up and he's holding up the phone again.

'RORY! Will you stop recording fecking everything?!'

I make a grab for the phone, half playfully, but my hand clips the table, which must have a short leg because it wobbles more than it should, and the next thing the contraption that Rory brought down for one of my pints starts to totter. It's a wooden frame around a glass and the glass is a kind of a cone. I reach out to try and steady it. But I send the wooden frame flying on to the tiled floor and the glass cone breaks in bits on the ground. And no one cheers like they would back home. It's very quiet in the pub and the barmaid looking over at us.

Rory waves at her. He's not even blushing. Youngsters don't mortify at all now. The barmaid comes over with a half-cross look on her face.

'My mother is very sorry, Caroline,' he says. 'She is a bit jet-lagged.'

'Oh, OK, yes, all the time zones to Ireland. I get brush for you. You are good boy to bring your mom on holidays, but maybe it's her first time to drink Belgian beer. Very strong, yes, Mom?' I see now she's a good bit older than Rory. 'He is a good boy, Mom, is he?' She is sort of cleaning in and around my feet.

'I'm ever so sorry,' I say, and I am all over the place, fussing about it. I try to pick up a shard for her that's near my foot, but she shoos me away, telling me I'll cut my hand. She's too late. I'm still scrabbling on the floor and I feel a spike of pain and sure enough my right thumb is starting to bleed. I don't think anyone sees, so I shove it into a napkin by my side. It doesn't feel sore, but when I look down the napkin is red. I'll have to get to the loo soon.

After it's cleared up she brings over two more quare-looking pints. Rory takes a big slug out of one of them as if he hasn't had a drop of liquid in days.

'Will you go easy, Rory? You're too comfortable altogether with all this drinking.'

'Mam, I'm in my early twenties. This is my prime. I am a sesh-machine. So anyway, Mother dearest, you were saying how I'd want to watch myself with young wans getting their claws into me before you nearly glassed me. What was your point exactly? Tell the class.'

'No, it's just that wans these days, they're way more, you know, way more than they used to be, I don't know, how do I say it . . . forceful, assertive . . .'

'Do you think they'll force themselves on me, Mammy? Don't let Freya hear you victim-blaming.'

'I'm not, I'm just . . .'

'Look, Mammy, there's no girl on the scene at the moment and, anyway, you probably should know that . . . well, it's just that . . .'

'GUYS, OH MY GOD, YOU ARE SO CUTE. I WISS MY MAMAE COULD COME TO DRINK WITH ME.'

The two lads from the flat have walked in and the Brazilian lad, whose name I've forgotten, has made a bee-line for our table. He seems better. It's my first time seeing them with their tops on. They do look very stylish. It comes more naturally to them lads. There aren't many gay people in Kilsudgeon. Or not ones that are 'out', as they say. There are certainly no fellas around the place looking like these two lads. The Brazilian lad is wearing pure-white trousers – a terrible colour for stains to be wearing to the pub, but he's kept them clean so far anyway. They're gone too small for him because they're only down to his calves – yellow leather shoes and no socks. Then he has a kind of pink jacket with *Pink Ladies* written on it and an almost-see-through T-shirt. I couldn't wear that material. Not now, anyway. I'd scare people. JP is a bit more conservatively dressed, but it's still very stylish. A white T-shirt and a hoodie and jeans with rips that are supposed to be there.

The Brazilian lad sticks out a hand. My handshaking hand is bleeding beneath my leg and I don't want to stain his trousers. Thank God I wore the black slacks for the trip, even though they were too warm. I give him my left hand.

'Left hand, cool, like secret society.' He puts his other arm around the boyfriend's waist. Him and JP seem to have made up and are all smiles. I remember his name now.

'You're in better form, Fabuloso,' I hear myself say. I know straight after I say it that his name isn't Fabuloso, but I can't think of any other options. The Belgian monks have me by the hair.

'Fabuloso! *Meu Deus!!!* Can we keep her, JP, please, please, please? I get drinks. What you want, Lady Fabuloso? Young boy, you take more of this Kwak. So funny, you Irish, you come out here and you all drink this type of thing and it too strong for you, no?'

'Ah, we can handle it all right,' says Rory.

'Aiee, hey, OK, man, come with me to the bar and help me handle these beers I buy for you to say sorry I totally show you my balls earlier.'

'Are you all right, Ann? You're gone fierce pale altogether,' JP asks.

The drink and the bleeding aren't mixing well at all.

'I'm grand, JP. I'm just going to go to the loo, if you'll excuse me.'

They give me room to get out. I try to hide my bleeding hand in my pocket but there's no pocket in this jacket, so I hide it behind my back. I'm not that well balanced so I lurch out of the booth and the floor isn't where it should be and, before I know it, I am on my backside in the pub with my legs in the air like an dog wanting a tickle.

And just after, I see a tall, tanned man in a suit who looks very familiar coming into the pub. Then the lights go out for me.

10.

A GAY ICON

I open my eyes after some very strange dreams about people not wearing socks and a pint glass made out of scaffolding I am reaching out for while Tracy is telling me my probation isn't up. It seems to go on for ever. The first thing I am aware of is that I am staring up a man's nose. He's like a polished-up version of Patsy. He isn't looking at me but seems to be talking past me. He has my head lifted on to a cloth of some kind. JP and Rory are looking at me as well. Fabueno is standing a little bit further away, out of the discussion. It's coming back to me now. The broken glass, JP the gay lad from Kerry who puts on a continental accent to talk to his Brazilian boyfriend, who isn't called Fabuloso. I close my eyes again, trying to get back to the dream where everything makes more sense.

'Whisht? She's back to us again. YOU'RE BACK, MRS DEVINE.'

Our MEP, Mick the Lamp, is dabbing my face with a tissue and looking at JP, talking to him as if I'm still not back.

'I think she's in the clear, but you never know. You see there's a little bit of *history*.' And he makes the drinky gesture. 'I'll tell you more about it later, JP.'

Rory avoids my gaze.

'It's not easy, is it, Rory? My own father had his problems too. You're very brave. Patsy told me about how you got the disadvantaged grant, but I see it now in front of my eyes.'

A few minutes later we are around the table again and finally there is tea in front of me. I am relieved to see that the tea is in a mug and not a contraption. Mick is addressing the group.

'Anyway, it's great to have you here, Rory. I have to apologize for the accommodation mix-up. When Patsy told me you were on the way, I had my man JP here go in and explain to the Brazilian lad that the time was up on the lease. That's him there. He's Fabuelo. The man has no English at all and JP was just helping him out while he got himself settled in the city.'

The Lamp addresses Fabuelo in a Spanishy voice.

'You find apartment, Fabuelo? Yes? You move somewhere else, yes? Many, many places live in Brussels, no?'

Fabuelo seems to go along with it. '*Sí, señor*,' he says, sounding like Speedy Gonzales. Even I can tell he's taking the mick out of Mick.

Mick turns his head slightly and talks to us out the side of his mouth.

'Ah, he seems a nice poor divil. Not a word of English, I'd say.' He gives Fabuelo a thumbs-up. 'Good man, Fabuelo. Like football, yeah? Brazil, Belgium, hah, big game, yes?'

I catch JP's eye and he winks at me, and I know it's the Country Wink to tell no lies but not to be saying anything unless asked and I give a little nod to show I've received the message. *Roger that*, as the fella said.

As Mick turns back to us, Fabuelo is making a little praying-hands sign. I let him know with my eyes that Ann Devine won't be doing any squealing about small hand towels or tattoos or k-holes or any other kind of holes.

'He'd be a bit on the skittish side, Ann,' says Mick confidentially, 'so JP is proceeding carefully. You know the way with these lads. But we'll sort it all right, don't you worry. An apartment is what the Boy Wonder was promised and an apartment he will get. You must be very proud of him, the way he has made a life for himself, despite your own difficult circumstances. JP told me ye were out and about, so I made it my business to welcome you formally to Brussels.'

I don't do anything with my face, but it's a struggle. I thought I'd left that story behind me when Rory was heading off to college last year, but it's back again. Patsy had got Rory into university in Cork with Leaving Cert results that Denis called HMV because it had so many CD's on it. Patsy did up an application that made out Rory was disadvantaged, and to avoid a means test they cooked up a story that I was *frequently passed out due to the effects of prescription drugs*. By the time I found out about it, it was a done deal.

After some more tea a concerned-looking woman comes into the pub. It turns out she's The Lamp's assistant and she says to The Lamp not to forget his meeting. She looks doubtfully at the motley crew around her man, as if we're about to damage his reputation. Especially me, with the hair gone askew and a bloodied napkin on my hand. Women my age shouldn't have bandages on them unless it looks like it was done professionally. The Lamp tells us we'll be good to move in later that day and JP promises that he'll get it sorted. After The Lamp leaves, we stay for another round.

'You wouldn't see this craic in Kilsudgeon, would you, Ann?' says JP.

'You'd be surprised.'

'Well, I wouldn't see it in Lyracompane anyway.'

'Do you get home much?'

'Yerra not much, but I'll go in a few months. I'll chance it.'

'Does your mother know about the . . . ?' I'm trying to choose the words.

'About the what, Ann?' He looks deadly serious.

I have a flash of panic. 'I mean, about you not being, about you being, you know . . .' I'm clearing my throat.

'What, Ann?'

Then I see him and Rory exchanging looks and smiling.

'YOU SCUT. Letting me think I'd said the wrong thing.'

'You're gas, Ann. The look on your face!'

Fabuelo leans around again and pats my knee.

'Do not listen to this *puta*, Ann, he is, like, also all the times messing with my head. JP, have some respect for our queen, man.'

'You're a gay icon now, Mammy,' says Rory.

'My mam has a fair notion all right, Ann,' says JP. 'Mothers pick up on shtuff, don't they? She says, *How's your special friend, the Brazilian?* I'm bringing him with me for the first time later on. I wonder what they'll make of him. Lyracompane wouldn't be noted for its gay scene. T'will be like the feckin *Birdcage* with him around the village. If I can get him to line out for the Junior B, we'll be made.'

When we get back to the apartment Fabueno starts packing up a few bags. He pulls a big, floppy-brimmed hat out of one and puts it on, modelling it for me.

'What do you think, Miss Ann? I am like Billy Porter?'

'You're the spit of him,' I say, not knowing who Billy Porter is.

'I wish I could stay with you guys right now, you are so cute. We smoke some, drink some Cachaça. I tell you about

93

Brazil. I miss my mamae, but you know Brazil verrry homo-fobico. She knows who I am, but my papae, so macho. He hate me.'

'That's sad, Fabueno.'

'Thank you, Miss Ann, for not telling the man that I am, like, living here a little longer than I should be and JP is my boyfriend.' And he plants a big kiss on me. He has a lovely smell, godblesshim. I don't get kissed much by good-smelling men. I'm going to find out what he's wearing and dowse Denis in it.

They leave, and I can relax at last. We watch the news with biscuits and tea. I'm exhausted. Rory pulls out the couch to sleep. Only, might I add, after I asked him to. He had already set himself up in the bedroom. Chivalry is dead. I doubt *he's* gay anyway. He's not good enough to his mother.

The next morning Celestine picks us up. He tells me that he is praying to Jesus for my struggle with the Devil. I tell him Patsy's not that bad. Rory's all excited. Today, Mick the Lamp is bringing us on a tour of the Parliament.

When we arrive, JP is there to meet us. Rory pretends he is going to an important meeting.

'John,' he says, 'do you have the documents? And this is my attaché, Lola,' pointing at me, and JP laughs and I enjoy the buzz of it all. We walk in through a large courtyard with tall grey buildings all around. There's a place called a Parliamentarium on our left. JP says it's a museum about the Parliament. Imagine going to a museum for the Dáil, but JP says they are stone mad for politics out here. Students go to learn about it.

'They're professionals out here,' he says. 'Not a load of chancers like back home.'

Me and Rory look at each other.

'No harm in being both,' says Rory.

'But we're not going into the Parliamentarium,' he says. 'That's for the little people. We're going right into the Parliament and having a nose around.'

We walk across a big open space with curving walkways and I see that Rory has lost his smart-alec face and is just agog.

'It's like a cathedral of politics, Mam,' he whispers. 'Imagine this was your job.'

As we go into the Parliament itself we have to pass through metal detectors. I wasn't expecting any metal detectors until the airport again, so I haven't gone through my pockets. And sure enough, as I approach, what do I pull out? Only a bloodstained tissue from yesterday. I'm trying to put it in the bin, but it sticks to my hand and, just as I'm trying to get it off, of course Mick the Lamp appears like magic.

'You are better, Ann, are you?' He grips my arm, just as the bloody tissue goes in the bin. I'm sure he saw it and it confirms all he suspected.

'Don't believe what you've heard, lads,' says Mick, handing out badges on strings after we go through the metal detectors. 'Those people who say, *Europe is all straight bananas*, and the like. This is the centre of power.'

He brings us up to where Rory will be working. It's buried in the building and after about twenty corridors and beeping through doors I'm lost completely. I see a few people with Irish heads on them who Mick salutes, but I don't know if I should know them. They might be big cheeses here, for all I know. I see a woman who looks like Angela Merkel in the distance.

'Is that who I think it is, Rory? Merkel?'

'Mam, please,' he says, and sure enough she comes out of a toilet with a full bin-liner. Even the cleaners look statesman-like around here. And why shouldn't a cleaner look like a statesman, I suppose? Their job is nearly more important.

Rory's desk is in a spacious office with a window and I can see from the *Up the Kingdom* mug where JP works.

Mick sits down at the desk. 'You'll be here, young man.'

'What will I be doing?'

Mick is vague. 'A bit of this and a bit of that, Rory,' he says. 'You'll be shadowing JP here for a lot of it. Learning the workings of the place.'

Rory looks a little disappointed.

'But anyway! You didn't come all the way to just look at an office. Let's go and see where the magic happens.'

We troop back through the corridors again. Rory seems a little slumped around the shoulders. But when we get into the Parliament the sight of it perks him up again. It's huge. The seats seem to go back for miles.

Mick shows us where they speak and all the little earphones on the desks to translate it into whatever language you like. I could do with that in my own job, especially some of the older people. I wouldn't know what they'd be saying half the time.

We watch as Rory walks around the auditorium. Gazing up at the size of it all.

'And how is Patsy, Ann?'

I'm thrown by the question. How *is* Patsy was the way he said it.

'You would see him a bit, wouldn't you, through Rory?'

'Ah, Patsy is himself,' I say carefully.

Mick looks like he's thinking this bit of wisdom over.

'I wonder has he lost his touch a bit, Ann? You know, there was talk he was very nearly caught out last year.'

'Oh, is that right?'

'They reckon there was a TV company did a number on him. They got him to look for a bribe. Didn't you hear the talk?'

I look away. I'm sure my face is giving me away.

'And I heard another story about a will and a Yank woman. I wonder is the poor man overworked? He takes on so much, doesn't he?'

'He gets involved in a lot.'

'Surely in your position you must have heard talk about the Yank?'

'There'd be a lot of talk around Kilsudgeon, Mick, about a lot of things. I don't pay attention to all of it.'

'I know, Ann. And you have your own struggles to bear as well too. I only hope that Rory is in good hands, you know.' He grips my arm again. He's mad for the arm-gripping.

Rory comes up to us, nearly giddy.

'Go up there to the podium, Mammy, and I'll do a video of you. G'wan, Mammy,' he says when I start huffing about it.

When in Brussels, I suppose. So I walk up to the podium. I see JP go up around the back. The screen behind me lights up. Rory is in front of me with his phone. He's doing a selfie video. He's got his vim back.

'OK, so I'm here at the European Parliament. Here is Kilsudgeon hero Ann Devine about to speak truth to power.'

'What will I say?'

'Something inspiring, Mammy.'

'Well . . . I'd like to thank you all for coming here . . .'

It's just me and Rory and Mick the Lamp and a few cleaners.

'It's not a wedding, Mam. You're talking to millions.' He whoops. 'NOW WE'RE SUCKIN' DIESEL.'

I look around, and JP must be after twiddling something because I'm up there on the big screen looking at myself up there on the big screen.

'Quick, Mammy, say something there and I'll test the translation.'

I start saying, 'Well, you know now, we're very happy to be in Europe, unlike the English.'

I'm getting into the swing of it. Rory is filming away and listening in on a headphone.

'It's working, Mammy. The fella is trying to translate it, but he says he doesn't speak culchie.'

'What?'

'Joking, Mammy.'

I get down from the stage and sit in seat number 19. There's a label on it of the fella who normally sits there. An Italian, Zanni. It's like school. I wonder does he have to turn up more because he's up the front? Rory walks up and down the aisles, finding the names of the Irish MEPs. I don't know who half of them are.

Mick announces that he wants to show us their swanky canteen and after that he will love us and leave us. We go in, and the staff all know him in there and he has their names too. *How are you, Shu lin?* here and *What's the craic, Sunday?* there. Even speaking in French the odd time, or I think it's French. Whatever he says, he says it comfortably anyway. He's very comfortable. He's like a Hollywood Patsy Duggan.

'Everything you want under the sun. Forty different cuisines on the busy days. You can have Vietnamese food and get a plate of stew as well. It's only mighty. I don't be going on about this now around election time. The Dublin media back home have their knickers in a twist about this, but it's hard work all the same so you'd need the sustenance.'

He doesn't look like he needs much more sustenance. The man is as sleek as a house tabby. The white hair is immaculate. Europe has been good to him.

'And this is my good friend, the *maître d'* Uriel.' He has his arm around a young woman in a chef's outfit. 'This is Rory Devine and his mother, Ann, who I was telling you about.'

'We are so proud of your journey, Ms Devine.'

'My journey? Oh . . .'

She's talking about it in the American sense. Is there anyone here who doesn't think I'm off my head on tablets?

'We are going to take good care of Rory. We promise.'

'We are,' says Mick. 'It'll be like a second home for him.'

After goodbyes to all the staff and getting their congratulations for turning my life around, myself and Rory start to make our way to our digs. On the walk back he's talking away like mad about being at the heart of it all and I have a light-bulb moment about Mick the Lamp. Maybe he's the best of a bad lot. If Rory got on well here, it might start to drive a gap between him and Patsy. Mick doesn't look like he takes on too much. Corruption would be too much effort for him. He might even know The Professor.

Bing!

Rory has put a message into Extended, a video of me speaking to the European Parliament.

It's a reply from Fidelma. Fidelma! *That's great, Ann.*

That's a turn-up for the books. Europe has been good to me so far.

11.

NEITHER OF US HAVE ANY IRISH

That evening they are all heading out for dinner but I pretend that the hangover has hit me a second dose. I'd only be cramping their style. Rory doesn't seem gutted that I won't be there. He is all excited, picking out clothes.

'Are you sure you won't change your mind, Mam?' he asks, hoping I won't, I'm sure.

'I am. I get tired of being around people after a day or two. They could be the nicest people in the world. It's like a bra. No matter how comfortable it is, there's always a time when I get tired of keeping up a front.'

When Rory is gone and I have time to breathe I sit for a while until the sound of the street outside gives me the bit of 'go' to head out on my own for a walk.

I just amble with no destination in mind. I haven't walked this slowly in ages. I'm always dashing. I get fed up walking behind a tourist. *How could anyone walk that slowly?* But that's the way I'm walking now. With no particular place to go, as the song says. I have my little map and I'm wandering the little squares. I feel as *safe*! Is this what tourists feel like in Dublin? I'd be always on the lookout, getting a sixth sense for where the gougers are, tense all the time. Whereas out here I don't know what a Belgian gouger looks like, so I'm trotting along and there could be a Brussels gangland fella walking next to me and I wouldn't know. I peek at menus without trying to attract attention, saying 'No, thanks' to fellas selling me roses.

'Beautiful lady,' they tell me, 'you like rose?'

'Where would I put it?' I tell them.

Big, disappointed smiles out of them, big smiles out of me. The hangover is wearing off. I imagine myself as the wan out of that book, what's it called? *Live, Laugh, Love* or something. The husband fecks off on her and she decides she's going to be a Buddhist and eat like mad and find some young buck to sort her out.

Rush, Worry, Eat in the Car, that'd be the name of my book.

There's no one here I know, so I can stop in any pub I want and no one will say, *There's Ann Devine going into a pub on her own.* But then I start to lose my nerve. All the restaurants that I walk past are coupley. Maybe I should just get a sandwich. And then a thought strikes me.

Fuckit, says the thought. *Fuckit, Ann*, it says again.

I stop at the corner of a square outside a restaurant, take a deep breath and take a seat without being asked. A young lad comes straight out with menus and soon after with water and a basket of bread. He puts bread in front of me and, when he's gone, I make an absolute disgrace of myself with the bread and the pale butter.

I sign up to their Wifi. I'm gone a bit addicted to the smartphone. There's 145 updates on the Neighbourhood Watch WhatsApp group.

Van going around selling eggs.

They were trying doors earlier.

I bought eggs off them earlier they're ok
The eggs?
Bike for sale, Worth 400, will let it go for 100.
Hey everyone can we keep the discussion solely for security issues
08so-andso has left the group
A photo of a child's face.
Sorry guy's Saorlaith got my phone. Lol.

'You are 'ungry, madame,' says the young lad. He's not bad-looking. Could you imagine if I got myself a toyboy out here? I don't know would Denis mind so much, as it wouldn't be anyone he'd know. *Take some of the pressure off me*, he'd say. I ask him what wine he'd recommend, like I'm a wine expert, but what I really mean is what wine would you recommend for the Likes of Me. He reels off a few names from a list and says what they would go with and I tell him I'll try the second one he mentioned and he repeats it, and I say that'll be grand.

He brings it out with a few nuts in a bowl, including the cashews and the Brazil nuts which I wouldn't be gone on normally, but they are gone in seconds. The wine is the right temperature. It's like a neck warmer on the throat. I breathe out like I've never breathed out before. Gazing out over the square, I'm as relaxed as can be. I take a look at the food menu and pick out mussels, because no one will know if I don't like them. But when they arrive I do like them. Only they're very messy and I get splashes on my good blouse, but what harm? There's no eating in mussels, though, so I get the menu back and order steak. I could be up to sixty euro at this stage with the bill. This will be one to keep from Denis. Just suiting myself. Sunglasses on my head, like a friend of Stephanie's. I ask for more bread to wipe the plate. I smell something in the air from out on the street. A woman is looking at her phone, leaning against a pole. Fags. I could murder a fag now, but this isn't a place I think you could go bumming one off someone like a teenager. I ask the young lad where would I buy cigarettes. He seems to know I'm not a full-timer.

'You can get zem about fife minuts walk,' he says, but then he offers me one of his. White filters on them, like in the films. Taking fags off a young lad. He gives me a little smile and all. Jesus, Ann Devine, you're making a pure Shirley Valentine out of this situation. He lights it for me.

Oh, this fag is lovely. I can feel my blood pressure dropping. Imagine if we just retired out here. But on what, of course? We haven't a bean. We'd have to ask Kevin for some of his Dubai money. He's all that's left, now that Jennifer is spending it like it's going out of fashion.

There's a couple having a huge row a few tables over, and the wan gets up and tells your man something along the lines of that's he's some type of a bollox in French. He's shouting back and then she walks off. Or not exactly, but she fairly laid into him about whatever he had done. An ashtray goes flying. I half turn to nudge Denis about it before I remember he's not there.

I take a photo of the wine glass to send to him but move the fag out of the way. Not that he'd go mad, but he might use it to get him to be allowed to do something he shouldn't do later, and I don't need to be handing him any licences. Ould lads' health is more precarious anyway. That's my excuse. He'll still be gone before me.

He's after getting a smartphone as well, and all he has to do when he gets this is just touch the screen and the photo will appear and then it'll go somewhere on the phone and he'll lose track of it and he'll never find it again, but he'll get the gist anyway. We've sent each other a few photos now. Just funny things we might see out and about. Not sexy ones. I wouldn't know how to angle the thing, and who'd want to be looking at your bits? I don't understand that carry-on at all. If he sent me one, it'd be to ask if he should see the doctor about it.

We should do this ourselves more often xx, I say in the text.

Two x's for Denis. We're married a good while.

Send, and up it goes. Would you think I'm silly, but when the messages goes off I imagine it leaving the phone and landing on Denis's. I still, after all these years, think about the message like a little letter and imagining his face when he reads it. According to the text I got when the plane landed, it'll only be thirty-five cents, which is cheaper than a postcard.

No reply, of course. He doesn't have the phone on much and says they're a curse. He's right. He seems very happy without it. I put mine away for a while. It gets dark. Still no reply from Denis, but there's a WhatsApp voice message from Geraldine.

'Oh helllllooooo, Ann. Glad you could join us. How is your – what is it Mam calls it? – gallivanting? Gadding about on the continent. Well, now who's the irresponsible one, Ann? I'm sitting here in the car, Ann, outside the church. She's in there now and she says she's saying an extra prayer for me. I might get a "Hail Holy Queen" out of her. You'll be lucky to get a "Glory Be".'

'Thanks, Geraldine, I owe you one,' I write to her. She replies with another voice message.

'No prob, sis. Joking about the prayer. You'll get a decade, I'm sure.'

I'm feeling fairly decadent anyway. I ask for another cigarette off the 'Maggie May' character and try to relax again. The responsibilities come from all angles at my age.

The phone rings ten minutes later.

'Shite shite shite shite shite, Ann,' says Geraldine. 'Fuck. Ann. Fuck-fuck-fuck. I'm on the way to the hospital. Mam had a fall on the way out. I said did she want a hand and she said no, and then she tripped on the kerb before I could get round to her and she's after doing something to her hand.'

'Oh oh oh,' says Mam in the background.

'Are you OK, Mam?'

'Tell her I'm fine.'

'You're not fine, Mam, that wrist is up like a balloon.'

'What's going on, Geraldine?'

'And my hip, Ann.'

'What happened her hip?'

'I don't know. Mam, we're going to the hospital now. The ambulance would take for ever.'

'No, you should have waited for the ambulance. They know how to move you after a fall.'

'Well, excuse me, Brussels, if I didn't do it exactly right. I think she'll be fine. I've checked her energy.'

'Keep your eyes on the road, Geraldine, and don't mind your reiki,' says Mam.

'Gotta go, Ann.'

I ring Deirdre and ask her to meet them at the hospital. I need a bit of sense on the ground. I sit back down. I'll have to change my flights now. How do you do that?

I send one to Family: *Mam had a fall can you get me an earlier flight home.*

There are more texts. Did the universe get wind of me being too relaxed? There's Ann now, having a great time. We'll need to put a stop to her gallop.

And then the phone rings. It's Gordon. I wonder is someone dead. Why would he ring when I'm away?

'Hello, Gordon.'

'Oh, sorry, Ann, are you away? I heard an unusual ringtone.'

'Yes, Gordon, I'm in Brussels, with Rory. Helping him get settled in.'

'I suppose you've heard the bad news?'

How does he . . . ? She must have fallen in front of a few. Maybe someone saw Geraldine's car outside the church and called the guards.

'I did, Gordon. A bit of a shock. You're very good to call.'

'I had to call. We're going to need all hands on deck for this.'

'Well, Geraldine is with Mam anyway, the poor thing. She's is a bit upset all right.'

'Of course, yes, your mother would be particularly affected by this. But it's not just her. It's a blow for many more.'

What others? How many people tripped over this kerb?

'We'll have to get a committee together,' he's saying.

'A committ— wait, Gordon, what are you ringing me about? Is it about Mam falling?'

'Did your mother fall? I'm sorry to hear that. No, I'm talking about the post office. We've heard they're going to close it.'

The penny drops.

'It will be the death knell of the community. We're going to have to put together a committee. Father Donnegan was on to me about it. He said to me, *Gordon, we don't always see eye to eye, but the Tidy Towns is the one group that are active enough and ye need to be the core of the opposition*. I must say, it was very mature of him to come to me like that, a sign of a more deferential Church, I have to say, and in fact this could . . .'

His explanation is costing me a fortune in roaming.

'Listen, Gordon, the line is bad enough because I'm so far away, you know?'

He doesn't take the hint. My plan is to not be on the phone.

'Hello, Gordon? Hello? The reception is terrible here, I can hardly hear you.'

'I can hear you perfectly, Ann. That's strange. I was only talking to my sister a while ago and she's out in Spain. They've a house there.'

I lose my nerve.

'No, it's OK again, Gordon.'

'Anyway, Ann, we should do something.'

He talks about a *war-room* and a *sub-committee* and that *we won't take this lying down*, although I feel exactly like lying down.

'Now, we'll need to be at the centre of it. Can you drive it while I'm away?' It'll need that bit of Ann Devine magic that you showed last year if we want to save our post office.'

I promise I'll *drive it* and give him a short bye-bye-bye and hang up before he replies with more byes, and then I'm shot of him.

'Would you have another fag – I mean, a cigarette – there, Elijah?'

He hands it over, but I think he's starting to worry about whether I'm one of those women – what do they call them? – is it pumas? He hands me the lighter to light it myself in case I pull him on to my lap. I could assure him now that nothing is further from my mind. I am the opposite of frisky.

This time, the smoking isn't long and luxurious. I horse it as if I were out the back of the convent during the Inter. Cert. and my friend Leona was asking for *the next go off it*. The one evening where I was suiting myself entirely. Anntime. And now a whole pile of things to worry about come at me in five minutes.

There are no more photos to Denis of wine glasses. I pay Elijah, give him twenty euro for the rest of his cigarettes and walk back to the flat, take off my bit of make-up because I don't want to be making their sheets manky, but then again, Fabuelo was nearly wearing more make-up than me last night. When I get in I light one last cigarette off the gas

107

and smoke it out the window. The smell will be gone before Rory comes back.

It's nearly dawn when he comes in, crashing around the place in a fierce state. Humming whatever was the last song out of the place he was in.

'Blugggghh Take your mama out tonight gonna show her Pfffffffwhat it's all about.'

The breath out of him is nearly flammable.

'Mammysletstalk mantoman jawant toast?'

He looks like he's about to get in beside me until I tell him in no uncertain terms that he's not four and get back to bed. He staggers out again, the door closes and I hear snoring.

I doze for a couple of hours and wake up to a text message from Deirdre telling me she has a new flight home for me and that Mam is comfortable on a trolley and she's with her to let Geraldine go to work and that Denis will meet me at the airport.

I do most of my packing before Rory stirs from the couch. I go in, and he's sprawled with a bit of toast in one hand and the butter – the butter we brought over with us – on the cushion next to him, and it would have melted, only the place is quite cool, and I wonder why that is and I see the future political kingmaker has left the door wide open to the hall and there's a confused-looking woman, dressed immaculately, looking in at me in my Penney's dressing gown and slippers.

'Hello.'

'Bonjour, madame.' She looks in. I know the type. She's dying to ask. 'You make a party last night. Is your friend OK? I hear him fall at ze door. I do not know this man.'

'It's OK, I'm his mother.' I don't think that reassures her much. I don't think her English would stand up to a full explanation in the Kilsudgeon dialect about JP the

Continental from Lyracompane, Fabuloso and Mick the Lamp.

And neither of us have any Irish.

Rory farts in his sleep. That seems to be enough to reassure the neighbour he is OK, and also it scares her dog, which had been sniffing the door saddle. I can close the door.

After removing the butter and finding it the right level of soft for toast and tea with UHT-shite milk I wake Rory and proceed to very gently lambast him for getting into a state, tell him that his granny is in the hospital and that he should take it easy on the drink because his granny would be worried about him. The usual bit of guilting you do to try and get children to behave themselves and a load of other advice that I know he won't take, but I give it anyway because I'm his mother and it's my job to read out the Health and Safety notices so I'm not sued. I don't think he's fully awake. He also has a bit of a bruise on his neck, which I don't ask about, because I stopped asking my children about bruises on their necks after the first teenage disco Deirdre came back from, looking like a vampire had been at her.

I sit down and ring the taxi man.

12.

A BIT SHOOK TBH

The taxi drops me at the airport. It's not Celestine but another fella called Blessing, who knows both Celestine and Patsy. He also thinks Patsy is a man of God, but he hasn't heard yet about my fictional drug habit.

'Airport very busy, madame. Everyone leave Brussels *pour vacation.*'

He gets out, hands me my bags and dawdles a bit, so I give him a few euro of a tip. I look around me to try and get my bearings. At least I'm cheered up by where he drops me. There's a huge sign above my head. *Kiss and Ride,* it says.

Oh, that's a good one. I take a photo of it with the phone. I'll send it on to Denis. Just for the bit of devilment, to take my mind off Mam. Deirdre has told me since that Mam has a broken wrist and a bruised hip and is, as Freya would say, *a bit shook tbh.* Freya and her mam are due up for a visit later.

I go inside. I'm a bit disoriented. I don't think I've ever negotiated an airport on my own. Denis isn't good in them either, but between us we muddle through. I look up and try to find Zone C – or is it B? I have to find the email. It is very crowded. True for you, Blessing. They *are* all leaving Brussels. I see a few pink, odd-shaped heads that look Irish, and by following them I get to the desk. In the queue I send the WhatsApp.

I saw this and I thought of you haha maybe u ll get one or the other if you ve the place tidy xx

I send it off up into air and go through the security.

Bing! Bing! Bing! says the phone on the conveyor belt. Bing! it says, coming out the other side.

Denis is replying quickly. It must have livened him up. I put on my shoes and see what he has to say, but he has nothing to say. I have WhatsApp'd *Kiss and Ride* and a dirty invite to the Kilsudgeon Tidy Towns group. To twenty or thirty of the pure nosiest residents of Kilsudgeon. It landed straight after a discussion about the post office closing. The last message before mine was from Gordon.

Hello everyone, you may have heard the news by now that there are plans to close Kilsudgeon post office. Our Vice Chairperson is away at the moment but I have contacted her and she will be on to us soon with her thoughts on how we can fight this every step of the way. Personally I think there are two strands to our approach Number 1 is . . .

But the group has to page way down to see Gordon's other strands because my *Kiss* strand and *Ride* strand arrived in to start the party. All the Bings! are everyone else in the group having a right oul laugh. Even the driest shites are in top form over it.

I go for both options LOL

Fair play Ann that'll get the attention of the media.

You'll go viral again Ann.

Fair play ann.

That one is from the Nolan twins. When did they join? Oh, for God's sake. The last two people in the world you'd want to make a mistake in front of. They work with Denis on the lorries and they're like subtitles on every single thing that goes on around the place. *Fair play* seems tame. But they wouldn't be great at the typing. Then they get into their stride. They must be sitting together, because the messages come from them in exactly the way they'd say it.

Denis will be in no fit state on Monday.

He's not in any state any Monday.

That's true.

Now we know why.

He's very tidy though.

He should join the group.

Will you be taking this on parsnip Ann or is there a committee for this too?

That arrived after a bit of a delay. They must have been thinking that one out. Only the autocorrect made a balls of it for them. 'Parsnip' instead of 'personally'.

The white van is back.

At least someone else has posted to the wrong group. That was meant for the Neighbourhood Watch. There's a message only for me from Gordon, and he's asking if I *meant* to send that to the group. What does he think I meant to do? Do I look like the kind of person who responds to the news about a post office closure by promising my husband he's going to get looked after when I get back from the continent?

Bing!

The group is still replying.

How do I delete it, I text to Gordon.

Except I don't send that to Gordon. I send that to the group as well.

Too late now, says one of the twins.

The secrets out, says the other.

No wonder they're all keen to go to Brussels.

The youngest lad is gone out there, another person explains.

Explaining *our* family news to someone else in the group.

087suchandsuch is typing.

Oh God, what now?

A WhatsApp from Freya just to me. I forgot that she's in the group too.

SCREAMING Auntie Ann! Seriously cannot deal. Just given us an idea for our podcast this week. And she puts in the monkey with the hand over its face picture.

I reply that I'm glad she's inspired, but could she please help me delete the thing. She sends me on instructions and eventually I calm down enough to delete all the messages and reply *sorry* and that *I'll be back soon to look at the post office.*

Then there's another flurry of texts from people who've missed the whole rigmarole and are raging.

We've a screenshot, says the twins.

Don't worry, Freya texts me. *None of these boomers have a clue how to do a screenshot.*

Thanks Love.

But I do know how to do one!!!! And she sends it to me.

Freya don't you dare.

Joking. Anyway, just going up to see Nana. See you soon.

There's a new number in the group. And they are after writing a big message.

Hi, everyone. Iseult here. Sorry but this is not the time for joking, we need to get serious about the post office closing. It is the heart of Kilsudgeon. What is our plan?????

Now Gordon's back on. *Hello Iseult yes it is serious and we will be having a public meeting with public representatives which myself and Ann will organise – any thoughts Ann?*

My thoughts are that I am looking up at a gate that says Baku and there is time for me to go and buy a ticket and stay there until they all feck off, but that won't do. I summon up the spirit of Tracy and type bullshit.

Agree 100% Gordon. I am working towards that as we speak.

That shuts them up for a while. I work on a gin and tonic in the Laughing Shamrock in Brussels airport. But Iseult putting me in my place has made me blush all the way up my face, which I'm still basting in when going up to board the flight. There is sweat on my forehead, and I can feel it on my neck, too.

By the time I get on the plane I'm a wreck. A lady asks me if I'm a nervous flyer and that makes me flush more. I sink back into the seat, trying to concentrate on an article in the airplane magazine about a city I'm not going to ever get to go and see now because I'll be looking after my mother. WhatsApp or no WhatsApp, the post office closure is a disaster for Kilsudgeon. The place has always been in the doldrums. If the post office goes, it'll be another empty spot on the street.

When I come through Arrivals, Denis is there to meet me.

'I've tidied the place,' he says with a big wink.

But he sees my expression and knows it'll be just *Kiss* for the foreseeable.

13.

I'M NOT A CHILD, LORRAINE

Mam smiles up at us. Geraldine, Freya and me are sitting around her in the ward.

'I'M A MARTYR FOR MY RELIGION, ANN. CAN YOU SWITCH THAT HEARING YOKE ON FOR ME? That's better.'

The wrist is broken. Her hip is OK, but she's bruised. Devotions, of course. Always bloody devotions. That's where they all fall down. Devotions or Blessings of the Graves. Shaky old women leaning on other old women for support, tripping over something that should have been fixed.

We're in ward 4F in the County Hospital. There are four others in the ward. Two are out for the count. The television is on. Val Furnish is shouting at it.

'THE COUNTRY'S GONE TO THE DOGS.'

'Tis you said it, Val,' says little Bridget Salmon.

Val is laid up with what looks like a hernia, from what I can tell from a quick glance at the chart when I was tying my lace. Bridget is perennially in here with some affliction as that family were always a bit delicate, but she could also take a sudden turn requiring hospitalization if she heard Val was laid up. There should be a film written about the two of them. Bridget constantly calling around to him with bits of shopping and talk and Val acting like she's just being a good neighbour. The Twins told me she even changes his bedclothes. But I doubt they've ever so much as shaken hands. We think. Sure, maybe it's like the *Kama Sutra* up there with them. But I doubt it. Not with his back.

'The kerbing. I saw the kerbing and I said, *Mam, mind the kerbing* – didn't I say that?'

Mam doesn't reply. Geraldine is fussing around her bed. Rearranging things in her locker that don't need rearranging. She's rattled and blaming herself. I know the feeling. When something happens to an old person in your care, you're always your own prime suspect.

Val Furnish roars at the television again.

'THAT'S THE START OF IT NOW. THE FEMINISTS. THEY HAVE THEIR ABORTION, THEN THE NEXT THING THEY'LL BE COMING AFTER US WITH THE EUTHANASIA.'

I don't know how he's getting all this from the news with the sound turned down. The report looks to be something about turf-cutting.

'True for you, Val.'

'CARTED OFF TO THE KNACKER'S YARD. TURNED INTO GLUE.'

'Glue is right, Val. A tube of Bostik. That's all we are.'

Mam looks straight up at the telly. I know she's not happy there's a man in the ward. It's supposed to be same-sex wards but the nurse told me they're rushed off their feet with the heatwave.

'THEY WEREN'T HAPPY WITH LETTING THE GAYS GO AT IT. OH NO.'

'Don't let me go like that, Ann,' whispers Mam to me from her chair, not taking her eyes off the telly.

'Like what, Mam?'

'Shouting at the telly in a hospital. If I get like that, will you put me down?'

'You're going nowhere, Mam. It's a broken wrist. I will not be putting you down. I'm not a vet. And Val has been shouting at tellies all his life. Since they got rid of *Live at 3.*'

'It's the way it broke, Ann. I could feel it go on me and there was no stopping it. Do you know what I mean? No give in it at all. Like it was waiting to snap.'

'You should be doing yoga, Mam,' Geraldine cuts in.

'Well, I'm not going to start now, am I?' says Mam, quite sharply, even for her.

'Jesus, Mam, there's no need to snap at me. I was only trying to help. I could teach you a few poses.'

'When you're in the pain I'm in, Ger, you'll understand.'

'It sounds like you hope I will have that kind of pain, Mam.' Ger looks hurt. She goes off to the loo. Freya watches her go and then crouches in near Mam.

'Here, Nana, this'll cheer you up.' And she starts showing Mam something on her phone. 'So, Nana, your eldest was basically on the rip in Brussels. Rory said she was paralytic on Belgian beer, and he made a video as well.'

This is me . . . Ann. Over here in Belgian with Rory, helping start his internment.

'And this is her addressing an empty European Parliament.'

Well . . . I'd like to thank ye all for coming here . . .

'And this is her SEXTING Uncle Denis. Would you be able?'

'Kiss and Ride.' Mam reads it out. 'What's that about, Ann? I thought Ger was the wild one.'

At least we're not talking about Mam's demise. Geraldine comes back.

'You could have hit your head and died, Mam, if I wasn't there. You should put in a claim.'

'I will not put in a claim, Ger.'

Mam is not from a generation who put in a claim for compensation. If something bad happens, it happens, and it was your fault. If you came home from school with a red arm from a teacher's strap, it was your fault. If a dog bit you, you must have been annoying it.

'The Church haven't a bob, Geraldine.'

'They have plenty, Mam. In the Vatican. Put in the claim, Mam. The kerbing was broken. Then you can go private.'

'We were never claimers, Geraldine. You claim if you want. I suppose ye want a share of it, do ye?'

We leave it go. She's cranky with the pain.

Nearby, Val shouts, 'AND THE POPE VISITING IN A FEW WEEKS AS WELL! WHAT ARE WE SUPPOSED TO SAY TO HIM NOW? MAKING A SHOW OF US IN FRONT OF THE WHOLE WORLD.'

A nurse comes past, and straight away she has Val Furnish's number.

'Ah, Val, what are you at at all? Getting out of bed there, and what are the trousers doing on you with the catheter still in? What were you thinking? You're more trouble than a toddler.'

'I'M NOT A CHILD, LORRAINE.'

'Hard to keep a good man down, Val,' chips in his admirer.

'Bridget, my love, you're not supposed to be here. You know that. This isn't your ward, is it? Where are you supposed to be?'

'Four C.'

'That's right, my darling. Now can you go back now, please, to Four C, like a good woman? Why are you down here at all? Are you trying to seduce poor Val, and him already laid up enough?' Lorraine winks across at us.

Bridget scowls and mutters to Lorraine that *Four C is a ward with a load of old people and there's a smell off that ward*.

'There's no smell there, Bridget, it was only mopped an hour ago. And anyway, you told me you've no sense of smell, so what are you on about, girl? I think you're only blackguarding.'

Bridget looks like the jig is up and shuffles out the door, banging the walker off bed frames and trolleys. She's not happy about being kept away from the man she loves.

'Find someone who looks at you the way Bridget looks at Val,' says Freya out of the side of her mouth.

'And the state of you, Val, shouting at the television in a hospital ward and patients trying to sleep. Are you going to be like that all the time?'

'Is it against the law now to stand up for your beliefs, is it, Nurse? Did the management tell you to keep me quiet? And the two foreign nurses as well. Taking away work from the Irish.'

'The management told me to put you out on the road, Val, but I felt sorry for you. But if you talk about Meena and Benilda like that again, I'll tell them to go ahead.'

She winks at us again. Lorraine spends the next while attending to Val, and he quietens down now there's no one to impress. He looks over at Mam after a few minutes.

'Terrible, isn't it, Margaret?'

She says it is, but doesn't say specifically what, so I'm not sure what he or she thinks is terrible. But when you're old and in hospital, something always is terrible. She looks very small in the bed. Hospital shrinks the old people, even after a few hours.

The glass of wine in Brussels seems very far away. This is it now, Ann. The start of it. Mam's first fall. We got away

119

with it for ages. She is as hardy. She might be bound up like Nefertiti from time to time, but the woman is a machine. Still out in her garden fighting dandelions and shouting at pigeons to keep away from her few bits of lettuce. It was only that she never learned to drive that she didn't head off adventuring.

'Putting us down, Margaret.'

Val is back again.

'Who told you that?'

'It was in the magazine there at the back of Mass.'

'What magazine, Val?' I ask him.

Val waves *It's Faith!* at us.

Lorraine sniffs the air and goes over to Val again. She closes the curtains and we can hear her scolding Val gently.

'Ah, Val, you swore blind to me you didn't need cleaning up. Now look at you.'

A smell wafts over us. I know that one only too well.

Mam turns back to me with a scowl on her face. 'I should have got a private room, Ann. I thought I was due a private room. You were supposed to post off the insurance.'

Actually, I wasn't supposed to post it off. I remember asking Mam straight out if she wanted me to look after it for her, but she said no.

'AND THEY'RE CLOSING THE POST OFFICE AS WELL, MARGARET. YOU'LL SEE FOREIGNERS IN THERE NEXT. PRAYING TO MECCA'

Mam looks at me in alarm and I realize this is the first she's heard of it.

'It's only a rumour, Mam.'

'I suppose I'll never go to one again anyway. They sort all that out for you in the home.'

'In the home? A nursing home? Ah Mam, will you stop with that?'

'Bring me to the toilet, will you?'

I go over to the toilet in the ward to open the door.

'Not that one. Bring me down the hall. I don't want to be listened to.'

I have to listen to her. The poor thing. The fall didn't shake up the old girl's digestive tract, unfortunately, and the two of us are in the disabled toilet staring at the wall listening to her groaning away.

'No bit of dignity now,' she says to me.

'Don't mind yourself, Mam. I've seen and heard far worse.'

'They were strangers, though, Ann. This is different.'

'I'm sure you watched me, Mam.'

'That was sixty-five years ago.'

'Mam! I'm not that old.'

'How old are you again?'

I remind her that it's not sixty-five. She still doesn't take it well.

'Bad enough. Oh God, I nearly have a pensioner for a daughter.'

More groaning. Eventually there's some sort of resolution, but I wouldn't call it satisfactory.

Ger watches as I come back with Mam. I get her settled and we go out for a cup of tea and leave Freya to keep Mam entertained by telling her what she knows about the world.

'The nurse has said she can leave in a few days if there's someone there to mind her. They just want to keep an eye on her. Such a thing to happen, Ann. I feel terrible.'

'Listen, love, don't be beating yourself up. It's the same with children. If we felt bad about every bump and scrape, we wouldn't go out the door. Put it out of your mind now.'

'You're too good, Ann. I'm sorry about the WhatsApp message. You know I was joking, don't you?'

I tell her about the trip and bumming fags off a waiter in a square and she laughs at my Shirley Valentine act.

'You know, Ann, there's people out there, like, if you're ever looking for a bit of variety. Or a bit of strange, as they call it. And you didn't want to be lying to Denis . . . well, in my angels business I got to hear a lot about what's *available* . . .' She taps her nose.

'Don't be ending the sentence there, Ger. What are you talking about?'

'Swingers, Ann. They're all over the place. You wouldn't believe the meet-up groups I've come across in the hotel business. Rampant, it is, Ann. And it's even more rampant out the country because the houses are bigger.'

'Oh God, could you imagine Denis in that situation, making small talk? Worrying about where he has parked in a bad spot.'

'There's plenty of parking at a swingers' night, I'd say, Ann.'

We are giggling away like we haven't in a while.

'I'm sorry about your trip, Ger.'

'What do you mean?'

'You know, with Mam and all, she'll have to move in with me for a while, and then I suppose Freya can't, really. I mean, you'll have to postpone the trip for another bit . . .'

I trail off, hoping she'll jump in.

She hesitates and starts taking great interest in a hygiene sign.

'Ann . . . I don't think I can. This trip isn't refundable. It's not with any kind of a tour. It's all very informal. I've already paid over the money. And this really is the right time for me and . . . and do you really want me to look after Mam? Look at what happened the first time I was left alone with her, you know?'

Geraldine still has the fear of old people. She's had to work so hard all along and I did a good bit of minding of Freya, even when she was very small, that she's never really

122

took to the grubby business of caring. I see her around Mam. She's kind of stiff, as if she's afraid to touch her. We have old people made out to be so frail and odd that we can't bear to help them around in case they break or leak.

That was the half of why the reiki-massage-holistics didn't work out for her. She wanted to do all this massage, but when the first fairly ripe farmer came in with bunions she wasn't able for it. It's her personality is the thing. She charms people and makes them feel good. Which is a great skill in itself. But not much good in a toilet situation.

'It makes sense, doesn't it, Ann?'

'Are you two fighting over me?' says Freya, arriving beside us. 'I hope it's about who gets to have me.' She has a quivery little smile.

'That's it, pet. Your mother and me were just figuring out the logistics.'

'You're a star, Ann.' Geraldine hugs me and heads off with Freya.

123

14.

THE NCT MAN'S DAUGHTER

'Holding the fort again, Ann? You're some woman,' they say to me as they walk in. The Nolan twins. 'Is this the *Kiss and Ride* spot, Ann? You'll need a sign.'

'She'll need a sign surely.'

I'm standing at the door to the hall, waiting for people to come into this meeting about the post office. A couple of nights ago, after I left Mam in the hospital, I sat down and took a deep breath and organized it. I still get in a panic about inviting anyone to anything, in case they don't show up. But they are here. I have a small table in front of me and I'm collecting email addresses. I read somewhere that you can't do that any more or the GDPR will be on to you. But we'll be down their list anyway.

It's a beautiful evening. Shirtsleeve weather. Even though many have walked, the car park outside the hall is packed. Denis is outside, directing traffic – I can see him – with enthusiastic waving and tapping of bonnets, saying, *That's grand, you'll do there*. And the odd shout if people get too close. And one scrape off a wall and a woman mortified about what she's after doing to the Hybrid. It's a bigger crowd than any I've seen for a meeting around here. They're geed up about the post office.

This is the one thing that has brought every isolated farmer and bachelor and widow and spinster down from the mountains and up lanes out of hollows. You'll know them by the driving. The ould lads who drive in a high gear and judder around the place and the old women with Micras who sound like Formula One because they wouldn't change up from first gear. I can see Denis grimacing as he hears them. He is convinced that no one knows how to change gear in this country. He won an award once from a lorry company for fuel economy and he still says it's his greatest achievement.

There's some smell of smoke in the summer evening air. It hangs around mixed with the bit of honeysuckle that's growing on the hedge around the hall. Christian Dior should do a bottle of it. Fags and woodbine. And the crowd here tonight are the last of the tarry smokers, the age of them making a mockery of the health warnings on the packet. They'd rather die of fags than boredom. They won't be vaping. The closing of the post office would kill them faster with loneliness than any Rothmans. It's great smoking weather, though.

I leave the sign-up table and start trying to edge people in. There's no sign of Patsy. Rory told me he was trying to get a flight back from a conference in the Cayman Islands and that the meeting was organized too soon for him and that that is somehow my fault. I sit up on the stage, uncomfortable as anything. Gordon takes the microphone and gets the meeting going.

'Thank you all for coming now at such short notice. You can see the depth of the concern for our beloved post office.

125

I thought we'd start with a little history. Interestingly, it was in 1892 that Kilsudgeon post office . . .'

The murmuring starts straight away. I take a deep breath and just interrupt.

'Gordon, we might throw it open to the floor there, to let people talk about what the post office means to them.'

And so he does. One by one, the old people who don't go out, except to go to the post office, tell the room what it means to them. Nellie Riley says she doesn't see anyone from one day to the next. Mossy Burns says it was the first trip he made after he got the bit of depression. It's pure emotional in the room after that.

Gordon gets up after a good quarter of an hour of these stories. 'For any members of the media here, I want you to listen to that testimony and understand the depth of the feeling. We would urge everyone to start writing to their . . .'

'BOLLOX!'

Kilsudgeon would be a tame enough place politically, but it seems one well-timed *Bollox* can be enough to take the stopper out of the bottle. It's Davey Finnerty.

'This is only a talking shop,' he says. 'Where's the action? Where's An Post? Where's Patsy Duggan? I'll tell you where he is. In THE CARIBBEAN.'

This sets them off. Shouting and clapping. Davey never got this when he was a Communist.

'WHERE IS THE POSTMASTER?'

Gordon tries to intervene. 'Well, I know, er . . . David . . . feelings are high. We hope to meet stakeholders . . .'

'STAKEHOLDERS IS RIGHT. WE NEED STAKES THROUGH THE HEART OF OFFICIAL IRELAND.'

The claps are not as loud for that, as people try to figure out what he means.

'DO WE KNOW IF THERE IS TRUTH IN THE RUMOURS ABOUT IT BEING USED AS ACCOMMODATION FOR ASYLUM-SEEKERS?'

Gordon is stumped. 'I hadn't heard any rumours about that . . .'

In fact, no one had been talking about it, but now that Davey has planted it in heads, I can see people muttering to each other, *Did you hear . . .* The thing about rumours is you only just need to say there are rumours and then straight away there actually are rumours. And I think Davey knows this. Everyone seems to forget you couldn't swing a cat in that post office.

A loud, clear voice cuts through the hugger-mugger.

'Can I speak, please?'

'Of course, Iseult.' Gordon looks relieved.

'Thank you.'

Iseult Deasy stands up and pauses. You'd think she forgot her lines, but no, it's the acting. Now she has everyone's attention. She gets out into the middle of the room and walks up on to the stage and eases the microphone out of Gordon's hand. Even the young lads at the back are quietened. She has a bag with her.

'This post office is not just bricks and mortar. It is memory. It is our life.'

The word 'life' hits the crowd and they respond. Plain language. We all have a life.

'If it closes, it is the death knell of the community. For those of you who don't know me, I am Iseult and I am one of the returned. I returned from New York to make a life here, but my government wants to send me away again. I am a symbol of the future, and the post office closing is something we're not going to take lying down. What hope is there for the next generation? Amelia, can you come up, please?'

Amelia comes out of her seat and walks up to her. Slowly. Honestly, the *drama* these two manage to create.

'*This* is the next generation.'

She's the same generation as her sister. Although Amelia was a 'surprise', and we all know they can happen.

'My sister was lucky enough to be chosen to meet the Pope and bring a message to him. And the message she'll bring is *Our Community is Dying*.'

The crowd drink in that line. Then Iseult takes out a Kilsudgeon Gaels shirt and dramatically lets it fall to the ground.

'We won't need this any more. We won't be able to field a team. We will be decimated. We need to fight. We need fighters. Like Ann Devine!'

I happen to be scratching my ear when all attention swings to me. I try and turn the scratch into a thoughtful stroke of my chin and give a small wave at the same time. I must look very odd, but Iseult doesn't dwell on me for too long.

'Let's do something for the next generation,' she says, and there is a big clap. The meeting breaks up with Gordon reminding people to put in their email addresses, but no one is listening. They are surrounding Iseult with *Congratulations* and *Fair play to you for saying it* and that it's *True for her about the foreigners*. Even though she said nothing about foreigners. This giving out about foreigners is making me uneasy. I hope it's just people getting carried away.

She comes up to me while I'm putting away the chairs.

'Ann, I hope you don't mind me pointing you out. I just think more people need your get up and go. When is the next clean-up? I'd love to join in.'

'Well, we weren't . . .'

'You're a powerhouse, Ann.'

There was no other one planned. But now that I'm a powerhouse I'll have to crank the shagging thing up again.

When we get home, Geraldine is there. She's going first thing in the morning, so they're saying goodbye at our place. Freya has a look that I don't recognize at first because she's such a tough cookie. I realize she's sad. She'll miss her mam, even though they're always at each other's throats. But it's only natural mothers and their teenage daughters should be that way, for a few years anyway. I'm glad that aunts get special dispensation from their nieces. I couldn't argue with Freya for an hour, let alone a few years.

After Ger has gone I make some cocoa and Freya cheers herself up by laughing at what neighbours have put up on the Kilsudgeon Tidy Towns Facebook page.

'The medium is back, Auntie Ann.'

Sure enough, Dee Wills has posted: *Talk To Your Deceased Loved Ones To Get Closure.*

'Look at this though, Auntie Ann. *Iseult Deasy has tagged you and 345 others in a post.*'

'What's she saying?'

Freya reads it. '*I am feeling so many emotions right now, guys. For my village. The place of my birth. I've acted all over the whole world and it's always Kilsudgeon that calls me back.*'

There's a flag at the end of it.

'What flag is that, Freya?'

'Sweden, but I think it's meant to be the Kilsudgeon colours too.'

'*I've just come from our parish hall. I remember the first time I went there as a small child to be in the kids' production of* Rent. *I was never happier than when I got to perform in front of the village I love . . .*'

The Kilsudgeon Dramatic Society. Some egos came out of that place. They're defunct now. A huge row over ticket money that went missing after *Oliver*. The fella who played Fagin got accused of it. Then they found the biscuit tin underneath a table, but there was bad feeling over it.

'When I look at the crowd, I see that we need leadership. And I look to our elected representatives and I Don't See Leadership. And when The Celts pulled out last year. NO EXPLANATION! Decisions are being taken miles away . . . Every day in our post office, a million stories are told, news is passed on, the community COMES TOGETHER AS ONE. When we lose that, WHAT DO WE HAVE? WHAT DO WE HAVE? WE ARE STRONG TOGETHER. WE CAN DO THIS! How can we look at THE NEXT GENERATION!!! IF WE DO NOTHING. WE MUST FIGHT THIS. SPIRIT OF KILSUDGEON. WHO IS WITH ME?'

There are a lot with her: 400 likes, 35 shares. That's good. No one ever shares anything I put up on the page, apart from one time I put up a video about a bear knocking on the door of a car, and everyone loved that.

FAIR PLAY TO YOU GIRL U ARE DEAD RIGHT.

PATSY DUGGAN WAIST OF SPACE.

WHERE WAS HE SUNNING HIMSELF WITH ALL HIS MONEY.

'Oh wow, Patsy's getting dragged, Auntie Ann.'

It's all coming out now about Patsy. I've never seen so much criticism of him in one place before.

It gets even more ugly further down, though.

Dey will luk after asylun seerks but not dere own.

No wat u mean.

But Iseult, fair play to her, is back on straight away.

Hey, everyone, this is not about them versus us, it's about our post office. Let's keep it civil, ok guys.

The comment disappears. I didn't think 'Wilfred BREXIT MEANS BREXIT Dean' was a local anyway.

'Iseult is going to be best friends with a load of racists, Auntie Ann.'

'Ah, that's just online. They're not local.'

By the time we snap out of it and stop looking at the phone there are a thousand likes. Freya says that's big. I tell Denis about it later on.

'She could give Patsy a run for his money. She could get elected over it. And then where would our golden boy be, Ann?'

A good question, Denis, I think.

15.

NOT ENOUGH WOWING

The house feels different when I bring Mam in the door after she leaves the hospital. She's been in it many times over the years, but now I see her looking at it with different eyes.

'The hall is terrible cluttered – you could trip on something, Ann.'

I usher her into the kitchen, get her into a chair and put tea in front of her, and no sooner does she sit down than she wants to be brought to the toilet. When we come back she finally sits down to the tea.

'These chairs are awful uncomfortable, Ann.'

And so it goes on for a while. It washes over me. I've dealt with far worse in my work.

'Don't be making the face now, Ann. I can see it even with my eyes not being the best.'

'What face, Mammy?'

'I see the face you made when I wanted you to bring me to the toilet. I'm a burden. Ring up your own place there and we'll get someone.'

'You will not be getting anyone out of Mellamocare, Mammy. The mortification, if I couldn't look after my own mother.'

'Well, stop the faces.'

'Mam, that's my face. I'd have to get plastic surgery to have another face. What face would you like me to have if you tell me you have the runs and need to get cleaned up? I'm not going to be Mr Motivator.'

She seems to like the bit of needle in me and doesn't grumble as much for a while, and Freya arrives in anyway, which cheers her up.

'How's your radio show, Freya? Where would I get it? Is it on RTÉ?'

'Podcast, Nana. You can get it on, like, whatever is your podcast provider, you know – iTunes, Acast, Soundcloud.'

'Freya . . .'

'Sorry, Auntie Ann. It's on the internet, Nana.'

Mam takes this as explanation enough.

'Lossie is away in the Gaeltacht so I have to do the next podcast on my own.'

Lossie is Lasairfhiona, Freya's only friend.

'It's sooo hard. Like I'm just talking to myself for an hour.'

'Sounds like being a mother, Freya.'

'Ooh, burn.'

She grabs a biscuit and skips upstairs to Rory's room. I watch her leave. When my back is turned there's a crash.

'AH THE BASTARDING HOOR OF A YOKE!'

The mug is on the ground. There is tea all over the place. I clean it up and refill Mam's mug and bring her over to the Soft Chair and install her again with the tea within reach.

'It was my good arm that got done, Ann. I could never manage a mug with my other arm. That's it now, Ann. The start of it. You might as well put me in a home. I felt it as

133

soon as I got the fall. The body didn't have it in me to mend myself. There's a lot more behind me than ahead of me.'

I've seen plenty of old people after getting turns and I'm not buying it.

'Mam, will you stop being so dramatic. You had one fall. Give it a chance to heal. You'll be grand. Eat a biscuit there and get a bit of sugar into you.'

'You're only thinking about the biscuits, Ann. I hope you're not going to go huge like you did before. You put on a bit abroad in Belgium, did you? I thought myself now when I saw you coming into the hospital. Especially around the face. You might as well take the biscuit now. I don't want to be getting fat into the bargain.'

The fall must have shook loose some old thoughts out of Mam's head. She was always watching us like a hawk for fear we'd turn into hapes. *You won't get any man by eating biscuits, Ann*, she used to say.

There were fewer big women around forty years ago than there are now. I told her there were plenty of women bigger than me doing very well for themselves man-wise. Mam never agreed with that. And anyway, I did get Denis eating biscuits because the first thing he said to me was *Are you eating those?* at a bit of a party after a funeral. Mind you, it was a few weeks later we got together. You don't just fall in love straight away after a proposal like that.

There's a soft knock on the back door.

'It's probably Bim,' says Mam.

'BIM?! What's he coming in around the back for?'

'I told him c'mon away over. He'll have a few of my things from the house.'

I open the back door and, sure enough, there he is. He walks in past me, all full of purpose and business, as if he's the man to put manners on the situation.

'An awful shame to see such a fine cut of a woman laid low,' he says. 'Well, Peggy.' And he goes over and gives her a kiss! 'You should sue them, Peggy. Over that kerbing. It wasn't laid right first day. I remember the day they were doing it, Peggy, and I saw the man that was doing it and he wasn't doing it right. A desperate job.'

'Is that a fact, Bim?' says Freya, arriving in. She's back wearing her Repeal jumper. Freya is practising what she calls active listening for her podcast, but she does it to take the piss out of anyone halfway countryish.

'True as I'm standing here, Ferdia. Shur the thing was spalling first day. The fella threw down only about thirty mill of sand underneath the thing and the kerbstones after it. I was watching him. I walked past first and I was asking him was he going to make the trench deeper, and he says to me, *I make trench as deep as I make it.* A Pole. You'd think they'd know about trenches. I went back to the car then, and I was watching him for a few hours, actually. He didn't see me at all. I had the seat put back.'

'You were like Columbo, Bim.'

'Shur someone has to keep an eye out, Ann. There's lads getting jobs now shouldn't be let near a brush, never mind a kerbstone. I have your bag, Peg.'

And I see that he is holding a Lidl bag. I see clothes belonging to her peeping out of the top of it. He was packing for her? Does he have a key? And in a plastic bag? Coming out of the house with a plastic bag of clothes. Mam shows no sign of minding.

'You were lucky you weren't worse injured, Peg. You've a strong case to get money out of them. Big money. And you can be worse injured by the time you get to court, if you know what I'm saying to you, like. Put on a bit of a show for the judge. My brother has a spare neck brace.'

Mam is listening intently to him, as if it's the first she's heard of the idea.

'And you know, Bim, this one here was out in Brussels while the whole thing was going on. On the town in Brussels while her poor mother was laid up.'

She is doing this to get a rise out of me now, and it's working. Bim looks at Freya and seems to notice the jumper.

'All on holidays now from school, Freya, is it? And all the campaigning finished as well?' Bim asks her.

'There's a lot more we have to do, actually,' says Freya, and before I can stop her she has Bim filled in on how we need to keep the pressure up on legislation and how the North is next. We all pause to take it in. She has used up all the talk in the room.

Bim gives Mam a look. 'Some changes around here, Peg, isn't there? Hard to keep up with it. Not the way it was, is it? I suppose nothing stays the same.'

He's talking like they're the same age, but he's younger than me. But he turned fifty when he was ten.

Mam's face closes up. She looks through Bim and then looks at Freya. It's hard to know what she is thinking.

'Sit down, Bim, and take the weight off the floor.'

'Is that tea hot?' he says, and picks out a banana from the fruit bowl and slides into Denis's favourite chair.

Freya announces she has to go and leans over the back of Mam's chair and gives her a big hug from behind. Mam gives her a kind of ferocious hungry kiss that's aimed for the cheek, but the force of it puts it mostly across Freya's nose. But the contact has perked her up. I get a few kisses like that the odd time from my old people. So anxious for the human contact they'd nearly eat you up.

Bim is wiring into the banana with his mouth open. It's a wonder he doesn't . . .

136

He does. He grabs the remote control beside him and turns on the little kitchen telly. Mam stares straight ahead. I hope she might be thinking of making him redundant for a while. The news is on, and it looks familiar.

'Oh, that's Kilsudgeon.'

'This series of post office closures is happening right across the country. Even Kilsudgeon, a small town that achieved notoriety last year as the setting for the ill-fated Celts *TV blockbuster, has not gone unscathed. It, too, will have no post office within the next few months and locals will have to take their post office business to nearby Drumfeakle. And they are not happy.'*

Mam looks worried.

'A spokesman for An Post has said that customers can avail themselves of a wide number of online services.'

'Online. What am I going to do with online? Sure you hardly know online, Ann.'

They interview the postmaster, Danny Maher.

'There'd be people in here just for talking. The whole day. Having a bit of gossip. They might have even forgotten what they came in here for.'

Danny is talking a good talk, but he doesn't look too gutted to be going. He never wanted that job. His mother was the postmistress before him, and she would lap that stuff up all day long. But Danny was off in London before he got the call back to base to take up the job when his mam got crabbed, and you could see he didn't ever have much enthusiasm, listening to old people's life stories as they bought a stamp.

'All set for the Pope, Margaret?'

'I don't know, Bim. This daughter of mine won't get me tickets.'

'I *told* you, Mam, that we're getting the parish tickets so we can all go up together.'

She won't be told.

Bim slurps the last of his tea and looks around him. I want to edge him out without throwing him out. Mam is in the kind of mood to take his side. He opens the paper. Nicely settled into the hollow of the seat Denis has spent years making. When I've just about given up on hunting him out the doorbell rings.

'Ann, hun, how *are* you?'

The fragrance hits me before Stephanie Devine-Rourke's hug does. She is careful not to ruin her make-up so her cheek just glances past me. We're kind of stiff in the hug. I think all those Rourkes are a bit stiff with the likes of us. As if we'd smudge them.

'I meant to come earlier, as soon as I arrived, but there was a touch of jetlag because, actually, I came via Mumbai – we were organizing an event out there? I had to iron out a few wrinkles on the venue? And of course I was already missing the kids so we had a Skype call with me and their granny and grandad. And of course they'd love to Skype their other granny and grandad too.' And she gives a sweet little smile that I almost fall for because, well, she is a very charming woman when she turns it on.

We walk through to the kitchen to Mam.

'Hello, Margaret, I am *so* sorry to hear about your little mishap. I had a fall too, actually, skiing in Dubai – I'm sure you've heard about the indoor slope? The pain. I was in agony. But I had an event the following day and popped in the Tramadol and . . . Oh, I didn't realize you had company.'

Stephanie's arrival in the room flummoxes Bim. She's too much for him, with her scent and her active hair. He starts to mop up bits of the banana from his overalls.

'Stephanie, do you know Bim?'

'Nice to meet you . . . Bim?'

The Rourkes wouldn't be the kind of people to let a spailpin like Bim into their lives.

'Thanks for the tae, Ann. Look after yourself, Margaret. Drop me a text there, if you need anything.'

And quicker than if I'd called the squad car, he's gone.

Stephanie looks around the kitchen. Her face seems to flinch a little as she takes in Denis's chair and his spare boots on newspaper.

'I thought you were planning on updating this place, Ann.'

I mentioned it once a few years ago. Just to get her off my back, as she was nagging me to *update*.

'We did Rory's room last year. I can show you if you want.'

She shakes her head as if she's seen it all before.

'Classic error, Ann. Piecemeal redecoration never works. You are just going to end up with a series of different moods. Consistency is key if you want flow. When I'm decorating a venue I start with a blank canvas and apply the same emotion throughout all the spaces.'

Mam has gone silent. She's still sore at Stephanie because she suspects she was only asked to Kevin's wedding as an afterthought.

Her phone rings. 'Oh, that'll be Jen.' She walks out to the hall to talk to her.

'That's some perfume she has on,' says Mam. 'You'll have to light a match after she's gone.'

'It might explode.'

We share a smile. Stephanie is back in.

'Jen says hi. She's looking forward to a good old knees-up with her fave sis-in-law at Viv's wedding. Mutual friend – you wouldn't know her – getting married in a big do in Lackan Castle. It's been completely transformed. You know the people who did Lissalee Lodge and Spa?'

I don't.

'A lot of my clients reach out to me about there, so I'm really interested to see what's going on in Lackan. You know the Al Shabar group?'

I don't.

'They have the Drumnalsa stud over in Flesk. They are a key partner for a lot of my product activations.'

There's not enough wowing out of me, so Stephanie gives up trying to impress me.

'Annnnyway, so Jen's my plus one. It'll be good to catch up. Her company are big supporters of the whole Not for Profit space, so we'll have a bit of a chinwag in our *gúnas*, girl to girl. She's great, Jennifer. You must be so proud of what's she's done. Although, Declan . . . what do you *make* of him, Ann?'

I'm in a bind. It looks like we think the same thing about Declan. I soften up a bit. And from the sound coming from Mam's stomach I think she is softening up too. Stephanie pretends not to hear.

'Yeah, so the wedding is only the day before the meal. And, like, I know we'll be in the absolute *horrors*, but at least Declan's booked Slaughterhouse, so he's not all weird. It's literally the only place that isn't *awful* for dinner. I thought we should all get together. It'll be good to get a night out for Deirdre as well. Deirdre just needs a lift, don't you think? She looks old, Ann.'

'Where did you see Deirdre?'

'Oh, on Facebook, and I keep telling her to put a filter on some of her photos. You should do it as well, Ann. You don't need to be showing the world all your secrets. We women have to put on a brave face in a hostile world. I can give you some tips if you want. We could have a makeover day. Or *even better*, we could all go shopping!' As soon as she says this she claps her hands together with the enthusiasm, as if she has just had her best idea ever. 'Let's do it before the wedding!'

Mam blows her nose with an impressive honk.

'And you, Margaret, too, as well of course. Can't forget Margaret.'

'I've the runs, Ann. Can you bring me quick.'

'I guess I'll go,' she says.

I wonder did any of the Rourkes ever have the runs or did they get someone else to have them for them?

16.

PEASANTS DOWN THE TOWN

Hey gang, just to let you know we'll be getting a pile of tickets for the Pope's mass in the phoenix park. Throw me a text or drop into the parochial house if you want to be included. Sound. Joe Donnegan.

I send a text for ten tickets for whoever in the family want to go and I show Mam the text and say, 'There now, are you satisfied?' But she's grumpy that I have to head off to work and leave her.

Freya is minding her while I'm out. She has instructions to ring if there are any eruptions. My niece FaceTimed her mother last night, who told her about her layover in Paris and Bombay and how she was already feeling more Zen, and Freya held the phone away and rolled her eyes. She likes the chance to roll her eyes.

As I am going out the door my phone buzzes again to tell me Tracy has emailed to say that she would like me to fill in a three-sixty feedback form to show how, after my Sylvester visit and the Brussels trip, *we had worked together to resolve a multi-faceted rostering anomaly in a way that boosted skills acquisition, facilitated a work–life balance for you, the carer, and, most importantly, fostered an atmosphere of collaboration up and down the vertical.* She is obviously mad keen to get that award back.

My rounds pass without incident, except that Nonie is still giving me dog's abuse over Mam's wrist. Was I not there to mind my own mother? I was in Brussels, was I? What business had I going to Brussels, leaving her to be scrubbed raw by a *child*? (They'd sent a trainee on my rounds when I was away.) And do I know what would soften my cough now? Nonie putting in a *complaint*. And what good was the Tidy Towns if it didn't keep the post office open, and she'd heard it was Scientologists were taking it over.

Brian assures me again on the way out that she won't be making any complaint. He says the trainee was a sweetheart. He shows me where the complaint was written out on the back of a begging letter from the Missions, but he wouldn't be posting it, and he doesn't think she wants him to.

It's nearly five in the evening by the time I am up to Sylvester. He is out pacing in front of the house. He ushers me in. He's anxious to show off the place.

'Look, Ann,' he says. 'You can see the floor now, and I have the cats warned to do their business elsewhere. Haven't I, cat?' He wags his finger at one of them. The cat leaves through the open door and jumps up on the windowsill to look in at us.

The cleaners I'd organized have come in and carved a bit of clearing in the house, so at least I know I won't be getting Ebola off a chair. It smells a bit better too.

I make myself useful, giving him a check-up and then doing an inventory of the house to see what he's eating. He needs a Big Shop. He seems to live on tea, beans and fairy cakes.

143

'I thought you'd have lots of recipes from your time abroad, Sylvester.'

'Have you ever lived alone, Ann? It's very hard to get up in the morning. You're the reason I'm up at all today. You're my routine.'

He watches me as I poke around the cupboards. There are food jars with punts on the price tag. I find what I take to be some of Lady May's drink. I dare not open the bottle in case a spirit comes out.

'I stopped drinking after she died, Ann. We drank expensive stuff. *Drink with me, Syl,* she'd say. *We'll have the stuff I can't drink in front of the peasants.*'

He sees my face.

'She said "peasants" only as a joke at first. *That's what they want me to call them,* she says. *They want someone to hate, like they hated Daddy. I made them uncomfortable in the pub when I went in. They knew I knew that, but I went anyway.* And then I came along, she said, and shook her up a bit.'

I'm fierce nosy about this story, but he changes the subject.

'My dear and close cousin Nonie is not a fan of yours, Mrs Devine. She is positively apoplectic at the mention of your name. What would be the cause of that at all?'

'It's nice to be talked about, Sylvester.'

'My dear cousin is a mystery to me, Mrs Devine. We were never what you would call close. I do remember her being a giggler, Ann. A lively little thing. But something happened when she was in her thirties . . .' He trails off and starts picking at a fingernail.

I egg him on very gently.

'When would this have been, Sylvester?'

'I don't know, thirty or forty years ago, Ann. She was a happy-go-lucky kind of a woman, but then she just turned one day. Maudlin. What is it they say in these parts? She went sour. Have you siblings, Ann?'

He's changed subject again. Very frustratingly for me. I wonder does my face show how peeled out I am for the gossip. But I answer anyway.

'Four, Sylvester. Two here, two in London.'

'FOUR! That's practically Protestant, haha. Thirteen of us. Did you know why I was called Sylvester? They were out of names at that stage and I got the name from an uncle who had gone off to America and joined the circus. The circus was called Sylvester's and my mother called me Sylvester as a poke in the eye to my father, who she said should have *tied a knot in it after twelve*. We hadn't a shilling, Ann. Many nights I went to bed hungry. That is why I wear this.' He does a little Laurel and Hardy turn to show off his suit. 'I was so often in rags or dirty clothes during my childhood, Ann, that I wanted to look my best whenever opportunity struck.'

'Do you want me to look at your feet, Sylvester?'

He sits down and I take a deep breath and take off his shoes, hoping he'll carry on with the story. His feet are fairly ripe. I get a basin and give them a good wash. He has gone silent again for a few minutes as I dry the feet.

'A lovely suit, Sylvester. Is that for special occasions?'

'It was Lady May's father's. But I was wearing one like it the day I met her. You see, I used to come back every year from abroad and, in the time that I had been away, she had installed herself in the pub. Did you ever hear how we got talking? Oh, you'll like this.'

'I guarantee I'll like it, Sylvester.'

'She had her own chair by this stage. Lady May's throne. Over in the corner near the charity box for St Martin of Tours. She was there, wearing a long black coat. The rum in front of her. The only one to drink rum in the whole place. The Captain Morgan's was just known as Lady May's Bottle. The local denizens agog while she told them how to cook a quail or how much a gillie should be paid. She was playing up to her role. What they expected of her.

'And who should stride in only myself. Back from the ships. Ready to tell the mountainy men about adventures, Ann. But now I had competition. And the thing about it was, Ann, no one had ever picked up on anything I'd said before. I greeted them all and launched into a tale of high adventure from years gone by. She let me talk for a good long while. And then she stopped me. She says, *Did I hear you correctly? Sylvester, is it? You say you went from Macau to the Spice Islands and then you stopped in Sri Lanka, is it?*

'*I did*, I said, but I wasn't as sure this time. But she had me then. *Go on*, she says, giving me more rope to make an eejit of myself.

'*Well, it was a good while ago, madame*, I said.

'*I thought it was last year this happened. You said you were just back from Trincomalee. But there's no port there any more. My uncle had a business importing tea from there, and it was gone during the civil war they had there. We still have a house out there.*

'And all my audience were on to me in a second, Ann. *You're caught rotten, Sylvester Barrett, you clown*. And just like that, it was gone, Ann, my mystique.

'I *was* caught out, Ann. But it would have happened eventually anyway. The internet was the death knell of the raconteur. Everyone has all the facts now, but no one knows anything.'

He bites into a fairy cake.

'So anyway, I move my chair down to her and we get talking. *You're no more a seafarer than Mr Magoo*, she says quietly.

'Excuse me, madame, I said.

'I'd keep your voice down, sir, for your own sake. I know you. You're only spouting off names of places.

'I reject your slander, I said, but I was smiling.

'Call me Lady May, she said.

'Well, Lady May, I might have got it wrong about Trincomalee. I'm sure your uncle would put me straight.

'I've no uncle. I don't know one iota about Trincomalee, but I guessed you knew less. And I was right.

'She *was* right, Ann. I knew the game was up. I whispered to her I hadn't been further than Cricklewood for thirty years. That I made up the seafaring stories to amuse myself. I learned all I know from Alan Whicker. Only Lady May knew that. And now you.'

'I won't tell a soul.'

'But she liked me, Ann. *We're both playing parts in this village play,* she says. So she let me move my caravan in, and neither of us went up to Johnny's more than once or twice a year after that.'

'You were missed.'

'Maybe, Ann. Johnny put on *National Geographic* for the lads, and that was more informative than I ever was, and they can watch *Loose Women* to get the rest of their vitamins.'

'They can, Sylvester.'

'We lived together for three years before she got cancer and died. I minded her every day, Ann. I wouldn't let any of your carer people in because I'd have to share her. And she didn't want any local touching her unless they were bringing rum. And I drove the Rolls! For years pretending I had a Rolls and now I was going down to the shop every day for sliced pan and rum and After Eights. *I want to go out in style,* says Lady May. I stayed with her until the day she died. She said to me to give up the drink and take up chamomile tea and she'd see me on the other side when it was my time. *Don't let anyone else into this house*, she says, *unless they're as big a pain in the posterior as me.* And that was that.'

'That was that.'

'My feet feel wonderful, Ann. What are you doing to them? Are you sanding them?'

'Just a bit of filing, Sylvester. My sister taught me.'

'They wanted me out of the house, Ann. The English side of the family. Legal letters arrived with Such-and-such & Sons on the envelope and I knew they wanted their ancestral pile back. But I just ignored them and, after a while, the letters stopped. So here I am. Lord of the manor. That's my story. I buried twelve brothers and sisters, but not one of those funerals affected me like I felt after she went. I nearly did myself in a few times up here, Ann, only for the cats. I'd hate to do that to them.'

He takes another bun and I dry his feet.

17.

IT TAKES A VILLAGE

'What did I say, Ann?'

Denis is holding up the *Kilsudgeon Sentinel*. We are all four of us sitting out the back and it's a Thursday night, so Denis is having his Thursday routine of cans and the local paper. Mam has her eyes closed and is dozing a little, as if drinking in the evening sun.

'She's some operator.'

I can see a picture of Iseult in a kind of animal-skin bra and knickers. I squint at the headline.

CELTS ACTRESS AND LOCAL WOMAN GOES VIRAL WITH POST OFFICE FACEBOOK POST

Denis reads it out. 'Iseult Deasy, the local woman who has captured the imagination of the area with her impassioned plea for Kilsudgeon post office to be retained, has promised there is more to come from the campaign. In her most recent post, Deasy, twenty-five, says that the support she has received from as far away as North Carolina and Alabama in the United States has heartened her. "So many people have contacted me saying how disgusted they are that once again the elites are trying to break the spirit of Rural Ireland."

'Actress Deasy starred in the ill-fated *The Celts – Hound of Destiny*, the pilot of which was shot in Kilsudgeon last year, before the delay-plagued production finished abruptly, leaving a number of unpaid debts. Deasy played warrior princess Tlaghta, a role that was condemned in *Faith!* magazine. Deasy now says the role was not "in keeping with the values of Rural Ireland", and she regrets it. "I am focussed on bringing back the true Irish countryside," she told our reporter. Deasy is the daughter of Ignatius "Iggy" Deasy, who runs the National Car Testing (NCT) centre in Drumfeakle.'

The phone goes doollaly again.

'You need to switch off notifications, Auntie Ann. Your phone is owning you,' says Freya. With her own nose buried in the phone.

'What about you?'

'I'm young, I can handle it. But all of this screen time is not good for the ageing brain.'

I return to my phone. I've given up on my brain at this stage.

Iseult Deasy is Feeling Blessed with Kilsudgeon Tidy Towns and 145 others.

Hey, all, just an update to say thanx so much for all your support. I knew Kilsudgeon would not stay on its knees and would speak truth to powerful elites. Watch this space for the next steps in our campaign. Looking forward to working with the TT on the next clean-up. Keep the faith!!!XXXX

There is another beep. An email from Iseult. The girl will be in my dreams next.

Hi Ann. I don't seem to have got the email about the clean-up yet. Maybe it's in spam. My email address is iseult.kilsudgeon-fightsback@gmail.com.

I *have* added her to the mailing list. I just haven't sent an email yet. To iseult.kilsudgeonfightsback@gmail.com or anyone else. I rouse myself with a groan from the chair and go into the sitting room to send this cursed email. I have to put more pep into it now because I can feel that girl watching me. Am I being powerful enough against the elites?

Late Summer Clean-up – Let's make Kilsudgeon Tidy Again!!!! is the subject. Then I delete some of the exclamation marks. They'll think it's not me at all.

We're taking a break from the Tidy Towns this summer, but that doesn't mean we can't get the place looking lovely.

We're loving this quote from HumbleWholesomeQuotes.

I've got fierce into these quotes on Facebook these days. They're handy for when someone dies and you can write it up on their page if you can't make the funeral. You know the type, *They are up there with the saints, making a spot for you* and *You've just made a friend on the other side who might be a better friend than they were on this side.* That kind of thing. There's ones with angels as well, but I keep away from those. You don't want to be inviting angel people on yourself. They're very hard to shake off. Ger tells me she still gets fairly angry letters about why she didn't keep up her subscription to *Head of a Pin* magazine after she went through an angel phase. The money has gone out of angels, she said. The mental health stuff took over.

The one I put into the email says: *It takes a village to tidy a village.* It has a picture with people picking up rubbish and having a picnic. I press Send to the list and pray to the angels I haven't made a bags of it.

I go out to the other three out the back. Denis has since retired another can. Freya is standing at the back of Mam's chair. They're pored over the phone. Mam squints at it.

'Here she is, Nana, the religious influencer queen. Auntie Ann, did you know the meme in the email had Jesus in the middle? Hashtag Auntie Ann Inspo.'

'Well, maybe Jesus would be in the Tidy Towns if he was around.'

'Ann, don't be taking his name in vain.'

Freya makes the picture bigger on her phone and shows me. I look at it and, sure enough, it is Jesus with the reacher picking up rubbish and there's a tiny sign saying *Litterpickers for Trump* in the bottom corner.

My phone tells me I have a WhatsApp from Iseult.

Great work, Ann. I knew you were a doer, not a talker. Great to see you there. I hope to bring some friendly faces.

'Should we be giving the boy a call?' says Denis.

'Facetime him, Auntie Ann. Catch him out.'

I do, but Rory doesn't put on the video.

'Yeah, Mam, well, what's the craic?'

'We're all here, Rory. Me and your dad and Nana and Freya.'

'Put on the Facetime, Rory cuz,' chips in Freya.

There is a cough and a snort on the other end and, when he speaks, he sounds rough. 'Hah? Ehhh . . . hang on a second there . . . I'll call you back.'

He doesn't seem happy and before he hangs up I can hear him grumbling that the fucken fibre broadband is too good. We got it in last winter.

Bubbubububububububububup says the phone after a few minutes. I answer, to unveil Rory in all his wrecked glory.

'Say hello to your nana, Rory.'

'HELLO, RORY.'

'Hello, Nana, how's the arm?'

'I'VE TERRIBLE PAIN, RORY.'

'You don't need to shout, Mam,' I tell her. 'You look tired, Rory.'

'Yeah, I've been working hard.'

A small puff of smoke drifts across in front of him.

'Are you smoking, Rory?'

'Eh . . . no, Mam . . . ehhh . . . someone brought out rashers to JP there and eh . . . we're frying them, and it's just a bit smoky . . .'

The lie hits us all around the same time. Even Nana blinks.

'Is it breakfast time back home?' says Denis.

'His brain is fried,' says Freya.

'How's the job going with the Lamp?'

He scratches his head and yawns.

'Yeah, it's grand, like, not a bother. Bit boring. I might come back. Or maybe I'll take it handy and see what happens.'

'Is that all you have to say, Rory?'

'Ah Mam, early days yet.'

'Thanks for coming to my TED talk,' says Freya.

I have no idea what she's talking about.

'Yeah so, Mam, ehhhh . . .' and he kind of giggles.

'RORY, THIS IS NANA, ARE YOU GETTING ENOUGH TO EAT? YOU'RE GONE SHOCKING THIN.'

'I'm definitely hungry right now, Nana. I don't know what's causing it.'

There is laughter in the background.

'We're going out doing another clean-up, Rory. I sent out an email.'

'Huge news, Mam. Ehhh, Mam, I have to go now. The . . . ehhh . . . rashers are ready.'

There's more laughter in the background. I can hear JP say, 'Do you want another bit of smoky rasher, Rory, or will I put it out?'

His face disappears and we all just sit there looking at the blank screen. So much for Rory learning the ropes of power in Brussels.

Bing! No, it's not Rory back on, just more about the clean-up.

Good luck with the tidy, Ann. I'll be with you in spirit but the wine tour beckons. Watch out for Iseult. We don't want her taking over the whole show. Gordon.

18.

WITH RASHERS ON HIS LAP

It's been a few days since our nice night out the back with Denis and Freya, but Mam's gone moody again in the meantime. She says it's the pain at night, keeping her awake. But I'm not so sure. It should be better by now. I see it in the mornings. She has a Face on her and she looks for things to be cranky about.

'Do you not like your toast, Mam?

'It's black, Ann.'

'There's only a few burnt bits. I'll scrape them off.'

'But it will still taste the same.'

'But that's what you used to do for me.'

She crunches the toast, glaring at it as if it had just given her cheek, and then looks around her room.

'Did you pick that colour yourself for the walls, Ann? What kind of a colour is grey?'

She has a point. It was Deirdre told me to go for something other than magnolia, but I'm not conceding anything.

'It's not grey, it's an off-white.'

Burnt Smoke was the official name of the colour. I didn't even tell Denis that at the time. And there's no way I'm telling my mother a wall is called Burnt Smoke.

'It's very dour, Ann. Bim did my walls a lovely yellowy colour. But I can't look at these walls at all.'

I let it slide. Her complaints were up before she was. She reaches for the tea on the tray and grimaces again.

'How would you describe your pain, Mam? On a scale of one to ten?'

'I don't know.'

'Is it *annoying* or *more than annoying*? I just need to know for the pain scale so I can figure out your tablets. Is it *moderate* or *severe*?'

'I'm miserable, Ann. Where is that on your scale?'

There's nowhere on the pain scale that says *Driving me mad but she'll live.*

Mam takes a slurp of tea.

'Do you have them tickets yet?'

'No, Mam.'

'Make sure you get them now.'

She asks me about the tickets for the Pope four times a day. But it's strange. She's not excited about it. Every time she hears about the Pope's visit on the radio, she looks sad. There is something else going on with her besides this. She's had pain before, but it didn't make her miserable.

It's Mam who suggests it first, as I'm helping her get dressed.

'I'm sick of being cooped up, Ann. Bring me out on the rounds.'

'I don't know, Mam. I'm not supposed to. They're very strict on the regulations there.'

'But you're always bending the rules. What would they say if someone was to tell them you were doing cash jobs?'

My mother blackmailing me. And she looks as innocent as anything.

'C'mon, daughter, bring me out for a spin anyway.'

I agree, and you should see the pain scale go from ten to zero in a second. She's a pure Lazarus.

We start off at Neans. They've never been close, but they've had no falling-out so they're only delighted to talk away to beat the band. They knock a good twenty minutes of chat out of who's dead and who should be by now. So-and-so, who they don't like, *has cancer and isn't it terrible but the cancer would be slow enough with that wan as she took her time about everything herself.* Big, cheeky laughs out of them. Then it's on to the next generation and who is a disappointment to their mother, who has her father's heart broke and how the young people don't understand. I want to join in, but I'm too young. It's strictly over-eighties only.

'This one here is always on the phone, Neans,' says Mam.

'Ah, I suppose Ann's busy, Peggy. She's always dashing around.'

'I'm dashing around minding the pair of ye.'

I give Neans a wink, but she doesn't flinch. She won't break the code of the old.

'We were all busy, Neans, but we weren't on the phone.'

Guilty as charged. I've no comeback on that. I'd better get back to work.

'Now, Mam, I've to give Neans a wash there, so I might move you into the other room for a while.'

'Stay where you are, Peggy. I'm not a bit shy. Look away if you want. All our lives we were told cover up, isn't that right?'

'True for you, Neans. Let it all hang out, girl.'

So now I'm simultaneously the young wan and the ould wan in the room.

'You've a good one there anyways,' says Neans, gesturing at me.

'Keep saying that, Neans. She might believe it, coming from you.'

I wash Neans as the two lament the post office closing. And also All the Crime. I don't know where they're hearing about crime. Probably down the post office, when they used to go.

We leave Neans and head up to Johnny Lordan. He is mortified he didn't have notice of our arrival.

'I've curry on my britches, Ann, and you bring a woman into the house.'

'But *I'm* a woman, Flash.'

'That's different, Ann. Ah, why didn't you ring ahead? Get out, dog!'

The dog gives him a look to suggest that things were going fine until women started visiting. There's no sign of the daughter. Mam and Johnny talk politely about the weather and the various things that are a *disgrace*, but there's no confiding. We don't stay long.

After we get into the car Mam has only one thing on her mind.

'Bring me up to that tangler there in the Big House, Ann. I was never in that house.'

I ring him first in case he has curry on him, or worse.

He answers with a gruff, 'Unh?'

'Sylvester, it's Ann. Are you decent?'

'I'm always decent, Ann, but not always wearing clothing.'

I tell him my story and he says, *It would be an honour if you brought the good lady, the queen mother, and she could be assured of a most gracious welcome but would you give me a little while to prepare.*

When we arrive up, he's sitting outside on the deckchair, basking in the heat. He springs up out of it so fast I'm sure he'll aggravate his back, and how would I explain that to

Tracy? *The client injured himself greeting the carer's mother, who had visited him out of pure nosiness.*

He comes down the path to greet us. He takes my mother by the hand and leads her towards the house. Is it my imagination or is that a shirt I've never seen before?

'You're all style, Sylvester.'

'Well, it's not every day you have two beautiful women paying you a visit.'

I roll my eyes and, as I roll them over, I catch sight of Mam giving him a good old glad eye.

'And the Lady May's dear old dad, last Lord Eldermere, has donated this shirt. Feel that quality, Ann, look.'

He holds out the left tail of it. He smells strongly of camphor.

'You're up on your feet, Sylvester. Ann was saying you had a bit of stiffness,' Mam says coyly.

'I don't want to be a slave to the crutches, Margaret, my dear woman. We hurry ourselves into the grave, don't we?'

'True for you.'

'Are you going to show us around? I'm dying to have a look. I remember this place years ago, when May Lorda-mercyonher was only a small girl, and her father threw the Christmas parties for the children. I never got to go to the parties, Sylvester. My mother was a ferocious IRA woman.'

And Mam tells Sylvester about how a Black and Tan tried to have his way with my grandmother in a field when she was a schoolgirl and only that she was holding a knife for thinning turnips she managed to put the run on him, but then he came around with a gang of his comrades and kicked in the door of the house and had to be hauled out of it by a commanding officer. This is all news to me.

'It's a pity because I'd have loved to have gone to the parties here, Sylvester. They had treasure hunts and Pass the Parcel and Blind Man's Buff, and they played Charades and everything. And all the children came out of it with little bags. Small oranges and Peg's Legs. I never got over not being let go.'

'Well, why don't you come around with me? Can you manage the stairs?'

And my mother leaves the crutches with me and practically gallops up the stairs after him, with her good hand on the bannister. I hurry up after them. He is telling my mother about how May had half of it locked up because she never got over the father's death. One room was filled entirely with newspapers from when he was alive. She wouldn't throw them out because she thought she'd lose more of him.

'We all go a bit quare when someone dies, don't we, Sylvester?'

'We do, Margaret.'

I am nervous about the pair of them injuring themselves and breathe a sigh of relief when Sylvester doesn't suggest having a look up in the attic.

'Care for an aperitif in the drawing room, milady?'

He ushers us towards the main room. I'm scuttling after them when I hear a knock at the front door and go out, and who's there only Bim. He doesn't look happy. He tries to lean in past me.

'Is herself in there? There was no one at home when I called.'

I'm about to ask him how he knows we are here, but since his story about staking out the kerbing man, I'm fairly sure he followed us.

'I have rashers,' he says, holding them out as if no further explanation was needed.

'But we're all right for rashers, Bim. I did the shop yesterday."

'But the streaky ones, Ann. Peggy says you only have smoky ones and they don't agree with her.'

So Mam is complaining about the food and ordering rashers from Bim as if he's Kilsudgeon's Deliveroo?

Sylvester calls down the hall. 'Who is it, Ann?'

I don't know how to explain that it's Bim and that he's here with streaky rashers for Mam.

'Bim's here with streaky rashers for Mam, Sylvester,' I shout. Sometimes you have to tell it like it is.

Sylvester is smooth as you like, even though he doesn't know Bim from Adam.

'Come on into the drawing room, Bim. Any friend of rashers is a friend of mine.'

Bim starts striding up the hall, but he slows down as he starts to get closer to the open door of the room. He wouldn't have much experience of being invited into drawing rooms and seems to lose his nerve. I follow him in, almost nudging him through the door.

'Rashers,' says Bim again as he goes in, holding them up.

'You can never go wrong with rashers,' says Sylvester. 'Only we've moved on to the scones.'

And I notice for the first time that he has laid out a spread for us. The cups are clean and the food is fresh.

'And you know the old song, Bim. "I Can't Go Back to Savoury Now".'

He starts singing this funny little song about a man whose daughter wouldn't finish her dinner and he only found out when he was on to the pudding. I don't like being sung at, in general, but Bim's face, which is a mixture of perplexed and resentful, makes it worth it.

We sit down and I take a moment to drink in the scene around me. Sylvester sitting in a big ornate chair, Mam perched on a couch looking quite girlish, Bim slurping tea from one of Lady May's dainty little china teacups with rashers on his lap.

'Them cups are cruel small,' he says.

He has a point, but no manners.

'How're they all with you?' says Mam.

There are a scattering of siblings in Bim's house who are variously old and grumpy. They float in and out to get away from their families. A few aren't married so they never leave. Bim would love the space of Mam's house if he ever got it.

Bim says they are all fine and then launches into a description of a court case about a boundary dispute between someone called Cronin and, confusingly, someone else called Cronin, not related. We listen for a long time, losing track of it.

'. . . but the thing was, the daughter stood up in court and told her father Pat Cronin to drop the case against Cronin because she was doing a line with a son of the other Cronin, and he wouldn't see the grandchild again and the judge told him listen to the daughter because he'd seen her buying a plane ticket, and Cronin withdrew the case. You should know them, Margaret. They're over your way originally. Pat Cronin. And Gerry Cronin?'

Mam says she doesn't know any Cronins, and that's the end of the story. Bim seems to regret not picking a better story. Every now and then Mam and Sylvester throw a smile at each other.

Eventually, Bim picks up his phone that none of us heard ringing, says, 'Yeah? G'wan, I'll be up to you in a second with the blocks,' and leaves.

'I will anxiously await your next visit,' says Sylvester as he sees us to the door half an hour later. And he kisses Mam's hand.

'I enjoyed that,' says Mam in the car on the way home. She's in better form than I've seen her in a while.

'Bim's some character. You know he asked me whether I had the house all in the will and everything and how I'd lose the whole lot to the government if things weren't right. Is that true, Ann?'

'Don't talk to me about wills, Mam. You do what you want with that place.'

I'm lying, of course. But we're getting on well and she likes this kind of talk.

'Only one place left to go now, Mam. Nonie's. Are you ready?'

She point-blank refuses to go into the house. She will not even stand for it.

'I'll wait in the car.'

'Is it because of how she treats me?'

'How does she treat you?'

'I tell you all the time how she treats me.'

'It's not all about you, Ann.'

I don't ask any more questions. Mam has the Face on her again. And I've Nonie to endure and a clean-up to get to.

19.

THEY SMELL A BIT ORGANIC

Ann could we meet for the clean-up at the Lios field? It's a symbol of the abandonment of Rural Ireland.

I don't raise an objection. It's great to have a bit of young energy about these things, no matter what Gordon says. And a bird in the hand is worth two on a wine tour.

The Lios field is where they were making the *Celts* TV show last year. This was the show where Iseult was in her furry underpants. After they ran out of money, they left it in an awful state. There's an old ruined crannóg in one corner and they dug a massive hole that was supposed to be a 'fight pit'.

Denis wants to come with me. His first clean-up in ages.

'I'm just being a supportive partner,' he says.

'You're here for a nose.'

'Actually, I'm very environmentally friendly.'

'Pure tight, more like it,' I say, but I'm glad to have him. Freya stays at home with Mam. She says I'm getting too close to the dark side by mixing with Iseult.

The heatwave this summer is right up Denis's street. He loves any kind of rationing, so now he's having the time of his life saving water. Denis wants to flush the toilet with water from the shower. *Grey water* is the new thing. It's given him a purpose in life. I've had to draw the line with him reusing teabags. *We don't need that amount of tea leaves for one mug. Only about a third of a teabag is needed,* he said. *Well, I notice you sort yourself out first,* I told him. He said that was *a first* and pinched my backside. The scut.

We are the first to arrive. Noel opens the gate for us. There isn't much talk out of Noel these days and I see he's got old since the uncle died. He has the smell of a man living by himself. He wouldn't have anyone to wash for him, the creature. He thought someone would buy the Lios field and build houses, but there's nothing happening now. Every fella with a bit of land thinks they're sitting on a gold mine.

Cars start to arrive. Iseult arrives in a Civic driven by Davey Finnerty. Denis reads my mind and wonders out loud are the two of them *on the go.* She comes over to me.

'Ann! This is fab, isn't it?' She opens up her arms. 'This place has so many memories for me. I just wanted it to be part of the rebirth of Kilsudgeon. Oh and c'mere, I *never* knew that Rory was out in Brussels with Michael.'

'Michael?'

'Yes, Michael – Mick the Lamp, as you might call him. That's *gas* now. Mick's a cousin of Dad's. They would have been as thick as thieves back in the day. Mick's working hard for us on the post office too. Which is more than Patsy is doing, Ann. I don't mind saying it to you, but I think he's losing it around here. I think we need a change. But it's so great Rory's out there with Mick. Mick will teach him some things Patsy couldn't, you know?'

She looks up as two more cars come into the field, raising dust as they do.

'Looks like the guys are here.'

'The guys' start to gather. There is a tall, fine figure of a man with black hair and a bushy beard. He's carrying a stick that at first I think is a walking stick, but it looks more like a staff. He has a long T-shirt yoke with Celtic designs on and it says *Brehons Online* on it. His name, it seems, is Toirdealbhach. He spells it out for me crossly. I've never seen him before, but I have seen the type. Celticky. Shiteing on about Druids. I remember in my work there was a daughter who wanted to give herbs to a sick father a few years ago and he used to tell me to sneak the Panadol into him when she wasn't looking. With Toirdealbhach is a red-haired fella with the sides of his head shaved, like he was just out of the Christian Brothers. Except for the ears. Ears don't stick out now on young lads like they used to. There's a youngish boy around Declan's age – a black hoodie on him even though it's roasting. After him comes a youngish fella. He has a bag on his back and very black sunglasses. A woman then, a similar build to me with a load of grey hair in a ponytail and big work boots. A few older men with stern, humourless faces hop out of a grey Passat. One of them has a bandage to his face as if he had just come from Outpatients. A man with a fisherman's hat and a grey beard, sort of stubby. As he approaches, Denis whistles gently.

'Ollie Holland,' says Denis. 'I wondered what happened him. He was a Dutch fella who drove a truck around here years ago, but he was done for no tachograph and then went off out the Gulf in the oil rigs. They say he tried to get Somalis to kidnap him one time for money and he got rumbled. What's *he* doing around here?'

An older man with a shorter beard is next. Denis describes him to me as having a Retired IRA look. He gets out of an old Volvo with a much younger, European-looking woman and a gang of three young lads and a girl I take to be his children. About ten cars pull up in total, each one letting out some sort of variety of oddball, as far as I can see. Everyone seems to be wearing dark clothes that are too warm for the day, apart from the odd green T-shirt. The first locals are Iseult, Davey and Val Furnish, the man who was shouting at the television when Mam was in hospital. I look to see Bridget and, sure enough, she is there, standing next to him, proud as Punch of whatever it is he's doing. They made a quick recovery.

'They've stepped it up since the hospital,' I whisper to Denis. They are hand in hand.

'Ah, Ann, don't be putting thoughts in my head.'

'You're gerontophobic, Denis. Fear of the elderly. People are looking for a bit of a squeeze at all ages.'

Iseult appears next to me.

'It's so great to see this movement happen organically, Ann.'

They look like they smell a bit organic as well, but I keep that to myself.

'These people just circled around me and Davey. And you are here, representing the Tidy Towns and the local people of Kilsudgeon. You're our ambassador.'

Denis mutters something about *Ferrero Rocher*.

I start handing out hi-vis, but Iseult's crowd have brought their own and have put them on. They have slogans on them, but none about litter. *Irish Yellow Vest Brigades Direct Action NOW! SMASH THE GLOBALIST ELITES! KICK OUT SOROS!* I don't know where I'll put them for the photo or it won't get into the *Sentinel*. I don't know what clean-ups they've been on before.

There was *huge traction* on social media, Iseult tells me. My friendly little announcement about the clean-up on Facebook has been shared in a lot of angry places. Clean Up Irish Corruption, Take Out the Trash, Cleanse Ireland are all joining in for our little town. I have that light-headed feeling I get when I think I'm not really in control.

The locals finally show and my head clears up. There's about ten of them. Denis's fellow lorrymen – the Nolan twins – are there. I think Denis must have given them a nudge, but they are not their usual selves. They're unsure about cracking jokes in front of the strangers. My friend Sally is there, who I haven't spoken to in a while – it's been such a tizzy recently. Laura Moore, Flora's friend who's running the book club now, arrives. She'd be quite *grand*. She comes up and asks me would I like to join the book club and I get a little thrill but play it cool. I still haven't been to the book club. I haven't read anything longer than a text in I don't know when.

I decide it's time for me to kick things off.

'Right, ehmm . . . who's for the Garragh Road? Laura . . . good woman, you'll take a few with you. And the Twins, will ye head towards the village? As always, we pick along the road into the village and you bring the rubbish bags to the layby at the Cafferkey's old shop, and then . . .'

I hesitate. I have all the locals sent out and now I'm left with Iseult's organic group, and they look at me, pure surly. Ollie Holland, in particular. How am I going to tell a Dutchman who tried to fake his own kidnapping where to go? Iseult takes over, though. She suggests they clean up the Lios field itself.

'This is a magical place,' she tells them. 'The Fairy Tree is said to be a gateway to the Underworld.' She says this with an actory flourish. But they love it. Toirdealbhach goes to inspect the whitethorn bush and comes back, looking wiser.

'I feel a huge sense of the ancient here,' he proclaims.

We start picking up rubbish around the field. And we find the holy grail. A bag of rubbish that's torn open, and there's an envelope with a name on it. Davey comes up and looks at the envelope and squints at the address.

'That's not an Irish surname,' he says. 'This is part of the dumping that we're hearing a lot of from non-nationals.'

I ask him for the envelope.

Mrs M Ro Chen

'Chinese,' he says as I look at it.

The only Chinese I know around here is the lad in the Grey Lotus restaurant, and I'd be very surprised at him. He sponsors the camogie, the odd time. Harry Win. Win-win, they called the sponsorship deal.

'That's Marian Roche,' I say. 'It's just a mistake on the letter. Look, it's an ear appointment. The N is missing from the next line of the address.'

He doesn't seem convinced. 'It's a big problem in rural Ireland now. Non-national dumping.'

'Well, all the rubbish I've seen in my days picking it up has been very Irish,' I tell him.

Iseult pats him on the arm and he relaxes a little.

'We're all on the same side,' she says.

By the time we are done there are ten bags of rubbish and the field is immaculate, apart from the falling-down fake crannóg and a fight-pit in the ground. My nerves are better. I have Litterpicker's High now. The temporary sense of doing a good thing, even if there'll be rubbish back again next week. I've lost my fear of the Strange High-vis Crowd.

'Well done, everyone, that's mighty altogether. We can get the council to collect those bags here, Iseult, and then we'll go up to the pub for tea and biscuits.'

I'm treating them like old friends. The clean-up seems to have softened them as well. A few look like they could do with the fresh air. The young lad with the black hoodie has discarded it and has a black T-shirt underneath.

'I've a better idea for what to do with the rubbish,' says Davey with a sneaky grin.

He tells everyone to pile the rubbish into their car boots and bring it down to the village. 'To show how bad the dumping is,' he explains. We get into our cars and head in. But Davey doesn't stop at Cafferkey's shop. Instead he parks outside Patsy's constituency office and starts arranging the bags outside the door. The rest pull up and start to do the same. I get out.

'Davey, what are you doing? We can't leave them there. Patsy'll have a conniption.'

'Let him,' says Davey. 'We're just bringing the corruption home to him. This is a message from the people. We will not take it lying down.'

'But he didn't do the dumping, Davey. We can't be leaving rubbish outside his door.'

But they're not for turning, no matter how much I argue about it.

'We'll leave it for now,' I say to Denis. 'We'll go up for the tea and biscuits and come back later and move it, before Patsy sees it.' In the meantime, I have a more serious problem. Stephanie, my glossy daughter-in-law, has followed up with her threat of a girls' day out.

Stephanie has added you to the group Girls And Gúnas!

Hey, everyone! I was thinking we HAVE to spend more time together. It's a SCANDAL that we're not close. So what brings the girls together? GÚNA SHOPPING! Jen, Ann, Freys, Dee, fancy coming on a girls only shopping trip? Me and Jen need something for the wedding, and let's get suited and booted for Jen's 30th birthday bash lol. Xxx.

I see that Freya is typing almost immediately.

Sorry, can't make it. Stephanie. RGDS 'FREYS'

No worries, hun.

Freya has left the group. Stephanie is typing.

Wow lol. Freya gone already? Gen Z much? Ann, Dee and Jen, are you in? How are you fixed?

I'll go, but I'll be buying buttons, Steph. Kids orthodontist visit on Saturday. Absolutely dreading it.

Ann?

There is no reply from Ann because Ann is trying to figure out how to say no because Ann hates shopping for things to fit her arse at the best of times. Jennifer seems to guess.

(private message) *Mam, do go. Stephanie is trying her best. Accept her bid. x Jen.*

What does that mean?

Lean in, Mammy.

?

Just go to the fecking shop.

Hello Stephanie, yes, that'll be lovely.

Oh SUPER!!! It will be a BLAST!

Blast it. And in the pub I'm wedged in the corner beside Iseult, listening to them all discussing the ways in which rural Ireland is under threat. The data centres, they say, are the next thing. Facebook will have an army soon. You'll see. And where did they read about this? On Facebook. But they all listen to Iseult when she speaks. She's the leader of the gang.

We extricate ourselves to go down to get the rubbish bags, but it's too late. Patsy rings me, and he is hopping mad.

'WHAT DO YOU THINK YE'RE DOING, DUMPING THE BAGS OUTSIDE MY FUCKING DOOR, ANN? HAH?'

'Patsy, I meant to . . .'

'AFTER I GIVING YOUR SON A JOB IN BRUSSSELS.'

'Well, we never asked to . . .'

I can hear him breathing for a while on the phone. He's rattled.

'What's going on, Ann? Is this who the Tidy Towns are hooked up with now? The High-Vis and the Yellow Vests? Is this the craic?'

Finally, I get a word in edgeways and explain Davey Finnerty and how we were going to move it afterwards.

'You should have put your foot down, Ann.'

I try to explain that it's hard to put your foot down with people you've only just met and that I thought it was better to put my foot down quietly later when no one was around, but he's not really having it. What I don't mention is that I also found the whole thing quite funny and that I'm sort of hoping it'll mean that he never gets my son another job. I think it's a good idea to keep some things to yourself.

'And why did you organize that meeting so bloody quickly anyway, Ann? The one about the post office? I was on my way back.'

'It was Gordon.'

He sighs. 'Gordon, of course. He doesn't have any political acumen at all, that man. Well, he's stirred up a wasps' nest here anyway, Ann. Unleashed forces. It's all very well to be shouting about The Establishment, Ann, but what are you going to replace it with, hah? Answer me that.'

I don't answer him that, but then I have a brainwave.

'Why don't you organize your own meeting, Patsy? You can tell people what's happening. There's rumours flying around left, right and centre. Maybe you can bring a bit of the Patsy magic to bear on it?'

The mention of Patsy magic calms him down – like magic, actually. He likes the idea.

'Now you're talking, Ann. Of course. The Patsy magic. I'll show these fly-by-nights what real local governance is. Right so, send out the email again there.'

How did I end up serving two masters? I should have put my foot down.

20.

RIG-OUTS FOR ALL OCCASIONS

Mam grumbles through her shower, but I insist she needs a good wash before Stephanie picks us up for the *Gúna Girls* trip. I am too rough with her hair, according to Mam. And the shampoo got in her eyes and it's *hurting her something fierce*, even though it's the stuff for toddlers. But now she's all wrapped up in a towel and enjoying having her hair dried. Her form returns and we're ready for our spin. Freya watches us, amused with herself.

'Would you not come along, Freya? You've nothing else to do, with Lossie gone. You could study our – what is it you say? – our species?'

'No, Auntie Ann, I might catch Basic off you.'

Me and Mam sit outside in the morning sun waiting for Stephanie. She arrives in one of those SUVs and winds down the window. Deirdre and Jennifer are already inside. Jennifer gets out so we can hoist Mam into the front. I struggle a bit to get Mam up into this fecking JCB of a yoke.

173

'Sorry about the step up, Margaret,' Stephanie says as Mam gives one final grunt while I heave her into the front seat. 'This was all that was around at home. Dad's in the electric car because he wants to do his bit for the environment.'

Jennifer gives me a longer hug than usual.

'How was Brussels, Mam, apart from the Parking and the Riding? And yes, I saw the photograph. Freya sent it round in the . . . I mean . . . to us each, individually. She did not send it to a WhatsApp group you are not part of. Not at all. Anyway, sorry you had to cut it short.'

'I was sorry I broke my wrist, Jennifer,' Mam chimes in.

'Oh Nana, don't worry, we weren't forgetting you.' And she kisses her the cheek.

I get in beside my daughters in the back and Stephanie sets off.

'ROAD TRIP!' she yells. She's quite lively. 'I'm so happy you're coming along, Ann. This is my specialty. Event shopping. You're in good company. I was out with one of the Maktoums last month. Let's go, girls! I have the aircon up ladies, is that OK?'

Mam says she is cold and doesn't want to get an earache and Stephanie turns it off and we all swelter away. I see Mam has sweat on her face, but she won't admit she was wrong.

La Rochelle Ladies Independent Boutique is an institution around these parts. It's in a place that used to be a creamery half a mile from a small village called Corducklin, or Turducken, as it got called one Christmas and the name stuck. It's in the middle of nowhere but people come to it from all over. Her slogan is *Rig-outs for All Occasions*. In fairness to Marian Roche, she's made a great fist of it, but you need to have your story straight with her before going in. She is the nosiest woman in the wide earthly world. It's best to decide before you go in what information you are willing to give her because, if she gets you on the hop, she'd have you well and truly filleted.

If you went in to be kitted out for a wedding, by the time you walked out Marian would know the table layout, the vows, the page boys' names and the likelihood of the marriage going the distance.

The likes of Stephanie don't interest her. She's an open book and wants everyone to know her business anyway. But as soon as she sees me her eyes light up. She's nearly drooling.

'Ann Devine – hello, stranger. Are you going to the same wedding as the two belles here?' She points at Stephanie, and Jennifer, who has arrived in with Deirdre. Deirdre doesn't seem to be included in the belles, but maybe Marian has her in another category. She'll have you in 'Maid of Honour' territory a few years before you're ready to accept it yourself.

'And who is *this* young lady? Is that you, Peggy Hoare? Am I finally granted an audience with the dame herself?'

'Ah . . . dame, I'm no dame,' says Mam gruffly, but I can tell she loves that kind of talk.

'I hear the young lad is out in Brussels, Ann. He's sharp as a tack, that fella. Waltzed in here one day during an election, handing out flyers. Charmed every woman in the place. Got about ten votes for Patsy and a cup of tea out of me. And what he doesn't know about clothes. Send him over to me if it doesn't work out, we'll find a use for him. And I hear your sister is gone too? Well for some isn't it, and young Freya is down with you, I believe? She's another gas character. She'll have us all marching some day, hah? And you heard, I suppose, about the post office? I heard the meeting was a dead loss, and will you be campaigning yourself? I suppose you will, Ann. You're very caught up in this kind of thing. You should go for election.'

She splits us up. She's going to look after me and Mam and she gets a shiny-looking younger girl to assist Stephanie and Jennifer and, no doubt, Deirdre too. Marian isn't going to let anyone out without them spending. She brings us into a consultation room.

'I have this for the mature ladies,' she says. 'You can be yourself here, Ann, without some little slip of a thing gawping at the lumpy bits. Amn't I right, Peggy?'

'True for you, Marian.' Mam has warmed up. 'That young girl is only going to be picking up hangers, Ann. Stephanie Rourke will decide for everyone.'

'Now, ladies, let's start with a cup of tea.' And she waves over another girl in ripped jeans to make it. 'Plenty of milk, Peggy?'

That's sealed the deal for Mam, and she smiles yes. It's rare when someone understands the old need lots of milk in their tea.

'You're going to this birthday party for Jennifer, are you, Ann? I thought first you were going to the wedding as well, because it's a wedding you should be invited to. Didn't you look after the grandmother one time? You did, you know, oh you did.'

I had forgotten it, but yes, she's right, I did mind that horsey lady once upon a time. Marian is like the internet and the reception is always high-speed.

'Now, I think for a dinner you'd want something understated. Would you go sleeveless in this weather, Ann? Would you chance it? I suppose you wouldn't be a sleeveless woman? Would she be sleeveless, Peggy?'

'She should wear sleeves, Marian,' says Mam, the first time she's ever discussed sleeves. Marian eases me out of my cardigan.

'We've lovely ensembles just arrived in, Ann. And Deirdre, she's a powerhouse, isn't she? A powerhouse. They're gone quiet above in Spearlon. Aren't they? A niece of mine works there. She's underemployed, she was telling me. Underemployed, Ann. I'm sure Deirdre is the same, is she, Ann? Now would you be a fourteen or a sixteen? What do you think of these? These are Lulu Bordeaux. A lovely two-piece for the dinner. It's very flattering around the bodice.' She's tucking the jacket around me. 'You must be ferocious busy worrying about four generations, Ann. But now you're going to have some Ann-time.'

I think she's implying something about the state of the T-shirt I arrived here in. I hadn't really thought about the fact I'd be changing clothes.

'It suits you, Ann,' Mam pipes up. Looking me up and down. 'It trims you a bit.'

Marian laughs. 'Oh Ann, mothers have us measured well, don't they? And what about yourself, Peggy? Would you like something nice to go with your grand hair? Is that another one of your creations, Ann? Doesn't she have you turned out lovely, Peggy?'

Best of luck getting Mam to buy anything, I think to myself. She won't see the point in a new thing if she's after writing herself off for the knacker's yard, as she has told me repeatedly over the last while.

'Would you have a flowery skirt, Marian?' says Mam.

Marian nearly falls down with the surprise.

'WOULD I?' she says. 'You have come to the home of flowery skirts, Peggy. AMY!' she bellows out into the shop. 'Bring some of the Marc Shamois, please.' She sizes Mam up. 'Eights and tens, Amy! We have a tidy woman in here.'

'Marc Shamois, that sounds dear,' says Mam without conviction.

'Nothing is dear any more, Peggy. Fast fashion has us all broke. And what about blouses? What about this one?' She

177

pulls a light blue out of the pile Amy has brought in. Amy must know to bring everything in. The blouse has frills around the collar.

'That's lovely,' says Mam. 'Lantana. What do you think, Ann? Would I wear this the next time you bring me up to Wilderbrook?'

Marian's eyebrows go up. She's like a beagle with the sniff of a fox. Mam realizes too late she's after saying too much. Marian says nothing for a while. She comes back to where I'm struggling with the trousers of the Lulu Bordeaux, helps Mam out of her old skirt, and while Mam is leaning on her shoulder she catches her with a quick jab of a question.

'Wilderbrook, is that Sylvester's – well, Lady May's – place?'

She gets nearly the whole story out of us. We manage to leave out Bim, because I don't know who he's related to.

'Poor old Bim will be distraught, Peggy. Doesn't he do a few jobs for you?'

Worse than the internet she is, because you can't switch her off.

Stephanie peeps in and whistles at Mam in her new skirt.

'Switzwoo, very chic,' she says. 'This place is amazing, Marian. I've always said you find the real gems in the provincial places.'

Marian straightens up her face. 'We are not provincial, Stephanie, we are central to everywhere. We had people in from Dublin the other day.'

'Oh, Marian, so sensitive. How right you are.'

I marvel at how some people can talk straight and move on without blushing or fretting.

'Anyway, Ann, let's get a look at you. Is that a Lulu Bordeaux? I've seen sheikhs' wives wear that, Ann. The cut is lovely and really dampens down the hips, doesn't it?'

No harm in dampening the hips, I suppose. I feel like one of those women on telly getting a makeover and every Tom, Dick and Harry on the set seems to have an opinion on her. I've never gone shopping with so many people looking at me before. Normally, I go to Dunnes on my own, come home and say to Denis, *What do you think?* and Denis says, *Is that new? What was wrong with the old one?*

'How are you getting on out there, Stephanie? Is everything to your satisfaction?' asks Marian tightly.

'I can't find anything, but Deirdre's found a summer dress and Jennifer's still looking. She has her heart set on a Lavish Jack, but I don't think it's her. Anyway, let's see you on the catwalk, Ann.'

I walk down through the shop.

'Work it, girl,' says Stephanie.

I do the faintest rumour of a sashay.

'It isn't the mart, Mammy. Put a bit of zhush in your pelvis.' Jennifer doesn't mince her words.

Even Mam laughs at this. I do a twirl and take off the cardigan and sling it over my shoulder like Shania Twain would.

We go back in with Mam for her frilly blouse and flowery skirt and then Marian announces tea and macaroons.

'I look to differentiate myself everywhere,' says Marian. 'No one else does macaroons.'

At the end of the expedition Deirdre is first up to pay with a new jacket.

'A hundred and forty? I thought it was reduced, Marian?'

'That wasn't on sale, pet,' says Marian. 'I can't let it go for less.'

Deirdre gets her card out, and then there's a beep. We hardly pay attention to it until she tries it again and then the same beep. Marian takes the card and gives it a wipe. But the card isn't being declined because it's dirty.

'I don't know, Deirdre, it just says *Contact your bank.*'

Deirdre looks mortified, and Deirdre is never mortified. But now she is crumpled. She scrabbles around in her bag but doesn't have the cash, and ATMs have closed faster than post offices around here in the last while. Jennifer steps in and pays, but Deirdre looks shook about it.

The car is quiet on the way home. Deirdre looks out the window. Jennifer tries to joke her out of it.

'It was probably just Hughie going mad on Ali Express, Dee. You know what he's like. He needs a new look every week.'

Hughie has had the same look since he left school.

'Not now, Jen,' says Deirdre, and that's that from her until she's dropped off.

'I'll suss her out, Mam,' Jennifer promises. 'I'll see you again for the wedding and my terrible birthday dinner.'

Stephanie drops her to the train station and us to home. I invite her in, but thankfully she doesn't accept. Mam and me relax over tea and she announces that macaroons agree with her. It's just one surprise after another.

21.

THIS TOWN RUNS ON SILAGE

Another warm evening. Another angry meeting. Except I'm not sitting collecting email addresses. Patsy isn't the only one trying to get back into the limelight. Father Donnegan is after making the post office closure a 'parish matter', so he ended up organizing the meeting. I'm sitting in the crowd with Denis and Freya, and I'm fine and happy for myself to be out of the focus.

The crowd gather like before, but I can see a few more of the Duggan clan clustered in. You would always know them if they were on their own, but in a gang even more so. They are a big-headed, shovel-handed clan. Even the women. The heads for thinking of ways to make money and the hands for holding on to it. A few of the Duggan councillors are there with chains on. It's an impressive showing. There won't be any mistakes this time. The hall is full again with the same types who were at the first meeting. A good chunk of them are glad to have anywhere to go at all. Father Donnegan looks around the hall and says to whoever is near him that he supposes we'll start.

'Good evening, everybody, and thank God again for the lovely fine wea—'

He is interrupted by a kerfuffle at the back of the room. I know who they are as soon as the first sweltering, dark-jumpered young lad comes in carrying a bag. It's Iseult and her clean-up crew. They stand at the back of the room. She waves and mouths *hiiiiii* silently at me like we're great pals. Her gang flank her at the back of the room. There are more now than there were – a few more druidy lads have joined Toirdealbhach. The room just became a lot hairier.

Father Donnegan clears his throat and continues.

'Now, the first item I want to talk to you about, before we get on to the main issue, just to say that we are awaiting our tickets for the Pope, but in the meantime we have some very good news. Patsy Duggan has told me that two special train carriages will be added to the Dublin train at Kilsudgeon junction. Kilsudgeon will be travelling in style! Thank you, Patsy.'

He begins clapping, but only the Duggans take it up. It peters out. Father Donnegan, used to half-hearted Mass clapping, doesn't notice it and ploughs on.

'Before we begin I want to welcome Simon Murtagh from An Post, to outline for us what the current position is. Give Simon a big Kilsudgeon welcome.'

The welcome is smaller than the one for the extra train carriages and there are boos.

Simon Murtagh looks like he lost a bet to be here. His voice is watery. He tries to thank us – *thank us!* – for coming. He also *understands our concerns*. He wants to explain *as best I can the rationale for the restructuring*.

Rationale for restructuring – that sets the crowd off.

'Restructuring, my hole,' says Cathy Garrigan, a woman not used to saying 'my hole' too often.

'We have a plan for this area.'

Huge, bitter laughs roll around the hall. I'm glad now that I didn't have a chair on the stage. Simon tries to continue that it was all due to a *miscommunication*, but the voice is not right for the occasion.

'Coming down here from Dublin,' is being muttered around the place.

'I'm not from Dublin. I'm from Kerry,' he protests.

'You weren't long losing the accent when you have betrayed your own people,' says Andy Grogan and slaps his cap on his knee. 'The trip down to get the pension is the only bit of socializing I get.' He's almost shaking with anger.

The man tries to explain again. 'There is a streamlining process going on,' he says.

'AND YE PAID FOR A NEW SIGN FOR THE FUCKING THING LAST YEAR!' And Andy walks out.

A big sign that said *Connecting Our Future. An Post in association with Zemitar the Cyberspecialists* went up last week. When the lads putting it up were told it was closing, they said it was the first they'd heard of it and they'd have to put it up anyway *because that's what it said on the workplan.*

'That was part of a different programme under the previous CEO,' Simon tries to explain to the back of the man as he walks out. 'If you could look at some of the bullet points in your handout, we have outlined . . .'

But his handout hasn't been handed out. If I'd been involved, I would have made sure, but there was no one with an eye for detail organizing this. And anyway, this crowd has no time for handouts or outlines. We've had a few consultants outline things for our benefit over the years and then they went back off home with their mileage. He would have been better off saying, *Lookit, we're making no money off ye and that's all we care about now, so get used to it. The half of ye that use the post office will be dead in a few years anyway,* and then running out the back door.

But no one ever says that to us. The truth would kill us. But at least it would be quick.

'Rural Ireland is a cornerstone of the organization's blueprint for the fu—'

'WHERE IS THE POSTMASTER? HAVE YE DONE AWAY WITH HIM ALREADY?' someone shouts.

He's getting nowhere with this line of question.

'What have you to say for yourself, Patsy?'

Patsy wants to let him finish, but the hall will be burnt down if he doesn't say something quick. He gestures to Simon for the mic.

'I can assure you I will not stand idly by and watch this post office be closed. The Duggan name stands by it. I have made several representations at Cabinet level . . .'

'And what are you going to *do*, Patsy?'

'As I said, I have been on to . . .'

'Been on to who and what did they say?'

'Well, he said he understood our concerns and . . .'

Davey interrupts him. 'I heard they don't want to touch you, Patsy. You're old news. You're damaged goods. The game is up, man.'

Davey is no longer the outsider he used to be. He's gone mainstream.

Patsy looks a bit stunned by this. This isn't the Patsy who waltzed up to the house a few weeks ago all smiles and handshakes sending Rory off to Brussels.

He tries to calm the crowd. 'People of Kilsudgeon, people of Kils— Have I let you down in the past? Who has worked hardest for this community and will continue to do so? Who has got extra funding for the sewage treatment? Who took a stand against the water charges? Who got the . . .'

But he's drowned out by shouting. Father Donnegan tries to chip in from the side. He stands up and makes *calm down* gestures with his hands.

'Lads, now, please, if we could have a bit of order. We are all on the same side here.'

It quietens a little. The older locals stop joining in the shouting. But not for long. Toirdealbhach shouts out, 'NO TO CORRUPTION!' and someone else takes it up and soon it's a chant for half a minute. Iseult is on her feet and the noise miraculously dies down.

'I have a question for Patsy Duggan.'

She has a microphone. But there was no microphone handed out. I think she's brought her own. But where's she getting the power for it? I notice that the young lad next to her with the bag is twiddling something in it. A black box the size of a small safe. The sound is coming out of that. She's playing championship hurling here and poor old Patsy is only togging out for a challenge match.

'I have a question for Patsy Duggan,' she says again. 'Would you like to hear it?' She turns around to include the people behind her.

'Talk away, girl,' says someone.

'Who here votes for Patsy Duggan?'

'Excuse me now, Ms Deasy . . .'

'As you're always saying on the telly, Patsy, *I didn't interrupt you.*'

'But you d—'

'Who voted? Don't be shy.'

A few hands straggle up.

'OK, that's a bad sign, Patsy.'

More snickering in the crowd.

'For those of you who don't know, I'm Iseult Deasy, and I have had enough. And unlike some people, I'm not here to make promises I can't keep. I am here to make only one promise to you. I will stay and fight with you to keep your post office open. We are going to raise such a fuss they won't dare mess with Kilsudgeon again.'

The applause starts with her 'entourage', but locals soon join in.

Patsy tries to talk again. 'Now, now, Iseult . . .' But there's no now-nowing her now.

'He doesn't want you to know that he, Patsy Duggan, will actually BENEFIT from the post office closure. Who wants to hear about that?'

Patsy's face is like stone. The colour is going out of it. I think it's shock. I see it in old people after a fall.

'That is a lie and DEFAMATION,' he manages to shout, but she's moved on. She's back into the aisle. Owning it, as Freya would say.

'Who here has been dispossessed or repossessed? Who here votes for Patsy Duggan but hasn't got a thing out of him in a long while? But all the time, he looks after himself. I can't say any more, but I have seen documents.'

'What documents?!'

He's halfway to a full-on conniption now. There are bits of spit on the side of his mouth. I don't know if she has any documents, but the thing with Patsy is that you could accuse him of anything and you might be accidentally right.

'I will not listen to these lies,' says Patsy, but he's weaker.

'Who wants to hear about *real* solutions?' says Iseult.

'Lies,' Patsy mutters, and reaches for water, but there is none. Larry Leach goes off to the little kitchen in the hall to find him some and Patsy looks even more isolated now that his handler is gone.

'I want to hear what this lady has to say . . .' says one of the book-club women. Helen, I think she's called. There must be a strong feeling in the room if the Quality crowd are talking out.

'Kilsudgeon needs to send a message that rural Ireland will not TAKE IT ANY MORE! We are TIRED of being TAKEN FOR GRANTED by the ELITES in DUBLIN.'

She's flying now. But just at that moment she's nearly knocked out of kilter because it turns out her own crowd are a real pick'n'mix. Ollie Holland wants the mic.

'I haff to tell you guys in Kilsudgeon. It's time to wake up and shmell the coffee ya? You have the immigrants coming here, ashylum seekers or what they call themshelves, it's a big problem. You got to fight this thing ya.'

Iseult eases the microphone away. She smiles at him. 'Thank you, Ollie. I think we can hear the passion in your voice,' she says.

An ould fella in the druidy group starts shouting about Ireland needing to reclaim its Independence and starts reading from the 1916 Proclamation. He is drowned out by a short, dumpy woman shouting, 'As a mother, a local mother, I just think the whole thing is a disgrace.'

I've never seen her before, but she gets a few claps for that. It's a safe enough bet that at least something is always a disgrace. And if you say, *as a mother*, you get extra points. But then she says, 'AND THEY'RE USING THE FLUORIDE TO KEEP US DOCILE,' and the clappers pause mid-clap.

Patsy loses it then and starts shouting that they are all tin-hatters and he won't be spoken to like that by a shower of blow-ins who are vandalizing his property with graffiti and scratching his car.

'I'm not a blow-in, Patsy,' says Iseult. 'I came back from New York to help my home. I'm sorry you feel threatened by a young woman just starting out in her career. I'm sorry, Patsy, that you feel paranoid about graffiti, and we all condemn it, but I'm sure you have lots of enemies after thirty years in politics. But I will not say sorry for one thing. Being passionate about this community. Who here feels powerless? We all want some power back. And I have the solution.'

The young lad who's with her – I place him now as Davey's younger brother – nods at her, and a light appears on the wall on the side of the room. They even have their own small projector. Such a dainty little yoke, the size of a pound of butter, not like the generator Gordon uses when he's doing Tidy Towns committee presentations to me and the cat.

'This is my vision for rural Ireland. A new movement for Ireland. Nuatha. The *Nua* is "new", and then it's like the *Tuatha* from the Tuatha De Dannann, the original free Irish. Here is what Nuatha believes in.' Each time she clicks, a slogan appears with a photo next to it.

Direct action against cuts, with a photo of protestors in hi-vis.

Culture. Irish dancers appear next to this.

Sensible Environmental Strategy, not PC stuff!!!, with a photo of someone hugging a tree.

End to Political Correctness. There's a photo of a snow-flake.

Respect for our culture and religion. More dancers and the Pope appear next to this.

No 5G, and a picture of Chernobyl in an absolute heap.

There isn't much reaction to the 5G. We're only just after getting the 3G. But Davey and the rest of Iseult's gang are applauding every picture and cheering. Iseult clicks again and *DIRECT ACTION* fills the screen in big letters.

She doesn't give us any time to digest what direct action means. She carries on and puts up another picture. It's the post office.

'Now tell me, what do you see in that photo?'

No one replies.

'What is it?' she repeats, louder.

'Mpostffffice,' mumbles someone in the crowd. It's very hard to get a Kilsudgeon crowd to shout out one of those answers, in case it's the wrong one. A lot of older people would still have a dose of PTSD after saying the wrong answer to a schoolteacher with a leather strap years ago.

'It's not just a post office. This is the beating heart of the area. I remember buying my first stamp there. I'm sorry . . . I'm just a bit emotional.'

I look at Freya and her eyes nearly roll out of her head. I give her one eyebrow just to silently tell her, *Mind your face, you don't know who's looking at it*. She does a fake yawn and pretends to shoot herself in the head.

'I'm sorry . . .' says Iseult, wiping her eye. 'OK, Iseult, composure,' she tells herself. 'What does it mean, the post office? Community. Local power. It's not something that can be sold to the highest bidder. Something that can be commoditized. What would have happened if the British tried to take your post office? Would you let the Black and Tans back?'

'Noo!' We're on surer ground with this. It'd be fair to say people would rather not have the Black and Tans back.

'Would you let them occupy and sell your identity?'

This No is smaller. She needs to keep the questions simple for a Kilsudgeon crowd to stay shouting.

'Will you let them destroy your beautiful countryside and environment?'

More hesitation. This town runs on silage. It'll run on silage until the Flood comes. And no amount of promises of wildflower meadows are going to change that any time soon.

'Will you let them close your post office?'

'NO!'

Now we're talking.

'Then be here on the day they want to close it down – in two weeks' time – and we'll show people that the spirit of Kilsudgeon is alive and well!'

Davey is on his feet, chanting at Patsy, 'DIRECT ACTION NOW.' They've stolen Patsy's thunder. He has been going on about sending messages from rural Ireland for thirty years.

At the end of it, Patsy and Simon, the post office man, are looking forlorn on stage. They slope off as people surround Iseult to congratulate her.

Freya nudges me, looking over at the tight knot of campaigners talking in a corner.

'Mentallers, Auntie Ann. And I don't like using that word. But they are cur–ay–zeee.'

She sees Iseult detach herself from the group and sidle over, so she stops. Iseult is high on praise. She high-fives me and Freya, who just responds without thinking and then puts her hand away in case anyone else comes up.

'Wow, Ann. Can you feel the momentum?'

'You certainly shook them up all right.'

Patsy glares at me from the stage.

'I am so happy to have your support, Ann. You are the beating heart of the community.'

She's a fierce one for beating hearts. Me and the post office beating away.

'I'm going to put an end to the rule of Patsy around here, Ann. His time is up. See you on Save the Post Office Day!'

Patsy goes out the side door. I think about Rory turning into Patsy and maybe ending up in a meeting like this in a few years' time. Patsy's had that vote sewn up around here for twenty years. If you didn't want to vote for That Crowd or The Other Shower, Patsy was the choice. But it all ends badly, doesn't it?'

'What do you think, Freya?'

'So many feelings, Auntie Ann. She might be, like, sound and I'm loving the Patsy take-downs, but the people around her . . . I dunno.'

'Every family has its oddballs, Freya.'

'Yeah, about that. Check this out. Declan's sent on the deets for the dinner. He put it in Extended.'

I read it off her phone. *Hello. this is Declan. A reminder that dinner is booked tomorrow night for Slaughterhouse & Winch for Jennifer's birthday. Bye, Declan.*

'What's he put underneath?'

'It's Ryan Gosling saying, *Hey, girl, Happy Birthday*. His gif game is sooooo . . .'

'Basic?'

She waves her hands over her face. 'Oh my God can't breathe, I'm welling up. My baby said her first word.'

22.

STRONG VIEWS ON PALLETS

I knew we were too early. Denis cannot abide being late into a meal.

'I want to pick my chair,' he says. 'I like to be facing out the way. Don't like people sneaking up on me.'

'Is this from your training in the Black Ops?' says Freya.

Even Mam, a woman who sits in the hall waiting for a lift the day before, thinks we're too early. When we go in, there's no one else from the party there. Jennifer has gone with Stephanie to pick up Declan from the train. They are both ropey after the horsey wedding the night before. Deirdre will be late, I'm sure of it.

A young lad comes up to us, not wearing any socks.

'Hey, guys, how are you tonight?'

I don't reply. I'm not a guy.

'Booking forrrr . . .?'

We're all looking at each other. Declan booked it.

'Is there a Declan?'

'No Declans here, I'm afraid, guys. Do you guys have a surname?'

It dawns on me that Declan and Jennifer are going out a year and a bit and I never thought to find out a surname. Freya looks Declan up on Facebook.

'This is him . . . Oh pull-ease,' she whispers, and shows me the phone. 'Declan is even weirder on Facebook. It's a load of conspiracy videos and he's changed his name to Declan Truthman.'

The young lad at the desk gets called away, so he advises us to move over to a row of seats and hands us out menus. Denis looks to see if there's beef.

'Sure as anything now, there won't be beef,' he says. 'Oh, there is. Probably raw.'

After five minutes Stephanie breezes in, with Jennifer and Declan dawdling behind. She's beautifully turned out again. The shoulders are all brown and there's no handprints so it must be real. Most of us – even Jennifer – look a bit dowdy next to her. I'm going to make the effort to tell her. You should always try and be the bigger woman, I think. Especially when I'm already the bigger woman in a lot of scenarios.

'That's a lovely dress, Stephanie. You didn't get that off Marian.'

'Thanks, Ann, no, God no, Marian Roche wouldn't have this. Yeah, it's a midi by Maya. Now,' and she whispers, 'I got it at the Dubai mall. I like it but time flies and it's already feeling a little bit last season now, so I'll be refreshing soon. I mean, I could completely get away with it for a few years in Kilsudgeon, but I think I'll Marie Kondo it after this. Now, will we get our table?'

'The booking is under Rourke,' she says to Shoeless Joe. 'I rang again to get us upgraded. We're all Rourkes tonight. Could you imagine?!'

Stephanie looks at me in my new gear. She approves, I think.

'I love the two-piece, Ann. It's very . . . you.'

We're shown into the restaurant. Denis lets out the sigh he's been expecting to sigh since he heard we were going here. Slaughterhouse & Winch have expanded into the place next door. And the place next door used to be a garage. Denis is in his element for complaining.

'I got a Fiat 121 fixed here one time. Paudie Pitstop had it then. Poor Paudie would get another heart attack in his grave if he saw it now. I wonder did they fill in the pit.'

We sit down.

The floor is just the bare concrete and the pipes and ducts are all painted with big slogans. DISRUPT EVERYTHING, says one. YOU ARE NOW.

'Is this your kind of thing, Freya?'

She shakes her head. 'Trying too hard, Auntie Ann. Look at that hole.'

They haven't filled in the garage pit. There is one table for two down in it.

Denis peers in. It's Petey Welch, the mountainy farmer, and his daughter Isla.

'Will you have a look at the alternator while you're down there, Petey?' says Denis. 'It was making a noise on the way up there. I'd say she's gone. That Škoda was a bad buy.'

Petey is unimpressed.

'What kind of a fuckin' yoke is this at all, Denis? A restaurant with a hole in it.'

'Ah, stop moaning, Daddy,' says Isla. She is taking selfies against a mural on the pit wall. It's of Russian-looking wans holding hammers. THE PAST IS FEMALE, says the wall.

'Come in for Insta, Daddy. This place is iconic.' And she puts her arm around him and hauls him back in the chair. He still has a puss on him, so that won't do for Isla's photo. She's having none of Petey's moaning.

'You've such a resting bitch face, Daddy. It's Mam's anniversary. You know well she would have wanted you to be feeling like an eejit. And don't you have the morning off the milking tomorrow, and this is the thanks I get?'

'I'm in the pit of despair, Denis,' he says, but he smiles, or grimaces, for the photo all the same.

They're a great pair. Isla is keeping him alive. She's stone mad for the farming. She was drawing silage for a contractor during her Junior Cert. Now she's a bit of a social media star. agrihun, she calls herself. She put eyelashes on her tractor and the internet was all over it.

'Hi, Isla.' Freya waves shyly.

'Hey, Starbar,' she shouts up. 'We still good for the recording soon? I heard the one you did about Patsy's repeal video. It was fire, girl. Drag him, hun!'

'Oh my God, yes, totally. We can do a mutual.' Freya is beaming. 'I was just setting up the studio – well, Auntie Ann's sitting room – today.'

'What's a mutual, Freya?' I ask as we go to our table.

'I'll be on her podcast and she'll be on mine. You have to around here because there's no one to interview.'

The restaurant is rammed. It was mentioned on *Nationwide* last week. They were doing a bit on Ireland's Abandoned Middle – the new tourist area for places that got left out of the Wild Atlantic Way and Ancient East. The 'Hipster Heart of Ireland', they were calling Drumfeakle. They didn't take that too well around our village. Kilsudgeon used to be the place to be because of the Zank factory and everyone laughed at Drumfeakle because it used to be nearer the landfill, but then the landfill closed and Zank closed and now Drumfeakle thinks it's Berlin.

We are sitting at a table that used to be an old workbench, by the looks of it. The menus are in a vice. Everything here seems to be made of pallet. Our table has a streak of blue paint across the end of it. Denis strokes it admiringly. He's terrible fond of pallets and hates to see them thrown outside.

'Not a bad place for a pallet to end up. There's a lot of history in a pallet. Great to see them getting the use out of these.' He seems to be directing these remarks to Stephanie, who smiles but wouldn't be known for strong views on pallets.

Mam eases herself on to a butter box, but then she gets stuck because, in leaning over, her miraculous medal somehow got through a gap in the table and then, when she leaned back, the medal stayed under and she's tied by her string to the table. This is not what she needs now at her hour of life. I'm sure she isn't the first to get a miraculous medal stuck in a pallet in this place. We manage to disentangle her, but she looks like she won't enjoy anything after this.

'OK FOR DRINKS, GUYS? HI, I'M JAYDEN, I'LL BE YOUR SERVER TONIGHT. LET ME TELL YOU ABOUT THE SPECIALS.'

I have a feeling I know him to see from Freya's school, but the accent is pure Yank. They're all American now. Deirdre reckons it's because children are all reared on *Paw Patrol*.

'Server,' mutters Denis. 'They're gone from the altar into the restaurants.'

Jayden doesn't seem to hear.

'SO, FOR STARTERS? WE HAVE THE GOURMET MAC AND CHEESE?' And he rattles off the specials, which we don't listen to properly.

Deirdre and Hughie arrive in a fluster. Deirdre looks stressed. Even Hughie seems uneasy. Normally, Hughie is the calmest man you could meet. 'Be all the same in a hundred years,' is all he ever says. He got a grand easy job twenty years ago with Vantic, who make collars for light fittings, but they all say it won't last. The Chinese could make them on their lunchbreak. Some sleep their way to the top. Hughie napped.

'How are you, Deirdre? Is Nora looking after the two?'

She nods. 'So they'll be awake till all hours and up to ninety on Fanta and Chipsticks. We'll come back now after this and she'll hand them over and say, *Oh, they were as good as gold*, and the pair of them strung out.'

'But she's good to mind them, all the same, Deirdre,' Hughie chips in.

'Well, then, she should put them to bed. She'd have more time for herself,' Deirdre snaps back.

'It's hard to get small children to bed,' I say.

'Try minding them some time, Mam, then you'll see.'

'Zing,' says Freya into her menu.

A few minutes later Deirdre whispers to me, 'Sorry, Mam, I didn't mean that.'

I mutter half of nothing to let her know it's fine and I start into telling her about life with Mam out of the side of my mouth. The way we mothers all learned how to give out about someone in the family while sitting a foot away from them. You'll see us at it, when we're talking without moving our lips. Throat-talking, Denis calls it.

'. . . and don't get me wrong, Deirdre, it's all fine, but 'am can 'e a 'it 'ifficult a' 'imes. 'ery inde'endent.'

But Deirdre doesn't seem to be listening and I don't want to go higher. Mam's hearing is like an owl's now when it suits her.

'What's the matter, Deirdre?'

She's looking at a photo on her phone.

'Ah, nothing, Mam.' And she shows it to me. It's a snap from her mother-in-law of the two watching the Tractor Channel on telly and eating crisps. Deirdre breathes out a sigh and looks at Hughie, who just shrugs.

'If she gives them any sherbet, I will have words with her. Their teeth are costing us an arm and a leg as it is.'

'What's wrong with their teeth?'

I'm interrupted by Mam asking me is there any mash on the menu.

'What's a sweet potato, Ann? Does it have sugar on it?'

'You had them before, Mam, an orange thing.'

'Wasn't that a turnip?'

Denis and Mam join forces now on how there's nothing for them to eat.

'It better be a nice turnip,' he says. 'Eight euro for a bowl of it.' He thinks that by taking her side the odd time he's making it easier in the long run. I think you've to take a firmer hand with parents once they go beyond a certain age. Your mother is not your friend.

It's the one thing I'm looking forward to about getting old. Acting the maggot and watching the children dance around.

'Carpaccio of alpaca,' he proclaims, as if that sums it all up.

'There's chicken there. A compote of it.'

'BUT THERE'S FRUIT WITH IT. If I wanted fruit with my dinner, I'd have brought an apple in my pocket.'

'Don't you eat pork and apple sauce, Denis?'

'I don't.'

'I made it last year.'

'I didn't eat the apple sauce.'

'Well, who ate it?'

'I gave it to Rory. Margaret, will we go out to the chipper?'

Now Deirdre joins in.

'I'm nearly tempted to go to the chipper myself, Mam. The prices in here! I don't know, Hughie, we might share a starter. What do you think, Hughie?'

'I'm starving, though, Deirdre. I've been saving up space for this.'

Deirdre doesn't normally talk about money. She turns back to the menu and stares, as if trying to get the prices down.

Jennifer and Stephanie are deep in conversation. I can hear only bits and pieces. Things are being *rolled out across the Gulf* and *transfer pricing is key*. Freya is staring at her phone with headphones on. I glare at her to try to get her to take them off, which she does, but she rolls her eyes – *epically*, as they say – and puts the phone within reach.

'What are you doing anyway, Freya?'

'Editing, Auntie Ann.'

'Don't be editing now at dinner, Freya. It's bad manners.'

These are the sentences you find yourself saying to children. *Don't be editing at dinner*. I remember saying to Deirdre when she was four, *Don't be scratching yourself down there at Mass*.

But I like it, she says.

God doesn't want to be looking at you scratching your front bottom.

Why is he looking at me? she says.

There was no reply to that, really, when I was trying to keep Kevin quiet and find coins for the collection at the same time.

Declan comes in then, before I've a chance to ask Deirdre about teeth. He sits next to Jennifer, but as we're an odd number he has no one opposite him, and he looks happy with that.

'I think I'll have the bread and dips, and you can have what you want, Hughie, but you'll owe me,' says Deirdre. She is like a wasp tonight.

'That takes all the craic out of it, Deirdre.'

'Craic is off the menu, Hughie.'

I have never heard them sniping at each other like this. I wonder is she having another baby? She always said she was *done done* after Ailbhe.

'What is it, Deirdre? You're very cranky this night.'

'I'll tell you what it is, Mam. It's the children. Both of them. They need orthodontics. Their teeth are up in a heap.' She takes a big slurp of a pint. 'My two heroes each need five thousand euro worth of work done on their bockety teeth. What was it they called it again, Hughie, the thing the orthodontist said they had?'

'Anterior and posterior crossbites,' says Hughie.

'They both have it – both of them – can you believe that? Functional appliance orthodontics. Full fixed braces. Up in Dublin is the only place it can be done. Unless we go off to Hungary for a dental holiday. But you wouldn't know what they'd come back with from that. Teeth in their ears or something. What I can't understand is how they ended up with such mutant teeth.'

She's glaring at Hughie like it's his side of the family that's responsible for the mutant teeth gene. His teeth seem fine. Without thinking, I feel my own teeth with my tongue. There's a few gone down the back. But no one notices. Like the back of an orchestra.

'And then there's Hughie's news. Tell them, Hughie.'

Hughie clears his throat and explains that there are cutbacks at Vantic and there's talk of redundancy. Vantic were bought out by some big American crowd who want to shake things up.

'So you see, Mam, we're not having the steak tonight.'

The boy is back now, taking the orders. My mother orders a steak. 'WELL DONE, I don't want to be getting food poisoning.' And then she looks at me triumphantly, as if I've been feeding her raw meat all this time. She's a funny old bird.

As the orders go around the table, Deirdre turns back to me.

'Hughie knows himself he won't make the cut. And they've no union, so he'll get the bare minimum.'

We both look over at Hughie, who is talking to Denis about whether it's faster to go the main road or the back road between two places.

'I love him to bits, Mammy, but Hughie wouldn't have been pulling up trees when he was there.'

'I heard that, Deirdre,' says Hughie.

Deirdre isn't as good at talking out of the side of her mouth as I am. It takes years of practice. She mightn't have the orthodontics for it.

'You were too nice, Hughie. That's all I'm saying.'

I can well imagine some Yank coming in to Vantic and finding easy-going Hughie foostering with a load of folders and trying to cover for lads who are off sick with a sore finger for a year.

'So that's the story. Ten kay in dental to be paid sometime this year or they'll look like ould lads.'

'And what about your place? How's it going there?'

'My place!' She laughs. 'No, nothing doing. I'm very quiet in there these days. Nigel is still doing the poor mouth. *Margins are tight*, he says. And I know well they've a house bought out in Spain. I'd say he'll sell up for the quiet life. I could be out on my ear too. I'm feeling underemployed.'

'What do they want good teeth around here for?' says Denis, not helping. 'They're not going on telly, are they? Adam will be at the mart, and it won't be *his* teeth they'll be checking. It'll be the cattle's.'

'Daddy, I am not letting my children grow up looking like they're down from the mountains. I want them to get on in life.'

Denis leans back and I know he's got a joke to let out and I pray it's Stephanie-friendly.

'The anterior posterior can bite you in the arse.'

Deirdre puts down a bread roll. 'Very funny, Daddy. Are you giving us that for free? Do you know what would be more use now? A few bob, Daddy. Do you or Mammy have any to spare? No, I thought not.'

Poor Denis blushes. The money is a sore point with him. He knows he'll never have a lot of it with a job driving a lorry and is mostly happy about that. But every so often it gets in his face. Especially not being able to help out the children with something.

Deirdre looks for somewhere else to give her attention and the bread basket is in for it.

Stephanie straightens up from her chat with Jennifer.

'Oh my God, why didn't I think of it before? Come to Dubai, guys. Come. To. Dubai!'

Deirdre lets out a little laugh at the very thought of it.

'I'M SERIOUS. I've just been telling Jennifer that it's hopping again out there, but . . .' she looks over at Declan with a smile '. . . she's all loved up here. But you two, bring the family for a while. Ride out the storm and make a bit of money. And the dentists are cheap too!' Stephanie looks very pleased with herself. 'I'm going to text Kevin right away and see what he can do. And Hughie, you're an engineer, aren't you?'

'Ah, a bit of a one. I'm more project-managing now. Production line, ehh . . .' He fades out.

'Sell yourself more than that, Hughie! And Deirdre, you're office manager? I can literally think of four, five jobs available for you right now.'

'I thought that place was gone a bit sour. I saw something online about people out of work.' Deirdre is doubtful, but there's a tone of interest in her voice.

'Only if you don't know anyone. Both Kevin and I are *screaming out* for good people. And the Irish are turning their backs on it. C'mon!'

We're all a little stunned at this. Mam is even silent. Stephanie can be very persuasive. She's in Events, so I suppose she'd be good at making things happen.

Bing! She checks her phone. Her nails make a little clicking noise as she pages through it, and her bracelet clinks off it too. She has very noisy hands.

'That's Kevin. He says, *Sure, work away, how's Mam?* Ah bless, you can take the man out of Kilsudgeon . . . I'm serious, guys. Come to Dubai, it'll be just a great experience for the children.'

'But the schools . . .'

'They can go to school with my two! Oh, I'm so excited by this. Why didn't I think of it before? We're always saying the cousins don't spend enough time together.'

'This seems like a fairly extreme way to go about it, though,' I say. 'A play date would do, Stephanie.'

'Ah, I don't know,' says Deirdre.

'Guys, this is serendipity. You deserve a little bit of paradise.'

'Paradise,' Freya snorts. I've seen that look before. Stephanie hasn't, though. She doesn't know what she's doing. She pokes the bear.

'Oh, you'd love it, Freya. The shops are amazing and there's people from so many countries there, and the boys there – and I'm not being gross – but they are fiiiinne.'

Freya gives her a look that would kill a geranium, but Stephanie just barrels ahead.

'There's this water park, oh my God. Kevin went up one of the slides and he DRAGGED me up . . . I took my life in my hands.'

Freya mumbles something about your life being in your hands if you had to build it.

Stephanie doesn't get it. Or chooses not to.

'Yes, anyway, so if you were out there, then Ann, you could visit too. Ohhh, we could go in dune buggies. Oh, this is so happening.' She claps her hands together.

Freya puts down her phone and is rolling her eyes. 'Paradise if you're not from Bangladesh or a woman or gay.'

'Oh, Freya, I think that's all overblown. I, personally, as a woman, I've never had a problem there.'

'Pff white people,' says Freya.

'I have a friend from Delhi who works in IT, and she loves it there.'

'How many gay friends do you have, Stephanie?'

'A few, actually. I mean, obviously, they're *careful*, but you know, well, it's just a different culture to ours. You just have to be respectful.'

'Respectful, yeah, OK, whatever.'

'Oh, Freya, you've a lot to learn. We all have to live in the world. When you're older, you'll understand, hun.'

I should step in, but she's not my child. The rules are different. Deirdre has told me horror stories from school about parents falling out. Some fourth-class mother gave out to another child for putting a sandwich in her child's hair, and the next thing a solicitor's letter arrived, suing for defamation. *In the course of the exchange you called my client and her family 'a shower of tramps reared in a ditch and what would you expect with the father riding half the parish?'*

Freya carries on. 'Big Repeal campaign in Dubai, was there, Steph?'

'Freya, listen to me now, we're having a family dinner here now. While there's still any of my family left here, OK?'

I say that a bit sharper than I meant. And the table goes silent.

'Fierce building going on out there,' says Denis to fill the silence. 'I was watching it on the Discovery. They've an expo, and they're building a new city for it. They're some lads for the building.'

'So, OK, guys, who's having the fishcakes?'

Jayden is back with the starters. When they're finished with the *is everything ok?s* Denis asks if they've ketchup to go with his chicken wings. Jaden tells him they make their own ketchup and Denis looks suspicious.

'Ketchup isn't something you make yourself,' he says. 'It should be made in a factory.'

But he tries it and pretends not to love it, and soon we're all eating away and chatting about things that don't involve the Constitution or workers' rights in the Gulf. Which is how I prefer it when I'm out for the night.

Declan gets up from his chair, sits down again, then gets up and walks around the table and squats between me and Deirdre.

'I want to ask you something, Mrs Devine.'

I notice that he looks different. The clothes are new. He's wearing some sort of scent, which he never normally does because, according to Jennifer, he's a bit allergic to things.

'Well, Declan, how are you?'

'Yes, Mrs Devine, the thing is . . .'

I hear her before I see her.

Iseult.

'ANN DEVINE AND FAMILY! How great to see you here. Oh my God, Stephanie, is that you? And Jennifer? Is this *The Real Housewives of Beverly Hills* or what? The glam, girls. It's FAB. Ann, I won't disturb you now. I'm just having a little celebratory cocktail out in the bar with some of my team.'

205

She comes in close to me, displacing Declan, who scurries back to his chair.

'Ann, we just got some good news on the funding front from some of our American contacts, so we're all set to get Nuatha off the ground. By the way, loved that meeting. A little bird told me you suggested it to Patsy. A masterstroke. We needed to flush him out. Oh, here's my co-star here.'

Davey walks in, looking uncomfortable. He looks around at the group. He's not dressed for family dinners. He just has a hoodie with a fist on it. Davey was in Jennifer's class in school, but it's Declan he spots. He seems to know him.

'Declan, mate . . . good to see you again . . . Did you see Paxman's got another video out? Some really good stuff, you should check it out.'

'Anyway,' says Iseult, 'we've got a gang outside, so better get the party started, in more ways than one, haha.' And off she skips.

'Keep the faith, brother,' Davey says to Declan as he slouches out after her.

'How do you know him, Declan?' says Jennifer, but she's talking to his waist because Declan is on his feet. And tapping his glass. He's blushing ferociously.

'Now, I'd like to raise a toast. Please stand.'

'Oh wait, Declan, Rory is on Facetime,' says Jennifer. She holds up her phone so he can see us. Declan rubs his face with his hand.

We all squint at Rory.

'What's going on, fam?' he says. 'Are you all finally eating something other than spuds? Denis, have you had the beef?'

'Keep it down, Rory. Don't be telling the world our business.'

'Ah, Mammy, fair play to you, you're still standing. Some woman for the sesh, you are.'

'How are you anyway, Rory, you look . . .'

I see it now, the small beginnings of a beard.

'Rory, what is that on your face? Do you even have the follicles?' says Jennifer, laughing.

He *whatever*s her and says he called to wish her a happy birthday and that she can relax now because she's over the hill and she has less choices. He says something else then, but we don't hear it because Declan is clearing his throat and saying, 'If I could ask you to make a toast . . . Stand up, please, for a toast.'

We are slow to get up. Only Stephanie and Jennifer are used to it and are up straight away. Kilsudgeon isn't a place for standing when everyone else is sitting. You're only making yourself a target. The rest of us are still crouching as he continues speaking.

'I'd like to toast . . .'

I see Petey's head turning around.

'. . . we're here to celebrate . . .'

Mam isn't standing yet.

'Tell me when he's going to do something. He talks too much, that boy,' she says.

'We're all here for Jennifer's birthday. She's thirty, but I think she looks younger. And I think she won't look thirty for at least two years.'

'The old romantic,' says Jennifer, and we all laugh.

The laugh is still floating around when Declan says, 'But the main reason I am standing up is that I am going to ask Jennifer something very important.'

'OK, Declan, relax, love.' Jennifer's kind of hugging his hand.

'No, Jennifer. I want to say it.'

Oh Jesus, he's fishing around in his pocket for something. It can't be. He pulls out . . . a piece of paper. The relief.

'You are a special person,
Who has changed my life.
I am a man today because of you

I love you I hope you love me too.'

And then he goes into his pocket again! The relief was temporary. Out comes a box and, when he opens it, there's a ring in it. This is DEFINITELY not Jennifer's scene.

'You've changed my life, Jennifer. Now . . .'

'Oh Declan,' says Jennifer. But not in the way you'd think. It sounds very much like, *Oh no, Declan* and not a *Gone with the Wind* Oh.

'Will you spend the rest of it with me?'

'The rest of what?' says Mam.

'Jennifer, will you marry me?'

Jennifer drops the phone with Rory on it. He shouts, 'What the fuck's going on, lads? All I can see is the ceiling.'

Jennifer looks at me. I can't help her. I can't be shouting NO at her.

'Oh Declan,' she says again, and gives him a hug.

'Is that a yes?' he asks.

She doesn't say that but just gives him the hug and, by the look on her face over his shoulder, I wouldn't count on it.

The rest of the restaurant assumes it's a Yes because there's a big cheer.

Isla has the phone out.

'The Gúna Girls will have to make another trip, and you're definitely coming this time, Freya!' says Stephanie, squeezing Freya to her. Freya looks like a cat that doesn't want to be picked up. But she doesn't scratch.

'More expense,' says Deirdre.

'Lads? Hello, I'm on my back here,' says Rory through the phone.

'We all are, Rory,' says Denis.

23.

TERRIBLE FOR THE ALGORITHM

People are coming over to Jennifer to hug her. I can see agrihun, her face lit up by her phone, the two thumbs going at it hammer and tongs. It's already up before the ice cream comes out. Freya comes around to show me. There are already replies.

agrihun: *Oh my god, guys. Just saw the most adorable proposal. See my next post for video.*

betterwithouthim: *U are such a tease. agrihun.*

agrihun: *soz babes, now is terrible for the algo. Tomorrow after milking! Xxxohoxhox*

'Some night for the parish, Auntie Ann,' says Freya, in a country voice.

When the crowd dies down a little Jennifer gives me the signal with her eyes. Outside. Now.

'I must put on a lick of make-up. Will you come, too, Jennifer, after all the emotion?'

'Good idea, Mam.' She waggles her face, gives Declan a weak smile and holds it together until we get to the loos.

And *of course* they're unisex. Of all the times you need not a sight nor sound of a man, and these bare-ankled bastards have us 'mingling' outside the cubicles. Jennifer goes into one. I hear her from outside.

'Oh Mam, fuuuuuuuuuuuuuuuuuuuck.'

I go searching for a cleaning sign, which I put outside the door.

'FUCKSHITFUCKSHITFUCKSHIT.'

'OK, ease up now on the language, Jen, will you? Are you that upset about it?'

'Mammy, I'm having a panic attack over it.'

She takes breaths. I run out and get her water. She's recovered a small bit when I get back. Sniffling at herself in the mirror. I join her in the cubicle and shut the door behind me.

'I couldn't say no at the time, Mam. I didn't know how he'd react. I'll just delay it out for as long as possible until I see what happens.'

'Can you do that?'

'I'll take the sting out of it. Amortize the debt, as we say in finance.'

'And what about the parents? Can you amortize them?'

'I don't know what I'm going to do about them. What an eejit, to ask me in front of everyone. Who does that any more? I knew I should have spotted something. Did you see my face when I saw what he was going to do? I knew it. I'd seen him watching a video from Madison Square Garden, and the girl says yes in that. I could have shown him a hundred where the woman says no and the man is absolutely crushed and has his soul destroyed. That would have sorted him out. What am I going to do, Mammy?' She's forgotten about amortizing.

I can hear people complaining outside about cleaning in the toilets at this hour.

She gives her make-up a touch-up. I start talking loudly about hats.

Back at the table, it's calmed down a little. I go over and sit next to Declan and give him a hug.

'I didn't know you had that in you, Declan.'

'Opportunities are there to be taken, Mrs Devine.'

When we get to the closing time Denis asks for the bill. I can see by him he's been nursing what Deirdre said about money like a loose tooth. But he's too late. Jayden tells him it's been taken care of. I look at Stephanie, but she shakes her head.

'I wouldn't want to interfere in a family thing, Ann,' she says.

Declan says it was him. He *has* changed. He didn't so much as buy a toilet roll when he was with us. Now he's the Secret Millionaire, going around surprising us.

The whole party get a minibus home. Even the designated drivers needed wine to steady themselves.

I'm at the back with Jennifer and Mam. Freya in front with Stephanie. I can't tell if they're speaking, but they're not throwing slaps. Deirdre and Hughie are in the row ahead, definitely not speaking. Hughie gave out to her when he got sticky toffee pudding and she was tutting and worrying about teeth and money.

Thank God, Denis and Declan are up the front with the driver. Denis is full of drink and is anxious to make small talk after a night of Big Talk. So he goes to town on the taxi man across a wide range of topics and the lines drift back to us mixed with snatches of 'Night-time Hitz with Billy Fitz' on the County FM.

'NOT A BAD DAY.'

'Shitshitshitshitshit, Mam.' Jennifer is whispering *shit*s into my ear. Mam dozes on my left shoulder. I made her turn down the hearing aid thanksbetogod.

'THE FARMERS ARE LOOKING FOR RAIN.'

'You'll have to say something. You can't lead him on, Jennifer.'

211

'YE WERE HAVING A MEAL?'

'I know, Mam. I'll wait to see what Desdemona says.'

'THEY KNOW HOW TO CHARGE.'

'But it's your decision.'

'I want to see what she thinks of his proposal.'

'THE HELPINGS ARE SMALL, I HEARD.'

'If she thinks it's a mad idea, we might be able to let him down gently together.'

'OH, STOP. A SPOON OF MASH. A SPOON!'

Now this next tune [cough] is a great song from the main man himself, Tommy Nonnigan, and it's called, 'If I Had the Kind of Money You Think I Have'.

'You can't string him along, Jennifer. That's not fair. And you'll only send him even more into the Jeremy Paxman whatshisname. The guru fella. I'd say he's only waiting for the likes of Declan to be spurned.'

'NO ICE CREAM, THOUGH, WOULDJA CREDIT THAT?'

'DINNY WOULD HAVE THE ICE CREAM.'

'HE'D GO TO THE SHOP FOR YOU.'

'Oh, I know, Mam. This is it. He'll turn into one of these MGTOWs. Men going their own way. No, I do love him, Mam, but I don't know if I want to marry him or not. It's too early, and I probably might have come around to the idea if he hadn't asked in front of the whole parish.'

'I SEE ON FACEBOOK THEY'RE GOING TO DO ANOTHER MEETING ABOUT THE POST OFFICE. YOUNG DEASY.'

'SHE'S INTO THE DRAMA.'

'What possessed him anyway?'

'THE FATHER LOVED THE DRAMA, TOO, THE NCT MAN.'

'IF HE THOUGHT HE LOST A FIVER.'

'THEY'RE A COUSIN OF MICK THE LAMP, YOU KNOW.'

'THE FUCKER FAILED ME OVER A STICKER ON THE WINDOW.'

'A RACKET.'

She fiddles with the ring. It's enormous. Even Stephanie was impressed with it.

'You could pay for your niece and nephew's teeth with that,' I tell her.

She smiles and looks out the window as we pass Patsy's driveway. There's a car parked outside.

Jennifer looks out the window as a silage-man hurtles by in a flash of lights, a huge trailer behind him.

Now a special request for a special lady from . . . well, he doesn't say his name – it just says the Wilderbrook.

Mam perks up for that. It could hardly be . . . As if I hadn't enough things to be worrying about.

'Don't forget them tickets for the Pope,' she says sleepily, closing her eyes again.

My phone lights up. It's a message from a new number.

Delighted with the big news. So happy and can't wait to meet you soon. Des and Phil xxx

'Jen . . .'

'I know, Mam. Just tell me everything will work out.'

'Poor Jen. Your old Mam can't fix this, I'm afraid. It's Big Girl stuff.'

'Mam, please?'

'OK . . . Jen, it'll all work out in the end.'

I don't believe a word of it.

213

24.

ONE MINUTE YOU'RE ON THE *LORDAMERCY*

There's no sign of Jennifer and Declan the following morning. I can hear them chatting from time to time in Jennifer's old room, where they're sleeping, but I can't make out the words. I give up looking for excuses to walk past the room. But I make a big noise about getting Mam up and about and ready for Mass.

Father Donnegan looks distracted during the service. He loses his place in the missal a few times, doesn't know who the readers are, forgets to bring out the communions. There's something bothering him. Mam whispers there's talk he's being replaced. The bishop wasn't happy with him not reading out the abortion letter during the referendum. Father Donnegan claimed he didn't get the email, but the bishop wasn't buying that.

I've been at Mass more in the last couple of weeks than the previous few years. Once Mam got more mobile, she wanted to go back. A lot. It's like a boot camp with her. 'I need to get myself right for the Pope, and I can't pray in your place, Ann. There's too much distraction.'

I've mainly been just sitting with her, enjoying the peace and quiet. The prayer went out of me a few years ago. I don't know how it happened. There were just a few Sundays around when me and Denis woke up and looked at each other and said, *Are we going?* And neither of us answered and we fell back asleep and . . . I'd like to be able to tell myself a better story than that – that I read a book and it opened my eyes – but that's all it was. But I've a few things to pray about this morning. What do I ask for, though? *God, can you stop my daughter from going to Dubai to make a bit of money for herself and get away from her mother-in-law? Can you help my other daughter figure out how to keep her mother-in-law without getting married to the mother-in-law's son? Can you help me figure out how to keep my son out of trouble without me getting into trouble?*

I'd say Jesus would be saying, *You're holding up the queue there, Ann, and you're not coming up on our system.*

The rest of the Mass passes in a kind of trance. One minute you're on the *Lordamercy Lordamercy Lordamercy Christamercy Christamercies* and the next thing you're sitting back waiting for the 'Go in Peace'. Mam, as usual, looks a different woman after it. She's lively on the way out, touching the arms of her pals to get news off them. I eventually extract her from a group of them worrying together contentedly about the post office and get her into the car. As I'm going around to get in my side a familiar shape strides towards me. Patsy. Again.

'Ann, will you hold on a while? I want to talk to you.'

'Patsy, I have to bring the boss home. She'll roast in the car.'

'That's grand. I'll follow you home and we can talk there.'

And he does. The man treats our house as a constituency clinic. I get Mam home and rouse Denis away from the papers to look after her. Jennifer and Declan are still not up, from what I can tell. Patsy and me take two chairs out the back. There is that lovely stillness of a warm Sunday.

'The heat is mighty all the same, Ann.' He takes out a fag and lights it. He must still be shook. He'd only normally smoke around election time. I'm dying to ask him for one, but it's just after Mass and my mother is inside the house.

'What do you know about Iseult's group, Ann? You'd be fairly close to them.'

It's an odd question, since he was bawling me out of it after the clean-up, and I start to say that it was just a clean-up and I tried to move the rubbish, but he cuts me off.

'Look, I know you're only doing your litter carry-on and you got caught up in them and I accept your apology.'

'But I wasn't going to ap—'

'But I've been thinking about this whole thing. You probably saw in the meeting, I just let them show their cards. Don't interrupt the enemy when they're making a mistake, isn't that what the Chinese fella said? Sun Tzu.'

That's not how I remember it. I seem to remember Patsy and the Leech deep in conversation at the end saying, *This is fucked, lads*. But memory can be subjective, I'm told. Patsy obviously remembers it different.

'Iseult is smart out in many ways – she could be very good for around here. The bigger parties haven't snapped her up. She could be an independent TD like me one day. But she's young and, whether she wanted it or not, now she's surrounded by a load of loolahs. Davey Finnerty, like, for God's sake. Since when was the likes of him to be standing up at meetings in the parish hall? Accusing me of things I haven't even done, Ann! I caught him once, Ann, taking a shite on one of my posters. Taking a shite, Ann! That's a different feckin level, isn't it?'

'Janey.'

'And the others around her. Ollie Holland. The Flying Dutchman. Paying Somalis to kidnap him and no one would pay a ransom. Or the other clowns, in their Celtic fancy dress. No, she'd want to be careful – they'll drag her into something. And I know what they're saying, you know. Do you think that Rory is the only one working for me? I have my sources. I *know* what people are saying. They're saying Patsy's lost his touch.'

'They're not saying that, are they, Patsy?' I act innocent, even though I'm thinking of a conversation with Mick the Lamp where he said the very same thing.

'They're saying Patsy is surplus to requirements. The government don't need me for the votes. That I don't know the way the wind is blowing. Look at the abortion thing – people will say, *Oh, Patsy Duggan has no principles, he let Rory put out the two videos.*'

He's blaming Rory for the videos?

'Well, look, I don't know a damn thing about abortion. I have no children and I won't either at this stage, so I won't be saying anything to anyone, but the Church people need to be able to talk to me so I have to play for both teams. There's too much ideology in this country. Ireland has no room for big ideas. You need small ideas. Anyone comes in with big ideas is trouble. I see it with Iseult's gangs and the Celtic oul shite. These protestors, Ann, they don't know how the deals are done. I'm working away on the post office, but there's no way in the wide earthly world I'll be telling Davey Finnerty or anyone else what my strategy is. They think they'll bring me down and that'll fix Kilsudgoen? They won't, Ann! Iseult Deasy is only out for herself.'

That last line makes me smile. I can't help myself. Does he hear himself?

'I know what you're thinking, Ann, but everything I do is for Kilsudgeon. And if I get an ould commission along the way, so be it. But Deasy is a snake. The father is the same. He was taking money hand over fist to pass the car tests only it got covered up. The Deasys are worse than the Duggans. And, what's worse, they want to be like us. Well, they won't.'

I'm mightily confused now as to who *they* are, but Patsy grabs my attention back again.

'But if we're to get control back of this, Ann, you'll need to stay on side with Iseult. You're the only sensible one she'll talk to. Rory agrees with me. He says, *Mam will talk sense into Iseult. Mam can bring the community together.*'

'Rory said that? About me?'

'He did, Ann. He said to me, *Mam's a carer, she's used to talking to people who are mental.*'

I must remind myself to talk to Rory about appropriate language to describe my clients, but that's for another day. I feel a bit of pride all the same.

'So you'll stay in with them, will you? You can be dropping hints that Patsy might have a bit of a plan for the post office and just kind of sow the seeds of doubt with Iseult. When she starts to waver, the rest will fall away. Separate her from the herd, Ann.'

'I'll do my best, Patsy.'

Now, I don't know whether I will or not. But I'll play both sides for the time being anyway. Maybe it's not Rory who's the kingmaker around here. Maybe it's quiet old Ann Devine in her new two-piece from Marian's boutique.

Patsy goes away. I go inside and Jennifer is there, drinking coffee, watching telly. The newsreader is saying the Pope's Mass in the Phoenix Park is sold out.

'Well?'

'I'm OK, Mam,' she says. 'I'll figure it out. We had a good chat.'

'So is he going to take back the ring?'

'Shhh, Mam, no, nothing like that. It's OK, Mam. I'll figure it out.'

Good, I think, because I'm busy bringing a town together.

25.

ANN-ANN

Jennifer and Declan slope off *before the second hangover hits,* as Jennifer says. No sooner are they gone than Deirdre calls in with the two children. I put on cartoons so we can talk.

'How are they after their sugar?'

'Oh, stop, Mam. Still awake when we went back. Adam with his face stuck in a fairy cake. Norah up with him, saying his routine is all off, as if it's my fault. *Adam!* I won't tell you again. Cop. On.'

Adam is pucking his sister for no particular reason.

'I've a good mind to leave his teeth grow out through his nose. That'd put a stop to his gallop, if he looked a bit gammy. He wouldn't have too much confidence to be going out getting into trouble.'

'Your nana was like that. She didn't want us getting too glam when we were going out. *You don't want them to be seeing ye too easily girls,* she'd say. *Make them work a bit to find out what ye're like.* Are his teeth that bad? I can't see much wrong with them.'

'The whole side of his jaws, top and bottom, are growing at the wrong angle to each other. The dentist said he hadn't seen the like of it since he went off building houses out in the Philippines after a typhoon. Honestly, Mam, I feel like it's my fault. I should have spotted it when they were growing up.'

'They were fond of the soo—' I stop myself too late.

'Yes. Mam. I *know*. Thanks. The soother. That was Nora's doing. I should have put my foot down, but it's too late now, isn't it?'

It sounds like all the Devine women need to go on a course about putting their foot down.

'So Stephanie was on to me again this morning, Mam.'

'Oh. And what did she say?'

'Well . . . she said if we were really interested she would get straight on it when she went back. She knows already of a job I could do, and Kevin might have something for Hughie. We could live with them. They've loads of room. It's too warm to go now, but by the autumn we could go. If we wanted to.'

'And what did you say?'

'I said we were serious.'

'Oh. I see.'

'I'm bored, Mam. Bored and no money to do anything about it. Amn't I allowed to want more out of life, Mam? Do I have to be *solid Deirdre*? Solid Deirdre and Sound Hughie rearing two children who are going to be solid and sound. Look at Auntie Ger. I used to think she was a flake, but now I'm thinking, feckit, she's dead right. Why shouldn't she go off to India learning yoga? And Freya all the better for it. And Mam, I think me and Hughie need a bit of a kick in the arse too. Ten years married, Mam, and we have *nothing* to talk about. Did you ever get bored, Mam? Of your life with Daddy and the four of us?'

221

'Well, there always seemed to be a child on the way.'

'Maybe you and Daddy gave yourselves a kick in the arse.'

'We must have been doing it wrong.'

'You're a filthy oul wan, Mam.'

I'll miss these chats if she goes. I must have a sad look on me because she tries to reassure me.

'Mam, nothing's definite. We're just *thinking* about it, and it could be months yet. I'm sorry about what I said about the money. Is Daddy OK about it? He looked awful hurt for a while.'

'Your daddy never wanted money for its own sake, only for what it could do. But he never had anything specific in mind that he wanted to do with it. So we never chased money. Ye could have turned out a lot worse with more money and ponies.'

'Yeah, Mam, about Stephanie. She was asking me, *Does Ann not like me?* She was hurt over you saying she was taking your family away. Stung, Mammy. You might give her a ring, or talk to her or something. You're not the type to have rows, Mam. You've no practice at it. You're a diplomat. And tell Freya not to be sniping at her either.'

Deirdre and the children leave half an hour later. I nearly squeeze the children too hard when I'm saying goodbye. It hits me that I might only see them a few times before they go. I feel lonely. I ring my friend Sally Considine, who I haven't spoken to in *ages*. She picks up on the second go.

'Hello stranger,' says Sally. 'I've hardly seen you at all this summer. I hear you're mixing in new circles.'

'Oh, stop, Sally.' And I tell her my woes about my four children, mother, niece, the local TD and a closing post office.

She clucks just the right amount and takes my side where necessary and says nothing when I'm being unreasonable. As a good friend should do.

'It would be nice to have a bit of a distraction from it all, Sally.'

'I'm finding the days terrible long, Ann. And Donal doesn't exactly shorten them.'

Sally is a widow and Donal is her only son. A bachelor who is well into his forties. Fine and happy living with his mammy and no hurry to move out. A mournful oul slob. Her words, not mine.

'I'd be lost only for the book club.'

'I keep meaning to go.'

'Do! They'd love to have you. They're fairly *grande* for around here. You know a few of them.'

'I do. I'm almost certain I got clothes in the charity shop that belonged to one or two. What are ye reading at the moment?'

'Don't mention the war! It's *The Wife's Wife* by Zoron Malesttra.'

'It sounds difficult.'

'Ann, it's an ordeal. I'm on a page now that is just describing how they make almond paste, and it goes on for ever. I'd be faster buying the ingredients and making it myself. But it's the wine and the chat I go for.'

I have my second brainwave of the month.

'Sally, do you think I could come and do you think I could bring a friend?'

'I don't see why not. Why don't I text Laura, who's hosting it, and ask? Who's the friend? Is she presentable?'

'Too presentable, Sally. It's Stephanie Rourke.'

Sally whistles. 'I'll have to wash my hair for that, Ann, maybe get a new blouse. Hang on two tics. I'll ask Laura now.'

Within a few minutes she rings back and reads out a text.

'*We would be delighted, Sally. The more the merrier.* They'd be intrigued about you, Ann. You're sort of prominent but you don't be out socializing with them, so they don't know what to make of you. I'll drop up the book to you later.'

We say our goodbyes and I steel myself and ring Stephanie.

'Hello, Stephanie.'

'Who is this?'

'It's Ann. You know, Ann. Ann-Ann.'

'Oh, *Ann*! Sorry, I answered you on the Bluetooth.'

'How are you after last night?'

'What a night, Ann! So much to unpack . . .'

I blurt it out. 'Would you like to go to book club with me?'

'Ehmmmm . . . wow . . . that's . . . ehm . . . random. Who would be there?'

I name the poshest people I think might be at it. I won't tell Sally I left her out of the list in favour of Laura Bracken, Lily Corcoran and others from the golfy, tennis, bridgey crowd.

She makes a clicky thinking noise at the other end.

'Um . . . yeah. So, it would actually be super-useful for me to meet some of those ladies. A lot of women your age are starting to branch out, travel a bit more, and we're trying to get your cohort to Choose Dubai. When is it?'

'Tomorrow night. Sorry for the short notice. We wouldn't have to read the book. It's *The Wife's Wife*, so it's way too hard.'

'Actually I read that on the flight over, so that's perfect! Well, thank you, Ann. That's a nice invitation. I might even head back to Marian's now for a gúna for it. Care to join me?'

I politely but very quickly refuse. I've done enough outreach for one day.

As it happens, I end up wishing I'd said yes and gone with Stephanie, because I get a panicky phone call from Tracy. Brian has a doctor's appointment and needs someone to sit with Nonie while he's gone, and Patricia, the girl Tracy had arranged to do it, has just called in sick. I'm not her first choice. A succession of people *can't make it* or, to be more accurate, can't stomach it, and so it falls into my lap. I always feel my own stomach tighten when I have to go up there, but today I feel a little edge of curiosity too. Sylvester had said to me that Nonie *changed* all those years ago. She went sour. And I suppose I've been thinking about her as the girl she once was. What happened to cause that sourness?

There is a taxi outside their house and Brian is at the door, waiting for me. He waves and gets into it and goes off.

Sometimes Nonie's a bit rambly and I can get away with a visit where she hardly registers I'm there. But today she's spoiling for a fight. When I step through the door she's in the hall, glaring. She aims her first one at me, right between the eyes.

'I heard the daughter is getting married to that boy from Dublin. The fella that doesn't talk. He must have money. The women in your family all married above themselves.'

I take a deep breath. 'Good morning, Nonie. How are you? Brian is off gallivanting?'

She ignores what I say and I edge her chair out of the hall and into the kitchen and busy myself getting her tablets out and a snack to have before them. I ask to put on the radio. She says don't. Then she asks me am I putting on the radio or what am I doing? And how did I ever get a qualification in nursing? There must have been an amnesty. Was there an amnesty? I tell her no and, for the umpteenth time, that I was in the Middlesex Hospital in London and they didn't find anything wrong with me, and she says they must have been stuck that year. We've played this bad-tempered game before.

But for all this, she still lets me wash her upper body and her face and brush her hair. I ask does she want make-up, and she says Brian does a much nicer job and I'd make her look like a banshee. I don't know what she's basing that on. I wear no make-up on the job.

I suppose you could call the way she treats me bullying, but can you be bullied by an old woman who is stuck in a chair and gets sores on her back and has to be helped to the toilet? We are an odd pair. I am doing the most intimate of jobs, tenderly, and she's there barking at me but still letting me. She even goes quiet when I'm brushing her hair, as if she's soothed by it.

When Nonie is all spick and span, I check if there's washing up, but Brian has the place spotless. A neat man who has devoted his life to her is not going to be leaving teabags in the sink. I sit down and we watch *Gals Gab*, the morning show that does be on before *Loose Women*. They are deep into a conversation about whether you should ask your boyfriend to wax you. Nonie won't let me change the channel.

'Will Denis do that, will he, Ann?'

I don't answer that one. Because an email has just arrived in on my phone.

FATHER JOE DONNEGAN PP KILSUDGE – high importance!!

I open it. Father Joe is shouting all the way through.

TICKETS GONE DISASTER

HELLO ALL

MY DEAR PARISHIONERS, IT HAS COME TO MY ATTENTION THAT DUE TO CIRCUMSTANCES BEYOND OUR CONTROL OUR APPLICATION FOR PARISH TICKETS FOR THE PAPAL MASS AT PHOENIX PARK WAS NOT PROCESSED AND WE HAVE NO PARISH TICKETS. I WOULD ADVISE YOU TO MAKE YOUR OWN ARRANGEMENTS TO OBTAIN A TICKET.

YOURS IN JESUS,
JOE DONNEGAN PP

'Oh, shite.' And I said it out loud.

'What is it, Miss Hoare?'

'Nothing, Nonie. Nothing for you to worry about.' But I'm shook. I'm never shook around her. She's perturbed by the new development.

'Spit it out, Ann.'

She sounds almost kind. I tell her about the tickets.

'That's bad news for Margaret. She would have loved to see the Pope. It's sold out, you know.'

'Yes, Nonie.'

'She'll be very disappointed. And you could have got her the tickets.'

'I could, Nonie.'

'Five hundred thousand tickets, they say. Gone.'

She starts laughing. 'Oh God, Ann. After all these years, Margaret won't be going again. Oh, that's a good one.'

Some little switch in me goes on. For the first time, I lose it with Nonie.

'What is the matter with you, Nonie, hah? What's going on in your bitter little head?'

'You're shouting at me, and you a carer. You should be ashamed of yourself.' She has tears in her eyes now. And I am ashamed.

'I'm sorry, Nonie.'

'I'm reporting you, Miss Hoare.'

She's always threatening to complain. She gives me the silent treatment then and we watch the rest of *Gals Gab*. While I wait for Brian to come back, I compose myself by checking all my 'notifications'.

The WhatsApp groups are going mad over the tickets – Family, Neighbourhood Watch, Tidy Towns, even Neighbourhood High Alert (the breakaway Neighbourhood

Watch one for people who thought the original one wasn't worrying enough about crime). They're all asking about the tickets. Asking me! As if I'm Ticketmaster.

My phone is full of Iseult too, but not about tickets. She's set up a joint protest on the day of the post office's closure. *Kilsudgeon Tidy Towns and Nuatha Invite you to Fight Back.* And by the looks of things she's invited lots of people. Gordon is texting me *Nuatha????* from his wine tour.

I meet Brian in the hall as he comes back in. I tell him how I snapped at Nonie.

'There'll be no report,' he says. 'We need you now more than ever.'

26.

WHO IS SHE RIDING?

Denis drops me and Sally up to Laura's for the book club. The front yard is full. I can see Stephanie's tank parked up already. The night is warm and the front door is open. The sound of women talking floats out along the hall. Laura welcomes me in.

'Ann! So delighted you could get here. We're out the back. Your lovely daughter-in-law is already here. Thank you so much for bringing her along. We could always do with new blood.'

She guides me down the hall and out to the garden, where eight or nine women are gathered around a table. They are horsing into the wine already. Stephanie is the centre of attention. She's standing behind three of them, showing the ladies something on her phone.

'I am telling you, girls, this is way more achievable than you'd think. Come see us all in Dubai, haha.'

There'll be no one left in Kilsudgeon by the time she's finished.

She comes over and gives me a hug.

'You were so good to come at short notice, Stephanie.'

She has her copy of the book tucked under her arm with bookmarks and Post-its and the whole lot sticking out of it. I take out my own copy that Sally had dropped up.

A few more arrive. I sit tight to Sally. She would be of the same status as me, although she's more comfortable in that set. I'm nervous. I flick through the book, desperately trying to remember the few pages of it I read last night.

As we sit around the table, there's very little talk about the book. A lot of time is spent on what so-and-so's child is up to now, and I'm taking in congratulations for Jennifer. The story goes around about the proposal and I don't let on Jennifer was cursing into my ear in a toilet and crying into a gin and tonic on the back porch. They start talking about the post office and, the way they have it, I'm leading the campaign to keep it open because Iseult Deasy has told everyone that's the way. No wonder Patsy thinks I'm his inside man. The conversation drifts then to the rumours about what they're going to do with the post office and how Iseult said on Facebook there'd be asylum-seekers moved in there. Pamela Power says she wouldn't have *anything against the refugees, especially the grand Syrians we saw on the news, it's the others.*

'Eastern Europeans,' proclaims Alice Meagher. 'Did you know the latest now? The Moldovans are stealing turf out of sheds and mixing it with hash. They call it *cutting it*.'

'They'll cut the turf, but will they foot it?' I say, joking.

Alice doesn't get the joke.

'I don't know, Ann. I wouldn't put *anything* past them.'

There are mutters of agreement about things they *saw on Facebook*. Vandalism and stealing fireplaces and stealing dogs. I don't know what I've wandered into here. Is this who Iseult is appealing to? She doesn't need any mad Druids or Davey

Finnerty around her at all, as far as I can see. Kilsudgeon high society are all set to join a new party. Freya would not like me staying silent here.

'Every group has its troublemakers, I suppose.' That's the best I can manage. It sounds weak.

Laura gently eases us away from the vandalism, and a few other isms too. I am fit to eat my hand at this stage, and I drink my wine too fast. If she had a few nuts, it would keep my hands busy, but we're waiting for canapés that are in the oven. Already I can feel myself being a bit warmed up. *Mind yourself, Ann, don't be having another Brussels*, I tell myself. But that was beer. Wine is different. It has a habit of sneaking up on you. I hope I don't have to say much. Eventually, mercifully, Laura goes in and comes back with a tray of sausage rolls and other nibbly bits and taps a glass.

'Now, ladies, we'll have to talk about the book before we get too well on. What did ye think? Who wants to go first?'

Sally has assured me they won't ask me about *The Wife's Wife*. It's about a woman who has some sort of a gift, but I don't know yet what it is. And she turns up as a different person all through the ages – as a queen in one bit and then as a man fighting for ISIS. And there's one chapter I glanced at where she's a fish. *Devastating*, said the *New York Times*. The only bit I can remember for definite is a bit of sex early on, but even that lost me.

'Now, Ann and Stephanie, don't worry, we won't expect you to contribute to the discussion at such short notice.'

'Actually, ladies,' says Stephanie, 'I *binged* on this on the flight over.' And Stephanie launches into a discussion of the book. 'I met the author in Sharjah, at a corporate literary event I was curating, and I'm so glad because that helped inform my own view.'

The women hang on Stephanie's every word. This is a nicely turned-out room, but she's like someone off the telly.

'It's really a fascinating exploration of what it means to be a woman. This is something I've always been interested in, the complex interplay of gender identity and culture. Because Dubai is soooo multicultural. A real melting-pot. She combines, I guess, the historical background with some very contemporary points . . .'

And so on. Stephanie finishes a big long sentence with the word 'dialectic' in it and, when she has them in the palm of her hand, she gives them me on a plate.

'But here I am, taking over things. Ann, what did you think?'

'I suppose . . . as you said, Stephanie, it was . . . good, like . . . there were good bits in it . . . you don't know what is going to happen next, I suppose. With the different . . . ammmm . . . places, and then she's, well, yes . . . then I think does she turn into a man for one bit . . .'

Someone coughs. I lose my train of thought completely, which is easy because I don't have any train of thought. I'm desperately trying to remember the only bit of the book I read.

'. . . and the bit on the ship, that was good. You really know you're on a ship, like. It's windy.'

I dry up. They're looking at me. They say, don't they, about time slowing down when you're under stress? There's no sign of that happening. But maybe the wine hits the right bit of my brain at the right time, and *in vino veritas* and all that.

'Lookit, girls, I have to admit . . .'

G'wan says the wine.

'. . . I . . . I couldn't make head nor tale of the shagging thing. Honestly, I'm sorry now and on my first time here to be acting the gom, but for the bit of it I read, and I'm sure the woman that wrote it is very clever, but she lost me completely. You'll have to move on to the next person because I'm no good for this.'

There is silence. Thanks a million, wine.

'Oh, thank God,' says Laura, and bursts out laughing. 'I couldn't read it either. Fair play to you, Stephanie, you're a better woman than me, but Ann, I'm like you. I was dreading talking about it.'

Aileen Salmon, a woman I've never spoken to before, says, 'Ann, I thought it was a bag of shite. Stephanie, I'll try to give it another go based on what you said, but I can't promise.'

They all chime in then. Alice Meagher says she hardly slept last night for worrying about the book and thank God someone put her out of her misery.

'And did any of ye get to the first sex scene?'

'Which one was that, Carmel, the one with the fisherman?'

'Here it is, girls. Hold on.' Carmel has been licking her thumb and paging. She looks at us over her glasses. 'As if I didn't know exactly where it was. Wait now.'

Dirty laughs ripple around. Carmel makes a big show of clearing her throat.

'*She lies back, examining her own form, distractedly aloof. The sfumato-like shadow across her proud form delicately flutters as her lover drowsily gets up, dresses in his diaphanous gown and proceeds to the bureau, where he resumes his work. Conjuring words from ephemeral thoughts. She goes to the window and stares at the . . . oleag . . . oleagan . . .*'

'Oleagenous,' says Laura.

'. . . oleagenous *vista below as his rhythmic typing echoes around the wooden frames of the house. She cries out as a pang strikes her. A soupçon of doubt. A thousand miles and a thousand years away on a ship, someone hears her invocation across the four dimensions . . .*'

'Awful stuff,' says a woman whose name I don't know. 'And I hate them books written in the present, you know,

I do this and I go over to the window. I mean, like, it obviously happened already or we wouldn't be reading about it in a book.'

'True for you, Bernie. That was the way we all started reading books.'

I get a rush of wine to the head and open my gob again. 'And then, like, *who* is she riding if she thinks that's what happens? Denis would be asleep. He'd no more type afterwards than he would drive a train. Out for the count.'

There is no reaction for a second. Feck, I think, I've gone too far. But then there are howls of laughter.

'*Who is she riding?*' says Laura. 'That should be the name of the book. Oh Ann, you're a scream. They've no idea of the real world, do they?'

We have a right old time of it for the rest of the night. They are nicely indiscreet. Very personal about themselves. I slow down on the wine. I won't be sharing everything just yet. They're used to each other, no problem talking about hormones and whatnot.

'So what about Denis? Does he take Viagra?' One of my new best friends, Gobnait, lands this one on me out of the blue.

'Not that I know of anyway.'

'Oh, Ann, you'd know.' And they all laugh and I laugh too.

One of the women is a divorcee, it turns out. She's only starting going out and she's full of tales of the latchikos that are out there. I don't envy her at all. God, I don't know what I'd do without Denis.

'I went on an internet date last week,' Sally says quietly. 'Donal gave him the third degree when he came to the door. *What do you do for a living?* he says to your man, as if Donal does anything for a living.'

'What did he do for a living?'

'He was an oil man. Heating oil, not the rich kind. I think Donal is afraid he's going to lose his mammy to someone else.'

'Donal needs a kick up the arse,' says Laura. 'You've done plenty for him, Sally.'

'Ah, I know, Laura, but he's a bit helpless.'

After another half an hour Stephanie announces that she has to go. She hasn't been drinking. I walk her out.

'I had such a lovely time, Ann. You know, it can be a bit lonely in Dubai. I get lonely, too, Ann. There isn't much fun out there. A lot of arseholes. And the children my children meet. Spoilt. I won't keep Deirdre, I promise. I just . . . well, I wanted a bit of company for a while. Do you forgive me?'

We say goodbye with a hug. I feel lighter.

When I go back in, Laura is holding *The Wife's Wife*.

'Before we get too merry, girls, what are going to do with this?'

'Take it to the charity shop,' mutters someone.

'I wanted to read the gangster one anyway,' says Alice. 'I love the gangsters.'

Unless you think they're stealing turf, I say to myself.

'What about the one with the Dublin crime boss escaping to Dubai?'

'*Sheikh Evac?*'

Laura is about to say more when the doorbell rings. She goes out to the hall. I can hear a man's voice. It's Denis. Oh feck. I told him I'd text him to get me, but it must be gone late.

The next thing, Denis is brought through, blinking, into the light. The women are giving me winks.

'He looks like a man who doesn't need assistance all right,' says the divorcee. She's joking, but I can see her eyeing him up. I try look at him again objectively, to see what she sees. You're supposed to do that, they say in the books. Just ogle your partner. It's hard to get into the habit. And Denis doesn't help with his ould jumpers. He puts on an innocent face, but I'd say he loves the attention.

'A fine deck this,' he says to Flora. 'I love natural wood.' This is too much for some of them.

'So we heard, Denis,' says someone, and there's an awful filthy cackle out of us.

'Can I give anyone else a lift?' he says.

'You've already given us a lift, Denis,' says Laura.

Our departure is marked by a round of hugs and kisses and promises to come back, and I am told several times that I am *gas* and a *scream* and a *tonic* and other good things besides. I might even read another chapter of *The Wife's Wife*. I need something to help me sleep.

27.

LOW-KEY LOLLING

I've a busy day ahead. The full normal roster of work, which means another dose of Nonie, after the unexpected extra visit the other day, and Mam needs her hair washed again. She's very sweaty in the head these days with the heat, even though she's frozen. The thermostat goes on older models after a while. On top of all that, Freya and Isla will be using the house as a *studio*. I'll have to get the place ready. They'll be doing selfies around the place and the last thing we need is the whole of the internet looking at a pair of Denis's underpants poking out from under a cushion.

I get started with Mam, to get that job out of the way. Of course, there's only one thing on her mind.

'MAKE SURE YOU GET THE TICKETS, ANN. I. DO. NOT. WANT. TO MISS THE POPE COMING AGAIN. DO YOU HEAR ME NOW? I *HAVE* TO BE THERE. GO EASY WITH THE SHAMPOO, ANN.'

'Mam, for the last time, I am not too rough with you. I've washed a thousand heads. Will you just relax into it? Now, is the water the right temperature?'

We take a while to agree on the temperature.

'Your nails are a bit battered, Mam. Will I give them a going over while your hair is drying?'

'DO, SO. DON'T BE PUTTING ON ANYTHING TOO BRIGHT. I'M GOING NOWHERE.'

I give her head a final rub of the towel.

'GO EASY, YOU'LL TAKE THE HEAD OFF ME.'

There is no way that neck of hers would give way so easy. It's the hardest thing about her. I give it one last rub, give her ears a squeak and pop in the hearing aids. She doesn't resist. She holds her hands out, examining them.

'I always had nice hands, didn't I, Ann?'

'You did, Mam. You still do.'

And she does. They're young enough hands. Mam always looked after her hands. She always liked her arms, and a good bit of the rest of her body, to tell you the truth. She might give out a bit about Ger and her ways – *She always suited herself, that wan* – but Mam was never a martyr. Ger has more of Mam's grace. I'm a bit lumpy, like poor old Charlie.

'We were supposed to go the last time, Ann,' Mam eventually says.

'Go where, Mam?'

'To see the Pope. John Paul the Second. The Polish fella. Do you remember him?'

'I do remember him, Mam.'

She's silent again for a while. I think this is because she wants to be given a nudge.

'It was October, wasn't it?'

'Thirtieth September, 1979. It was all arranged. But then . . .'

238

There is a knock to the door. I can tell from the knock it's Bim. He goes *Bang-bang ba-bang-bang*.

Mam hasn't heard the knock, it seems. I might try and sort this out myself.

'One second there, Mam,' I say. 'I must just get the nail-varnish remover.'

I go out to the door.

'Well, Ann. Is herself around? I was hoping to get a word with her.'

'It wouldn't suit now, Bim. Can I pass on a message to her?'

'No, I'll get her again.'

'She'll want to know the message.'

He fiddles with his ear. 'There's talk.'

'What talk?'

'Nonie is going around saying things.'

'What going around is Nonie doing? She's housebound.'

'Well, she's saying things.'

'To who?'

'To me.'

'When did she see you?'

'I was there doing a job on a door.'

'Well, what's the talk?'

'About Margaret.'

'What's Nonie saying?'

'I can't say, really. I should tell Margaret myself.'

'She's in the bath.'

She's not, but it's all I can think to get rid of him. He doesn't question why a decent Kilsudgeon woman like Margaret Hoare would be having a bath in the morning, like she was Princess Margaret.

'What did she say about my mother, Bim?'

239

He looks around and rubs his mouth with his hand. 'That your mother should be ashamed of herself, going around to Sylvester's.'

'Sylvester's? I brought her. What's the harm in that?' I'm bluffing now. I shouldn't have brought her with me on a work visit.

'Taking advantage of Sylvester, Nonie says.'

'What? What does she think we were doing? That's some imagination she has.'

'Now, Ann, you know what she's like.'

'And you know what she's like, too, so what did you go telling her we were up there for?'

'I. Did. No. Such. Thing. Ann.'

I straighten up and start drying my hands on a tea-towel, as forcefully as I can.

'You did, Bim. You were stirring it. Well, you can forget about visiting Mam for a while. If your visits are upsetting me, I don't know what they'll do to her.'

That shakes him, as I'd hoped.

'Now now, Ann, I'm only telling you what she said. She was spitting, Ann. Spitting. She said it was your mother's revenge on her to be going after Sylvester.'

'Revenge for what?'

'She wouldn't say. She said your mother would know.'

'I'll pass on the message, Bim. Thanks ever so much.' I'm pure sarcastic with him, but he mightn't know sarcasm. Bim has only the one speed on the gearbox.

As I close the door on him I hear the door into the sitting room close behind me, so I walk down the hall slowly to give Mam time to get away, but she's still sneaking away when I get in. Somehow, she has found the remote control. Which I can *never* find when I am looking for it. She's after pressing the wrong button, so she's there fretting in front of a big blue screen.

'WHAT'S THAT HDMI THING? I WANT THE ANGELUS. I WANT THE ANGELUS OFF THE TELLY.'

'It'll be a while, Mam. It's only ten o'clock.'

'Say it with me anyway, so.'

And off we go. I can just about hang in there with three bits. She goes into the 'Hail Holy Queen'. She's taking me through the long grass now, lads. The 'Hail Holy Queen' was a prayer I could never get a handle on. It's the first time the two of us have prayed together in our house since my father died. Two ould wans. Praying together with the smell of acetone around the place and HDMI floating around on the screen. When we're finished, I turn off the telly and check her head to see has the hair dried.

'Now so, Mam. We'll get your nails done up nice and then I'll give you a blow-dry.'

'You got shut of Bim, Ann.'

'I did, Mam.'

'What did he want?'

'Telling me he meant to drop something off and that he forgot to bring it.'

She doesn't buy it. As I finish her nails she opens up the past again.

'It was your father, Ann, the poor man.'

'What about Daddy, Mam?'

'He wanted me back up on a pedestal, Ann. He was terrible ashamed over the Court Case.' And she goes quiet again.

'He says to me, *I won't have you standing around with the rest of the hoi polloi.* That was the way he'd be, you know.'

'I do know, Mam.'

That was Daddy. The man for the big gesture.

'He wanted to make it up to me.'

Mam's eyes are closed. I wonder has she dozed off. But her forehead is scrunched up, as if words inside that she hasn't said yet are paining her.

Then we have a nicer interruption because right then Freya decides to start her day. She comes in, headphones on, sees us and naturally thinks straight away it's about her because she's fifteen.

'There's something heavy going down here. Is this about the podcast?'

'No, love.'

'Look at this fine girl sleeping away on this lovely day. Go out there into the fresh air, Freya,' says Mam.

The moment is passed for now and I've to go on my rounds. Neans and Babs Cronin are asking me when should they turn up to the post office for the protest and will I be organizing transport? I tell them I'm still *ironing out details*, like I have a notion of what's going on. I do my breathing and march straight into Nonie's, expecting fire and brimstone, but she doesn't say a word to me. The mouth is set closed all the way through. Normally, I work out how happy she is from the levels of sniping but, today, nothing. Maybe she's happy the message has been sent.

Except, just before I go, she says, 'So that's it, is it, Ann? That's how ye get back at me? Through Sylvester.'

I don't stay around to ask questions. I head up to Sylvester. There's no reply at the door. I let myself in. I shout around the house, but there's nothing. An awful thought strikes me. Has something happened to him? Is that what Nonie's words were about? I go to ring the office and then I see that I have a text from Tracy. This is it now. She's found out about the visit. But no.

Hey hun Sylvester rescheduled due to appointment. Will tomorrow do?

I'm too relieved to be cross.

28.

'CHILDISH GAMBINO' IN IRISH

By the time I get home, a strange scene awaits me. Freya and Isla – agrihun – are in the sitting room with Mam. Freya and Isla are sitting next to each other on the couch, with a microphone on a stack of books between them. Mam is across the way in her favourite chair, reading her missal and looking very settled. I can tell from the look on Freya's face that Mam's presence wasn't part of the plan.

The first person to say hello to me isn't even in the room. It's Lossie, who's on the laptop, looking out at the other two.

'*Conas atá tú*, Mrs Devine?' she says.

'Lossie? Eh . . . *ceart go leor*, I suppose? You must be still in the Gaeltacht?'

'*Fan noimead*.' And she goes off to close the door behind her. 'Sorry, lads. I have to speak in Irish all the time here or I'll be thrown out. It's super-fascist here. They already sent Zane Hartigan home.'

'Zane? No way!' says Freya.

'Yeah, we all have to sing "Childish Gambino" in Irish and we're all there going, *Yo fear gorm, faigh d'airgead, faigh d'airgead*, and Zane was like, *Tá sé sin LOADASHITE*. He was on a warning already.'

'It's so tough being middle class. You have been through so much.'

Lossie laughs. 'Oh, shut up you, Freya, you'd be down here in a heartbeat, shifting all round you at the *céilí*.'

Freya glances at Mam in her chair and then at me. There's no stir out of Mam. She has no intention of going anywhere.

'Mam, do you want to leave these girls do their thing?'

'No, Ann, I'm grand. Don't mind me, girls. I'm too old to be offended now.'

Isla smiles. 'Yeah, actually, I record some of mine out in the milking parlour. It's a trend in podcasts now, family in the background – adds to the richness. Remember my bit on putting on fake tan for a night out and then doing the milking? I couldn't shut Daddy up in it, and it was the most downloaded one. Authenticity, babes.'

Freya accepts this. She likes agrihun a lot.

They finally get up and running. Freya starts the introductions.

'Welcome to *The Culchie Feminist* with me, Freya, and . . .'

'. . . me, Lossie.'

'We're coming to you live from Kilsudgeon Studios.'

'Your Auntie Ann's sitting room.'

'My Auntie Ann's sitting room and . . .'

'. . . the GAELTACHT, where I am TOTALLY ILLEGALLY speaking English, *ag troid igcoinne an* power! Oh shite, sorry, someone just walked past.'

'A LASAIRFHIONA, AR CHUALA ME BEARLA ASTU?' There's a voice from somewhere else in the room.

'*Nior chuala tú faic, Clodagh . . . Chogair*, lads, I'll have to go. It's too dodgy, unless you want to do the podcast in Irish?'

'Sorry, L, we have, like, four listeners. I don't want to lose them. I'll get you at the end for the Newsround.'

'Sound. *Slán*.' And Lossie is gone.

'OK, everyone, hope you heard all that. Lossie was live from Irish school there, but we still have AGRIHUN! Aka Isla Welch. Welcome.'

And they start talking about Isla's career as agrihun.

'The first video was just me lipsyncing . . .'

'Love a bit of lip-syncing.'

'. . . on a silage bale.'

'Uh oh, cancelled. Silage is soooo bad for biodiversity.'

'I know, right? But Daddy's gone too old for hay. I wanna, like, turn the whole farm into a nature reserve one day, but . . . you know . . .'

'Gotta do the numbers.'

'Gotta. Do. The. Numbers.'

I'm enjoying this chat, I have to say. It's a great way of getting local gossip. These girls don't seem to give a hoot who's listening because Isla goes TO TOWN on some young lad who said she had *nice tits for a small girl*. And then they talk about her mother and when she died of cancer and Isla cries a little.

'Ah, the poor girl,' says Mam from the chair, and Freya has to introduce her 'audience', and she gets us to clap and Mam claps one hand on the side of the chair on account of her bockety arm.

After about twenty minutes Freya says 'thank you' and I think they're done and I get up to see would anyone like a sausage sandwich, but Freya says no, Isla is going to interview *her* next. So they switch the whole thing around and

Isla starts asking questions. And I see why Freya is anxious about Mam being there. Isla is asking her about the referendum campaign and taking abuse from ould lads on the street. Freya is cagey and glancing over to Mam to see her reaction. Mam is listening.

'I . . . I, well, I did a few leaflets.'

'Are ye talking about the referendum?' Mam asks.

This is it now, I think to myself. The row we all avoided during the campaign.

'Wasn't it great all the same?'

And that's all she'll say. The two girls stare at each other. Then at Mam. I stare at Mam. Isla coughs.

'And the big scandal of the parish, Freya,' Isla says, changing the subject. 'What do you make of it? No tickets for the Pope. What's the goss on that, Freya? Where are the missing tickets?'

Oh no! Why did she have to bring that up? They've no discretion at all, these influencers. I can see the news hitting Mam like a wave. She lets out a wail.

'Ann! You said they'd have tickets.'

'Mam, I thought . . .'

'I knew I should have written off for them.'

'We were promised . . .'

'I have to go to it, Ann. I *have* to.'

'We'll sort it, Mam. I promise you.'

She stares straight ahead then starts speaking to I'm not sure who.

'I have to see that Pope, Ann. There hasn't been a day goes by, Ann, when I don't think about it.'

Why is she so upset about the Pope?

'He says to me, *You're not going to be standing out in the rain with the locals. I'll get us a VIP*. Do you remember him going on about the VIP? Your father's VIP letter was to arrive in the post. We all waited for it. But we never ended up going. He swore blind to me he'd sent off for it. That was Eddie the Pump's way of making it up to him after the Court Case.'

I look at the two girls as if to say, *I'll explain later*. Mam is still talking.

'*If you keep my name out of it, Charlie, we'll see right by you. I know a few people in Opus Dei. We'll have you serving Mass to the Pope and Margaret doing the offertory.* And I was high as a kite again, thinking I'll be up there for all the world to see. Back up on show, after hiding my face for years after the Court Case. We waited for the postman, day in, day out. Nothing. Your father was selling detergent for a while, and he'd come home and he'd know from my face there was nothing.

'The day before the Pope was supposed to be in the Phoenix Park, I nabbed the postman. I said, *Are you hiding letters out of jealousy?* He said he wasn't, that he didn't know what was in the post. I was shouting at him that there should be a letter there with "Opus Dei" on the outside of it.

'Charlie came home that night, and I ate him, Ann. I ate the poor man alive. He'd let me down again. And he was crying, Ann. I said some shocking things to your father, Ann. But he'd let me down. I told him to go off to Nonie.'

I have to ask. 'What about Nonie, Mam?'

'I think your father was carrying on with Nonie.'

I feel like everything in the room is very far away. For some reason, my attention is fixed only on a half-dead geranium in the window and the whirr of the clock, which I normally wouldn't hear because it's supposed to be one of the silent ones. Even the girls are quiet. Affairs happened on *Dallas*. JR had affairs. Not Daddy. I mean, he was a charmer, but not for one second would I picture him sneaking around the houses. A car parked for too long outside one area. Affairs are for other families. Except for Ger, who told me there was a married man in the area whose wife was an awful wagon and he was lonely, and she *saw* him a couple of times, but only *a bit of a smooch*, she said. But that was different. No, Daddy was not supposed to be a man to have an affair. And with *Nonie*? Oh God. I can't go up there again.

'Mam?'

'Ann, he told me on his knees he didn't go near her. That he was only up there doing a few jobs. You know your father never really had any kind of a proper job. He was always just tipping away at something. And he could have been good at anything. I kept saying will you go working with Paddy Furlong or Andy Lynch or one of the big operators around and get something steady, and all he would say is, *Charlie Hoare is his own man and he'll make his own way.* That's why I have a soft spot for Bim, because he's his own man too. Even though he hasn't an ounce of charm. Your father had charm. Everyone liked him, and some liked him too much.'

'Such amazing content,' says Isla, almost in a trance. But the shocked looks on me and Freya tell her a different story and she corrects herself. 'Um . . . so . . . um, yeah, I guess that's probably off the record.'

'Bring me for my nap, Ann,' says Mam. She looks hollowed out from letting out the news.

When agrihun is gone and Mam's asleep I sit in the kitchen digesting. Freya comes over and brings me tea, which is rare for her to do unbidden. She puts a hand on my shoulder.

'Thanks, pet.' And I put my hand on hers. 'Are *you* OK, Freya? It's a bit of a shock, isn't it?'

'Yeah, it is . . . ehm, Auntie Ann, I'm after doing something you won't like.'

She opens up her laptop and shows me an email. It takes me a while to see what I am looking at.

WORLD MEETING OF FAMILIES 2018 CLOSING
MASS ORANGE ROUTE CHAPELIZOD
ENTER & EXIT VIA CHAPELIZOD GATE SECTION
Phoenix Park C7
26/08/2018 15:00
MS CAITLIN MORAN

'What's this, Freya? Did you get a ticket? Who's Caitlin Moran? Is she Maura Moran's youngest?'

'Keep scrolling, Auntie Ann.'

Page after page after page of tickets pop up. Then she opens another email window. More tickets here, this time addressed to Lindy West. She opens another one, this time twenty tickets for Chimamanda Ngozi Adichie. I definitely don't know any Adichies.

'Freya, what's going on?'

'A hundred tickets, Auntie Ann. Me and Lossie did it as a joke, and we kept on putting down these names of famous feminists and they never stopped us. It was fun. I didn't know that it was going to mean no one from Kilsudgeon could go. So, Auntie Ann, can we just, like, give the tickets to, like, Nana and you and . . .?'

'Freya, forward me those tickets. We're going to have to send them to Father Donnegan and pretend it was a mix-up.'

She makes a face. 'Leave my name out of it, pleeeease?'

'Well, Freya, whose name are we putting on this? Malala?'

'My rep is toast, Auntie Ann.'

We write the email together. Freya is looking over my shoulder and sighing when I make the slightest pause while looking for a key.

'Just let me write it,' she says, but I'm not letting her near it because I know she'd ignore my advice.

To: fatherjoedonnegan55@eircom.net
Cc:
Bcc: freyakahlo@gmail.com
FW: ORDER COMPLETE: WORLD MEETING OF FAMILIES

Dear Father Joe,
Wait till I tell you what happened

'Are you trying to write the most Irish email ever, Auntie Ann?'

~~Wait till I tell you what happened~~
You're not going to believe this

'He won't.'

~~You're not going to believe this~~
The spam folder is an awful curse of a yoke

'I wouldn't open with it, Auntie Ann.'

~~The spam folder is an awful curse of a yoke~~
She's only young she didn't know what she was doing

'HEY! I knew exactly what I was doing.'

~~She's only young she didn't know what she was doing~~
I have a bit of good news for you. Unbeknownst to me, my niece Freya was ordering tickets for her nana and the rest of the family and she meant to ask for 10 but she accidentally put in 100 . . .

'No one will think I'm that much of a dumbass.'
Right so, Freya, I'll change it to *My pagan niece tried to steal the whole parish's tickets just to spite ordinary, decent Catholics.*
'OK, OK.'

. . . she accidentally sent off for 100 tickets instead of 10. Didn't it go into spam and she's only just after finding it, so she's very happy to pass it on to the parish. She won't be able to attend herself because . . .

'I'll be sacrificing goats in a black Mass.'

. . . she has to visit a friend who is leaving to go to Australia.

'Lying to a priest, Auntie Ann. Tut, and I cannot stress this enough, tut.'

'That's only happened since *you* moved into the house. Nana is supporting the referendum, I'm lying to priests, you're like *The Omen*.'

And SEND!

Father Donnegan rings me back almost straight away. He is bursting with the good news. He thinks Freya has saved his job. He wants to mention her in the newsletter. He'll try and get her a chat with the Pope. Freya watches me, aghast.

I manage to talk him down from cloud nine. He can barely contain himself. Five minutes later . . .

****FATHER JOE DONNEGAN PP KILSUDGE *****
SUBJECT: FEEDING THE MULTITUDE

HELLO ALL
'They all ate and were satisfied, and the disciples picked up twelve basketfuls of scraps that were left over.'
THERE HAS BEEN A MIRACLE! THANKS TO THE HEROIC EFFORTS OF ONE OF OUR BRIGHTEST YOUNG PEOPLE, WE NOW HAVE TICKETS TO SEE THE POPE. WELL DONE, FREYA.

He doesn't go into any detail. I'd say he knows well what might have happened. A girl who tried to take Germaine as her confirmation name doesn't start ordering tickets for the Pope as a fifteen-year-old.

'I'm ruined, Auntie Ann.'

'You'll get your reward in heaven, Freya.'

'Can I get it in bitcoin instead?'

As for my father and Nonie, it'll take more than an email to fix that.

29.

ELDERLY AFFLICTION BINGO

Mam is over the moon about the tickets and she doesn't seem to wonder what her godless granddaughter was doing ordering a hundred of them. The good mood wakes up other parts of her brain too. The next time I get ready to go to work, she wants to come.

'Mam, I've to go up to Sylvester now. Can you manage the tablets by yourself?'

'What tablets?'

'Your afternoon ones. The Voldarine and the Spartol. Two tablets for the blood pressure they found the last time.'

'I don't feel any difference with them.'

'That's the point, Mam. They're keeping things on the level. Just take them now, won't you, like a good woman?'

'I find them very confusing.'

'They're not that confusing, Mam. I've left you the bit of a sandwich. You just need to take them with food, so eat the sandwich and then there's two blisterpacks there, and when the blisterpacks are gone, you've taken them. There's nothing to forget. And Freya is around too. When she wakes up. You can thank her formally for the tickets.'

'I might drop them or something, and she'll be off galli-vanting with her friends.'

'Mam, Freya doesn't be gallivanting. She has nothing else to do.'

'I don't think you should leave me alone. I felt a bit funny this morning.'

'You were on your own all day yesterday when I was up with Nonie.'

'But I felt fine yesterday and I've forgotten how to take the tablets since. I'm gone very forgetful. It's the first thing that goes when you're on the way out. Did you say who it is you're going up to see, any harm in asking?'

She knows very well how to take them tablets, but who could blame a woman for wanting a spin out of the house and spending a bit of time with someone her own age? A man, to boot. I just wish I didn't have to be there, like a spare wheel.

'Lookit, Mam. You could get me into trouble, and with Nonie going around accusing you of all sorts, I can't be bringing you up there again.'

But she looks at me so beseechingly I can't help it.

'All right so, but you'll have to sit down low in the seat. I don't want you seen.'

Sylvester is sitting in the doorway, half in and half out of the sun, as we pull into the yard. I go over to him before extracting Mam.

'I hope you don't mind me bringing my mother.'

'MIND! Why would I mind? But Ann, I haven't a crumb to give ye. The cupboards are empty.'

Mam has hopped out herself and is shouting for her walker. I don't know where she's getting the hormones from.

We go inside. While Gavin and Stacey are reacquainting themselves, I poke around the presses and the fridge.

'You really don't have any food. What happened to the Tesco Man delivery that Mellamocare set up for you?'

'No sign of it, Ann.'

I ring up head office, putting a finger to my lips to warn Mam and Sylvester – who are giggling about something – to whisht. Tracy isn't there. Her secretary *will look into what happened, but The System is down.*

'I've been eating oats ever since yesterday morning,' Sylvester is telling Mam.

'Like a horse,' says Mam, with a dirty smile on her.

Jesus, give me strength for the next few hours.

'Like a horse is right, Peg. An old nag only fit for the knackers' yard.'

'You've a bit to go yet,' she says. 'I hope.'

'Can we go to Lidl?' he says out of the blue. 'I saw a stepladder I might buy. I was there yesterday on my travels, but I had no wallet on me.'

'Right, I'll bring ye to Lidl, but this is a one-off, OK? I'm not supposed to bring clients out. Tracy will have my guts for garters. And you're *not* going up any stepladders.'

I get the two of them into the car somehow – Mam insists on the back seat – and I go around the boot, trying to fit two walkers in.

Lidl is quiet. We are a sight going up the aisles. Me pushing the trolley slowly while my two elderly children go along after, commenting on prices and trying to put extra teacakes into the trolley.

'Get them there, Ann, they've a bit of marzipan as well as the double chocolate.'

'I am not giving you diabetes, Mam.'

'We might as well complete the elderly affliction bingo, Margaret, hah?' says Sylvester.

The two of them are egging each other on. I go off on a bit of a recce to try and speed it up. I round the corner of the herbs and nearly clank my trolley off some eejit going the wrong way around.

'Ann!'

The eejit is Tracy.

'Ann, how are you, hun? Fancy meeting you here.'

My two amigos are a little bit away. They're waylaid by the biscuits. Sylvester catches my eye and waves, but I turn away. They're too far away for me to warn them. I have to think fast. Tracy doesn't know my mother to see, and she mightn't know Sylvester out in the wild. There's a photo of him up on The System, but old people never look like their System photos. Mam knows the story with Tracy, but I can't trust her to keep her mouth absolutely shut or to say the right thing. My eyes are drawn to the array of stuff in Tracy's trolley, compared to the sliced pan, buns and rashers in mine. Tracy sees my glance.

'I'm on a clean kick at the moment. I'm trying to remove toxins from all aspects of my life. We put so much processed food into ourselves, Ann. It's no wonder cancer is going through the roof.'

She glances down into my trolley, practically bursting with cancer, and says no more on that matter.

I can hear the two approach. How will I get the message across? And what is the message? *Just don't get me into trouble.*

'Aren't they lovely, that pair?' says Tracy, pointing behind me. Sylvester and Mam have moved into our aisle and are closing in. Sylvester has picked up a leaf blower. He's off the walker, waving it around.

'Would you want one of these, Margaret?'

'I could do my perm with it,' she says.

'You've a grand head of hair. You don't want to be ruining it with a perm. Ann, what do you think?'

'Oh, stop. Haha. You're a divil.'

I can't mention his name.

'Aren't you going to introduce us?' he says grandly.

'Of course, yes. Margaret, Syl (I say his name with as much eyebrow as I can), this is Tracy, my boss in Mellamocare – sorry, Soothocare. You know, the place I work that I was telling you about?'

Could I not have picked an actual different name for him? Syl. What kind of a name is that?

'Boss! Oh, listen to her. We're colleagues. Hierarchy can be so disempowering.'

I stare so hard at them that, hopefully, they'll feel it nudging their brains.

'Very nice to meet you, Tracy. Ann's a real jewel of a carer,' says 'Syl'. 'I'm told,' he adds, and winks at me. Oh Jesus, Sylvester. No winking.

Mam links his arm. 'Yes, they all say that about her around here.'

OK, Mam, play it cool now.

'I wish she was my own daughter.'

Mammy, play it cool.

'What was it you said your name was?' Tracy says.

'Syl.'

'Oh, what's that short for?'

'Sylvie,' he says.

Agnieska, a local woman who works there, comes by, pushing a big square trolley full of doormats.

'Hello, Ann. Great to see you out, too, Margaret. Good to get out of house. How is Ann treating you?'

'Oh, we've only bumped into each other here,' says my mother.

Agnieska looks puzzled, but after twenty years she's still permanently puzzled by most of the natives of Kilsudgeon. *All these children, Ann, never outside. I ask my son would he like to bring friend fishing. No one fish in Ireland, he say. It is not a surprise you have famine.*

'You've a bandage, Syl. Did you have a bit of a tumble?' Tracy's tone has hardened ever so slightly.

'Nothing but a trifle,' he says.

'It looks like one of ours. Is it one of ours, Ann?'

I had never figured Mam for being a spur-of-the-moment kind of woman, but she manages to drop the packet of biscuits she's holding, and it bursts and goes over the floor. I stoop down to help her pick it up.

'A diversion, Ann,' she whispers to me.

I'm almost certain Tracy heard her, but she makes no mention.

'Well, I'd better pay for these concoctions before the yoghurt passes its sell-by date. It was lovely to meet you both. And Ann, I'll see you soon too?' she calls over to me.

I've edged away from them and I'm pretending to take a fierce interest in colouring books. As if I have nothing to do with my mother and the man I'm being paid to mind. And then she's gone.

'A sterling performance, Peggy,' says Syl/Sylvie/Sylvester. 'Worthy of an Oscar, my dear. I think we got away with that.'

30.

CLIENT MINUTE PER ROSTERED HOUR

Tracy: *Ann, can you come in at your earliest convenience?*

The text arrives shortly after I drop Sylvester and his shopping home. Sylvester was wrong. I didn't get away with it. *At your earliest convenience* has nothing to do with my convenience. This isn't my first rodeo. I've been in trouble in Tracy's office before. If it goes like the other ones, she'll start with some sort of a question that I can't answer. And then she'll answer it for me.

I get Mam settled and drive to the Mellamocare Local Area Office. The secretary gives me a glance of support and throws her eyes towards Tracy's door.

'Sit down there, Ann. She's in one of her moods.'

After a few minutes, Tracy waves me in. I sit down while she messes around with the mouse of her computer and puts a star next to a note in her diary. After a few seconds of very important things she has to take care of, she looks up at me.

'Ann, can I ask you a question?'

'Eh . . .' This is it now. The question with no answer.

'What do you hope to achieve in this job? What gets you up in the morning?'

I was right. The opening question designed to throw me. It's out of one of her books. If you were ever in Tracy's office, you'd see a whole shelf of business books with white covers and big writing on the front. *How to Explain Simple Things to Simple People* or *25 Ways to Make a Million* or *Getting to YEAH!* You'd never know she was working in a carer company. I could write a few of those business books myself. *How to Wash Their Backside When They're Slapping You in the Head. Difficult Daughters-in-Law. She Might Be Your Mother but You Haven't Lifted a Finger to Help Since 1998 so if You Don't Mind* . . .

She made us all read *Difficult Conversations with People Who've Made a Balls of Something*. I can't remember the exact title. But the big advice if you were about give someone a fierce lambasting was: start with a question that makes them think about where they are, so they are more receptive to feedback. So I know I'm in for it now.

'Well, I suppose, Tracy, like, I want to . . .'

She interrupts me straight away.

'So, Ann, you are already on probation. I will admit you have improved in your record-keeping. Your productivity in terms of the Client Minute per Rostered Hour is suboptimal, but in this organization we are dedicated to fostering diverse work schedules, so we've managed to align ourselves on that one. And I'd like to think I have made a personal journey in order to accommodate you, would you not agree? I have offered you the opportunity to work on prospects with Sylvester, and you've taken that opportunity. You can see I have often adopted an informal tone that hopefully has strengthened the teamwork bond, would you agree, Ann? But now, this latest incident. I sense a regression, Ann?'

I got lost halfway through her spiel. I heard *suboptimal*, which I presume is bad. But I figure it's best to agree.

'Yes, Tracy.'

'But you have abused the trust I placed in you. I extended my internal company credit significantly for you.'

'Eh?'

'I went out on a limb for you, Ann, after you endangered the brand.'

You mean when people found out the brand was going to try and bribe a TD to build a feckin Las Vegas over Kilsudgeon? But I can't say that, because no one really found that out.

'I'm sorry I endangered the brand, Tracy.'

'And now this. Where do I begin? Bringing the client out of the Agreed Care Zone. Encouraging the client to exceed Agreed Levels of Independence. Failure to Disclose Pre-existing Extra-Roster Non-relevant Client-care Commitments.'

I must have the blankest look on my face for this one.

'Looking after Margaret Hoare.'

'That's my mother.'

'But you didn't tell us . . . and, finally, Encouraging . . .' She clears her throat. I think she is winding up for the big one. 'Encouraging a client to fraternize with . . . *the carer's own mother.* Ann, how do you feel when you hear all that? Ann, that is unforgivable. Now, Ann, this is all written down in my report.' She points at her screen. 'That report is ready to be uploaded to Global Issue Resolution. Global, Ann. This is big. But I am not ready to send that report yet, Ann. Do you know why?'

'I don't.'

'I am going to give you another chance. Your *last* chance. For one reason. Do you know that reason?'

'Because my clients like me?'

'No, Ann. Because this organization empowers me to take initiatives myself. You are still on probation. You have one last chance to win me over. No more mistakes, no more revelations. I want us to be active partners on this journey. Can you do that, Ann? No more probation. Just direct. Woman to woman. One more chance. Let me down and you're out.'

She turns back to her computer and starts typing and making notes, and I take that to mean we're finished. I go outside. The secretary walks me out, signalling she wants the goss.

'How did you get on?' she says when we are out in the main corridor.

'I still have a job anyway.'

'For a while, anyway, Ann. There's another award she's in for. A HR one. I see her emails and she has nominated you as a special project. A test case for Compassionate Conversations for Non-adversarial Exit Outcomes. It means how to get rid of you without any employment tribunals. Don't ask. I'm sure it'll happen to me eventually, but then she knows I know too much. And Tracy has her skeletons too.'

'Oh? What are they?'

'I'm not telling you. They're for my own use, Ann.'

'Even for a few Double Deckers?'

'Haha, you cheeky thing. I'm not that easily swayed. And I'm eating energy bars now, anyway.'

'I've no bargaining chip over you at all so,' I say, laughing.

'That's right, Ann. We're paid shite, but secretaries hold all the power. And don't say "chip" in front of me when I'm hungry.'

We leave it at that. She's a good sort. I'm walking out to my car when the phone goes. I answer without looking and regret it. It's Iseult, ringing to fill me in on preparations for the post office protest, which is happening on Saturday.

'So Ann, I was thinking we could start first with the core group at the fairy field and then assemble with all the locals at the post office. Some of the guys want to harness the field's energy. You know the way it's supposed to be a portal to the otherworld? I mean, look, it's not for everyone, but I think the heritage angle will do huge numbers on social. And don't worry about the promotion of it – you just share it with your local crowd and I'll get my channels going. This is going to be *so* amazing. I can feel the energy from you on this, Ann. I'm so glad we're joining forces.'

Bzzzz. Incoming call. Jennifer. Place on hold?

Does it ever stop?

'We'll get our post office back, Ann, and when that's done I'm going to run in the next election against Patsy. Will you join with me on that campaign, Ann? Maybe we could get Rory away from the dark side?'

So Patsy's, Iseult's and my plans are all going according to . . . plan. But they can't all succeed in the end.

Jennifer has left me a WhatsApp message.

'Mam, it's Jennifer.' I can hear a big slurp. She must be ruining a glass of wine. 'Yeah, so I tried ringing and no one checks voicemail, so here's your first WhatsApp voice message. Congratulations on that. Anyway, Des wants to invite you up to stay after the Pope's visit, OK, so you're to come, OK? I need you here. Declan has picked a date, Mammy. A date. It's, like, fifteenth October, and I'm, like, what's the hurry? And he's talking about inviting Paxman to celebrate it.' I hear another big gulp. Judging by the voice, I'd say the bottle is in danger of being emptied. 'Like, obviously, I'm not going to put up with that, but I just don't know who I'm dealing with here, you know? And Des doesn't really see it and I don't know where to start. Just make sure you come and stay, OK? Get a taxi from the Pope out to here. Get Deirdre to look after Nana. Just make sure you come, OK? Promise. Bye, Mam.'

No matter what age they are, the sound of a child being unhappy hits me right in the stomach. It's like a baby's cry. I can't ignore it.

Bing! *Hey Ann, don't forget. Saturday! We start in the fairy field!*

I wish I could ignore this other woman, though. Fat chance.

31.

SMASH THE BETTING INDUSTRY

The Pope is in the country and we're in the Lios field again.
There are a good fifty of Iseult's people gathered now. Cars
are parked all along the road, and even a minibus has come
down from Dublin. They have banners furled at the moment.
It's the biggest number of them I've seen yet. I'm glad I've
brought Denis with me. This crowd has a meaner streak.
The first rain in over a month is falling. It's a gentle drizzle,
but Iseult's beardy men are delighted with it.

'This is the weather of our ancestors, Ann,' says
Toirdealbhach, in mighty form. He is holding an A4 pad
with writing on it. It's already dampening.

'Feck sake, Ann,' Denis whispers to me. 'This crowd are
away with the fairies. Are there any locals coming to take
the mad look off the place?'

'It doesn't look like it. I seem to be the only one in the
circle of trust.'

Iseult has her little microphone. 'Thanks to all of you for
being here. We are at the site of history, and making history.

Today, the post office is closing its doors cynically while the attention of the country is on the Pope. But I know where my place is – with my people,' she says to the crowd, even though none of them are locals. 'You know my own sister is going to be there to meet the Pope. But I won't be there. And I think we know, too, that this Pope is turning his back on the traditions that we hold dear.'

'Is the Pope not a Catholic?' Denis whispers.

'Shhh, Denis. We'll be rumbled.'

'This a special place in Celtic Ireland, the fairy field of Kilsudgeon. Where Ireland fights back.' She waves over to where one of the Proclamation man's young lads is spraying graffiti on a disused artic container. When they finish, I see they've written *Patsy Duggan globalist elite and George Soros*. There is a round of applause from everyone. We don't applaud.

'Now Toirdealbhach will start off the ceremony,' says Iseult.

'Let us walk to the tree of the De Danann,' says Toirdealbhach. He has us walking through the field to the fairy fort and one of the whitethorn trees. I want to tell them that there is no fairy tree, but we're in the minority here. All I want is for Iseult to start campaigning for an election like a normal young wan and get rid of Patsy, but she's going about it a quare way. We stop at a stump of a tree.

'We stop here, my friends, at this symbol of the destruction of our natural beauty. This sacred tree of Eiriu. A whitethorn, our heritage destroyed by European agriculture and the demands of the neoliberals.'

Denis is whispering to me the real story of the stump. 'It was a cousin of Tommy's who cut that down to spite Tommy and bring him bad luck. Imagine! As if the fairies wouldn't know. He got killed himself off the back of a motorbike. But that was the drink.' Denis doesn't believe in the fairies but, like a lot of people around here, he hedges his bets on them.

'IRISHMEN AND IRISHWOMEN: in the name of God and of the dead generations from which she receives her old tradition of nationhood, Ireland, through us, summons her children to her flag and strikes for her freedom . . .'

He's starting to recite the 1916 Proclamation. He must know it off by heart.

'. . . Having organized and trained her manhood through her secret revolutionary organization, through secret revolutionary organization . . . through . . . emmmm . . . hold on, lads.'

He doesn't know it off by heart. He fishes in his inside pocket and pulls out a piece of paper and squints at it and then scowls.

Oh for God's sake. Lads, does one of ye have the Proclamation?'

Someone hands him a sheet of paper.

'"Twas down by the glenside I met an . . ." Ah that's the song.'

Eventually he finds the right bit of paper and reads out the rest of it. He has the accent of a man that spent time in London, or an actor. I wonder does he know Iseult from the acting? The acting crowd would be harbouring a load of strange ideas. All that waiting around for work, I suppose.

'One hundred years ago we began the next fight for freedom, and I want to start a new century by reclaiming our sovereignty. James, do you have the seal?'

An old man comes up with a big kind of a coin of Patrick Pearse.

'James will now reclaim the country on behalf of Patrick Pearse.'

James holds up the big coin. It seems to be made of cardboard.

'I reclaim this country to the east' (and he points the cardboard clearly away from where the sun is), 'to the west' (into the sun), 'to the north' (he points it back to the east) 'and to the south' (he just points it up in the air).

'This lad needs a satnav,' Denis mutters to me. 'Ask Siri what planet has he come from.'

'*I'm sorry, I did not understand the question,*' says Siri. Thank God I have the volume low.

'Now,' says Toirdealbhach, 'I will invoke our ancestors.'

'Oh, stop the lights,' says Denis.

Toirdealbhach is dressed in full Bunratty Folk Park style today. He has a cloak covered in symbols on the front of it. *Brehon* is written on it in old Irish letters.

'The sacred land of Ireland,' he says, holding a big walking stick, 'is polluted by the foreigner and the globalist slavers. No more will we take this. No more will our Christian heritage be spat upon by the combined forces of Cultural Marxism and technostates like Facebook and Google. We must rise up to defend our homeland as once we defended it from the Dane and the Saxon. The killing of our babies is the latest step, but we will fight. We will fight! Éireann ABÚ!' he shouts, and thumps the stump of the tree.

The fairies won't like that, but everyone shouts out '*Éireann abú!*' There's a fella with a phone going around filming this. Denis and me try and keep well away from him, but it's hard to know where he's pointing the phone.

The ceremony is over. Fags are lit and Iseult is back over to me.

'Wasn't that amazing, Ann? The power of it. I could feel it in the soil. This is a special place. It's no coincidence that we're drawn to Kilsudgeon. Toirdealbhach was telling me that there are ley lines running through here.'

'I'm surprised they were allowed, because there was awful ructions over the pylons that time.'

She seems confused at this. Something is nagging me about what I've seen.

'What was it about the foreigners, though, Iseult? I work with lovely people from abroad.'

'No, Ann, this isn't about people, it's about the global giants – that's what's closing our post offices. We are a diverse group. Oliver is Dutch.'

'But Oliver was the one . . . at the meeting . . .' She walks away again to greet some other mad yoke. We get into our cars.

'Who are you after getting yourself mixed up with?' says Denis. 'The Tidy Towns are gone very political, are they? Is this a good idea, Ann?'

'I am going to just turn up and then head away, Denis. This giving out about foreigners is not on.'

'And wouldn't new people be good for a post office?' he says. 'Wouldn't they be sending parcels through it?'

'I don't think they think that way, Denis.'

By the time we park and get to the post office it's a real jamboree. They've draped a big sign in front of it: SAVE OUR TOWN. The primary school is there, with the teachers holding banners. Macra na Feirme people in tractors. There's a car from the local radio station. It's a Mini with a big plastic cow on top of it because they're sponsored by *FODDARKINGS – The Agri Feed Giants*. I feel better when I see this. Like Patsy said, there are oddballs around the edges, but we are *all* concerned. And no one's mentioning foreigners any more. Maybe the locals will take it back now.

Someone is talking into a camera near me. It looks like RTÉ's local correspondent. He must be new because he's interviewing the most long-winded man you could see. He'll learn eventually, but for now he's forced to listen to Neily No Comment, as we call him. He'll give the RTÉ man chapter and verse on useless information, but he won't make the news tonight, I'd say.

RTÉ man extricates himself from Neily, but it doesn't get any better for him because Iseult is next, talking into his microphone and her own. She starts slagging off the correspondent, saying he'll have to collect his RTÉ pension somewhere else now that the post office has closed and she can't believe RTÉ could afford to send someone here with the wages they're paying the top people and how they're next on the list when the people rise up. I presume she's joking. I can't imagine the locals of Kilsudgeon marching on RTÉ, unless they stop doing the Farming Weather.

More and more people arrive. The crowd is now the size of a strong funeral. Another banner goes up on the other side of the post office door. KILSUDGEON TIDY TOWNS + NUATHA = A CLEAN START FOR KILSUDGEON. They've even got our logo.

'Feck, Ann, you're in a coalition,' says Denis.

'I had nothing to do with this, Denis. I never said yes to any of this.' But then I didn't say no either.

At about a quarter to one Iseult starts to arrange the crowd by getting her own people to usher people along the pavement and out on to the road so that everyone can see her. Iseult gets the young lad with the amp to play a tune from a CD. I don't recognize it at first, but then I realize what it is. 'The Spirit of Kilsudgeon.'

She talks into the microphone as the song begins. It's a long journey to the bit with lyrics.

'Neighbours and friends, I was raised on this song. Will you join me in it?'

They do. They were all raised on this song around here.

> Twas in the year of 1920
> And the savage Saxon was in the country.
> Brave Kilsudgeon stood up to fight
> And sent the Tans into the night.

> Young Paddy Morris the volunteer
> Drew English blood from ear to ear.
> Glorious his march, stirring his fall,
> That his name forever shall walk tall.

Even I join in on the chorus. And me a blow-in.

> On our native land, our native soil,
> Kilsudgeon answered Éireann's call.
> No more beneath the English yoke,
> Their domination up in smoke.
> Kilsudg-eon, Kilsudg-eon,
> Your fields so fair and green,
> We'll fight the foreign armies
> With our gunpowder dry, our blades so keen.

She leads us through the other umpteen verses and finishes to a big round of applause.

'You know the story there, don't you?' Denis whispers. 'Paddy Morris was supposed to be a pure lunatic, he'd fight anyone, and he got into a scrap with an RIC man over a game of cards and slashed him with a bit of a mirror. They say the IRA shot him themselves during the Civil War, he was such a headcase.'

Iseult hushes the applause: '*And* I have a new verse.' And her voice rings out over the street.

> When it was time to shout enough,
> The Kilsudgeon took the smooth and the rough
> To stand up and shout. We will be counted,
> For as our abandonment has mounted,
> You won't take our post office, school or kill our street.
> Don't stand in our way, globalist elite.

It's not exactly the Clancy Brothers, but the crowd seem to like it.

As she finishes, Danny the postmaster comes out and starts bringing in the postcard stands. The timing is perfect. Straight away, Iseult gathers us in front of him as the last customer comes out.

'Iseult, how are you?' he says as he starts reaching up for the locks. He glances at Davey and the others as they crowd him in close.

'I couldn't be better, Danny,' says Iseult. 'Now do you know why we are here?'

'I suppose to protest about the post office.'

'Not protest, Danny. We are here to keep the post office open. How would you like that, ladies?' she says to the last two out, who have been dawdling inside. It turns out to be Neans and Babs. Neans is being pushed in her chair by her weekend carer, Tina.

'I . . . It would be nice, wouldn't it? We'll miss the place. I'd have to travel thirty miles to get my pension, and I don't know how I'd get there,' says Neans.

Iseult shouts into her microphone. 'That's right, people of Kilsudgeon. Our most vulnerable in society are not able to have the services they need. Well, we won't let this post office be closed.'

'How are you going to do that?' says Danny as he starts moving a State Savings information carousel in towards the door.

'We are going to peacefully occupy the post office.'

'Oh janey,' I whisper to Denis.

'On behalf of the people of Kilsudgeon I am requesting you give us the keys.'

'I will not. The post office is a bank. I can't have the likes of Davey running around inside. And him up in front of a judge every second week.'

'DO YOU HEAR THAT? THE POST OFFICE IS *LIKE A BANK*. RIGHT FROM THE HORSE'S MOUTH. AND WHAT DO WE THINK OF BANKS?'

The crowd growls.

'What time is it?' says Iseult suddenly. 'Ann, what time is it?' She picks me out. 'Ann, come over here and don't be so modest.' I'm nudged forward. I'd much rather go home.

I look at my watch. It's going slow.

'I make it five to one.'

Everyone is looking at me as if I've suddenly become official timekeeper for the town now.

'It's well gone one,' says Danny, looking at me crossly. 'Are you mixed up with these lads now, Ann? Is that the way it is?'

'LEAVE HER ALONE,' says Iseult. 'Ann Devine is a symbol of all that's right in Kilsudgeon. She came to me and said, *We need to do something*. She started this Tidy Towns, she stood up to Big Business.' I have no memory of saying any of this. Iseult repeats it. 'Ann rang me the other night and said, *Can we do something together, Iseult?* I said, *We can, Ann*. And do you know what the first thing is I'll do? I'D LIKE TO BUY A STAMP.'

'I've locked up the till,' says Danny. 'It wouldn't be open at this hour anyway on a Saturday.'

Davey Finnerty and his pals push him aside. Iseult wriggles past him into the shop and then another of her people goes in.

'WHO'S WITH ME? WHO WANTS TO KEEP THIS POST OFFICE OPEN?'

And before I know it there's a sort of push behind me. A surge of people. Danny is torn between trying to get us out and stop more getting in and I'm half spat into the post office. There is cheering outside and 'The Spirit of Kilsudgeon' gets sung again and more people break through. It becomes a community effort.

'SIT DOWN! SIT DOWN!' Iseult shouts. 'LINK ARMS! LINK ARMS!'

I am on the ground now and find myself linking arms with two fairly pungent young lads in hoodies and tattoos all over their legs.

'Fight the elites,' one of them says to me.

I'm desperately in need of the toilet, but you can't start a sit-in with a toilet break.

There's a party atmosphere in the post office now. There must be twenty or thirty crammed inside. It's like the week of the Christmas bonus. Davey Finnerty has gone upstairs and I can hear him and a few others poking around. It's then that I see the bags. They've brought in big rucksacks and sleeping bags and bags of cans. Every so often Danny the postmaster comes back in to tell people not to be going near the tills and that he has to take the money out, and he leaves with a load of jeers after him. The old folk aren't too loyal to him. 'He wasn't listening to us at all,' says one of the old women. I don't really blame him. There's only so many years you can take hearing about bunions on pension day.

Denis is leaning against a counter, looking at me with a mixture of amusement and astonishment as I sit there. I've unlinked arms with the two druidy fellas, as it's clear the 'fascist police' aren't going to try and kick us out any time soon. I'm worried about the banner outside. Gordon will have a fit if he hears of it.

Richie Hallinan the Trad Man arrives next with a squeeze box and, before we know it, a hooley has broken out. A couple of primary school teachers are there, so of course they start organizing people into sets. A primary school teacher can't pass up an opportunity to organize something.

There's a crash as the One4all voucher trolley falls over. A druidy fella is standing next to it.

'SMASH THE BETTING INDUSTRY,' he shouts.

'COP ON, Sean,' shouts Iseult. 'BE CAREFUL. Hearts and minds, remember. Vouchers aren't gambling.'

That's when we hear the squad car outside.

32.

MARTIN LUTHER SUPERKING

'What's going on, Danny?'

Sergeant Eoghan Gallagher is a big man, so with the big yellow coat he takes up a lot of the space that's left in here.

'They went in past me, Thomas, I couldn't stop them. This feckin . . .' And he waves over at Iseult.

'Does your father know you're here, Iseult?'

'I don't need his permission, Sergeant. I am defending the community, Sergeant.'

'Listen to me now, miss. I'm the one defending the community.'

'You're defending your interests, Sergeant. This is the community behind me.'

Richie starts up another reel until the sergeant silences him with a hand out flat. Then he turns to me.

'And Ann Devine, are you here representing the Tidy Towns? This is gone beyond window baskets now.'

I don't have a quick answer for him like the people you see on YouTube. You know the videos where there's a policeman saying, *Where are you going with the trailer full of scrap metal?* and there's a fella giving him cheek, saying, *I know my rights and I want to see a warrant.*

'We heard that you were mixed up with this crowd, Ann.'

That chills me a bit. Am I *known to the guards* now? I'll be *helping police with their inquiries* next.

'She's doing what I'm doing – representing the people,' says Iseult, who seems to be an old hand at this.

'Ann can answer for herself. Can't you, Ann? I'm sure you can.'

'Stop harassing her, Sergeant.'

'Are you going to be one of these professional protestors now, Ann? I've enough on my plate dealing with the loolahs besides having the bloody Tidy Towns rioting. What are ye going to start doing – throwing bedding plants?'

'WHAT IS YOUR BADGE NUMBER, SERGEANT?' shouts Davey.

'Ah, to hell with your badge number, Martin Luther Superking. Now and if I go out to look at your car, will I find it insured, will I? How many suspended sentences has that judge given you now? My badge number is on the tip of my boot and you'll feel it in your backside now in a minute. And get that phone out of my face.' He takes a protestor's phone and puts it in his pocket.

'GARDAÍ CORRUPTION, FASCIST COPS! GARDAÍ CORRUPTION, FASCIST COPS!'

Davey leads the chant. One of the primary school teachers is absent-mindedly mouthing it. The other one seems annoyed the set-dancing is over.

'Seriously, Ann, what are you doing, involving yourself with this shower of crusties?'

'THE CIA ARE ALIVE AND WELL AND WORKING IN KILSUDGEON.'

The sergeant starts laughing at this and says he wishes he had the CIA manpower, but there's no distracting this crowd. He turns back to me again.

'Look, we're all on the same side here, Ann.'

I finally find my voice. 'We are, Thomas, but didn't we all campaign for you for the extra guard? Would you not support us over that?'

'But you didn't occupy the Garda station when you were doing that.'

'We couldn't. It's locked all the time.'

The other protestors start laughing and cheering

'Denis, can you talk some sense into her? Or I'll stop your truck, too, every time I see it.'

'You'll find nothing wrong with it, Sergeant, and I don't mind stopping for the chat.'

Janey, even Denis is infected with the backchat.

There's a woman guard with him. Young Sheehan. She must be 'the good cop'.

'Ah, c'mon now, Ann, this isn't the way to solve this. Lookit, come away over with me.'

'SNAKES, ANN, DON'T LISTEN TO THEM!'

She doesn't put my back up, so I go over and talk to her. She's a small, squat little thing. A bit of a mini-me. I remember her doing debating at the talent show in the school. She was nailed on to be a guard that time.

'Well, Ann,' she says, and ushers me into the corner. 'I don't want to say anything now, but there'd be a few undesirable types in amongst them. They're not local, Ann. That Dutch fella, between yourself and meself' – and she goes very whispery – 'they think he might be into the . . .' She stops as he starts coming over to us.

WHATT IS THE POLICHEWOMAN SHAYING TO YOU?'

'We're going to leave now, because our presence is only giving them exposure, but I wouldn't stay around too long, Ann, OK?'

Meanwhile, Iseult is talking into her phone again. I can hear snatches of it.

'Hello to everyone on the live stream . . . the revolution in rural Ireland has begun . . . Here, in the unlikely crucible . . . Kilsudgeon . . . we are all Kilsudgeon today . . .'

'You better go home and mind Mam, Denis.'

'. . . on this weekend when Ireland is the centre of the Church's family with the arrival of the Pope . . .'

Denis asks if I'm going with him, but I say I'll follow on. I'm trying to see what they're going to do with that banner. Thankfully, it's been brought in from outside, so at least people won't be gawping at it, but I'm afraid they'll put it up again. Unexpectedly, as he's leaving, Denis gives me a hug. In public. What's going on with him? Has he had a stroke or a premonition?

'Mind yourself, Annie,' he whispers. The tenderness nearly undoes me. The big softy. He goes.

Danny comes in and makes a big show of taking the money from the tills, accompanied by the Sergeant. After a while, it quietens down. I see that the locals are drifting away, and soon it's just me with all of Iseult's gang.

They bring tables over to the door. They're giddy with their success. And it doesn't look like they have a plan of what to do next. Iseult has stopped with the streaming and she's deep in conversation with Davey. It's the only time I've seen him smile.

I go back to my place. With the guards gone, no one's linking arms, so we're just on a few chairs that have been brought down from the rooms upstairs.

A man I heard them calling Big Jay has taken off his Druid cloak now and looks half normal. He takes out a packet of cashew nuts and offers me some. I realize then I'm famished.

'Were you ever in a squat, Mrs Devine?' he says. It's the first time any of them has made small talk. I say no and he tells me about all the squatting he has done in Dublin in derelict houses that were empty of every single bit of furniture. I have to ask.

'How did ye go to the toilet if all the bathrooms had been taken out?'

'TravelJohns, Mrs Devine. Best invention ever for the revolution. The landlord, right? He had cut off all the water. We just did our jobs into this TravelJohn and this mate of mine drove over to the prick's house in Blackrock, threw them into his garden. Man, what a fucken laugh. The dude is there at some, like, garden party shindig, and my man Big Stu just throws a load of shit into the shrubbery. Big Stu is like – cos the landlord is this big, thick culchie who got lucky, no offence – "HOPE THIS REMINDS YOU OF HOME!"' He grins at me, takes a rollie and starts to light it up.

Davey is straight over. 'No joints in here, Jay,' he says. 'We don't want them calling it a drugs thing, mate, yeah? Let it settle, OK?'

Big Jay puts the fag into his pocket reluctantly. He sighs.

'We had some parties in the squat, though. Did you ever do mushrooms, Ann?'

'I did mushrooms one time for the Christmas dinner. For a starter.'

He starts laughing. 'For a starter!'

I continue, a bit puzzled. 'Denis doesn't like them. He says they give him indigestion. It's a shame, because they were grand with the bit of garlic and the oil. I was very proud of them.'

'You were proud of your mushrooms after you did them? This is gold, Mrs Devine.'

279

And then I cop on. Drugs. I tell him I haven't done any of those. He proceeds to give me a full rundown about how a fella might *do* mushrooms and what I might do as a beginner. I should be well hydrated, apparently.

'And would you ever have smoked the old peace pipe?'

At least I know what that is. I reckon if I hang around enough with this crowd I might get to have another go. But it's been a while. I wonder is it still the same stuff that we got one time at a Fleadh? But that could have been turf.

There's movement at the door and a familiar smell and voice comes in. It's Nawaz from the chipper. He's after taking over the running of it now, since Joe got a turn. Poor ould Joe had spent a lifetime nibbling his own supply and gone very big, and it was only a matter of time before it caught up with him. The arteries were like black pudding on him. They found him half into the freezer, holding on to his chest. When they were pulling him out he says, *Don't be throwing any of that out now, I had a shower this morning.*

Nawaz stands there, looking at me sitting next to the collection of characters.

'Well, Freedom Fighter Ann Devine, haha, how are you, my friend? I see you on the news. I bring some chips and burgers for all the heroes fighting for Kilsudgeon. The Tidy Towns army, no?'

'Good man, Abdul!' shouts Toirdealbhach. 'Bring us over the curry there.' There are laughs.

I think they are slagging off Nawaz. He doesn't seem to notice. He starts doling out the chips. Iseult is all smiles, and a few of the others gather around him. Then a few more lads emerge from the back of the post office. His smile disappears only for a second. He comes back to me.

'I even have a choice of Dairy Milks for you, Ann Devine. You see, nah? Nawaz doesn't forget the good customers. I hear the Tidy Towns are occupying the post office so I say,

Meenakshi, we'll make a special meal for them. You want to come over to this counter here, I give you first choice.'

He announces to the room, 'Very good customer. Haha, she gets first choice.'

He seems to be making a big fuss about bars of chocolate, but when I'm over there his manner changes.

'Do you know these people, Ann?'

I try and explain that it's sort of 'evolved' out of the litter pick-up.

'Yeah, OK.' He looks over his shoulder and says very casually, as if just making conversation, but not loud, 'Now where is the Dairy Milk? Here, one second, Mrs Devine, now let me see what else I have got for you. So, Mrs Devine, there are some pretty tough men in here, no? Maybe they come into my place causing trouble one night, hah? Ah, here we are, oh, it's a Golden Crisp, sorry. So maybe one or two of them tell me I should go back to my own country. No Turkish Delight, Ann, I know you'll be disappointed and, yeah, maybe these men say are you bring in sharia. You know Joe never wanted me selling the chocolate in the chipper.'

'He'd get heart failure if he found out.'

'Bad woman, Mrs Devine, haha.' And he's all smiles, but he grips my arm as he's leaving. 'Mind yourself, Mrs Devine, hah?'

There is sniggering as he leaves and it's loud enough that they want him to hear it. Davey says he won't eat the chips because you wouldn't know what spices there would be on them.

The Dutchman says, 'Thish is what I am telling you. The great replayshement. There'll be a moshque here. I guarantee thish.'

I sit eating the Dairy Milk, in bites. I should stand up for Nawaz, but I suddenly feel all alone. I text Denis to collect me. The banner will have to wait. I'm in the wrong place and I'm afraid.

I tell Iseult my mother needs me and she thanks me profusely for *making this happen*, and then she looks at her phone and squeals, 'Russia Today are here . . .'

I head outside. I can spot the Russia Today fella, a man in a dickie bow and checkie suit talking to himself with one of those selfie sticks. The world is full of people talking to themselves while talking to everyone, as far as I can make out. I see Denis and Freya are at our car. A few yards away, Mam standing next to Sylvester. He's talking and she's looking away from him. I go over to them.

'Well, Sylvester, you made it in.'

'I came in for a look, Ann. You have quite the weekend ahead of you, Margaret was telling me.'

'That's right. We're all set, aren't we, Mam?'

'She was at the door when I went home,' says Denis. 'She's ready to go and see the Pope now.'

'Are you going, Sylvester?'

'No, Ann. I am not a . . . believer.'

Mam says nothing.

'I was nearly on Russia Today, Ann,' says Denis. 'He wanted me to do an interview, but I said I hadn't shaved so I wasn't ready for his close-up.'

'That made his day, I'm sure, Denis.'

'He has plenty to talk to him. Youngsters were gathered around him, filming themselves filming him filming them. They all seemed to know about Russia Today.'

'Who's Russia Today, Freya?'

'Fox News for people who think they're too clever for Fox News. Auntie Ann, you absolutely have to get out of there. Me and some others have been on Facebook. The stuff up there is just . . . epically bad, Auntie Ann. Like, total fash. They're just using you.'

The dickie-bow man is nearly swamped with young lads looking to be interviewed. No one is afraid of a camera now. They're all set to perform. Some are carrying skateboards. Denis snorts at the sight of them.

'Look at them with the small wheels. You'd want shocks on a skateboard with the potholes. And they wouldn't have lights either on the road, like the cyclists . . .'

'Auntie Ann, Uncle Denis is having a seizure. He's talking about cyclists again. Give him his medication.'

'Take me home, Ann,' says Mam.

'Yeah, Uncle Denis, bring your wife home before she's radicalized.'

'We're too late, Freya.'

33.

THE DEVIL CAN TAKE ME

I put Mam to bed early, but as I leave the room she starts talking.

'He said he wouldn't be going near them so-and-sos, and he cursed them, Ann.'

'Sylvester?'

'He said all the popes were evil, Ann.'

'But he's a sailor, Mam, they've no interest in the Church. Or he just wants to cut out the middle man.'

'No, Ann, he told me I was foolish for believing in any of that stuff and that it wasn't going to make a blind bit of difference to Charlie. But I didn't tell him about Charlie for him to be telling me how to think. You know what men are like. You tell them something and they think that means you've hired them to fix it. You needn't bring me up there again, if you don't mind. I'll stay below in the house with *The Chase*. I like that Pope and I won't hear a word against him.'

Poor Mam. What do you say to an old woman with boy trouble? Plenty more fish in the sea? There aren't, and the sea isn't around for that long. Now is as bad a time as any to ask her what's been on my mind. She's half praying with the rosary beads. I can't tell if it's an official rosary.

'Mam? Can I ask you something? Do you feel . . .'

'. . . implored thy help or sought thy intercession . . .' I see now she's still praying, but it's so faint I can only hear the lips make the sound. She finishes the 'Memorare' and looks at me.

'Do I feel what, Ann?'

I start again. 'You know you said about the referendum, how it was a good thing? What did you mean?'

'You weren't around for the last one, Ann,' she says.

She's right, I wasn't. Me and Denis were in London for the first couple of years after getting married. He was on the sites for a while and I was nursing. Then I found out Deirdre was on the way and I said, *There's no way I'm rearing a child in London on my own,* and we came home.

'Eighty-three was terrible, Ann. We all voted against it. And I knew people, Ann, I knew women who couldn't have another child. Women who'd had men force themselves on them. And I *still* voted for it, and some of them did too. Do you know that your sister nearly killed me coming out and I begged them to tell me, you know, was there any way at all that I couldn't have any more? We wouldn't even say the words back then. This doctor says to me, he said whatever happened was God's way. *God's way,* Ann. They were so *cold,* Ann. But I still went with the crowd in eighty-three. I was afraid of going to hell, Ann. Well, this time I said to myself, there's no way I'm voting against another woman having some bit of a say. That's what I said now and that's the truth of it and the devil can take me. I hope he doesn't, of course.'

'You never said anything about it in May.'

'Ah, I was afraid someone would get a hold of it. Even Freya, godblessher. She'd probably have me in one of those videos.'

'What videos?'

'You know, where they have old people supporting it. Bim was showing me these videos saying, "Aren't they a disgrace? Wouldn't you think they'd have more sense at their age, going on video talking about gays or abortion?" Now I didn't say a word to Bim. He's handy for doing jobs around the place, but I said to myself, *You've the wrong end of the stick entirely about me, Bim.*'

She's quiet for a moment, watching me.

'I went to confession over it, Ann.'

'Over the vote? Who did you go to?'

'Donnegan.'

'How did he take it?'

'*You're not the only one, Peggy*, he says. I wouldn't be gone on Joe Donnegan, Ann, but he was good to me now. He says, *You're forgiven*, and I said the Act of Contrition. But, Ann, I wasn't sorry. Supposing I was wrong, Ann?'

'I don't know, Mam. I'm the same.'

'And I said to him, *Will you still give me Communion?* He says, *Peggy, I've given it to worse than you.* And I was thinking like, if it was around before, you know, Ger would have had one. And there'd be no Freya.'

'We don't know what's right, do we, Mam?'

'No pet, you'll never know, only what you feel.'

'True, Mam.'

'And I was hard on Ger when she was having Freya, you know. I was sorry about that too. I'll never mind a word that girl says, Ann, when I think of being angry at her and she only a little baby in the womb. I changed, too, Ann. I thought about what happened to women my age and some your age. Do you think ould wans don't think about these things, Ann? That we're just there sitting in our scarves saying the rosary? But the prayer gets me through.'

'Does it work, Mam, the prayer? I stopped praying when I didn't hear anything from it.'

'Ann, when your father died I needed a lot of help. I had no one.'

'You had us, Mam.'

'I didn't want to bother ye. You had Denis. And small babies, and Ger was . . . well, she was wrapped up in herself, and she blamed me too. For being cold to your father. But she never knew about Nonie. Otherwise, ye'd hate both your mother and your father.'

'No one hated you, I'm sure of it, Mam. Ger is just . . . well, there was a lot of things said.'

'The only one who kept me out of St Kevin's, the madhouse, was Our Lord. He's been good to me. Every day I asked Jesus for how to do the right thing. And Jesus was always good to the women. You see, Ann, I've had time over the last while. I've done a good bit of reading. You think I'm just an ould biddy with the runs.'

'Ah, Mam, I don't think that. It's just that you're so good to go to Mass I didn't think about you with all these thoughts. And you still are very keen on the Mass.'

'The prayers give me comfort, but Jesus tells me what to do. But he didn't say a word to me on the vote, and I'm worried, Ann. Maybe I'll hear him at the Pope. He's the only middle man I'll listen to. But don't say a single word about this to anyone, Ann. I want to have a bit of peace at Mass and not have people be pointing at me.'

I kiss her goodnight. She's right. I did see her as just a cranky ould wan who needed to be helped. More fool me.

34.

A GOUGER BEHIND EVERY ESB POLE

They say you can see for miles from Kilsudgeon Junction, but why would you want to? Even on a sunny day it's as *bleak*, and today isn't a sunny day. It's not even near Kilsudgeon, and there was talk of getting it called something else because it was giving us a bad name. It's next to a dump, and the seagulls up there would take the eye out of you. I don't even know if you could call them seagulls. They haven't been to sea in ages. Retired gulls, maybe. There was talk there might be a mix of crow in some of them too. That's all we need, the crows and the seagulls getting together. We haven't a hope against that type of cunning.

On either side of the track there are wrecks of old train carriages and the odd burnt-out car. There are latchikos who use the field next to the tracks to get the copper wire out of the cable, and there's always a kind of burnt smell there. And a bitter little breeze that'd go right through you.

It's a different story this morning as we catch our special soul train. There's a fierce buzz in the air. People are getting out of the cars with windcheaters and flasks of tea. The people-carriers are emptying children out on to the road with their flags and chairs. You'd forget that people love an outing and that they mightn't go to Mass, only on Christmas Eve. It's drizzling gently. There are eight of us in two cars, waiting for as long as possible. Me and Denis, Mam and Freya in one, Deirdre and the family in the other. Deirdre comes over and leans in my open window.

'I hope they'll let us in with our tickets, Mam. They don't have the name of a prominent feminist on them.' She nods towards Freya, who's glued to Twitter because it's *hopping* with the March for Truth, apparently.

'So how's Freya? How's our little local hero?'

'Literally, don't even talk to me right now about that, cuz. It is a hundred per cent mortifying. I wouldn't be surprised if I'm just, like, totally disowned at the march. Lossie is already there to me, saying that I'm enabling the survival of a corrupt institution. And on the other side of it, I can't even *move* without some old person saying, like, OMG, Frances, because, literally, *no one* gets my name right, OMG, Froja, you are sent from heaven. I'm litch an emotional wreck.'

'It's tough being you, Freya,' says Deirdre.

'Preach. But I know where I'm going today. March for Truth.' And she waves her little banner for that.

'Well, the highlight of your day is yet to come. Staying at our house tonight and being woken up by Hughie's father banging a harvester outside your window.'

'What's the harvester's name, Dee?' says Freya.

'You cannot be talking like that now in the Pope's carriage,' I tell her.

Deirdre is minding her this evening, while we're at the in-laws.

'And Nana, are you looking forward to meeting the Pope and Declan's mam and dad?'

Mam is coming with us to see Declan's parents after the Pope. That wasn't the original plan. It was very much Mam's idea, but we have to make the best of it. I was looking forward to a night off. I was up earlier, packing for her. But the change of plan was no bother to Desdemona. *We've loads of room*, she texted me.

Mam is watching the crowds and doesn't hear the question. Deirdre goes back to her car to begin unloading. Mam looks at her ticket.

'You know, Ann, the tickets your father was supposed to get me were real VIP ones. *Gold-rimmed cards signed by the bishop, Peggy*, he says. *That's how you'll know them in the post.* What do these say? Section G7? And are all of these' – she gestures to all the people milling around – 'here for the G7 as well? Is that close? G doesn't sound close, Ann. A would have been better. A sounds closer. They'd start at A, wouldn't they?'

'Maybe they're doing it back to front, Mam.'

'The Jesuits don't do anything back to front, Ann.'

We get ourselves out of the car and I'm startled by a whine from a megaphone. It's Patsy on the platform. He's reminding us that there is a special extra carriage on the train just for Kilsudgeon people and that he was the man who got it done, as if he'd welded the top and sides of it himself. He's already announced this on his Facebook page, and the angry reactions piled up underneath. This usen't be the way at all. Normally, he'd put up a photo of him shaking hands with someone and say he was *delighted to announce*, because Patsy was always delighted to announce things that had nothing to do with him. He'd take credit for a cow in calf, that man. But for all this brass neck, there used be no grumbling. Someone would write underneath, *Fair play, Patsy* or *Can you come out and look at the drain outside our house?* But now? *Scumbag elitest lapdog. Traitor. Mr Corrupt.* I mean, we all knew he was on the take, but no one was *saying* it. The train pulls in, rammed to the gills, but with one empty carriage for us. The driver gives Patsy a big wave. Maybe he did get it done.

As we are getting on he says to me, 'I see you're playing a blinder, Ann. We have them now where we want them. Iseult has lost it.'

We fill the carriage, but not all of us are going to the Pope. Freya goes off to sit with Lossie and Gary Cushin and a few others from Repeal Kilsudgeon. Eight of them in total, in two four-seats facing each other. The rest of us – God's chosen people – fill the rest of the seats. Freya is trying to keep a low profile, but this doesn't last long.

Father Donnegan gets up to do the rosary. Before he starts, he wants to thank *a very special girl who made this possible.* I can hear a small *Oh no!* from her end of the carriage as he calls out her name and beckons her up to receive a voucher. She walks up to him, the picture of mortification, wearing a top I hadn't noticed when we were going out the door that says *Respect My Reproductive Rights.*

The rosary only lasts one decade before the tea-trolley comes down, and they don't come back to it. Father Donnegan says they'll let the Pope do the rest of it. The tea-trolley fella is earning his money today. I don't think he's been in a carriage where there's as much giving out about the prices. '*How* much for a Fruit 'n' Nut? HOW MUCH?' is all he's hearing. Freya gets two KitKats sent down to her by Maire McMahon.

The trolley man goes and the sing-song starts. 'The Spirit of Kilsudgeon' gets a turn, but without Iseult's new verse. I relax a bit. It's nice to be back in the normal run of things. I go down to Freya with a cream Danish that another woman has splashed out on for her.

'Hello, Ann,' says Gary Cushin. 'I'd say Freya is the owner of the most miraculous medals in the whole Repeal Campaign.'

Lossie is laughing at her too. 'OMG, Freya, we have to do this on the podcast. How you've found religion.'

'Omigod, Lossie, you are SO funny. Can't believe Netflix haven't given you a special yet.'

Father Donnegan leads us out of the train as if we were in Lourdes. Even the Kilsudgeon For Yes find themselves shown how to exit Heuston Station.

Freya is all set to go with Lossie in towards the centre of Dublin for their protests, but Father Donnegan has got a notion into his head that there should be a photo at the entrance.

'Ann, a word in your ear. Would you be able to convince Freya to come with us as far as the park entrance?'

'You wouldn't be trying to convert her now, Father, would you?'

'Honestly, Ann, trying to keep the flock I have at the moment is a big enough job for me. Will you say it to her?'

I do, and she is not happy.

'No, Auntie Ann. No way. I'm going in with Lossie.'

'OK, I won't force you at all.'

But then Freya finds herself surrounded by three or four rosary types who are shaking her hand and wanting to thank her personally and saying, *You'll be our guide now, won't you, girleen, and isn't it great to see the young people involved and showing initiative? You lead the way there. You know better than Himself, hah?* And before she can say any more, she finds herself at the head of the delegation going out the door. I can't go with her because I have to get Mam into a wheel-chair, and by the time I do get up to her she's given up.

'I swear, Auntie Ann,' she says to me, 'I'm sorry I ever booked those tickets. And DON'T' – she points at me – 'say karma. That's a different religion.'

Denis and me take turns pushing Mam. We cross the Liffey and then go up Parkgate Street. Mam is muttering that she should have been in a mobility scooter and she was dying to have a go off one.

'The parish would have paid for it, Ann.'

'They were banned from the day, Mam. There wasn't room for the chargers. I told you.'

Freya is up ahead, trying to hurry the group on. Resigned to being late.

Mam is the first to mention the crowds. 'I thought there'd be more. I *could* have had a scooter. You'll be worn out pushing me, Denis.'

Denis replies that he's fine and well able for it, but there's a steep hill just inside the Park and he grunts his way up it. Mam ignores the swearing under his breath. Since she got her hearing aid she's found out that her family have been turning the air blue all along.

The park opens out in front of us. It's a damp green. There are stewards and recordings out of tannoys telling us to turn this way and that. A ripple of excitement goes through the crowd. Father Donnegan is warning us all to have our tickets ready. We are braced for queues. We were warned about queues.

'Have the tickets ready,' says Father Donnegan. 'Make sure you've the bags out now. Time to get rid of your cans,' he jokes.

The older people are fussing over bags and money and cards in purses on strings around necks, because it's Dublin and the country people are convinced that there's a gouger behind every ESB pole.

We get to the entrance to the Mass and . . . it's nothing. Just bored, damp young lads who barely give us a glance as we walk in.

'OK, let's have a photo so,' says Father Donnegan, and he martials a group of us with Freya in the centre. She's holding up her Truth sign in all of them, but he doesn't seem to mind. The Truth is the Truth, I suppose.

'Byeeeeee,' she says, and legs it back down the path. I dash to give her money for a taxi, ask her fifteen times to mind herself. She hugs me and then says I owe her *big time*, but she's glad Nana made it.

After the barriers, we take a second to look at the surroundings.

'Well, it's not 1979 anyway,' says Denis. 'Where is everyone?'

'Did we get the time wrong?' Mam says.

But it's only an hour to the Mass. The Kilsudgeon group goes to its paddock. And, of course, G is at the back. And there's no one in it. Or the one in front of us, or for acres ahead of us. We drift up towards the front, as far as we can go. Eventually, Kilsudgeon finds a square it's happy to occupy with the wrong ticket and people go in and set themselves up.

'Don't mind the rest of them. I want to look him in the eye,' says Mam. 'I want to be close.'

Denis, Mam and I keep on going up the front. Every time we stop and find a paddock that has a bit of room, Mam presses us on further up. We've left the Kilsudgeon crowd behind us in C. Mam wants A.

'And in the middle, Ann.'

After five minutes, we come right up to the VIPs.

'I'm going in there. I missed this in 1979, Ann. I am *not* being out in a paddock like a heifer. Your father promised me VIP and now I'm going to get it for myself and tell him about it.'

I push her up to a gate at the VIP entrance. A security man is there. I think he'll be fairly soft. You'd want to be an easy-going type for a church thing, wouldn't you? But as I get closer I see this man is not easy-going. I know by the weathered face and the confidence on him he's done a few of these before.

I shoo Denis away. 'We'll have a better chance if we're just two women, Denis.'

'You're right,' says Denis. 'He'd only be intimidated by me.'

I roll Mam up to the gate.

'Excuse me,' I say hesitantly.

'STAND BACK THERE. THERE ARE PEOPLE COMING OUT.'

There's a gang of people trying to get in and I try to get his attention. I want to get him away from the other chancers and explain my story. Because my story is important.

'Excuse me, I want to get my mother in there.'

'OF COURSE, MY DARLING, DOES SHE HAVE A TICKET? SHOW ME THE TICKET.'

'Could I just have a word over here?'

'I CAN'T LEAVE THIS GATE. CAN I JUST SEE THE GOOD LADY'S TICKET?'

'You see, that's the thing . . .'

'NO TICKET, NOT INTERESTED, ALL RIGHT, MY LOVE?'

'Well, you see, she couldn't go in 1979 . . .'

'NEXT THERE, PLEASE, THANK YOU, SIR. OUT, OUT, I TOLD YOU GET OUT.' He's talking to someone else now. A woman with a big head of curls.

'I'm going back into my mother, sir.'

'THEN GET THE TICKET FROM HER, SWEETHEART, ALL RIGHT?'

'Mammy, get the ticket there for the man,' she says to an older woman inside the barricade.

The woman shows him a ticket, but then he asks the younger wan for her ticket and threatens to throw her out as well.

'I don't know where it is. She's lost it, sir. She has it all right. We both showed your other gentleman, your colleague, the tickets.'

'NICE TRY, LADIES, I'VE BEEN HERE ALL MORNING.'

'On me mother's grave, sir, she was in when you were gone to the toilet.'

'I NEVER GO TO THE TOILET, SWEETHEART, I'M LIKE A MACHINE. NOW, LADIES AND GENTS, HAVE YOUR TICKETS READY, PLEASE.'

They're playing a sort of game with each other. There's a red-haired man there inside as well, too, sizing up the situation. The bouncer has moved on from the two women and I make a beeline for him again. He has no time for the amateurs like me. I try again.

'You see, there was a mix-up with the tickets . . .'

'THERE'S HALF A MILLION PEOPLE EXPECTED HERE TODAY, MISSUS, I'VE NO TIME FOR MIX-UPS. THERE'S A WHOLE PARK YOU CAN GO TO.'

'But you see, in 1979, the tickets . . .'

'STAND BACK NOW, MADAM, IN THE NAME OF THE FATHER, SON AND HOLY GHOST, ALL RIGHT, MY LOVE.'

And he gently blesses me while guiding me out of the way of a wheelchair woman who *has* a ticket. Denis is looking over at me and he decides he might have a go at persuading, but he gets within a few feet and the man is on to him.

'DO YOU THINK I HAVE NO PERIPHERAL VISION, LAD, DO YOU? I SAW YOU HANGING AROUND THERE FOR THE LAST TEN MINUTES. NOW, UNLESS YOU HAVE A TICKET FOR THIS WOMAN HERE THAT MATCHES THE DESCRIPTION OF A TICKET FOR THIS AREA, THEN I SUGGEST YOU JUST GO OFF AND GET A BURGER BECAUSE THE SHOW WON'T START FOR A WHILE YET.'

Mam looks forlorn. I turn to Denis to try and figure out what to do.

'We could try the next area, maybe get in with a few priests, Denis.'

We stare out across the field, hoping inspiration, or even a bit of a brass neck, will come to us. I put the brake on Mam, and me and Denis walk down a small bit. I turn back to her, but there's no sign of her. I get the panic I haven't got in years with a child at a crowd. The security man is busy with another family who are arguing over tickets.

I look over along the line and there is my mother, in mid-air, being lifted over the fence by the red-haired man I saw earlier. The chair is still outside the fence. He sets my mother down gently on a chair the other side.

'Be cool now, Denis.'

We sidle up and draw level with where Mam is. She's looking out at us from inside the railing with the same gleam in her eye as when she met Sylvester.

The red-haired man leans against the railing next to me. 'She's some woman, your mother. I wouldn't be lifting country women over railings normally, but she was very persuasive, your mother. She told me how she was done out of a ticket in '79. And godblessher she's as light as a feather.'

'But what about the wheelchair?'

'Why don't you sit in that, Ann?' Mam turns to the man who hoisted her in.

'We're ever so grateful to you. What's your name, if you don't mind me asking?'

'John Paul, ma'am.'

'Are you named after the Pope?'

'And half the minceir in the country, ma'am.'

'Denis, will you give John Paul a few bob there for his trouble, like a good man. He made me a VIP.'

John Paul won't take it high nor dry.

'Put away your money, you'll take the good out of it.' He nods his head. 'You'd have got in anyway. Look. The boss man is gone.'

Sure enough, the rest of his family are in. Maybe the security man finally caved and went to the toilet, because we see that it's a raw young lad in charge now and he's far more easily persuaded.

'A pile a room in here. Only on a power trip, that simple boy. Godblessye now.'

'What about the toilet, Mam?' I ask her. She waves me down to whisper to me.

'You put a pad on me, Ann. Now go off and find yere own spot. I'm staying here.'

'Grand so,' says Denis. 'I'm going to get a bit of food before the Mass.'

There's a stir in the crowd. A cloak of priests starts to move on to the stage. Things might be about to start.

35.

UP ON THE ŠKODA

I'm at a bit of a loss now. Leaning on the railings. A whole other family is keeping an eye on Mam. She's deep in conversation with John Paul's mother. They're going on about Blessings of the Graves. A guard moves me on because I'm blocking the path. I've arranged to meet Denis at the corner of D and C after he gets his pizza, so I have a few minutes to take it all in. In between all the enclosures are all these roads and people are rammed at the front of the railings to get a good look at the Pope because they expect him to come past. There are lots of people there, but when I look out across the far paddocks, even now with Mass nearly starting and a rosary in full swing, there are big open spaces. Who has all the tickets? Was it a load of Freyas?

But the people who are here are up for it. Mam must be having the time of her life now, praying outdoors with thousands of people. She never went to the Moving Statues, even though Daddy was all for it. They didn't do much together in the last years of his life. I wonder will this give her faith a top-up? I wish I had Mam's certainty in knowing what the Man Above thinks. Although she deals more with Jesus. *He's better with women*, she says. *But Mam, aren't they all the one?* I used to ask her. *Isn't that the Trinity? We all have our own way of understanding it*, she said to me. *I don't think that's the case, Mam.* But she wouldn't hear otherwise. Whatever it is, she's as happy as a clam now, ensconced in her seat, waiting.

As the rosary gets louder, I find myself saying it out of habit. It's soothing. What would Jesus think of me now, storming a post office? I give Him a word to say I might chat to Him again and look back out over the field, and some movement catches my eye to the left of the stage. There's a black jeep and there are guards running and then I see a white, boxy vehicle as well. It couldn't be . . . could it?

Denis is nowhere to be seen. I find myself running towards the commotion, drawn to it. There are a few other people skittering along as well. Fathers dragging children and nuns with every kind of colour of habit and skin skittering across the grass. They're young, so they must be foreign.

The moving ball of people is fully out from behind the stage now. I keep looking for barriers or something to stop the likes of me getting close, but there's nothing. You'd swear they were smuggling him out of the place. As if he threw a strop backstage and said, *No way am I saying Mass for this shower*. The crowd gets bigger but is still only tiny compared to the thousands pressed against the railings. At one stage a small boy runs across my heels and falls to the ground, but I keep going. The mother barely stops to pick him up. The convoy turns a corner unexpectedly, the crowd parts a little, and there he is, up on the Škoda. Smiling away and waving at the carry-on a few feet below him as if it was all part of the plan.

The crowd has spotted him and are galloping towards what they think the route is. I think he'll go left again, and I hold my ground. The guards don't know what's going on. An older guard beside me is on the phone to someone higher up who doesn't know what's going on either.

'Who in the name of God is driving that yoke?'

'Hah? No, the first we've heard of it. He'll drive over them. No, there was no plan. A pure disaster.'

Sure enough, the convoy turns towards me. I have my phone out to put on the video. Almost instinctively. My thumb is to and I dry it to get the thing woken up. He's the most famous person I have ever seen in the flesh. A South Americany nun tries to push across my arm. I'm having none of it. I use my big arse to gently ease her out of the way. I've never shoved a nun before, though I wanted to plenty of times when I was in nursing training. The phone is taking its time, but sure enough as the jeeps and the Popemobile draw near I have him in my sights. The man himself. Waving as the convoy ploughs on.

I'm full sure he's looking at me, or looking right *into* me. I imagine him saying, *I've seen your kind of Catholic before, Ann Devine. It's your mother that should be here. I'll go up to her and John Paul and his mother next. That's who I'm here to see.*

I don't know how someone hasn't gone under the wheels, the way the convoy is carving its way through the crowd. He's within feet of me. I reach out involuntarily, watching him on the phone, and . . . I touch . . . well, it's just the shoulder of the fella who's running alongside. He looks suspiciously for a second over his shoulder but seems satisfied I'm not ISIS, then he's gone. I touched the Pope's bodyguard. That's close enough.

The guards get control of the situation. They start herding people in behind the barriers, and soon enough the convoy is the only show on the road and everyone is back in their pen. But I'm still all fluttery after my brush with the Pope. I look at my phone because I barely looked at him in real life. I didn't notice at the time, but in the video I'm shouting, 'Pope! Pope! Look over here, Francis!' I'm surprised I didn't call him Francie.

I go back to Mam's spot and lean in to tell her my story. She says she saw him pass, but there were too many tall people around. John Paul offered to lift her up, but she said she didn't want to be on telly being hoisted up. I'm glad. She's had so much manhandling over the last while the osteoporosis will kick in somewhere on her and she'll break something in a stress fracture.

I show her the video like I'm a child wanting her to be proud of me.

'Didn't you get very close! Maybe you'll get a bit of faith back.'

The cheering of his procession drifts away from us as the Pope goes further and further back. They don't take him past the empty areas and, before long, he's back up the front.

I leave Mam again and find Denis with the rest of Kilsudgeon. It's a right picnic they're having in the drizzle. The sandwiches are long gone, the flasks are empty. They are wiring into the pizza just as the Pope appears on the altar.

'Pizza at Mass,' says Denis. 'Did you ever hear the bate of it?'

I shuttle backwards and forwards to Mam's enclosure a few times to see is she OK. Eventually, the security man from earlier recognizes me and gestures me to go and join her.

'Are you sure?' I say, surprised by his change of heart.

'That was then and this is now, love,' is all he says, so in I go.

I sit next to Mam, watching her watch the Pope. He is meeting the children of Ireland. And sure enough, there is Amelia Deasy, handing him a letter. Her parents are a little further back on the altar. And Patsy! Chummy as you like with them. For God's sake. He's managed to get his way on to that stage without singing any Latin. The hymns nearly convert me, though. No matter the turnout, thousands of people singing would melt you.

'He says a nice Mass, doesn't he, Mam?'

She gives me a cranky look. Even if there's pizza being eaten somewhere else, Mam doesn't tolerate idle chat at Mass.

The Pope asks for forgiveness for all the abuses and the woman translating for him puts it into English. I watch Mam closely. Her eyes are closed and the brow is wrinkled on her. Her knuckles grip the rosary tight.

We draw our breath at Communion. It is a fierce operation. There are people funnelling out with the hosts at a smart clip. They go out among the paddocks; left and right, they turn. Over and back.

'Four thousand ministers of the Eucharist, I read,' whispers Mam. 'They won't need half of them.'

We get Communion and then sit quietly for a while.

'I want to go, Ann.'

'Now? Mam, you never leave a Mass early.'

'I want to go. Get me into that chair like a good girl.'

I ring Denis to join us. He wonders has Mam had a fall, she seems so down. He pushes for a while. They talk about different types of drizzle and he holds an umbrella over her. He's the perfect man to know something's wrong and say nothing until it's safe to talk. He'd make a great spy if you wanted him to not blow your cover. *Oh grand, Dr Blofeld. Who do you have tied up there? James Bond. Is he a local? I wouldn't know him now.* And then, when the coast would be clear, he'd be untying ropes and discussing shark tanks.

We pass groups of people handing out free sandwiches. All the stuff that was expecting a bigger crowd. Bored soldiers are leaning against vehicles. The journey back through the park seems to fly by. Thousands are leaving. The type that always go early to get the paper. Soon the sounds of singing start to fade. We are back on to Conyngham Road, then Parkgate Street. Returning to normal life. There are people in shops buying pot noodles and fruit pastilles and all the small things of ordinary life. As if nothing is going on up the road. We go to the Ashling Hotel, near Heuston. Denis settles us in and fusses over getting tea and a few scones, and locates the toilets and all the little things that you'd notice weren't being done if he wasn't there.

Mam takes a big slug of tea and coughs a little because it's too hot.

'So that's it, Ann.'

'That's it, Mam.'

'Forty years, Ann. It's a long time to wait, isn't it?'

Denis comes to the table and I put out a hand to my side, flat, to let him know there might be Big Talk, so he leaves the small butters down without a word and goes off in the direction of a big telly to check how a football match is going.

Mam watches him go.

'I get cross with you for having him all the time, Ann. And not turning your back on him, like I did to your father. I miss him something terrible all the time. Even though he let me down. I feel bad for giving him the cold shoulder for so long.'

'But you thought he was carrying on with Nonie.'

'I thought I'd get a bit of peace today. But there was nothing, Ann. I heard nothing.'

'But the Pope had his apology, Mam.'

'No, Ann. I was listening out for Jesus.'

'Maybe there was too much noise, Mam.'

'I don't know, maybe I'm an eejit to be looking for one sign. I'm fierce tired, Ann. Did you ever feel so tired in your head you don't want to do any more? Just take to the bed and not wake up? I feel that way, Ann.'

'Maybe Jesus will talk to you later, Mam. When he's less busy.'

'My legs are sore,' she says, and goes silent again.

After a few minutes Denis comes back. He puts a hand on her shoulder, and she grabs it. I think they talk sometimes without me. I like that. I mightn't always be giving her the right advice. I send out a WhatsApp to let the family know where we are and we watch the white dot of a ball move around the big green screen of a football match at the other end of the bar.

And then, all of a sudden, the place is bustly. Deirdre and Hughie arrive and the children are worn out and cranky from walking and pizza, so they sprawl on the couch. Freya and Lossie come in all flushed and excited from the March for Truth, but Freya sees her Nana's head bent and fingers-to-lipses Lossie and they just make small talk. You can tell, though, they're itching to tell me about the March for Truth, and I can see smudges on the mascara.

'We all had outings, so,' says Mam. 'Isn't that grand? We all had a day out. And I was a VIP after all.'

I give her a kiss on her head and start getting ready for the trip to meet the parents.

36.

REMINGTON SOMETHING

The taxi driver thinks he knows where they are. I check my phone for the address, but it must have been said to me and I was meaning to write it down. I know it's 15 Remington something because I remember thinking *Remington Steele*, and I wonder what's Pierce Brosnan at now, because he was great in that. I wasn't gone on him in *Mamma Mia!*

But the taxi man knows Phil and Des. 'Everyone knows the two of them,' he says. 'Sound out,' he says. 'I'd be open-minded that way.'

I don't know what he has to be open-minded about, but I let him prattle on.

'I know these places like the back of me hand,' he says. 'A lot of the foreign drivers now, you'd be going around the houses with them. Up for the Pope, are ye? I was listening to it on the radio.'

Denis takes control of the small talk again, pointing out any problems with road layout or dereliction so that the driver can go on about it and say, *Well, you know what happened there, don't ya?* He knows all the gangsters in Dublin too. He was in school with them and they were all battered in the Industrial Schools and that's what had them the way they were, but they had a 'code', the old crowd. The new crowd are all off their heads on crack. That's a different story.

Denis agrees that crack is way worse *than the heroin* and that *it's gone like the Bronx.* Denis is mad for this kind of talk. Anything that suggests the Bronx. Any gangland news, straight from the horse's mouth, will be worth a lot at lunchtime in the gravel pit.

The houses get bigger and further back from the road.

'Now, 15 Remington Road, isn't it? Yeah, I've definitely brought them home a few times. A great couple for partying, the two of them. That's them there. You wouldn't be the usual people going in there. I knew Phil, but I never knew the other one.'

I don't see any sign of a granny flat. It must be around the back.

We get out slowly. Mam just has the walker now. The wheelchair went back on the train. I have sent a text to Jennifer saying we're here, and she's given me the thumbs-up. But they're not outside.

I ring the doorbell. It has a most unusual knocker. The door opens and a man answers.

'Hello. You must be Phil.'

He looks at me, almost through me. 'Right.'

He sees Denis and then Mam on the walker. 'Eh . . . three of you? I'm not really sure what she's going to do. OK. It's a flat rate, so whatever way you want to do it.'

'I'd texted Des and he said it was OK? Is Jennifer here?'

'Jennifer?' He shakes his head and says something about the agency. Declan must have got the oddness from the father.

'Well, come in so.'

He looks at our suitcases. 'You have your equipment in them? Ehh . . . fine, I guess.'

'Ah, just a few bits, you know.' I give him the apple tart I bought at the hotel. He stares at it like he's never seen an apple tart in his life.

'Now, if you could start in the kitchen and, when you're ready to do the sitting room, we'll move then.'

Denis whispers at me. 'I think we're in the wrong place, Ann. This is a different Des and Phil.'

'Excuse me, are you Declan's father, Phil?'

Phil looks very cross. 'Oh, for God's sake. Not again. That bloody driver. Was he a shortish fella, comb-over? Said he went to school with gangsters?'

'Yes.'

'I don't know if she's a close friend of yours, but can you tell her to use her full name, please. We keep getting people here looking to be measured. You're looking for Desdemona and Philip? That's Remington Mews. This is not the first time. They're up there.' And he walks us up around the corner and points us along the road to another house. A house where Jennifer is standing in the front lawn, staring at her phone, puzzled. We make our way up sheepishly.

'Isn't that a good one, Jennifer?' I say when we reach her. 'We had the wrong Remington.'

'Trust you, Mam, to go to the wrong house. I *texted* the address,' she says as she marches us up the path to the front door, where Desdemona and Phil are standing.

The place is massive. Two newish cars parked in the drive-way. There is room in the hall to stand and chat without knocking anything. A big St Bernard dog pads over, and he's clean. I scan Denis for stains, but in fairness he must have eaten the pizza neatly. I see my own trousers have some kind of a blemish on them. I'm hoping it's water. Time will tell.

Des doesn't have any blemishes. She has blonde hair that, even now, on a Sunday evening, looks like she is just out of the hairdresser's, and a gorgeous cream trouser-suit. Phil hangs back and has the same kind of awkward stance that I remember in Declan when we first met him. But Des gives me a big hug.

'Jennifer, will you go and fetch that boy? Ann and Denis, it's a pleasure and an honour to meet you and – I hope you don't mind, Denis, but – especially you, Ann, a local hero.'

I mutter a few *ah-shur*s. I don't feel like a hero at the moment.

'And here is the boy himself now,' she says.

Declan comes along the hall and, as he stands next to Phil, I can see he is his father's son. Des is all energy.

We stand there talking about the Pope and wasn't it a pity about the weather and the crowds were down, and Denis talks about pizza at Mass and for the second time today asks did they ever hear the bate of it? They hadn't heard the bate of it either.

The conversation moves into the lounge, as she calls it. I think there might be a separate sitting room. Des fusses over Mam. She gets her into a comfortable chair and puts a foot-stool down for her, and there's a sherry in front of Mam and she refuses nothing offered to her. There isn't a word about indigestion.

We sink into comfortable chairs. She brings out a spread of nibbly bits and names them for us. There is bruschetta and pinwheels and olive tapenade and salmon somethings, and this is only the warm-up before dinner. Denis and Mam wolf them down, no complaints. Des and her big blonde hair have woven a spell.

'Dinner will be at eight,' she says.

Imagine knowing exactly what time dinner is going to be!

Des plonks herself between me and Jennifer. She puts a hand on my arm.

'You know, Ann, I feel like I know you. Thanks for looking after our boy last summer. It was the making of him. And about time he was made. I think Jennifer still has a bit of work to do, don't you, Jen?' And she gives Jennifer's shoulder a squeeze.

I can see now why she doesn't want to break up with Des.

The doorbell rings.

'Excuse me, Ann,' says Des, standing up. 'I think I know who this is. The place is absolutely hopping this weekend because of the Pope. All my rural customers take the opportunity, you see, when they're in Dublin. I had them till nine o'clock last night.'

I am boiling with the nosiness. Jennifer is smiling at me. She's never said much about what Des did for a living. *She has her own business*, she always said. Phil goes out to freshen the tea. Declan has disappeared elsewhere in the house.

'Your face, Mam.'

'Well, I'm just curious.'

'It's sex toys, Mam.'

'It is NOT, Jennifer . . . is it?'

We can hear the two of them in the hall. The visitor is a woman from somewhere up the North.

'Here you go, Mona. Will you try one to see does it fit?'

'AH, FAIR FUCKEN PLAYTEYE, DESSIE, ME OLD MUCKER. THAT'S THE STUFF. THAT'LL MAKE ALL THE DIFFERENCE. AYE, I WILL TRY IT ON SO.'

And there is the sound of her going upstairs.

'I'M A NEW WOMAN, DESSIE,' we hear her say as she comes back down. Jennifer is giggling. She's happier than she's looked in a while.

'Come in, Mona, you might as well, as you're here.'

A woman comes in with a big cloud of silvery hair. She's a bit older than me. She's fairly hefty, but she carries it well. A big flowery dress and linen trousers.

310

She notices us. 'Oh, I'm sorry, Des girl, I didn't know ye had company. Where are my manners? There's me coming in the door swearing like a fu-fecking marine. Hi. Hello there, young lady,' she says to me, 'I'm Mona, Mona McCAUGHEY from Tyrone.'

'You don't need to be apologizing to us, Mona,' I assure her.

'Aye, I know, but ye can't be too careful. The town is full of Holy Joes this weekend. Not that there's anything wrong with that. I was there meself. But it's the hardcore that'd get offended by a bit of language. Shur, Jesus Christ, wasn't Our Lord Himself nailed to the cross? Wasn't he swearing away goodo? Do you think he'd give a flying fuck about what some big article from the backarse of Tyrone was saying?'

We agreed that, no, Jesus would not.

'Are you the in-laws? Dessies said yous were comin all right. And who's this fine cut of a man? Is this your husband, Ann? You're doing well there. A bit of a rival for Philly boy here. Us big women need a good strong man to hold on to, isn't that right, Annie?'

Denis is *delighted* with himself. He can't keep the grin off his face.

'Listen now, while you're here, girls, are ye going to get a fitting? Look at the support, girls.' And she puts her hand under her front and cups her boobs out at us. 'Women like me, big oul boobers carrying two stone upfront, Ann, we've been in the wrong bras all our lives and we'd be still at it, only for this miracle-worker here. The boob whisperer. I'm telling you, Ann, have you tried it? TRY IT! She'll change your life. Right now. Surely I'd better go.'

And off she heads.

'Would one of them do me, Des?' says Mam out of nowhere. 'I'd say I haven't been fitted right my whole life.'

'Oh, Margaret, it is one of my personal crusades! People think that the senior woman doesn't need a bra or even

311

deserve a nice one, or they just don't bother making them for her. You must see plenty of that, Ann.'

'I do, Des. No one cares how the elderly are dressed. I wish I could bring them shopping, but Mellamocare doesn't want them brought out.'

She looks at me for a second and smiles, and then Phil comes back with the tea.

After a half an hour Mam is dozing a little in the chair, so Des says she'll bring us to our 'quarters'. We are to be in the granny flat, and the two 'lovebirds' will stay in Declan's old room. Des brings us on what seems like a long walk through the house and out the back to the granny flat. Although 'granny flat' doesn't do it justice. It's like a whole other house. She leaves us to get settled.

'I'll sleep on the floor,' says Denis. 'It'd be a shame to ruin that bed. There's toothbrushes in the en suite. New ones. It's like America.'

We go back down for the dinner. It's the biggest roast beef I've ever seen. Denis is nearly crying with appreciation. Phil hasn't said much so far, but it seems he knows about wine and is telling Denis in great detail about it. Denis throws me the odd look that says he is gasping for a pint. He's out of small talk and it doesn't look like Phil is as interested in traffic, bypasses and parking as Denis is. I'm next to Des at the table. She wants to talk about the wedding.

'. . . when I heard about the proposal, Ann, I could have killed him. Imagine asking her in front of a load of people. I was mortified for you, Jen. I mean, I was surprised Declan would do a thing like that. But this girl is a star, Ann. She's just taken it in her stride, haven't you, hun?'

Jen gives me a watery smile.

'You know, Ann, I'm so happy that he is with Jennifer. I worry about him. I was always very busy with the business and I think I didn't pay enough attention to him. I put him in boarding school, Ann. I sent him away, and Phil was away with work as well.'

Phil looks uncomfortable.

'So Jennifer has been really great for him. Hasn't she, Declan?'

Declan doesn't seem to mind being discussed.

'Paxman has a new podcast on Kilsudgeon, Mrs Devine. He's really good on it. He says it's the battleground. Kudos for the occupation, Mrs Devine. You're doing good work.' And he . . . gives *me* a fist bump.

Des suddenly busies herself with distributing second helpings, giving out to Phil for not making sure Denis has enough spuds on his plate. Denis announces that the wine is mighty.

We finally get a chance to talk before going to bed. We're in the kitchen of the granny flat. Denis is trying out the channels and the smart TV. Every so often he announces the latest thing the TV has. Jennifer arrives in with a bottle of wine, and she's found a can for Denis.

'Mam, I don't know what to do. Declan's got worse with the Paxman thing. He met him again last week at one of his Slug Seminars.'

'Slug Seminars?'

'Oh Mam, remember I told you about Paxman's slug theory? So now he's saying men are oppressed by the image of themselves in the media, and say, like, if there was an endangered species, like if it was a wolf, it would get all the attention, but no one likes slugs. Even though they're vital to the world.'

'Salt'll get rid of slugs, Jen,' shouts Denis from the TV room. 'Hang on, I'll look it up on the telly. Internet on the telly!'

'Thanks, Daddy, we're all good for tips on actual slugs. Right, so Paxman runs these Slug Seminars. *Embracing Your Power*, and all that shite. Declan went along, and there were questions at the end and he asked him about organizing a wedding and Paxman gets this fucking BRAINWAVE, Mam, that maybe *he* should get into the business of wedding planning, but with men in mind, and stop all this bridezilla stuff "at source". AND he's getting a licence to perform the weddings himself, so now Declan comes to me saying we're going to be the first Lance Paxman wedding. I swear, Mam, I'm in an episode of fecking *Don't Tell the Bride* but, like, I already know all about it.'

'But you're not going to stand for that, are you, pet? Not if you're this unhappy?'

'No, I'm not, but I don't know where to start. Look at the set-up here. Look at Des – she's fabulous. Phil is harmless. I do love Declan – I just need a way of getting out of this without hurting anyone, including me. Any ideas?'

'Oh, Jennifer, you'll have to be honest with them.'

'Any other ideas, Mam?'

'Ann?!' It's Denis from the other room. 'Kilsudgeon is on the news! Come in quick.'

We sit and watch the reporter outside the post office. He's live in the dusk. Behind him is Kilsudgeon post office. Yellow Vest people all around the outside. A few guards off to one side. There are banners everywhere. Hanging from the upper-floor windows. KILSUDGEON TIDY TOWNS + NUATHA = A CLEAN START FOR KILSUDGEON and, right next to it, another one: IRELAND BELONGS TO THE IRISH.

'I see you're a racist now, Mam?' says Jennifer, not smiling.

My chest feels tight. I hope my in-laws are not watching the news.

It might as well be me up there on that roof with a sign. That's the result of my scheming now. There was me worried about Rory working with Patsy. And now look at what I've enabled. Well, this ends now, I can tell you.

37.

AMERICANS WITH GUNS

We have an early start the following morning. I have to get home to do my rounds in the afternoon, so we don't hang around the house for too long. Jennifer says she has a 'breakfast meeting' at work, which sounds like an awful thing to have to go to. Des has clients coming, but she's promised to measure both of us ladies for the big wedding. She says she can already tell what we need doing from the look of us.

I am still finishing my breakfast when she leaves, and I walk her out. She gives me a big hug.

'We're going to be bosom buddies, Ann,' she says.

'You must have a lot of them in your business.'

She shrieks with laughter. 'I knew you were good stuff, Ann. I like Jennifer and I like you as much.'

'And I like you more than I like Decl—' and I say it without thinking, but then my look of horror makes her laugh, again to my relief. I haven't ruined everything.

After our breakfast, Declan drives us to the train. He is chattering away about the news last night as we sit in the traffic. Well, chattering for him.

'Are you going back into the post office, Ann?'

'Yes, but only to get the bann—'

He interrupts. Declan *never* interrupts.

'They're all talking about it on Lance Paxman's live stream. About how you took on the big TV show and now the government. He says it's a turning point. I've emailed him saying I'm marrying into a Kilsudgeon family, and he said, *Keep the faith, brother.* My mam's dead against Paxman, but she would be, wouldn't she?'

He doesn't say what he means. At the station he gives me a handshake that turns into a hug.

'You're a hero, Ann.'

Seeing this, Denis makes his handshake unhuggable.

On the train down I am glued to my phone, but watching it with a pain in my stomach. All these people congratulating me on Facebook for giving the Tidy Towns 'teeth'. The fights going on in the Comments. A load of Americans with guns in their profile photos telling Ireland to *wake up*. Except Gordon. Gordon sees through it. The Church of Ireland were the first outsiders. He can probably see the signs. He sends me an email.

I was so surprised to see our name associated with that kind of thing, Ann. We'll need an urgent response. I'll be back next week. Can you put something up on Facebook disassociating us from the whole thing?

Rory is raging. *MAM WTAF?? Does Tidy Towns mean something different now? Who are you tidying? I'm coming home as soon as I can. Patsy sorting out a flight.*

Freya sends me a link to the Kilsudgeon Facebook group, where they are organizing a counterdemonstration, and a link to lots of articles about the alt-right and how they operate.

I'm nearly relieved that my own family are tearing strips off me. I must have reared them right.

I can't reply to everyone, so I reply to no one. When we get home I get Denis to mind Mam. Freya is still over at Deirdre's with her cousins. I sit down to write out a post for Facebook.

Kilsudgeon Tidy Town wishes to dissociate itself from . . . The phone rings. It's Iseult. I ignore it. Twice. Then she sends this.

Hello, Ann, call me. I have some information for you.

Reluctantly, I call her. She's unnaturally breezy and goes into a spiel before I say anything.

'Listen, Ann. Everything is going as planned here, but we need to get the local people more in the picture, you know? We need you down here, fighting with us.'

'Lookit, Iseult,' I say, trying to think of the right words, 'this isn't anything Tidy Towns wants to be involved in.'

'We all want to bring about change here, Ann, don't we?'

'Well . . . emm . . .'

'But you know, Ann, before we go any further, I need to check something with you. Because if we're going to be partners on this we need, like, full disclosure, amirite?'

She doesn't let me reply.

'So basically, I was asking Michael – you know, Mick the Lamp – about how *Rory's* getting on, and he was telling me something super-interesting about Rory.'

'Oh . . .'

'Yeah, so, apparently – and I know this is a sensitive topic, but I really need to know – Mick was telling me that Rory got a special, like, scholarship to UCC because of a tough upbringing because . . . and, like, obviously this is really . . .

317

difficult to bring up but I have to . . . because you have addiction issues? I am so sorry, Ann. And don't worry, your secret is safe with me. I think your struggle is very brave, but I just need to know that you are OK now, and I promise we won't say any more about it . . . unless . . .'

'Unless?'

'. . . unless, well, obviously, unless you relapsed and people were asking. I'd need to tell them. And I know that would have a real impact on your job, wouldn't it, because don't you, like, have to handle drugs for some of your clients?'

She's trying to blackmail me. My breathing grows shallow. Then I make it worse.

'I don't have a problem with drugs, Iseult. That was just something Patsy cooked up for the grant.' As soon as I say it, I know it sounds terrible.

'Yeah, I know, Ann. Mick was there to me before, like, *Is Ann on drugs?* and I was, like, *I can't think of anyone less on drugs, why?* And he told me the story and then I was really suss and now you've confirmed it.'

She listens to me breathing quickly.

'But you know what, Ann? We've been through so much together and every relationship has its skeletons. That's what comrades are, yeah? Every soldier has a past. It's about the future. So look, I'll see you back here for the sit-in, yeah?'

'No, Iseult, I want to . . .'

'Because the town looks up to you, Ann. You need to show that the town *is* behind us and our fight. But if they heard about what you did to get Rory into college, it would be such a betrayal of what we are about, Ann. I think they would feel let down. It's going to be a big night tonight. Gary Cushin and all his Marxist goons are doing a counter-demo and there's rumours the guards will try and end the sit-in and take us out. We need everyone on camera for that, Ann, if it comes to it. So I'll see you there, Ann?'

'Iseult . . .'

'Later, Ann.'

It's finally come back to haunt me. I let it happen. We could have turned down the grant or given it back. But I just let it slide. *You were always a bit wishy-washy, Ann*, my mother would say about me when it came to believing in anything. If my son is made in the image of his grandfather, then some of it is in me too. The harmless bit of a nod and wink. *Shur it's someone else's money.* And what is it I believe in anyway? Even the religion is a bit wishy-washy with me. There's Mam with her prayers and faith, hanging in there. Principles. And what do I have?'

Freya comes in the door from Deirdre's for her lunch. She's still got her T-shirt and flag from yesterday's March for Truth. She starts to tell me about it.

'It was so incredible, Auntie Ann. We just stood there, like, deathly silent. And they went past Magdalene laundries. Like, I'm glad Nana got to see the Pope, but I'm glad I went to that, you know? It's hard, isn't it? Obvs, I love Nana, but I guess we just, like, believe different stuff. What about that stuff I sent you? Do you get now why Iseult and her gang need to be cancelled? Will you come with Gary and the others for the counterdemo tonight?'

'I want to, Freya, but things are a bit complicated.'

'Auntie Ann?!'

'I just need to do one thing first, OK?'

38.

ONLY THE TRUE GAELS LEFT

I do my rounds. I can't help wondering is it for the last time. Sylvester is sheepish. He asks about Mam, but I don't tell him much beyond that she got on fine and she's tired now after her trip.

'Did I offend the good lady, Ann? Sometimes I let my mouth have its way.'

I promise him I'll pass on the message. It's late afternoon by the time I get to the post office. There's an RTÉ news van there, and the Russia Today man is parked outside the Centra, sitting half in and half out of his car eating an ice cream. He looks bored. The guards are parked there, too, with a truck loaded with barriers, but they haven't put any of them up yet. A few of the Nuatha people are gathered outside. I sit in the car, trying to see what's the quietest time to go in. It's five o'clock. They'll be doing something for the six o'clock news, no doubt, so I should go now. I have a hi-vis on so that I don't stick out. Imagine that.

Mary Cuddihy is coming out of the Centra now. I wait for her to go because I'll get stuck talking to her and she is as LOUD, even when she's talking about nothing. Once she slips out of view I stride up to the door, cool as you like. I have a bit of luck because Iseult is just inside and I wave to her and I can get straight in without anyone outside even noticing.

'Hello, Ann!' Iseult insists on hugging me, but the hug is cold as can be. The others barely look at me.

We go upstairs, where she has made a little office in one of the empty rooms. Davey is in there, and the Dutchman. There are a load of phones charging and they have a drill out and are putting up metal loops on the wall. I ask what they're for and Ollie Holland snaps, 'For chaining ourselves.'

Davey Finnerty walks over then, face like thunder. 'I see your son has been busy libelling us, Ann.'

'I don't know anything about that,' I say, and I don't. 'What's Rory up to now?'

'Him and your niece are posting up all sorts of shit about us and our cause. Well, I hope you have deep pockets, Ann, because when we get out of here we'll be on to our solicitors. My uncle, actually.'

'Solicitors? So you're anti-establishment only when it suits you?' It pops out of me by surprise. But I'm not here to make friends any more.

'Ann, Davey, leave it,' says Iseult. 'Rory is still under the influence of Patsy. That's what they want – division. Isn't that right, Ann? They want us fighting. So they gave us an ultimatum. Get out of the post office or we'd be removed this evening. And what did we tell them?'

'We told them to fuck off,' answers Davey. 'We want commitments from a minister that the post office will be kept open.'

I take a deep breath and say, 'What's with the banner on the roof about the Irish?'

Iseult looks to Davey. 'That, Ann, is the real threat,' he says. 'Our friends in Save Our Celtic Identity brought that.' He gestures over at another man I don't know, who is busy sorting chains. 'They said they heard the building was going to be used for migrants. That's the plan all along, Ann. We got there just in time. Who knows who could be moving in here?'

'Well, Kilsudgeon Tidy Towns wants no part of that. We have had people from all backgrounds doing our clean-ups.'

'I heard there was no one turning up the last few times before we came along.'

I've no answer to that.

'Anyway, I want *our* banner down.'

'How do you know it's the view of the majority? If you put a post up on Facebook now, who would agree with it, Ann?'

He sees me hesitate. I haven't heard much around here to encourage me.

'That's right. They wouldn't. If they knew a horde of foreigners were being put in here instead. How many Likes would you get for that?'

'What horde are you talking about? It's all just rumours. And anyway, Kilsudgeon is not a racist place, Davey.'

'It's not racist to want to preserve this country. It's nationalist.'

'But you have a brother in America, Davey.'

'He's working for the Establishment. He's a leech.'

I'm getting nowhere with this.

'Can I just take down our banner, please?'

'The window's stuck, Ann. I can't get it open.'

Davey is not for budging. He has a look in his eye I haven't seen before, and Davey has had lots of mad looks in his time. I go over to try the window, and it has nails in it.

'I'd better go.'

'Are you sure you can't be persuaded to stay, Ann? I mean, like, it's totally your own choice, but it would be seen as a bit of, like, you know, letting the team down? And there are special bonds here, like I was saying earlier,' Iseult says.

'Look, Iseult, say what you're going to say. I'm going. I'm not part of this any more. This isn't Kilsudgeon and it definitely isn't me.' My heart is beating quickly. I know what this means. But I'm not going to cry about my job now.

Iseult looks at me in a funny way. I think she might be pleading with me. She seems a bit scared.

'I think it's only the true Gaels left,' says the Dutchman.

I want to point out the obvious, but I don't. Not with the look in Davey's eyes. I go downstairs to leave and I can hear cheering in the main post office room.

There is chanting. 'Pax-man, Pax-man, Pax-man . . .'

Surely not? He wouldn't be bothered with here, would he? It gets louder as I get down the stairs, and I see what they are all cheering about. A familiar head is in the middle of the group and he appears to be reading something off his phone. It's Declan. I want to shout out, but he's in mid-flow. Davey and Iseult appear at my shoulder.

'. . . and he's sent me a message to read out to you. He has it on YouTube but he says the mainstream media will censor it and the snowflake commentariat will try and cancel him.'

The group murmur their agreement.

Declan starts to read. I have never seen him so loud and confident. It's a pity he got his confidence from this shower.

'Greetings, men and women of Ireland. This is a glorious day for Irish manhood and womanhood. We have stood firm against the forces of identity politics and the Dublin liberal media. The world is watching. Continue your struggle for Kilsudgeon and beyond. The identity of rural Ireland. This post office is just the opening skirmish. Before long you'll be fighting for your language, your culture, your masculinity, as they are being eroded by Big Pharma and the Feminist meat grinder.'

Declan's face is quite red with this. But with the effort of it, not the embarrassment. It goes on for a few minutes. Everyone gets a go. Politicians, the Church, 5G – even, for some reason, hybrid cars. I look around me. They are lapping this up. They are lapping him up. I'll have to get out of here now, and I'm taking Declan with me before it all kicks off later.

Davey goes over and hugs Declan. 'Respect,' he says. 'Joining the cause. We need more of your family to think the same.'

After a while the crowd around Declan goes back to sitting down. Someone hands him a rollie, and he takes a puff, uncertainly. Eventually I get a chance to go over to him, and he grins.

'This is it, Ann. The first battle.'

'Why are you talking like this, Declan? What's got into you? Does Jennifer know you're in here?'

He doesn't reply.

'Does she, Declan? Declan, c'mon, we'll go out of here. It's not our scene.'

'No, Ann, this *is* my scene. I was asleep for years. I thought it was shyness, but there was a lid on my life. It's a lid on a lot of men, Paxman says. Some of it is in us, but some of it is society not valuing us. This is about taking back control. You go on if you want, Ann. This is my place.'

There's no stirring him. He's scaring me. But I can't leave him in here. He's still the boy who got out of a car last year and stayed with us for two months. I won't see him turned into a Davey Finnerty. Shouting in court about foreigners. I owe it to his mother. And to my daughter.

It's gone eight o'clock now, and it's dusky outside. It's a cool evening, although the air in the post office is muggy. And very smelly. There is a toilet, but no shower it seems. One of the gang arrives back with shopping from Lidl and sandwiches are handed round. The food donations from the village have stopped. People might be supporting on Facebook, but not enough to bring in a hamper. Shortly after the food, we hear shouting from outside. It gets louder. It's another protest. About twenty or thirty of them, Freya at the front. There is a banner saying KILSUDGEON SAYS NO TO RACISM.

The gang inside rush out to hurl abuse at the other protest.

Wave if you can see me, says Freya on WhatsApp.

We look out the window and the guards suddenly appear and form a line between the groups. Davey comes downstairs, shouting, 'GET BACK IN! THEY'RE TRYING TO DRAW US OUT!'

The people in yellow vests who were outside come running, shouting. Immediately, they all spring into action. They start shoving furniture up against doors. A few people are already chaining themselves to the metal loops.

We're left alone without any jobs to do. I am glad now that Declan is still Declan enough to be flummoxed by all this drama. He stays stock still. I guide him over to a corner where we are out of earshot.

'Listen to me, Declan, because I'm only going to say this once. If you want to have any hope of marrying my daughter, you need to come out of here with me. Jennifer is already touch and go with you the way you are at the moment. She is this close to calling off the wedding. One word from me either way could make all the difference.'

I hope he still wants to marry her and wants to come with me because it's the only kind of pull I have with him at all. Declan just stares ahead.

'I'm sick of it,' he says. 'Mam, Jennifer, now you. Just women telling me what to do. *Oh, there's shy Declan, he'll need it sorted for him.* Mam does it to Dad. But Dad lets her. She's so strong. Paxman says alpha females exist. I just want to make my own way.'

'But Declan, just because you have a problem doesn't mean you should follow the first person who looks like they might solve it. They mightn't . . . Look, Declan, if I tell you something, will you promise not to say a word? Promise now?'

He nods.

'Declan, I got into this mess because I wanted to get Rory away from Patsy Duggan. And I latched on to the first person who might do that. Iseult. And I let her get control of me, Declan. I was weak myself, Declan. You were not weak. You were yourself, strong in your own way.'

'But I'm strong now and it's only a problem because Jennifer doesn't agree with me, so I'm wrong somehow.'

'Well, all I know is, Declan, you could be right, but if you're any bit wrong, then would you risk losing Jennifer over it?'

He says nothing.

This is tricky. Out of nowhere, Tracy's techniques pop into my head. *Ask a question.*

'Declan, can I ask you a question?'

Even that throws him. I don't even know what the question is.

'What's the question, Ann?'

'Eehhh . . . what . . . what is it you want?'

He breathes out noisily. 'That's a good question, Ann.'

Thank God for that.

'Like, aren't you just following whatever Paxman says? He sent you down to read out a message, Declan. Yes, I know, I know, it might seem that Jennifer can be very bossy, but she loves you, Declan. This crowd have no love about

326

them. They're just trying to stir up things for their own gain. They like broken things. They won't last. Maybe this Paxman fella might make a bit of money, but he won't be sharing it with you. Will you come with me, Declan?'

I think I have him. He looks at his phone, and the screensaver is him and Jennifer. He stares straight ahead and slides down the wall until he is sitting. I join him by a more awkward method. We're an odd pair, sitting on the ground while barricading and chaining's going on around us and *FASH, FASH, FASH!* is being shouted outside.

'What do you say, Declan?' I get up and put out my hand. He accepts it and hauls himself to his feet.

We move out of the main room, around the counter and to the corridor that leads to the back door. And there at the back door is Toirdealbhach, sitting on a chair, hammering planks across the doorframe and props into the floor. We're stuck. We try to act casual.

'Just having a look,' says Declan. I feel for the first time that I have an ally in here.

I try to ring Denis. Davey sees me with the phone out.

'Put it away, Ann. We need a tight message here. If you're in, we don't want anyone filming, unless it's Iseult.'

I send Freya a quick text while that's still allowed. *Stuck inside Declan here dont ask need help call guards. Dont want be seen get me out back door maybe.*

We go back to our spot and wait for I'm not sure what.

Bing! I put it on Silent but sneakily look at the screen.

Freya has added you to the group Devine Intervention.

There is a lot of thumping upstairs.

Deirdre: *What's this frey?*

Freya: *Auntie Ann is stuck in the post office with the Kilsudgeon KK. We need to get her out.*

Rory: *I am in a car breaking the speed limit as we speak. Skitchy at the wheel about to LOSE HIS LICENCE. We are 15 mins away. Hang on!!!*

Denis Husband: *Sskfsgfsgsfg*

Rory: *Denis, stop arse-dialling.*

Denis Husband: *Wil u ring me fridge can t do these buttons in the lorry*

Freya: *OK, boomer.*

08something (a number I don't know): *Ann, the guards are going to be in in half an hour PD.*

PD? Who is PD?

Me: *You added Patsy, Freya!!*

Rory: *I did Mam.*

Freya: *You sent that to the group, 007.*

08something (a number I don't know): *This is my other phone for this kind of thing.*

Rory: *Booty-call phone.*

Denis Husband: *nnnnnnnnnnnnnnnnnnnnnnnnnnn*

Freya: *I'll ring Uncle D.*

Big Jay, the druidy lad I met last time, staggers through into the post office carrying a bag, so I tell them I've to be quiet for a while.

Freya: *Roger that.*

Rory: *Going dark.*

'Lads, check this shit out. It's a bag of old letters. I found it in the back of the cupboard. Ann, this is your vintage. It's *ancient*.'

He empties the bag out on to the pallet table we are sitting at, a few bits falling through the cracks on to the ground. I pick up one. The letters were all stamped and, as I flick through them, I see they are all local addresses.

'And there's another bag back there. They're all from the same time, around September, October 1979. That's nearly forty years ago. Would you credit it?' He holds up the envelope. It has SAG written on it.

'What does that mean, SAG?'

'St Anthony Guide,' I say.

'What?'

'They'd write that on envelopes so that St Anthony would mind the letters.' There are blank looks all round.

Now he opens the envelope and takes out the letter.

'You shouldn't do that,' I say, even though I'm curious myself.

'They're probably all dead, it's so long ago,' he says, shrugging.

'I'm alive,' I say, but he's too busy eyeing up the contents. Good manners really are a thing of the past.

'*To whom it may concern*,' he reads. 'Hah, listen to that, was everyone royalty back then?' He clears his throat. '*To whom it may concern. I am writing in reply to your advertisement in the Sunday Press last week. I am a 35-year-old man and I have never had a girlfriend. I have met girls at dances, but I didn't click with them at all. In the last few years I have stopped going. I am worried I might have a thing for men.*'

Big Jay throws the letter on to the pile. 'Sap.'

There's silence after it. I think he thought it was going to be a great laugh, but the others don't laugh.

'The poor divil,' I say. 'How lonely it must have been for them.'

There are telegrams about sweepstakes, ones with a personal message for *a Mr Karl Steiner believed to be on holiday in the area.* I'm itching to open more letters, but it feels an invasion of privacy. I just look at some postcards. *Having a lovely time. Not too much rain. Killarney is very expensive.* And another one: *It was 90 degrees yesterday. Having a fabulous time in France.* I wonder who that was? It's addressed to Edwina Rourke from Siobhan. Of course! Stephanie's aunt writing to her mother. The Rourkes were the only ones going on holiday in the sunshine that time.

Big Jay goes out again and comes back with more bags. By the time he's finished there are ten bags in total. From what I can see they date from 1979 up until 1985. That was when Mary McCarthy, or Mary Stamps as they called her, was the postmistress. Kilsudgeon used to be a sorting office for a large area.

Mary Stamps retired around 1985, I think. Actually, she was nudged out because she was going very scatty. Towards the end she was unpredictable. The only thing she was guaranteed to do was the old age pension, but if you wanted anything else it was pot luck whether she would serve you or not. Postal orders, for some reason, used to really get her irate. People put up with her for a while because they felt sorry for her. Her son was killed over in America six or seven years previously and got the news in a telegram that came into the post office itself . . . come to think of it, it was in September 1978 that happened. I look through all the bags. All the postmarks are September. Some sort of madness must have come over that she hid these.

I'm surprised they've never been found before, but then Mary Stamps had lived over it and was replaced by Danny's mother, and neither she nor Danny ever lived here. They mustn't have bothered to look around the place. Danny was never that dynamic, I suppose. They say he was the last post office in the country to put in a laser machine because he didn't like 'fiddly buttons'.

'Davey, I need to get home to my mother,' I plead with him. 'I can go out the back door.'

He thinks about this for a second. 'It's barricaded. We're in for good now, Ann. You're part of us, whether we like it or not.'

'But Davey . . .'

I'm interrupted by more thumping down the stairs.

'More bags,' says the Dutchman. 'We find them in filing cabinet when we look for shome things to block the door.'

I nip off to the toilet to catch up on the WhatsApp.

Ann: *I can't get out the back door it's barricaded.*

08something: *I was on to Danny about it. i didn't say why. You could try the back window on the town end. But you'll need to block the lane when the guards start coming in. I can tell them the truck is ok.*

Ann: *Thanks Patsy*

08something: *Remember this now around election time.*

Freya: *Not now, Duggan.*

08something: *Excuse me now, I won't be spoke*

Denis: HAVE YOU A LAPTOP PATSY

08something: *N TO Like that*

Denis: *Ladder*

Freya: *FOCUS, PEOPLE. Uncle D, I will ring you. Patsy, is your ladder accessible?*

Deirdre: *Can't you just tell guards to let her out?*

Freya: *There's cameras there. If she's seen coming out it'll make her look like she's a racist.*

Deirdre: *It won't.*

Freya: *I've seen people cancelled for way less. I've cancelled for way less.*

08something: *Guard telling me Davey Finnerty won't let anyone in or out.*

Deirdre: *Such a bad idea.*

Freya: *Dubai is a bad idea.*

I have to mute the WhatsApp group. It's making too much noise. Davey is getting suspicious. We wait for a while.

My phone rings. It's Freya. I don't answer but I look at the group. It's gone crazy since. I scroll up through the messages.

Freya: *PAGING AUNTIE ANNNN?*

Freya: *OK, Auntie Ann, you got that? The back window at the town side goes on to a little balcony. Rory will be there with a ladder. And go to the lorry where Uncle Denis will get you. FREYA OVER AND OUT.*

Rory: *Just at the Feekle. Road safety ad shit going down here. Skitchy classic young male driver. Haven't even told him we're in a hurry. #truefriend*

Freya: *Classic Kilsudgeon.*

08something: *Ladder out back of constituency office. Denis. U can block lane. Was on to sergeant. Knows sensitivities. Has got me out of scrapes before.*

Rory: *U ledge, Patsy.*

Now I'm up to speed.

I hear the guards outside, shouting about our last chance before they forcibly remove us. The excitement builds inside. Iseult is on the internet, talking to the world.

'Hello, everyone, especially our friends in America having their lunch. As you can see, the state is attempting to suppress our direct action. This is an assault on democracy by the forces of Political Correctness.'

I whisper to Declan, 'Are you ready?'

He doesn't react.

'I'm going now, Declan. Follow me if you want.'

As Davey starts getting people to chain themselves to counters, I say I'm going for the loo.

'Again?' he says, looking very angry.

'If I go now, I'll last longer.'

Declan goes with me. They've no suspicion of him. As we leave there is a thump at the door. A shout goes up. The guards are roaring that they will give one last chance. They are told to shove the chance up their holes.

My phone buzzes in my hand.

Denis: *out back with ladle*

Denis: *ladder*

Rory: *With Denis now so you won't have to hear his wisdom any more on this channel. Outside back. Mam, do your thing.*

We hear another thump on the door. Declan and me are up the stairs, trying to find our way about in the bad light. We get lost temporarily, wondering which end is the town gable, but Declan figures it out from the sunset. We look out the window. It's in the next room. I try the door. It doesn't budge. I turn the key in the lock and it budges less. Declan, out of nowhere, plants a flying kick at the lock. It doesn't budge. I try the handle again, it opens. I was turning it the wrong way.

333

We are in a dusty room with more filing cabinets. The window looks seized up, but Declan grabs it and opens it. Rory is on the lane and sees us and comes over with the ladder. If there's any young lad who knows ladders, it's Rory, after years putting up Patsy's posters and pulling down other people's. Declan opens the latch and pulls up the sash. An alarm goes off. Shite. He forces the sash up. I look at the gap compared to me.

'You'll have to give me more than that, Declan, oul stock. My backside is the cat's whiskers. If it doesn't get through, I won't get through.' He grimaces and heaves it up another bit.

I attempt to squeeze out the window.

'C'MON, MAM!' Rory is at the railings. I have to sort of stand on Declan's back to get over the railing before I can get on to the ladder.

'Don't let me go, lads, whatever ye do. I'm not good with heights.'

'Let go of my head, Ann,' says Declan. 'Ah, fuck it, my hair.'

I let go of his hair with a *sorry* and then Rory is able to receive me on the ladder.

'Put your foot down. The right foot, Mam. The other right, Mam.'

It's like *Ireland's Fittest Family*, where you'd see all these young lads manhandling and roaring at their mams to throw her leg over a round bale.

Declan sees I'm safely out of it and he runs back in.

'Declan!' I shout.

No sign of him. Maybe he's made his decision after all.

There is a sound of crashing at the other side of the building, and shouting. But I am down and I am out. As I touch the ground, who should appear at the window above, only Iseult.

'Ann? Ann, is that you?'

'What do you want, Iseult?'

'Please take me with you! I'm trapped in this as well. I never meant it to go the way it did. It was Davey – he's the one who brought all the others in.'

'YOU KNEW WHAT YOU WERE DOING,' shouts Rory.

'Please, Ann. Remember what we talked about?'

'NO FUCKING WAY, ISEULT,' Rory shouts, and then he takes away the ladder.

'I will FUCKING END YOU, Rory!!!! AND YOU, ANN DEVINE!'

Denis revs the truck.

'What about Declan?' I say.

'We have to go now!' says Rory. 'The media will be trying to come around.'

Rory lays the ladder on the ground, notices too late that it's covered in Patsy's election stickers, and we run to the end of the cul de sac, where Denis has blocked the road so tightly not a sinner can see. We get into the cab and I climb behind Denis's seat to the little bed. It smells of Denis's side of the bed at home, only more so.

Denis punches the air and shouts, 'HUPPPPYAHBIYAAA! THAT'S SOME JOB, ISN'T IT, ANN? THIS IS LIVING. C'MON OUTTOFIT, YE FUCKERS.'

With the excitement, he's actually driven the wrong way, so we have to go three miles down the road before he can turn. Then he brings us back in the direction of home, past the scene at the post office, where the guards are still shouting in the door, the alarm is going off and some people in hi-vis are crouched on the pavement.

Denis drives us home via Johnny's for a few brown bags of beer and Rory runs into Nawaz for chips.

Freya: *Guys, Declan is on the ground outside the post office. I think he's hurt his leg.*

Jennifer: *What's going on, Mammy?!!! Why am I seeing Declan on the news fighting the fascists?*

335

39.

STILL KEEPING THAT DOOR OPEN

We are sitting around the kitchen table. Me, Freya, Denis, Rory and Mam. We are all on the beer. Apart from Freya. Deirdre is at the hospital with Declan. Freya is telling us what happened him after she was dropped home by Gary Cushin from their counter-protest.

'So we're all watching the guards break down the door and I'm looking at WhatsApp, wondering what the actual is going on, and then I see Declan at the window and I'm, like, oh no, he's on the dark side, and he's leaning out and I'm thinking, *No, Declan, no, don't shout something*, but he's untying the IRELAND FOR THE IRISH banner and there's a big cheer and I'm telling Gary Cushin, *Quick, he's one of us. He must have infiltrated*. And so we get them shouting, "NO PASARÁN!", which is this thing they shouted in, like, the Spanish civil war . . .'

'Thanks, teacher,' says Rory.

'Shut up, stooge. Anyway. He goes along the windowsill to take down the NUATHA + TIDY TOWNS sign as well – I

336

guess for you, Auntie Ann – and that's when he slipped and he kind of grabbed on to it and it sorta broke his fall? But not really. And he landed on his leg and now everyone thinks he's a hero against the Fash. Which he is. Now maybe tell Jen to delete literally ALL his Facebook activity for the last month. It's pretty shitty.'

I have to pinch myself as I listen to Freya fill us in on the missing bits of the story. This fifteen-year-old eating her chips after breaking her aunt out of a post office. We turn on the news and they are showing the scene again.

'Incredible scenes here in the normally quiet village of Kilsudgeon. A post office protest has turned very ugly indeed.'

Thanks be to God and his blessed mother and whoever else'll have me, they haven't emphasized the Tidy Towns aspect in it. I'm sure I'll have to do some amount of distancing, but at least I'm not being hauled out of there by the Guards, as we see happen to Iseult and Davy and a few others. I remember again Iseult's threat to 'end me'. I'll be talking to Tracy soon, I'm sure.

I've hardly had a chance to realize that Rory is home. I size him up. He has a bit of a colour. I think he's filled out. There's something different about him. It's not confidence, he's just more relaxed in himself. Or is it happy? I want to ask him about work, but there is a knock at the back door and Patsy wanders in.

'Still keeping that door open,' he says. 'Well, Devines,' he says, taking us in, 'what are we going to do with ye? You would think you were the most sensible family you could meet, and what are ye up to? Breaking out of a post office. Tell me, Margaret, you weren't flying a helicopter or something, were you? What hope is there for the rest of us, hah? I'm going to have to delete that WhatsApp group,' he says, 'or throw the phone in the river. Jesus, Ann, how did you get involved in such a scrape?'

'You know well, Pats . . . I don't know, Patsy. I kept trying to do the right thing but at the wrong time, or vice versa.'

'Brazen it out is the only way, Ann. That's what I do. You'll get used to it.'

'I don't want to get used to it.'

'*Now* do ye see how ould Patsy Duggan isn't the worst of them? Everyone might like the protest. It's great to be shouting, but who gets the deals done? It's the man in the know. Only for me having a good connection to the Garda sergeant, we were able to get you out, and we'll see right by Declan, too, don't worry. Isn't that right, Rory? We'll always have a plan if you give us a chance.'

'That's right, Patsy.'

I *had* a plan, but it was an awful stupid one. You can be scheming away, but you've no control over what someone else will do. And I read Iseult all wrong at the start. And the only way to get Rory to do the right thing is to tell Rory what the right thing is and let him decide himself. And how do I know whether it is or not? Maybe Patsy's way is the way of the country. My head hurts now. The tension is going out of it and the beer is coming in, but somewhere along the way they're throwing slaps at each other.

Patsy goes away and we start drifting off to bed. Mam hasn't said a word through all of this.

'Nice to have people round you, isn't it, Ann?' she says when I'm getting her into her nightdress.

'It is, Mam. Especially when you're in trouble.'

'No harm in a bit of trouble either, Ann. You find out where you stand.'

'You're not mortified by me?'

'No, I'm proud, Ann. But you should have rung me to say what was going on. I was here worried sick. I'm still your mother, you know. Be sure and ring the next time now.'

It's nearly midnight when the car comes in. It's Jennifer. She went to Declan in the hospital and brought him home. He only has a sprain and a bruised knee. She helps him into the house. They're hugging very close.

'I turn my back for a second and I find my fiancé carrying on with my mam,' she says. 'I thought I'd lost you, Declan. You were like a stranger.'

He's quiet again, but he has changed. You don't hang out a window ripping down nasty signs without it changing you. Paxman mightn't be doing the ceremony, but Jennifer won't have it all her own way from now on.

I finally go to bed at two. Denis is already there. I expect him to be asleep, but he's waiting for me.

'Your first go in the lorry in a while, Ann,' he says.

'Remember I used to go to work with you on my days off, back in the day?'

'And go to work on me too.' He giggles.

'I'll have more days off from now, I'd say.' I tell him the story.

'Ah, Iseult is all talk. She has enough on her mind now anyway. The gobshite.' He turns around in the bed to face me. 'Well, what did you think when you saw me in the lorry?'

'I thought, who's that handsome man coming to rescue me?'

'That's what I hoped you'd think, Annie.'

My headache goes away.

40.

POLICY NUMBER 5C

She wasn't all talk. She lets me stew for two days, and then I'm woken by a call from Tracy.

'Is it true, Ann?' she says without greeting.

'Is what true?'

'I got a message this morning, Ann, from Iseult Deasy, saying you have an issue with prescription pills. Given her recent activity, I assumed it's just a mistake, but I thought I'd check.'

'Oh.'

'You know Mellamocare policy number 5c, don't you, Ann? You are to disclose any potential reasons why you cannot administer client medication.'

'I never took a single tablet.'

'I'm sure an audit will tell us the full truth, Ann.'

She is silent for a while. I presume it's to give me space to apologize for . . . well, I don't know, because I haven't done anything. Anything obvious, anyway.

'I went out on a limb for you, Ann.'

'I know, Tracy.'

'You don't understand, Ann. I mentored you, and now it turns out you . . . well, all of this. I'm going to look very foolish. I hadn't bargained on this kind of outcome when I asked to put you on the Compassionate Conversa— I mean, when I gave you another chance.'

I'm struck by a sudden idea.

'I could resign, Tracy. I could retire. I'm nearly sixty.'

'I'll get back to you, Ann. We'd have to see what your entitlements are.'

'I don't care about entitlements.' I do, actually, but I care more about not being sacked.

'Well, in the meantime let's call it . . . eh . . . compassionate leave. We'll get a doctor's note saying you're stressed. I really did try my best for you, Ann.'

'I know, Tracy.'

I wonder what this means for her award. She probably deserves one after it all.

I go downstairs in a daze. My lovely little job. I lean on the kitchen worktop, looking out the back window. Rory comes in and finds me minutes later, still holding a teabag. He's holding his phone.

'You saw this, Mam?'

It's a text message to both of us.

You got the news, Ann? I picked the drugs angle. Easier to get you sacked. I'll keep the fraudulent grant claim for another day. And it looks like we'll be working together, Rory. Patsy v interested in what I found out about Rory's grant, so he's really happy to have me on the team.'

'Did she rat you out, Mam?'

'She did.'

'You're out?'

'On sick leave for now.'

'You're not the only one.'

'What do you mean?'

'I'm done with Patsy.'

'What?'

'I'm finished with him. I'm not working for him any more. I knew how he could turn on me when he blamed me for him putting up the wrong referendum video. And he said I shouldn't have left Iseult up the ladder. So he's blaming me for that too. It was Patsy who texted *her* to get out of there. He was scheming even then. He says we need the likes of her. She represents the young. And she's well connected. He's going to try and get her uncancelled. So that she's on side. I used to think having no principles was a good thing. But I'm out of there before I'm pushed.'

'Thrown under a bus, like your grandfather.'

'What?'

I tell him the story.

'You should have said that before, Mam.'

'I don't think it would have made a difference, the way you were then. We were all hoodwinked by someone, Rory. You would have done the same to someone else in a few years.'

'I got up to some shit, didn't I, Mam?'

'You did, son. And I stood watching.'

But I have him back now. And no job is better than that.

41.

GREAT, SNOTTY LUNGFULS

The house empties out over the next few days. Jennifer brings Declan home. On Wednesday, Ger arrived back early from India. She cut her trip short by a week because she was worried Freya was getting into trouble. I think it is my finest hour. That Ger thinks I'm a bad influence on *her* child.

'It's been emotional, Auntie Ann,' she said, as we waited for her mother to collect her.

'I love you very much, girleen, and you're always welcome,' I said, and she started bawling crying.

Rory has gone back to Brussels for a week because he had the flights and he wanted to *knock as much craic out of it as possible while pretending to work.*

After all the excitement, Denis and me look forward to our first Thursday night tradition in a good while. Takeaway and reading the local paper to see who's in court. It's my turn to get the supplies in.

It's just Nawaz in the chipper when I go in. He looks up and then busies himself with the pots at the back. It takes him a while to ask what I want.

'You must be glad they're gone out of it, Nawaz.'

'Yeah, next please, your order?'

Is he out with me over something?

'We might go mad tonight, Nawaz. Throw us out a snack-box there.'

He takes the cold chicken from the front and drops it in the fryers. The television is on Euronews. We both watch it. Not speaking.

'The world is in an awful state, Nawaz.'

Nawaz doesn't say a word. He finds some very important tasks to do with rearranging the chip-paper.

The No Comment bit comes on Euronews, so we don't even have anything to listen to. This goes on for another couple of minutes while he repeatedly checks the chips as if he wants them to hurry up.

'No Dairy Milk, Nawaz?'

'We are out of Dairy Milks.'

This is too much.

'Nawaz, are you out with me over something?'

He looks at me. 'How long we know each other, Ann? Ten years? And you didn't defend me when I need you. I bring chips to the Tidy Towns, do you remember, and chips to these bastard Yellow Vest fuckers? I heard them laugh. I know what they laugh at. Me. Like a fool, helping, and when I see the guys who cause trouble before, who call me Paki, I see you. Mrs Tidy Town. Hah? You say nothing. No word.'

'But I left, Nawaz. I tried to get the banner down. I . . .'

'You left to see the Pope first, not to do something about it. You do things to protect yourself.'

I can feel the colour rising up from my chest to my neck and face.

'OK, Mrs Devine. I understand it is difficult to stand up. Maybe you think, *What will people think?* But when you worry about your reputation, I worry about my windows or I worry my children get in fight.'

'I don't think that'll happen around here. Iseult had manners put on her, didn't she?'

'Read the paper, Mrs Devine. Already she cries about making mistakes. Blonde women crying always forgiven. She is local. Bangladeshi like me or Congo are not local. It's going to be more like this. Lucky for Kilsudgeon, lucky it doesn't have too many foreigners. See how you feel when thirty Nawazes are sitting in Danny's back room for only having tea. Or wanting a place to have prayers. You will see more protests next time. And I won't bring chips.'

'I'm sorry, Nawaz. I never thought . . .'

'I hope you're not going to cry now, are you, Mrs Devine? Like Iseult?'

'I won't cry, I promise, Nawaz, I won't.'

But I do. Great, snotty lungfuls of crying. For feck's sake. Nawaz gives me a napkin and stands there. I need another one. There's all sorts coming out of my nose now.

'Are you getting the poison out now, Mrs Devine?' He smiles.

'I . . . BLUB . . . am . . . BLUB . . . Nawaz.'

'Lucky we have no other customers, or I'd have to ask you to leave,' he jokes. 'Thrown out of a chipper, hah?

'The only thing I haven't done this week.'

I calm down.

'I let you . . . how to say, off the hook for now. You are human. We all weak sometimes. You are good weekly customer. No More Slaughterhouse and bloody Winch for you,

OK? Next time you bring family for Indian food here, from a Pakistani from Bangladesh.'

I tell him we'll have every remaining wedding in the family in his place.

'Good, good. Tell your niece I have all the vegan food, too, if she turns vegan. And anyway, Mrs Devine, it's not the foreigners you have to worry about, it's the Dubs. Coming down here, causing trouble.'

I buy the *Kilsudgeon Sentinel* in the shop for Denis. When I get home, I can feel Mam looking at me. I hope my eyes aren't giving me away. Whatever she sees, she says nothing, then she announces she wants an early night. Tactfully, maybe.

Denis settles into his chair, takes a big slurp out of his can and then reads the story out for me.

GDXJKWHU#RI#QFW#FHQWH#RZ#QHU#UHJ#UHW###
URQ#LQ#UHFHQW#SRVW#RIILFH#VWDQG#RII

Looking at the smiling, pretty, slim blonde (25), it's hard to imagine what a tumultuous few weeks she's had. Ms Deasy went viral last month for her impassioned plea for her community and succeeded in starting a strong protest and a political movement all in the space of a few days.

However, the protest turned sour when it was infiltrated by far-right elements and was ended when Gardai made several arrests, including Deasy herself. A moment she now bitterly regrets. 'I allowed myself to be manipulated when all I was trying to do was help the community, the whole community. I was also in a toxic relationship at this time with someone that I wanted to please. But I realize now that what we need is real unity and I've reached out to Patsy Duggan to heal the rifts and work together for Kilsudgeon's future.'

346

'It didn't look that toxic to me. She seemed well in control,' Denis says.

Ms Deasy became emotional at this point in the interview. Blinking through the tears, she said she would not stop fighting for the area she loved, but now she would do so with positivity.

Meanwhile, in the same incident, the young man who injured himself as he removed a controversial banner on the outside of the post office has been talking about his own ordeal.

Speaking by phone, Declan Carter, who is engaged to local woman Jennifer Devine, said he was just on crutches and the twisted ankle he sustained in the fall from an upper-storey window was healing well. He made no further comment.

'Fair play, Declan, tell them shag all,' Denis says approvingly.

Mr Carter's fall was partially broken by a number of Gardai who were attempting to force their way in at the time. It was not clear how Mr Carter gained entry to the post office. But he has been hailed a hero on Facebook for showing that Kilsudgeon is a welcoming and tolerant place.

'He had it in him all along, didn't he, Denis?'
'He might turn out to be the best of the in-laws, Ann. Maybe it wasn't Jennifer was the making of him. He just needed to lose the plot.'
'You should be a psychologist, Denis.'
'The mother, you see, Ann. She's like yourself. She wouldn't have reared a gobshite.'

This unexpectedly sets me off crying. He comes over and puts his arm around me. I tell him about Nawaz. And one thing leads to another and I tell him, in between snivels, that maybe I got involved with Iseult because I was trying to get Rory away from Patsy.

'You're like America in the Middle East, Ann. Going in for one reason and getting out for another.'

'Thanks, Denis. You have such a way with words.'

'But lookit, Ann, there isn't a malicious bone in your body. Everyone gets into scrapes trying to look after their family. I'd say Nawaz knows that too. But I wouldn't go accidentally helping any more wans like Iseult. Or it would look suspicious.'

'OK, Denis. That's good advice. I'm going to stay away from the far right for the foreseeable future.'

'That's my girl.'

He goes back to his chair and takes up the paper again.

'What's that about Patsy next to it?' I ask.

Gxjj dq#vhfx uhv#ix qglqj #iru#nlovx gj hrq#p hp ru| #fhqwuh

Independent TD Patsy Duggan has said he is delighted to announce a grant of €50,000 will be made available to set up the Kilsudgeon Memory Project on the site of the recently closed Kilsudgeon Post Office. At the centre of the exhibition will be selections from the more than 500 letters discovered in the post office during the recent protests.

I had clean forgotten the letters.

Mr Duggan said that these letters are a snapshot of the town from 1979 to 1985 and are invaluable to the whole country and will attract visitors to see all that Kilsudgeon has to offer. Mr Duggan did not elaborate on what else Kilsudgeon would have to offer but did say plans are afoot. 'Protests are all very well in the short term,' he said, 'but it is the elected officials who do the work of getting things done.'

Mr Duggan would not be drawn on reports that the construction firm owned by his cousin, Liam Duggan, would be involved in the refurbishment of the post office.

42.

ALL LONG STORIES AT THIS AGE

It's some job. But I'm glad to have something to do. We're in the community centre, going through all the letters from the post office and working out whether any can still be delivered. There's a few of us locals at it – me and Sally, Father Donnegan from time to time. Deirdre drops in too. She's taken a leave of absence so she has time to set up the move to Dubai. They're going in October. I can't believe it. She's like a new woman. She just seems . . . taller. I realize now she's been slumped for a good year. I just didn't see it before.

No one asks why I'm not on my rounds officially. It turns out people aren't half as interested in you as you'd think. I now have *four* cash jobs. Sylvester and Johny Lordan and Neans and Babs. So I can bring Neans and Babs to help with the letters. And I'm finally free from Nonie. I wonder how my poor replacement is managing.

Two days it takes us to get through all the bags, sorting each letter into personal and official, trying to figure out if the recipient is dead or not, and it's towards the end of the second day that I find them. Stuck under a pile of bills from the Department of Posts and Telegraphs. Two letters with a familiar surname on them. One for Charles Hoare, the other for Margaret Hoare. I think I know what one of them is anyway.

Mam is bustling around with the tea when I arrive back. She's excited to be going home soon. She's even looking forward to ordering Bim about, watching him make work for himself. But she'll see less of him. He's up with Sylvester now. There are enough odd-jobs up there at Wilderbrook to keep him busy for the rest of his life. He might even get the house. Sylvester says if he plays his cards right, he'll marry Bim so he won't have to pay the inheritance tax. It turns out what Bim was looking for was just someone to talk to. That's all we all want, isn't it?

I take the letters out of my bag and push them across the table to her. She frowns at the address and the postmark. She looks at me.

'Two letters to our house in Clonscribben, Mam. From 1979.'

She opens the one with the Dublin Diocese stamp on it. There is a card inside with gold edging. She reads it.

'*Dear Mr Hoare, we are writing to tell you that your application for a place in the Religious Enclosure at the Papal Mass has been*' – she looks up at me – '*unsuccessful.*

'Feck, Mam.'

'Oh, my poor Charlie. Would it have hurt him more to be refused than to never know? We probably wouldn't have gone if he'd been refused. He would have got all angry at them. *Them bastards in their bishop's palace, making a laugh out of Charlie Hoare*, he'd have said.'

It's funny to see her imitate his voice. She hasn't done it in years. She opens the other one. I see her face go from puzzled to understanding to hurt as she reads. She looks up at me and then reads it aloud.

'Dear Margaret,
  How are you? I am writing to tell you that your husband Charles has always been a gentleman towards me and never interfered with me in any way. I asked him would he come away with me and he said no. He was married to you and he loved you.
  Would you write to me, Margaret?
  Yours faithfully
  Nonie.'

We're silent for a minute. That's a lot to take in.

'All this time, Ann. Your poor father. He was a good man, and I wronged him.' She holds it and stares at it and reads it again and then looks at the envelope and then asks for tea.

My phone rings. It's Des.

'Sorry, Mam, I better . . .'

She waves her hand. 'Go on, go on.'

I walk into the sitting room and press the phone.

'Des, this isn't a great ti—'

'Ann, don't say anything, just hear me out, OK? I need to say thank you for saving Declan from those people. I really don't know where he was headed. Some of it is my fault too, Ann. I don't exactly know how, but it's always the mother's fault, isn't it? Whatever we do. I know Declan is different, but you and Denis and Jennifer have been the kindest to him in his whole life. I know you see him as odd, but you just get on with it. That's all we want for our son. Look, I don't know if they'll get married. Just don't let Jennifer break his heart. She'd break mine, too, because I'm mad about her. If she does right by him, I'll adopt her, haha.'

'Joint custody, Des. I've another daughter going to Dubai. I'm running out of them.'

'I promise. Weekends for you.'

'Once a month is fine, Des.'

'OK, so. Ann, now I'm also ringing because I'm expanding.'

'We all are, Dessie.'

She laughs.

'I know I have the right woman. Ann, do you remember the empty unit near the post office? It used to be a pub?'

'The Kilsudgeon Arms. I remember it well. A kip.'

'Ann, I get women from the country who travel sixty miles for what I do. But what about all the older women who don't want to come to Dublin? What if I came to them? And what if, when they came in, they were met by a woman who is – I hope you don't mind me saying so – of a certain vintage? A woman who isn't afraid of women's bodies, who's lifted another's boob, who's seen the mastectomies and odd shapes of old age? How would you like to sell bras, Ann? I would train you. And set you up down here. What do you say?'

What do you say to an offer like that? You don't say no, anyway. Not immediately. She says she'll give me time to think about it. I need it, because Mam is shouting for pen and paper in the other room.

I tell Des I'll get back to her, then I run to Mam, hunting down pen and paper and giving them to her. She sits down to write a letter to Nonie. She won't tell me what she's written. I see her finish it and she asks me for an envelope.

'Do you want a stamp, Mam?'

'I'll take it there myself, Ann.'

We drive to Nonie's. Patricia opens the door. Patricia is the Filipina girl at Mellamocare who took over my rounds. They all asked for her. They all wanted 'Asian Ann', Patricia told me, and Patricia says nothing about my cash visits.

'Who is it, Patricia?' calls Nonie brightly, and then she sees us and there is fear in her eyes.

We troop in awkwardly. Patricia gathers us in the sitting room and doesn't ask a single question and leaves us as she potters elsewhere in the house. She's *very* good.

Mam hands Nonie the letter she wrote.

'Forty years too late, Nonie,' she says, and also hands her Nonie's letter to Mam.

Nonie drops it and slumps back in the chair.

'Noonoonoonon . . . PATRICIA, TAKE ME UPSTAIRS, TAKE ME . . .'

Patricia comes in and looks at us.

'Long story,' I say to her.

'It's all long stories at this age, Ann,' she says.

'No, Nonie, stay, please,' says Mam. Mam leans in and puts her arm on Nonie's.

'Read it.'

Nonie reads it and starts crying before she's finished. Then she reads her own. God, I'd love to know what my mother wrote.

'I was a bad bitch to you, Ann,' says Nonie.

'I'll get over it, Nonie. But why did you keep me around? You could have got Patricia in years ago. She's better than me. Why did you have me there all the time?'

'I wanted you there, Ann, to look at you. You remind me of him. In your face, Ann. Your eyes. I wanted to look at you, but I couldn't bear it. I was forty years of age, Ann. I was desperate to have a child. You could have been like my child. I hated myself every day for being nasty to you, but I wanted to see you every time too. Just for the look of him. He never strayed, Margaret. Not for one moment. He was only friends with my brother. He said, *I'm sorry if I gave you the wrong idea, Nonie, but I'm mad about Peggy.*'

'Does Brian know?'

354

'Only you and Father Donnegan know. But I can die a bit better now.'

'You're not dying, Nonie. You can start living now,' says Mam, and she gives her a hug. And I swear to God, I don't believe in miracles or angels or any of that stuff, but you should see Nonie in front of me. She melts into Mam. The shoulders open up, the face relaxes. She's crying over Mam's shoulder, but the face is relaxed. I never knew her face could look so lovely.

'You'll visit me, Ann, won't you, even though you're not in the job?'

'I will, Nonie.'

'Please, Ann. Brian's not well. He's gone for tests.'

'We'll both come up, Nonie. Until you're sick of us.'

We leave, and I'm feeling wrung out by it all, but Mam has one more stop to make.

'Take me to your father, Ann,' she says.

So we drive up to see Daddy in Clonscribben graveyard. It's a still September day, with that lovely warmth you get when you're not expecting it. Charles Eamonn Hoare is in a good bit. A lot have died since him. We're dreading the state of the place when we go up.

But the gravestone is clean and there is a plant there. A calla lily weighed down with a small purple stone. Nonie must have been minding him.

'What did the mother-in-law want on the phone, Ann?'

I tell her about the boob whispering.

She considers it. 'You should ask your sister for advice on running a business. She's the sensible one now.'

'Thanks a million, Mam.'

Mam is very still. She shushes me. We listen in silence. She seems to be praying.

'Oh, Ann, I can hear his voice.'

I can't hear anything but the birds.

355

'I listened for him as well, at the Pope, but I heard nothing.'

'Is this Jesus, Mam?'

'No, I've heard him plenty since.'

'I don't understand, Mam.'

'It was Charlie's voice I wanted to hear.'

ACKNOWLEDGEMENTS

First to my beloved wife Marie, who cajoled, hugged, suggested, told me to cop on where necessary and gave all the love needed during the doubtful times. I hope I wasn't too much of a pain.

Thanks to my silly-funny and kind children, Ruby and Lily. There is nothing better for a day of writing where nothing happened than to have two small bundles bounce up the stairs wanting to WhatsApp piggy and mermaid emojis to their mammy.

Thanks once again to Faith O'Grady and all at Lisa Richards for keeping me on an even keel when I was actively searching for odd keels.

To Fiona and Rachel, my superb editors, who once again hewed/wrought/smelted – a host of industrial processes really – this book out of the earlier ore dirt and turned it into the gleaming steel beam it is today.

Thanks to a great team at Transworld in Ireland and London: Josh Benn, Kate Samano, Sarah Day, Beci Kelly, Tom Hill, Ella Horne, Fiodhna Ni Ghriofa, Aimee Johnston, Orla King (especially for a game-changing plot suggestion), Brian Walker, Sophie Dwyer and Jamie O'Connell.

Thanks to Ollie for another great cover. Ann thought the angle 'wasn't flattering' but the pen does add ten pounds, she's told.

Colm O'Regan is a columnist, broadcaster, comedian and author. He has published four books of non-fiction – the three bestselling books of Irish Mammies and *Bolloxology* – and published his first novel, *Ann Devine: Ready for Her Close-Up*, in 2019. *Ann Devine: Handle with Care* is his second novel. Originally from Cork, he now lives in Dublin with his wife Marie and daughters Ruby and Lily.

ANN DEVINE
Ready for Her Close-Up
Colm O'Regan

Meet Ann Devine, a riddle, wrapped up in a fleece, inside a Skoda Octavia.

Now that her youngest has flown the nest, Ann finds herself at a loose end. Until, that is, she is put forward for the Kilsudgeon Tidy Towns Committee.

Yet all is not neat and tidy in Kilsudgeon. There are strange sightings of people who aren't local driving 4x4s with a yellow reg, a man bun requesting kefir in the restaurant and a quad bike at a funeral.

What does this have to do with rumours of a brand new television series to rival *Game of Thrones*? And what will it all mean for Kilsudgeon's newly proposed town park?

A lot, as it happens.

As the town begins to fill up with the film crew, extras and a Hollywood star who is fond of the drink, everyone welcomes the chance to make a few bob and to finally get enough broadband to send an attachment.

Or nearly everyone. Harmony is threatened when the newcomers seem to be doing more damage than good and the last straw is when Ann's pride and joy – a floral arrangement in a boat – is trashed. She's about to discover what it means to go viral . . .

'Warm, charming and laugh-out-loud funny' *Irish Independent*

'Hilarious, warm, and bursting with chancers and charm in equal measure' Tara Flynn